Satis

RAE

faction

LAWRENCE

Poseidon Press
NEW YORK

Copyright © 1987 by Rae Lawrence

Published by POSEIDON PRESS,
A Division of Simon & Schuster, Inc.
Simon & Schuster Building
Rockefeller Center
1230 Avenue of the Americas
New York, NY 10020

POSEIDON PRESS is a registered trademark of Simon & Schuster, Inc.

Designed by Irving Perkins Associates
Manufactured in the United States of America

10   9   8   7   6   5   4   3   2   1

Library of Congress Cataloging-in-Publication Data

Lawrence, Rae.
Satisfaction.

I. Title.
PS3562.A915S2   1987   813'.54   87-9375

ISBN 0-671-60760-X

For rock and roll girls all over the world:
Jenny B.Z., Antonia K., Sally C., Annabel H.,
Francesca R., Maria H., Melody J., Amelia W.,
Genevieve S., Madeleine R., and Angelina P.

*A*t one point or another I had been in love with all of them—Rosaline, Marinda, Katie Lee, December—and for a brief time each had loved me back.

It was years since they'd been together in one place, but I still thought of them as this fabulous foursome. It was easier to remember them as they had once been—four daughters of four of the most famous men in America, all beautiful, all full of promise, all eager to voyage out into a world they had been brought up to believe was waiting just for them.

I hadn't kept in constant touch with all of them over the years, but one thing about having famous friends: you always know what they're up to. Even if you don't get a pale-blue air letter postmarked from a European capital, or an ivory wedding announcement engraved by Tiffany, or a letter scrawled late at night on the smooth white stationery provided to guests at the Beverly Wilshire Hotel, there's always *People* magazine and *Women's Wear Daily* and *Rolling Stone* to let you know what's up. Or what's down, the way things have gone lately.

But I'm going to try and put all that behind me, at least for today. It puts quite a lot of pressure on you, knowing that your wedding day is supposed to be the happiest day of your life. I feel happy, correction, I *am* happy, though I'm not the kind of person given to saying these things out loud. I have to admit I'm a damn handsome son of a bitch in this hand-tailored pinstripe suit with the pale-yellow rosebud pinned to my lapel.

The rosebud was her idea, a woman never truly thinks you're well dressed if she hasn't taken some small part in your sartorial decisions. The flower matches her gown, a yellow silk number with enough lace trim to have blinded an entire village of Spanish peasants. She looks terrific in it, but then she always looks terrific, and she always knows it.

Still, what it does to me, seeing her there at the far end of the aisle.

And here they all are, together in one room for the first time in years, in their proper pastel church outfits, arching their necks for a glimpse of the bride. In a pink silk suit, leaning back into her husband's protective arm, there's the one I loved first. In the blue polka-dot ruffles, fanning herself against the heat, there's the one who used love only when it suited her purposes. In an infinity of lavender pleats with a matching straw hat, there's the one who loved me longest, the one I once hoped to spend forever-and-a-day with.

And now, stepping toward me in time to a sweet strain of Brahms, here comes the one I love best, the one who loved me last of all.

*T*he perfect man could be anywhere, December Dunne thought, looking out the window, pushing back the long platinum hair that never needed brushing. He could be standing thigh-deep in a cool stream high up in Montana, fishing for trout. He could be in Boston, where this train was headed, finishing his second cup of espresso in a small sidewalk café, memorizing the succession of English royalty for his tutorial in history and literature. He could be in New York, where the train had just stopped to pick up another load of college students, buying the morning newspaper to see whether his story on a local politician had made it into the final edition.

Or he might not exist at all, but December quickly dismissed this thought with all the confidence of a seventeen-year-old who, away from home for the first time, knows herself to be on the edge of a great adventure. Or he might be on this very train, taking another look at the packet of registration material from Harvard that December had read so many times she could recite it by heart. The possibility filled her with hunger, and she headed up toward the dining car in search of a yoghurt or Pepsi or anything that would relax the knot that had formed in her stomach a little over an hour ago when her mother had left her and her one overloaded backpack at the Matawan train station with this single piece of advice: "Now honey, go out there and make us all proud of you."

It was easy to pick the students out from the commuters. They were younger and tanner and their clothes were pressed and clean. Jesus God, December said to herself, they're all wearing the same clothes, the boys and the girls: penny loafers and deck shoes, corduroy and chino trousers, cable-knit sweaters and those T-shirts with funny little collars and alligators appliquéd on the chest. You'd never know it was 1972 on this train, December thought, and suddenly she felt embarrassed about her clothes, her purple Mexican peasant blouse and her faded overalls and her high cork platform sandals that were worn down on the outsides of the heels.

She could feel them staring at her, and they weren't the kind of stares she was used to, stares for the prettiest girl in the room. They weren't admiring the platinum hair that fell in a sheet to the middle of her back, the smooth light pink skin, the high cheekbones, and the wide blue eyes that gave her the look of a beautiful Chinese princess painted over in a clear pastel palette. They weren't impressed with her long willowy body, made graceful by years of dance lessons, made powerful by summers of swimming in the strong surf of the Atlantic.

They were smirking: at the large hoop earrings that were so obviously fake gold, at the silly socks striped in rainbow colors, at the garish red nail polish with little flecks of silver in it. They think I'm cheap, a greaser girl, and she could picture what her dorm at Harvard would be like: room after room of country club girls in pastel man-tailored shirts and kelly green sweaters making fun of her behind her back. I'll never fit in, December thought; it would cost a hundred dollars to buy just one of those outfits, and a hundred dollars was nearly a third of what she'd saved out of her summer salary, it was all she had to live on practically till Christmas.

December bought a Coke at the counter and added a teaspoon of sugar so it would taste more like the Pepsi she preferred. She had worked enough cashier jobs so that she could instantly subtract any odd sum, like sixty-three, from a hundred. Thirty-seven cents, enough to buy a little plastic bag of potato chips: lunch. I've just learned my first lesson about Harvard, she thought, and I haven't even gotten there yet. It didn't have to do with looks, and it didn't have to do with brains, and it didn't have to do with how cool you were or how much drugs you did or how many boys you'd slept with, it all had to do with something else, something December didn't have. Money.

December made a mental list of all the things she knew about that these girls didn't. There were some things she didn't have the words for exactly, sexual things she'd learned from being with different guys over the past few years, that seemed like a good place to start. She knew how to drive very fast on an unlit road without headlights so that the police wouldn't be able to find you in case you didn't have a driver's license or the car wasn't properly registered or you just felt like kicking up a little trouble. She knew how to tell if a man was carrying a gun just from the way his clothes fell and, depending on where he was packing, whether he was likely to use it. She could determine from how straight another woman could look you in the eye and how much time she waited before looking you over, up and down, checking out your body and your clothes, whether that woman could be trusted with a piece of information about the man you were with. She knew the best places to meet the cutest guys: in record stores (by the records of whatever group the management was playing over the house system); on the beach (at the food concession nearest the lifeguards' parking lot); at a club (the pinball machine closest either to the public telephone or to the bar where the band was getting their drinks); in a shopping mall (the hardware department at Sears). These were some of the things these girls couldn't possibly know. Whether they would come in handy at Harvard was another issue.

A classical well-rounded liberal arts education was about fifth or sixth on the list of what December was looking for in Cambridge. She could have found that at Rutgers. And it wasn't just the chance to get out of New Jersey. She could have married herself off to someone on his way to Texas or California, or she could have just taken her chances and gone to New York City, getting a high-paying restaurant job, or maybe modeling, or just waited to see what developed, as a couple of her friends had done.

December Dunne was going north to reinvent herself. As what, she didn't exactly know. She surely did not want to be one of the country club girls on the train. It was something larger than that. It was something big enough to hold all the ambition and wildness she had been carrying around with her since she was a young girl. She had no special talents. She was smart, but she was not brilliant. She was beautiful, but she was not so naïve as to think that was enough.

Back in her seat, she looked out at Connecticut, the farthest north she'd ever been. She tried to summon up the enthusiasm she'd felt last night about a new life in a new place. Her family had moved around a lot when she was growing up, and December was used to pulling up stakes and starting fresh. It had made her confident, and it had also made her reckless, because she'd never had to face a mistake or embarrassment for more than a few months before she went on to a new place where no one knew who she was.

No one at Harvard knows who I am, she thought, and she began to peel the glittery polish off her left thumbnail. No one has the slightest idea, she said to herself, and for the first time since she'd left New Jersey she began to smile.

It won't take them long to find out who I am, Katie Lee Hopewell thought as she pulled the dry cleaner's plastic off the last of the ten silk dresses hanging in her closet. She had just finished unpacking, and not one of her three freshman roommates had even arrived yet. She congratulated herself on her cleverness, talking Daddy into lending her his corporate jet to fly her up from Lexington. She'd picked the second biggest bedroom in the suite (choosing the biggest might have caused animosity, and besides, this one had more closet space); she'd had time to scout the territory before the rest of her entrymates arrived.

She'd gotten the names of her roommates in the mail a few weeks ago, and she'd had the head of her father's personnel department check them out for her. A little advance information was always useful. Her father was in the hotel business, and with a Hopewell Inn franchise located in nearly every county on the East Coast, it had been easy to find out what she wanted to know.

Marinda Vincent was one of the Vincents from Richmond County, New Jersey. Her family had made their money in real estate and her uncles and cousins were all respectable lawyers and businessmen, some of them held public office, even, but everyone knew they were thick with organized crime and that you couldn't do a thing in the county, build a housing development or open a restaurant or even pave a road unless her uncle gave the nod to it. Katie Lee couldn't figure out what Marinda was doing at Radcliffe. Girls like her usually lived at home until they could be placed in a politically useful marriage to a proper and promising man from another large family.

Rosaline Van Schott was from old money, so old no one could really remember where it had come from, it had been so long since any Van Schott had worked for a living. Katie Lee had seen pictures of Rosaline's parents in the society magazines her mother received, on the pages dedicated to charity benefits and racing meets. Her father was a notorious drunk, having once made the comment, while being interviewed by *Life*, that the hardest job he'd ever had was "getting the ice bucket filled by eleven A.M."

Rosaline could be useful to Katie Lee, who was hoping to break in with what her father would have called the right kind of people. In Lexington they still remembered the days when her father was poor, when he'd gambled all his money on his first roadside motel, before the little signature rooftop bluebird was perched on motels at nearly every major interstate interchange in the country. Katie Lee knew she had a lot to learn, and she was hoping Rosaline would be able to teach her, or at least introduce her to the people who could.

The only mystery was December Dunne. She was the adopted daughter of a man named Willie Dunne, the operator of two local fast-food restaurants. He had married December's mother, Gloria, and December had obviously been part of the package. Beyond that the trail disappeared; either Gloria had changed her name or been married before—it was hard to find out, the family had moved around so much. Katie Lee wasn't concerned, she could guess what December was like: one of those serious public school girls who'd wonked her way into Radcliffe and who would spend the next four years wonking her way into law school or medical school. No fun there.

Katie Lee switched the light on her makeup mirror to "natural" and applied a thin coating of clear peach lip gloss with a small sable brush. She was her daddy's golden girl, and she looked it. Her flawless tan was set off by tiny diamond and gold stud earrings. Her round hazel eyes were flecked like a cat's with gold at the edges. Her long thick hair, once light brown, was now a rich warm yellow, streaked and highlighted with the sort of natural randomness never found in nature. She examined her roots; she'd need a touch-up in about a month and would fly down to Lexington to get it done. She didn't want her roommates to know she dyed her hair, and besides, André was the only one who could be relied on to do the job right.

Katie Lee looked at the list of things she needed to do before classes started the next week. She had to find a decent manicurist and a dry cleaner she could trust. She needed to find a garage for the little red MGB that had been her high school graduation present. And she had to get a detailed street map of Cambridge, because that was the first step in her plan: finding a site on which to develop her very own Hopewell Inn with her very own money. It would be a small but auspicious beginning, and then she'd be on her way, for Katie Lee Hopewell, just turned eighteen and arrived at Harvard less than three hours ago, intended to become the richest woman in the United States.

• • •

Rosaline Van Schott was absolutely terrified, but this was nothing new. She repeated to herself all the reasons not to be scared. She knew the car probably wouldn't careen out of its lane into an oncoming truck; Philip, the driver, had been with the family for years without getting into any kind of accident, and the car, a gray Mercedes specially ordered from Germany and rebuilt in the States to her father's specifications, was an extremely reliable machine. She knew that probably no one would try to mug or assault her once she arrived in Harvard Square; though Cambridge was a dirty and dangerous city, with subway trains and poor people, she had seen from maps and pictures that Harvard Yard itself was enclosed, shut off from the rest of the city, with tall metal gates and its very own police force. She knew that probably no one would accost her, or even try to talk to her, as she moved into her freshman suite; her mother was there to protect her, her tall, blond, efficient mother, the scariest person Rosaline had ever seen.

But once her mother had helped her line her drawers with scented lavender paper, arranged her soft Belgian shoes in neat rows on the antique wooden shoe rack, and copied out the telephone numbers of a doctor, a dentist, and an ophthalmologist located in Boston should any emergency arise, what then? What would happen when her mother left her alone with these three other people she had never met before?

"It will be good for you to make new friends," her mother had said, as though Rosaline had any old friends, any friends at all. It was a little game that Charlotte, who had the newspaper clippings and photograph albums to prove that she had once been the most popular debutante in New York, played with her strange and silent daughter: pretending that Rosaline was merely a younger version of herself, headed for a whirlwind social life with the offspring of other socially prominent families.

But they could not have been more different. Where Charlotte was tall and precisely groomed, with carefully painted coral lipstick and her hair coiffed and sprayed into a perfect blond helmet, Rosaline was tiny, and awkward, with curly reddish brown hair that had been cut bluntly at chin length in an effort to disguise its unruly thickness. Her bright green eyes, too large for such a delicate face, tilted up at the corners and were framed by heavy eyelashes that grew straight out just the way her eyebrows seemed to grow straight up. Her skin was sallow, the supposed legacy of a Spanish great-grandmother, and her small, full lips were drawn in the kind of constant pout that hadn't been fashionable since the 1920s.

Rosaline knew that Charlotte knew that Rosaline was a hopeless case. At the age of twelve, after one of her father's especially rowdy drunken tears, she had been quickly dispatched to a school in Switzerland; a few months ago, after Charlotte had received a letter from a worried headmistress, she had been just as hurriedly recalled to New York. Rosaline could not refute the headmistress's charges: that she had made no friends at all, that she showed no interest in the athletic program the school was famous for, that she spent hours and hours by herself in the woods behind the school, reading books and talking to animals, but mostly just staring off into space. Her grades had been excellent, but this caused Charlotte to worry even more, for she knew that the path to spinsterhood was usually lined with books.

So Charlotte tried, in the few months before Rosaline left for college, to give her a sort of crash course in how to be an attractive, eligible, and charming young lady. She bought her a dozen silk blouses, and Rosaline had managed to spill something on every one of them. She took her to Elizabeth Arden, but Rosaline broke out in hives when even the lightest bit of makeup was applied to her sensitive skin. She dragged her along to parties and luncheons, but Rosaline just stood awkwardly in corners, interfering with Charlotte's own good time. Eventually Charlotte began to feel Rosaline was working at unhappiness merely to spite her: today, for instance, after all of Charlotte's lectures on first impressions, Rosaline had worn a peach heather Shetland sweater that clashed deliberately with her kelly green cotton turtleneck.

It was Charlotte who picked up the room key from the custodian, who directed Philip on the moving of Rosaline's trunks, who preceded her daughter up the stairs and rapped forcefully on the door, which was opened by a girl who looked to Rosaline very much like a stewardess, and who reeked of Miss Dior.

"Welcome," the girl said, extending a hand to Charlotte as though she and not Rosaline were to be her roommate, "I'm Katie Lee Hopewell."

"How nice to meet you. This is my daughter, Rosaline," Charlotte said, pronouncing the name as slowly and carefully as a language instructor so that Katie Lee would be sure to get it right: Rose-a-leen, in the French manner. Charlotte looked at Katie Lee's shoes, which were new navy-blue pumps with gold buckles across the top that served no purpose. "Are you from Lexington by any chance?"

"Yes, those Hopewells," Katie Lee said, thinking that Charlotte looked even thinner than the photographs she had seen in newspapers, and also older, from too many seasons in the sun. "And you must be from New York?"

"Yes, of course," Charlotte said, walking past Katie Lee into the large living room. "It's a shame they've bricked up the fireplace."

"Well, it's not really a living room," Katie Lee said. "Someone will have to sleep here. There are four of us, and only three bedrooms. I guess we'll trade off, to be fair."

Charlotte looked inquiringly at Katie Lee, as though fairness were a concept that she had just heard proposed for the very first time. After the last of the trunks had been emptied, and a room had been selected for Rosaline, and Charlotte had checked the bathroom (no tub and one large stall that two girls could shower in at a time), and Katie Lee had made them tea on a hot plate whose use was forbidden in that particularly old historic building, Charlotte left for Vermont, where she was spending the weekend with one of Joseph's cousins.

Katie Lee lit a cigarette and watched Rosaline unpack some French paperbacks.

"Oh this tastes good," she said, exhaling. "I thought I should wait, you know, in case your mother disapproved."

"You didn't have to worry," Rosaline said, and when she smiled, for the first time that day, Katie Lee thought how absolutely perfect her teeth were. "She disapproves of everything." Rosaline began to giggle.

"Well, she's gone now," Katie Lee said, but Rosaline couldn't stop laughing.

"I'm sorry," she said, covering her mouth with one hand, holding an embroidered floral sheet with the other. "But I just realized I haven't the faintest idea what to do with this. I mean, I don't know how to make a bed. I mean, I know it must be very easy, because everyone does it, but I never have, but I suppose I can figure it out."

"Oh, don't be silly," Katie Lee said, and it was a phrase she would find herself saying very often that first year to Rosaline, who didn't really seem to know how to do anything at all except read books and write papers and speak in about four languages. "Here, look," she said, making up the bed, explaining as she went along, Rosaline acting tremendously grateful for every fold, every hospital corner.

Katie Lee was thinking ahead, to how Rosaline would invite her home for Thanksgiving at their Fifth Avenue apartment, or maybe even to their horse farm in Virginia. Rosaline would take her to a New Year's Eve party in some glamorous New York hotel, introducing Katie Lee to handsome, rich young men whose families had fought in the Revolution. She and Rosaline would go skiing in Switzerland over the February break, with all of Rosaline's friends from boarding school. Rosaline was a little bit passive—Katie Lee had seen it right away—and people like that were always attracted to Katie Lee.

Rosaline was watching Katie Lee, admiring how competent and forceful she was. She seemed so straightforward and friendly, not at all like the snobbish and sarcastic girls she had met in Europe. If I'm lucky, Rosaline thought, if I'm very very lucky, and not too demanding or pushy of course, and always smiling and never talking about anything too personal or depressing, then maybe, just maybe, Katie Lee will want to be my friend.

Marinda held the joint against the metal door of the bathroom stall until it was out completely, and then she returned what was left of it, nearly half the cigarette, to what she considered a brilliant hiding place: behind the foil that held her birth control pills. Her mother might find the pills, though this was unlikely—Marinda was very careful—but she would never think to peel back the foil to where the drugs were hidden.

Marinda had feigned severe physical discomfort in order to convince her parents to stop at this highway rest station, where she knew her mother would never follow her into the bathroom. Her mother believed that public bathrooms were rife with diseases and prostitutes and assorted vague and indescribable dangers, even here, in the middle of rural Massachusetts. When she had found out that her daughter would be living in a coed dormitory she had called an assistant dean to make sure that boys and girls didn't share the same bathroom, and then she had called the infirmary to see whether there wasn't a problem with any sort of fungus, such as athlete's foot. She was told that the biggest problem they had was a high incidence of yeast infections. Mrs. Vincent didn't know precisely what they meant, but since Marinda didn't have a kitchen, she was probably safe from this particular ailment.

In a dirty mirror lit by a single wavering fluorescent light Marinda checked her eyes for unusual redness. If only I had blue eyes, she thought, my whole life might be different. Her dark brown eyes were the exact color of the long, curling hair that fell in a thick tangle around her face and over her shoulders. Her skin was a burnished olive that in this light verged on the sickly green. Marinda picked a piece of ash off her loose dark sweater, one of several she owned in a futile attempt to disguise the large, low-slung breasts that men seemed to stare at—men she didn't even know, men she didn't even want to see, men who had no right to look at her that way—everywhere she went. She was actually rather slim, with narrow hips and long delicate bones, but no matter how much she dieted (and she was always on a diet) her breasts made her feel fat.

If only I had blue eyes and one of those little button noses, she thought. Her own nose, long and narrow and slightly hooked, as though it were pointing to her wide full mouth, could be seen on all the Vincents. We may be rich, she thought, but oh we still look like peasants. Peter had once told her she looked exotic and sensuous, but Marinda knew that your boyfriend was the last person you could trust on the subject of feminine beauty. She pulled her curling bangs forward onto her face. I look like I've just come from dancing barefoot in a tub of grapes, she thought. I look like I'll have ten children before my fortieth birthday. I look like the royal whore, the one who's kept stowed away in the hold of the yacht until after the guests have gone to bed.

Marinda had gotten just a little too high, and when she returned to the long dark-blue Pontiac, she thought it was just like getting into a space ship, a space ship taking her to a new and distant galaxy. Her father was the captain, crouched over the wheel, smoking a cigar, running one hand over the top of his head where his hair used to be. Her mother was Lieutenant Uhuru, the communications officer—a perfect job for someone who practically lived on the telephone. They were going to beam Marinda down to live among the aliens. It was a four-year program. Then she was supposed to return to her home planet and use what she had learned to help her own people.

Well, that's where they're wrong, Marinda thought. She knew that after college, and perhaps three years of law school, she was supposed to return to New Jersey and work in the family law firm or the family real estate business or maybe in local government. After a few years she would marry another Catholic—Italian preferably—who was ei-

ther very rich or very politically powerful or had the potential to
become both.

But Marinda was never going back. She had decided this on the
first night she had slept with Peter Johnson, her perfect boyfriend,
who at this very moment was probably eating lunch in the dining
room of his college at Yale. Peter was the one who had opened her
eyes to how oppressive her family situation really was and taught
her about Miles Davis and Eric Clapton and Kurt Vonnegut. Losing her
virginity was the first step down the road that would take her away
from everything her parents had planned for her. Peter said he could
take one look at a girl and tell whether or not she was a virgin, though
Marinda thought that what he really meant was that he could tell at a
glance whether or not a particular girl would sleep with him.

Of course he will be sleeping only with me now, Marinda reminded
herself, and when she got to Harvard Yard she was relieved to find
that there was indeed one tiny, private bedroom left in the suite.

"Of course we'll be switching during the year, just to be fair," the
girl named Rosaline said in a soft voice. They were sitting out in the
big room, Marinda and her father and Rosaline and Katie Lee, while
Mrs. Vincent was wiping down the furniture (she had brought along a
roll of paper towel and some spray cleaner from New Jersey) in what
would be Marinda's room. Katie Lee was smoking Winstons, dropping the ashes into a crystal bowl she had brought up from Kentucky.
Fresh red roses from a florist in the Square were arranged in a matching crystal vase.

"Hopewell Inns, hunh?" Mr. Vincent said, smiling. "We sold them
some land a few years back, though I don't think I dealt with your
father, not directly. They've done very well over there, from what I
hear."

"Eighty percent occupancy, sometimes higher when the convention bookings are strong," Katie Lee replied.

What a suck-up, Marinda thought, what a goody-goody—she's actually flirting with him. Mrs. Vincent came out waving a towel
streaked with dust high over her head.

"You see?" she said. "No one can clean like your mother—even
after the maid's spent all day in the house I can still find the place
she hasn't done."

Mr. Vincent laughed and looked at Katie Lee. "The Vincents can
always find the dirt nobody else can see," he said, "it's a family

trait." He invited the girls to dinner at a seafood restaurant in Boston, but his wife insisted it was time to head back down to Providence, where there was some family business to take care of.

On his way out he pressed a fifty-dollar bill into Marinda's palm and gave her a hug. "Take them out to dinner tonight, sweetheart," he said. "Be the first one to pick up a tab. It will go a long way."

"Yes, Papa," Marinda said. And in a way it will, she thought, it will buy three round-trip tickets to New Haven, Connecticut.

Being a handsome, intelligent, thoroughly charming young man who believed in wild young romantic love but had not yet found it, Schuyler Smith was growing cynical. Too cynical for my own good, he thought, taking another sip of bourbon in the warm September sun. He was sitting on a fire escape with his close friend and second cousin Teddy Rossiter, watching the Radcliffe girls go by.

"Look at her," Teddy said, nodding in the direction of a honey blonde carrying a bunch of bright red flowers. Teddy opened another can of beer; it was the only alcohol he could stand to drink—though, watching Schuyler, he thought he might try to develop a taste for bourbon. Teddy was a freshman—it was his fire escape, in Harvard Yard, that they were sitting on—and Schuyler was a junior; it went without saying that Teddy was to become his older cousin's protégé here at college.

"From the South, I'll bet," Schuyler said. "They all wear dresses for the first week until they catch on." Schuyler had just broken up with a girl from Georgia whom he had occasionally caught looking, for a few uncomfortable moments too many, at the advertisements for diamond jewelry in glossy magazines. She couldn't believe that Schuyler wanted to become a journalist—there was absolutely no money in it—and she had been consistently rude to his friends from the *Crimson*, the college newspaper.

A long gray Mercedes pulled up, and Schuyler first guessed the delicate, pale girl who emerged from it to be the younger sister of a freshman. But there was something nervous and awkward about her that reminded Schuyler of himself as an incoming freshman, and she was looking around the Yard with this expression that asked if it could really be true, she would be living exactly here, in these short brick buildings named after some of New England's most prominent families.

Teddy wasn't used to drinking in the middle of the afternoon, and he knocked over one of the cans, spilling some beer onto the roof of a blue Pontiac parked directly below them.

"Shit," Teddy said, but the girl who was unloading her suitcases from the back of the car just laughed—she seemed a little drunk herself. "I've never seen so many beautiful women. I think I'm having a heart attack." He clutched his chest. "But I die a happy man."

"If you're very, very lucky you may actually get to talk to some of these exquisite creatures," Schuyler said.

"Couldn't possibly," Teddy said, reaching for another beer. "Too terrifying, at least that one is."

She wasn't scary at all, she was just sort of ethnic-looking, Italian probably, but to Teddy, sequestered in New England prep schools for nearly all of his adolescent life, it was the same thing.

"Come on, I'll take you around tonight. You've got to take advantage of the first few weeks here—it's the last time anyone shows any semblance of being friendly."

"Sure, Sky, sure," Teddy said. "We'll just knock on some doors and you can tell everyone I'm your deaf-mute cousin, just out of the hospital, recovering from a near fatal disease, and they have be very nice to me and bear all my children out of pure Christian pity."

"We can visit my old room," Schuyler said, pointing up to the top floor. "I can't believe they let women live here now. I was such a nervous fool when I first arrived here, I think it would have been too much for me if I'd had to deal with actual female persons on a daily basis."

Schuyler could still remember every detail of his first day at Harvard, two years ago. He'd been wearing worn-out blue jeans over freshly polished thick leather boots, a plaid flannel shirt, a tan suede jacket, and his lucky red felt hunting hat. His prep school roommates had called him Cowboy for fun, and the nickname had stuck until a Saturday night a few weeks later when Schuyler had drunk his roommates under the table at a local Irish bar and told them that if they ever called him Cowboy again he would pump their dumb Eastern asses full of buckshot.

They didn't really believe him of course, but Schuyler had a way of saying something very quietly and seriously, hardly moving his mouth at all, that made you stand back and reevaluate whatever it was he had said. There was a surprising strength in him that he called up when people least expected it. He rarely smiled or paid compliments, but there was something about him that seemed brave and fine and trustworthy, like a movie character played by Gary Cooper: the last good man in town.

He even looked a little like Cooper with his long chiseled face, strong jaw, cool gray eyes, and the thick shock of light-brown hair that fell straight across his high forehead. He'd spent so much time in the sun as a child, he'd developed a permanent tan that even the severest Massachusetts winter couldn't fade. With his boots on he stood six feet two, but he was so thin—just one smooth vertical line broken by shoulders made muscular from working on his family's farm—that most guessed him to be taller.

His people weren't farmers, really. His father, the son of a Maryland banker, had been caught doing something shocking with the mayor's daughter, something that ruined the young lady's prospects for marriage, when word got around. He was thrown out of the house and created further scandal when he and the young lady, Schuyler's mother, eloped across the Virginia state line in the middle of a very hot July night. From there they went to Chicago, where Mr. Smith telephoned his lawyer to make sure his trust fund wasn't in jeopardy. The new Mrs. Smith wired her younger sister to send her clothing and some family lace on ahead to Montana, where they knew someone who had a cattle ranch and where the hunting was supposed to be very good nearly all the year round.

Schuyler had a photograph of his parents that he kept on his desk, taken right after they had built the big stone house that Schuyler was born and raised in. They were sitting out on the porch and Mr. Smith was reading from a leather-bound book while Mrs. Smith was crocheting a dark-green afghan that Schuyler could still remember the rough feel of, though it had worn out years ago, when he was just a small boy. It was a picture not just of his parents but of the kind of life he wanted for himself, a life that seemed so impossible from here, in dirty, hectic Cambridge, where everyone seemed to be struggling and competing and talking all the time, even when there was nothing to say.

Teddy was one of the few people Schuyler had met who also knew when to be quiet, except that now he was making a great deal of noise, hanging over the railing of the fire escape, waving to a girl who was walking toward them.

"Be cool, cousin," Schuyler said, though he could hardly blame Teddy: the girl was astonishingly beautiful, her long platinum hair waving as she walked. Schuyler sighed, for he knew that Teddy was

committing the worst possible mistake with a Radcliffe woman: letting her know that you liked her. Courtship at Harvard was supposed
to be conducted with an utter lack of enthusiasm by either party.
This girl was probably going to turn around and walk away from
them, or ignore Teddy's whistling as she passed, or tell them to fuck
off, if she were from New York.

Instead she marched right over to them and stood underneath the
fire escape and looked straight up and said, "I'd like one of those
beers if it's still cold."

Teddy held out a beer and said, "Come up and get it. I love your
hair, is it real? Oh, certainly it is. We have some bourbon too, we are
very respectable gentlemen, we extend to you our utmost hospitality,
and however much beer you want—of course it's cold." Teddy's hand
was shaking and he was leaning too far out over the railing. Schuyler
pulled him back onto the fire escape, and as he did so Teddy dropped
the beer.

Two flights down the girl caught it. In her left hand.

"Kiss my ass," she said, and then she smiled a great wide smile,
and then she turned around and walked off, just a second too soon to
see Teddy collapse from drunkenness and Schuyler smiling back.

"We can switch after a few months if you think that's fair," Marinda was saying as December hung her one presentable dress in the
living room closet. They were passing a joint back and forth, waiting
for Katie Lee and Rosaline to return with their take-out dinner.

"Sounds fine," December said. "I didn't have my own bedroom at
home either, I had to share with my sister."

"I always wanted a sister," Marinda said. "Instead I got five
brothers."

"We're back," Rosaline sang out, carrying the pizzas. She had never
eaten pizza, and she felt she was doing something daring and a little
naughty. She hoped she wouldn't make a mess of it.

"I made her wait outside while I bought this," Katie Lee said, holding up two bottles of California champagne. "He didn't even ask me
to show my driver's license, and I was a little disappointed actually,
because it would have been my first entirely legal purchase of alcohol."

They sat cross-legged on the floor, eating and drinking and discussing which courses they might take. Rosaline and Katie Lee were both
thinking about art history, and December wanted to take Shake-

speare. Marinda said her cousin Bobby, who was a junior in Winthrop House, knew all the easiest courses in every department.

"He calls them 'guts,' and he told me I should be sure to take at least one a semester." People were wandering up and down the stairs, knocking on doors and introducing themselves. They'd met their proctor, who was supposed to keep track of them in a semiparental way, and the girls who lived next door, and some boys from downstairs who were on their way to see *Casablanca*, which everyone agreed was one of the best films ever made.

"Well, I'm nearly drunk," Marinda said.

"I am most certainly drunk," Katie Lee said, though December could tell that Katie Lee was very sober and was just pretending drunkenness to make them all more comfortable.

"I am extremely and fatally drunk," Rosaline said, trying not to think about her father.

"I know a great drinking game," December said. "We usually play it with beer. It's really fun, it's called End Up."

"It doesn't involve hand-to-eye coordination, I hope," Marinda said.

"No, it's really simple. You pick something everyone wants, like a career. You take turns—like if it's my turn I describe the career I want, and then I have to drink the whole can of beer—in this case the whole glass of champagne—without stopping or breathing, and then I turn the can or glass over, end up. And if you can do that, you're supposed to get whatever it was that you said you wanted. That's how you end up."

"Oh, *careers*, how depressing," Marinda said.

"You can pick anything. Like, okay, describe your perfect man."

Marinda held up a full glass of champagne and pictured Peter. "Well, of course he has to be wonderful and brilliant and gorgeous and all that other stuff that goes without saying."

"Don't just tell us about your precious Yalie," Katie Lee said. "You're supposed to be telling us about your fantasy man."

Marinda thought a while. "Well, I do love Peter, but there's part of me that always—well, I'm a real sucker for a certain kind of guy."

"Keep talking."

"Oh, you know, these sort of tough, mysterious types that don't say very much. They look like they could be a little mean, even, to people they don't like, but they'd do anything for you."

"This does sound like Humphrey Bogart," Rosaline said.

"Well, like Humphrey Bogart in a Western movie, maybe," Marinda said. "Someone who just has this enormous inner strength that nothing can corrupt. Who will stand by you no matter what." She closed her eyes and drank up her champagne and turned her plastic cup upside down. "Your turn, Katie Lee."

"Now this is just between us chickens, but I want a man with lots of money."

"Oh, come on," Marinda said, "you have more than enough of your own."

"Exactly. If he has his own money, then I'll know he isn't after mine. And he can't object to my having a career and working really hard at it, because that's what I intend to do. He can't expect me to stay at home raising his children. And he should get along well with his mother, because men who don't respect their mothers never treat their wives very well. And I want someone with good bone structure and some height to him and light eyes, so we can have beautiful perfect children together." She drained her cup and turned it over.

Maybe she is a little drunk, December thought, or why would she have revealed so much. Unless she thinks being so calculating is completely normal.

"Yes, I want lots of children," Rosaline said. She had never had a boyfriend or even been kissed in any way that mattered; her expectations all came from books and fairy tales. "I just want to be swept off my feet by a dashing Prince Charming who carries me off to his castle in the woods where we live happily ever after." I need to be rescued, she thought, from my evil witch of a mother, and then she went on. "I want someone incredibly romantic. I want flowers and candlelight dinners and piano sonatas in the background. I want some more champagne," she said, spilling a little down her chin as she drank. "So when do I get my wish?"

"Any day now," December said, laughing.

"It's your turn," Marinda said, picking the mushrooms off the leftover pizza.

"The perfect man," she said, closing her eyes. "He has no fear. We go everywhere together, anywhere we want, we just go wild, but we're never afraid, because we're together." She closed her eyes tighter. "What does he look like. He has to be tall, because I'm nearly five ten. Let me think." The picture was just coming into focus, the way the movie camera pans in on the hero just as the opening music fades away. But there was no time to think, because just then two young men came bursting in the door, one of them visibly drunk, explaining how his cousin used to live here and they wanted to check it out, for old time's sake.

And December lost the mental image of this perfect man she had created and opened her eyes to see who had dared to break her concentration.

Leaning against the doorway, a suede jacket slung over one shoulder, a scowl on his face, his gray eyes looking straight at her, straight through her, there stood Schuyler Smith.

2

*J*ust last week the final leaves had fallen, giving Schuyler an unobstructed view of the Charles River from his narrow bathroom window. He stood there now, finishing up his early evening shave, trying to decide where to take his date for dinner.

There was a French restaurant up near Radcliffe with a decent wine list, but it was expensive and stuffy and a little too dramatic for a first date. There were plenty of places in and around Harvard Square, but for reasons he was at the moment too nervous to examine, Schuyler didn't really want to run into anyone he knew. He decided on a little Italian restaurant in Boston, one of those places you had to walk down stairs to get to, with checkered tablecloths and candles stuck in old Chianti bottles. It was the kind of place his friends made fun of: corny and romantic, full of couples staring into each other's eyes and weatherbeaten Italian waiters who brought you a free after-dinner brandy if they caught you holding hands between courses. It fit his mood perfectly.

Schuyler couldn't believe he'd asked this girl out, and for what seemed like the hundredth time that day he went over exactly how it had happened. He'd been checking a book out of the library and there she was, right behind him, twirling a strand of hair with her index finger. At first he didn't recognize her—it had been nearly a month since he'd met her, that night when Teddy got drunk and they went to visit his old room in Harvard Yard. There were her clothes in his old closet, her books on his shelf, her pink down comforter with the roses appliquéd at the borders folded at the foot of the bed where his red-and-black Hudson's Bay blanket used to be.

He had offered to walk her home, and there was something in the soft way she spoke, her voice trailing up at the end of each sentence as though asking a question, that made him feel protective and confi-

27

dent. Her innocence and hopefulness were so contagious that Schuyler found himself believing, as he hadn't for so long, that the world really could be a happy and simple place if you found the right person, as perhaps he just had.

I am going to move very slowly, he told himself, taking a fresh flannel shirt out of the closet. I am going to proceed very carefully with this delicate, frightened, absolutely wonderful girl. He buttoned his shirt all the way up, then undid the top two buttons, then refastened the next to last button, and then he softly sang her name, Rosaline, like a prayer or a children's song or a wish.

Rosaline couldn't decide what would be more absolutely awful, if he tried to kiss her or if he didn't try at all. If he didn't try, as no one ever had, it meant that she had failed in some way: she wasn't pretty enough or she hadn't flirted enough or maybe she had flirted too much. If he tried, he would know how inexperienced she was. He would never ask her out again. He would make fun of her to all his friends. He would write an article in the school newspaper about how this new crop of freshman girls didn't know how to kiss. The faculty would call an emergency meeting where they would decide to give compulsory instruction on kissing to all incoming Radcliffe students.

Katie Lee was going through Rosaline's closet, shaking her head.

"We've got to find you something decent to wear. Remember what I told you: don't talk about money, don't talk about your family, and don't talk about politics. Here, what about this," she said, holding out a black velveteen jumper with mother of pearl buttons.

"I've got matching shoes," Rosaline said, digging out a pair of black velvet ballet flats.

Katie Lee rolled her eyes. "We have got to get you some heels. First thing on Monday. And we have to buy you some new clothes. I haven't seen this kind of thing since the eighth grade."

"My mother picks out all my clothes. What color shirt do I wear with it?" Rosaline asked, opening a drawer full of cotton turtlenecks.

"You don't need a shirt under this, darling. It practically comes up to your collarbone."

"It's a *jumper*, Katie Lee."

"Oh please, I don't want to hear that awful word. Rosaline, you're nearly eighteen."

December came in carrying a bag of makeup. "Here's the change,

Rosaline. Remember, you can't rub your eyes when you've got this stuff on."

"What if I'm allergic?"

"Quit stalling, girl. He'll be here any minute," December said, laying out the makeup on Rosaline's desk. She noticed that Katie Lee had dolled herself up fairly nicely for a girl who didn't have a date; the room reeked of her perfume. She realized with an inward grimace that she had unconsciously done the same thing, changing to a clean shirt in the middle of the afternoon and washing her long hair early enough so that it would be dry by the time Schuyler arrived to pick up her roommate.

"You're so sweet to be doing all this for me," Rosaline said as December and Katie Lee fussed over her makeup.

December was thinking, We aren't sweet at all, but Rosaline is too nice or too naïve or too preoccupied to figure out that we're doing all this out of guilt. If they helped Rosaline, it would compensate for the way they'd both been preening in mirrors all afternoon, wondering what sort of impression they'd make on Schuyler when he arrived to pick up their roommate.

Katie Lee was thinking, I can't believe how beautiful this girl is and she doesn't even know it, which is probably the only reason I can bear to be around her. I wonder if Schuyler has a roommate or, even better, an identical twin brother.

But when he came knocking it was Marinda who, emerging swiftly from her room in a white angora sweater none of them had ever seen before, beat them to the door and welcomed him to their humble abode.

"Not so humble, I think," Schuyler said, taking in the framed prints and stereo equipment that Katie Lee had purchased with her father's credit card. "How have you been doing, Marinda?"

"Oh fine, you know, I was supposed to go to New Haven this weekend to visit my boyfriend but I've got too much work so I'm stuck here."

Schuyler took in the sweater, the gold bangle bracelets, and the velvet jeans.

Marinda blushed. "My cousin's giving a party tonight—he's a junior in Winthrop House—and I may go over there later."

"Hey Schuyler," December said, "Rosaline will be out in a minute." She gave him an intimate smile, as though there were some wonderful secret they shared, and when Marinda looked away Schuyler smiled back.

"How's it been going?" he said, though of course he knew: word of

December's sexual exploits had spread first through the freshman yard and then to the upper class houses in the first weeks after registration. There'd been a congressman's son, an assistant professor in the economics department, two members of the varsity crew, and one of the doctors at the university health service. But there wasn't anything sluttish about her, Schuyler thought, watching her smile. It was as though she had been the user and not the used; she seemed to sleep around the way a man did, taking the best of what was offered and leaving with no regret or attachments. There was something wild in her, as if she were daring a man, he thought, to catch her.

"Can't complain," December said.

"Our darling December never complains," said Katie Lee, sailing in on a cloud of Miss Dior, "even about having to sleep in the living room," she continued, waving toward the narrow bed that most nights remained unoccupied.

"Hello Schuyler," Rosaline said, staring at her shoes.

"Hello Rosie," he replied, and she looked up and smiled. No one had ever called her that, and the easy intimacy of the nickname made something inside her relax.

Schuyler took a step toward her, and in that moment he could see the entire progress of the courtship unfolding: this candlelight dinner and the pale-yellow roses he would send the next morning, a month full of such dinners and flowers and walks with Rosaline along the river, each time her step a little more confident, his holding her hand a little tighter, until she had grown up and he had grown younger, to that place where they would meet, at last, as lovers. He took her elbow and, without saying goodbye to the others, steered her out into the night.

Marinda was trying to see whatever it was that Schuyler had seen in Rosaline. She wasn't jealous, exactly; she had a steady boyfriend, after all, and had therefore taken herself out of what her mother would have called circulation. But somehow she felt rejected, the way she often did when a man she had confessed no interest in chose to go out with one of her friends. It was as though she wanted all these men to be secretly in love with her, to have some sort of unspoken fealty. *What about me,* she found herself thinking in these situations, *wouldn't you rather have me if only you could.* There was something she was trying to prove, something that had to do with power, something she couldn't prove with Peter.

"He's unbelievable, isn't he," December said, coming up behind her.

"What? Yes, he's cute, in a kind of cowboy way, if you go in for that."

December lifted her eyebrows. "Any woman who wouldn't go in for that is in serious need of medical treatment."

"He's just a boy, December," Marinda said. She felt it disloyal to Rosaline, somehow, to be talking about Schuyler like this. Sometimes December seemed to say any old thing that came into her head without thinking first if it were appropriate or kind or polite. Marinda was sure this sort of behavior would get her friend into serious trouble, though she couldn't say of what kind.

December shrugged. She had learned over the last few weeks that there was no such thing as an honest conversation with Marinda. Too many barricades had been erected around whatever it was that Marinda was trying to hide. Her boyfriend Peter, for example, was obviously sliding into a serious drug problem—that had been clear on his last visit to Cambridge—but when December had tried to bring it up, Marinda would have none of it. Marinda was always pretending her life was so perfect. So perfectly boring, is what December thought.

"What should I wear to this party?" December asked. "What kind of people will be there?"

"Oh, you don't have to dress up," Marinda said, thinking of the platform shoes and short skirts that December favored. "Jeans are fine. It'll be kind of a preppy crowd, but the pink-and-greens won't be there."

Katie Lee emerged from her room wearing kelly green trousers and a pink Shetland sweater.

"Uh, Katie Lee," December said, "watch out for the sand trap by the seven hole."

"You look fine, Katie Lee," Marinda said.

"Sweetheart, I look better than fine," Katie Lee replied. "Will there be some liquor at this party? Because I don't think I can live through another one of these Yankee beer bashes."

Marinda laughed. "Bobby gives the best parties," she said. "Don't you worry 'bout a thing."

Katie Lee was worried about December, who was inhaling something from what seemed to be diving apparatus, and she was worried about her new green pants, which were stained with red wine that some awful noisy person had spilled on his way to the bathroom. It was unbelievable how people were behaving. The son of a senator who had introduced antidrug legislation into Congress was cutting lines of cocaine with the daughter of an actress whose career had taken a nose dive into alcoholism. An heiress to a Colorado mining fortune was dancing the bump with two boys, one white, one black, whom Katie Lee had earlier caught kissing on the staircase.

"You look like you could use these," said a voice coming up behind her. Katie Lee turned to see what was being offered: a glass of dark liquor and a glass of clear soda, held by a tall, muscular young man wearing a neatly pressed dress shirt tucked into tan corduroy jeans. His deep tan, black curling hair, and strong nose were set off by eyes that didn't seem to belong to the rest of his severe face: clear, warm brown, and smiling, as though someone had just told a joke. He looked to Katie Lee like the kind of man she'd seen photographed in travel advertisements for the Mediterranean, the sensual sun worshiper stretched out on a rock over the ocean, the salt water still beading up on his smooth, dark skin.

"You must be a swimmer," Katie Lee said.

"How can you tell?"

"The shoulders," she replied in her best southern belle voice, "and the short hair."

"How do I know Marinda didn't brief you about me?" His voice was deep and his speech held no trace of an accent, as though he'd learned to speak from listening to television announcers.

Katie Lee tilted her head to one side and drew her lips together in a little pout, careful not to get any lip gloss on her teeth. "And how do I know she didn't brief *you* about *me*?"

"She did, actually. You must be Katie Lee. I'm her cousin, Bobby Vincent." Katie Lee stepped back, and he laughed. "You look surprised."

"Well, yes, a little. I'm not sure what I expected," she said, waving one hand at the smoke-filled room.

"Someone in a leather jacket, with a mustache, smoking foul cigarettes?"

"That's not what I meant. You look so—so healthy, that's all."

"You have to be healthy to keep this up. Anyway, we aren't as decadent as we seem. Most of these people will be responsible pillars of corporate society in less than ten years. But for now, well."

"If this is your idea of having a good time."

"I enjoy giving people what they want, and I thought you'd want this," he said, holding up the glasses.

Katie Lee took the liquor and sipped it. "This is my favorite," she said. "I know for a fact they don't sell this kind of bourbon in Boston."

"I have a case shipped up at the beginning of every semester. This is for you too," he said, handing her the club soda.

"I wouldn't dream of spoiling Kentucky's very finest with carbonated Yankee tap water."

"It's for your pants. To get out the wine. It's an old trick I learned from my mother. Here, I'll show you." He poured some of the soda on her pants where the wine had spilled, just above her knee, and when the bubbling had stopped he wiped it off with a cloth towel. Katie Lee was shocked that this strange person was actually daring to put his hands on her leg (she never used the word "thigh," even in her thoughts), but with all the wildness going on in the room she supposed no one would notice this. It felt sort of nice, actually, to have those strong athlete's hands massaging her; it must be something they learned at practice. She could see his shoulder muscles working against the fine thin cotton of his shirt.

"A host's prerogative," Bobby said, straightening up.

"It works," Katie Lee cried. "I can't believe it."

"It never fails," Bobby said, waving his hand to indicate he was moving on to another part of the room. "It's one of the most useful tricks I know."

"And just what were you up to with Katie Lee?" Marinda asked, handing Bobby a joint.

"I was just being the helpful host."

"You needn't bother. She's a professional virgin."

"You mean she gets paid for it? Or rather, for not doing it?"

"You know what I mean. She told me she was waiting until she got married, or at least engaged. She said I was a fool to sleep with Peter before he'd asked me to marry him."

"Is he going to ask you to marry him?"

Marinda rolled her eyes. "Give me a break. I'm only eighteen."

"Well no one graduates from Radcliffe a virgin. It's one of the university requirements."

"If I had to bet on anyone, I'd bet on Katie Lee," Marinda said. "I think she actually gets a kick out of it, you know, getting these guys all worked up, letting them go so far and no farther, and then giving them this little speech about sex and commitment."

"Did I hear you talking about sex?" said Bobby's roommate Carter, who'd come up to bum the tail end of the joint.

"Who me?" Marinda said. "Heaven forfend. Bobby, what were we talking about. I can't remember. Excuse me, I think the bathroom's free. They must have been in there for at least twenty minutes."

"Did I say something wrong?" Carter asked, running a hand through his long disheveled blond hair. "Did I interrupt some important family conference?"

"We were talking about her roommate, over there, the one in the pink sweater."

"Luscious, definitely luscious. And a virgin, I happen to know."

Bobby raised his eyebrows.

"She went out with Woody Stewart a couple of times. Drove him up the wall, actually. She's one of those girls with a master plan like you wouldn't believe. She wants to make a million dollars by the time she's twenty-one, and she's looking to hitch up to some serious money. Well, you know, Woody's got this monster inheritance coming to him, so he thought he might get some leverage with Katie Lee, but she told him he was a lazy fool for not trying to do something on his own. She drove him crazy, I have to say, it was sort of fun to watch."

"She's very pretty."

"Oh God, Bobby, don't even bother," Carter said.

"It's never a bother," Bobby replied.

"She's not your type. Though you're probably her type. You're probably the only person I know more ambitious than she is. Don't let her know about your money though."

"She already knows. She rooms with Marinda."

"It's not worth the effort."

"Maybe not," Bobby said, but he remembered how Katie Lee's thigh had first tensed and then relaxed under his hands, and he thought how much more interesting the cold Yankee winter would be if he figured out a way to spoil Kentucky's very finest.

December was sitting cross-legged on the floor smoking a menthol cigarette. In this little space, between a stereo speaker and an orange crate of records, it was too loud to talk, and December thought it might be time to head home. The crowd had thinned, and a few people had passed out in the smaller rooms. It was that moment in the early morning where you either sensibly pack it in or decide to drive right through till dawn. December wasn't tired, but she was weary of Bobby's friends. There was something mean about them, the way they never moved their thin mouths when they spoke and looked so bored when they danced, as though the world were a place that didn't deserve their best efforts.

A boy in a tightly tailored green velvet dinner jacket grabbed her wrist and pulled her to her feet.

"Oh, no," December said, surprised to see how thin he was after feeling his strong grip, "I couldn't possibly dance. I'm too beat."

The boy smiled briefly. His crooked teeth came as a shock, for everything else about him seemed perfectly put together. His velvet jacket—it must have been custom-made, December thought, to fit so well—showed not a spot of the evening's damages. Underneath he wore a kind of T-shirt December had never seen before, not the kind of thing that sat wrapped in plastic in the underwear department but something expensive that probably required dry cleaning. His jeans were different too; they were made of regulation blue denim but were cut like dress trousers. His boots were silver, and he wore a single silver earring in his left ear. His red hair curled in ringlets right down to his shoulders, and his eyes were wide and light. His mouth drooped at the corners, as though he were just about to say something very disapproving, and his skin was as fair as a young girl's.

"Of course you don't want to dance," he said with a British accent. December had not met enough Englishmen to identify all the regional accents, but his voice was so clear and his pronunciation so clipped that she knew he must be from the best place, wherever that was. London, she imagined. "No one could dance to this dreadful music. I am going out for breakfast, and I would be delighted if you would join me."

"You would?" December asked. "Why?"

"I always leave with the prettiest girl."

"Try again," December said.

"All right. Because everyone is waiting to see who you'll go home with. Your reputation precedes you—don't bother making faces at me, I'm sure you don't care a bit. And because it would annoy Bobby extremely if you left with me, and I'm in the mood to annoy Bobby because he borrowed my car last week and put a nasty dent in the rear left fender. I believe he's already promised you to one of his wretched roommates, or maybe he's sold you off, the unscrupulous Italian. And because an old girlfriend of mine is about to make a scene, and with you as protection she won't follow me into the street."

December giggled. "I like that last reason the best. You were pretending to come rescue me, but you're really the one who needs rescuing."

"For which I will repay you with a lovely meal at my lovely apartment."

"On one condition."

"What is that, Miss Dunne?"

"You tell me your name."

"Child. Alexander Child. Around here they call me Alex."

"It's a deal, Mr. Child," December said, taking his arm. He looks like a rock star, she thought, as they walked the ten short blocks to the tan brick prewar apartment building where Alex kept three lavishly furnished rooms.

"Don't be too impressed," he said, putting up the water for coffee. "This is really my cousin's place, he's had it for years, but we all use it when we need it. My father lived here for a semester when he was a visiting professor. My sister hid out here after her second divorce. I have it until I graduate, unless Cynthia's third marriage takes a dive, in which case it becomes hers. She's the eldest. December Dunne. Is your middle initial *A*? Then your name would be an anagram for Menace Under Bed."

"I don't have a middle initial. How long did it take you to figure that out?"

"No time at all. It's this peculiar skill I have—it may be my only skill, I'm beginning to think. Give me a friend's name and I'll show you."

"Rosaline."

"Lion ears."

"Marinda."

"Mad Rain. It's easy once you get going."

December looked at the bookshelves while Alex put together an omelette. They were filled with photography books, the kind of books you had to wash your hands before reading.

Alex came in with breakfast on a silver tray. "There's vodka in the grapefruit juice," he said. "My cousin's a photographer. It's his excuse to meet beautiful women. I suppose it's a better excuse than the one I offered you. If you tell me this is the best omelette you've ever had I'll be yours forevermore."

"It's the best omelette I've ever had."

"You haven't even tasted it yet."

"I'm not hungry. I hate breakfast. I'm allergic to eggs."

"Then why are you here."

"I was just following orders," December said, stirring the vodka up from the bottom of the glass. Because, she thought, you're mysterious and British and elegant and smart and I haven't tried that combination yet. Because you're terrifically good-looking, and you know it, and you know that I know it, and you're not at all arrogant about it.

"You're not as arrogant as you sound," she said, as though he had been following her thoughts.

It took him a moment to catch up. "No, it's the accent, mostly. Your accent, where are you from."

"New Jersey."

"I haven't had the pleasure."

"Well, I wouldn't exactly call it a pleasure."

"And what was it like, growing up in New Jersey."

"Pretty boring, I guess. It's just another place. No stories to tell," December said.

"You mean no stories that you care to tell."

He may be too smart, December thought. "I have no secrets," she said.

Alex refilled December's glass and lit a cigarette. "That's what people say," he said as he exhaled a ring of smoke, "when they're hiding the most dreadful secret of all. Let me guess. Mother was a prostitute. Father was her business manager. Brother is a drug addict, and sister is in a mental hospital."

December laughed. "My father is a boring businessman and my mother is a boring housewife and my brother and sister are still in a boring elementary school," she said.

"Well maybe that's your secret," Alex said, "that you're secretly a very boring person."

"That must be it."

"I don't believe it for a minute," Alex said without a smile. "I don't believe it at all."

December laughed again. "That's one of my mother's favorite expressions, actually, she's always saying 'Can you believe it?' You know, like 'Paper towel's on sale at the Grand Union for forty-nine cents, can you believe it?' 'It went down to four below zero last night, can you believe it?'" December imitated her mother's South Jersey accent, a hybrid of nasal Philadelphia and lazy rural Dixie. "'Ten thousand people died in an earthquake, can you believe it?' "

Alex joined in the laughter. He loved a good performance, especially at someone else's expense.

"What's her name," he asked.

"Gloria," December said. "Make an anagram of that."

"Easy enough," Alex said, pouring more vodka into December's glass. "Rio Gal. O, a girl. You try."

December pictured her mother's name spelled out in dark block letters against a white background, like a child's flashcards.

"Go, liar," she said.

"December's going to Harvard, can you believe it?" Gloria had announced one night at the dinner table. Though it was December who had applied to college, Gloria had taken the entire process very seriously, as though the admissions departments were passing judgment on her ability to raise her children. Her daughter's acceptance by the best schools was seen by Gloria as a vindication of every bad episode in her whole troubled life; every unlucky break and sorry setback had led to precisely this moment. It was all part of God's plan, Gloria believed, that the mother had suffered for the daughter's rewards.

Gloria had grown up on a blueberry farm in South Jersey, and by the age of sixteen she was pregnant by the best-looking boy in her high school class: Harrison a.k.a. Sonny Kidwell, another local farm kid, a born charmer who had taught himself to drive at twelve years old on his family's one Harvester tractor. He knew how to blow smoke rings and light a match on his jeans zipper and buy a six-pack of Carling's without any I.D. He seemed to know just about everything there was to know except how to hold down a job, and Gloria started baking pies for the local restaurants and diners in order to support herself and her new husband. From the day her daughter was born, December 31, 1954, Gloria promised herself that her daughter would have a better life.

Sonny Kidwell died when December was four, and Gloria swore it was the best thing that had ever happened to her. Within three months she had gone back to her maiden name, moved up to northern New Jersey, and married a forty-year-old Irish immigrant named Willie Dunne, who owned two gas stations and a small diner on Route 35. Willie Dunne had money, and after Gloria had borne him two children—Madeline and Willie junior—he didn't particularly care how Gloria spent it.

Gloria spent most of it inventing a new life for herself and December. She decorated the house in American colonial furniture from Sears, Roebuck and covered the walls with framed Currier and Ives reproductions and needlepoint samplers. For December there were toys and books and ruffled dresses and endless lessons in piano, tap dancing, and gymnastics. Gloria cut out a picture of Princess Grace from *Life* and Scotch-taped it over December's bureau to remind her daughter to "aim for the stars." She told December there were only two rules she had to follow. The first was always to try her best to be better than everyone else. The second was that she must never mention her father or their life before Gloria married Willie.

Ten years after his death Gloria still hated Sonny Kidwell for knocking her up and leaving her with a small child to support. "If it hadn't been for Sonny," she told her second husband, "I could have been anything. I could have gone to Hollywood, or at least to New York." It was her personal punishment from God, she believed, that December grew up to look exactly like her father: same sharp bones, same thick, pale hair, and hardest of all, same ice-blue eyes that stared and stared and never seemed to blink. Gloria used to think that Sonny was reading her mind, and as December grew up, she began to think December could read her thoughts as well.

But December learned early to pay as little attention as possible to her mother. She went to all the lessons, and she tried to do well at them, because she knew that as long as she did her mother would leave her alone. She learned to like boys early, and she and her mother struck an unspoken bargain: as long as December did well in school, her mother wouldn't question her staying out till dawn or going off in cars with boys older than she, sometimes by several years. In the third week of June at the end of her sophomore year, December was ranked first in her class. Two days later she lost her virginity.

Getting December into an Ivy League school became the most important thing in Gloria's life. They could afford the best now—Willie had bought franchises to two McDonald's restaurants, and the worse the economy got, the more people wanted to eat out someplace cheap. It was Gloria who sent away for all the school catalogues and chose which college exams to take and bought the pale-gray flannel suit for December to wear to her interviews. All she asked was that December take some speech lessons so that she wouldn't sound "like such a Jersey tomato" at her interviews.

When December read the applications that her mother had typed up on an IBM Selectric borrowed from Willie's office, she discovered that Gloria had listed December's real father as an attorney named Bentley Harrison.

"This is too much," December said. "What kind of name is Bentley?"

"It's a very respectable name," Gloria said. "Don't worry, they never check this stuff. You don't want to come off like you're the first person in your family to go to college."

"Oh great. What do I say when they ask me how he died?"

"They wouldn't ask such a rude question. If they do, just say he died in a car accident." She's right, December thought, they never ask you how your father died. Even her best friends, who knew that Willie was Gloria's second husband and December's stepfather but little more than that, were afraid to ask. December had used the car-accident story before, when pressed by a guidance counselor at school.

"Maybe I'll tell them the truth," December said. "That would be interesting for once."

Gloria grabbed her daughter by the wrist. "This is no joke. I've only asked one thing from you your whole life, and that's to forget about your father. When I married Willie he became your father."

"Stop, Mama, you're hurting me." December tried to pull her arm away.

Gloria tightened her grip. "You promise me you'll never mention his name in this house or anywhere."

"I was just kidding. Come on."

"You promise me. Promise your mother."

December's hand was growing numb. "Okay, okay, I promise."

Gloria released December's hand. "You know I love you, honey. You know I'm doing all this just for you."

"I know, Mama," December said. "I know."

By their fourth drink and the third David Bowie album, Alex and December were lying across the silk Chinese carpet, speculating on which jungle animals they would most like to be.

"Maybe one of those antelopes with the exotic names," December said. "Or a lion."

"Having trouble making up your mind between being the hunter or the prey?"

"Well, if you're going to put it that way, a lion, definitely. I have the mane for it."

Alex took a hank of December's hair and held it up to his face, breathing in. "Only the male lions have manes. Your hair smells fantastic."

"New shampoo."

Now Alex was moving his nose in slow, small circles in December's hair, along her hairline, back and forth across her forehead, around her tiny unpierced ear. "This is how the animals approach each other," he said.

"And what animal are you?"

"A black panther, definitely," Alex said. "No political implications intended."

"A black panther is really a kind of leopard, isn't it?"

"I don't know. They're the ultimate combination of strength and grace. They are both beautiful and rare."

Just like me is what he's going to say next, December thought.

"You know," Alex said, "you wear the most awful clothing."

"Well, thanks so much," December said. "Flattery will get you everywhere."

"You know I'm right, my darling," he continued, fingering the drawstring that gathered up the coarse bright cotton of her Mexican blouse. "You should be wearing silks and velvets. In blues, and grays, and violets. To play up that wonderfully pale skin and those gorgeous eyes. You should look like the ice princess in a nineteenth-century ballet."

"This sounds very decadent," December said, lifting herself up on one elbow. "And very expensive."

"Oh please let's not talk about money, it's the most boring subject. I shall have to take you shopping. Imagine yourself in a long blue velvet dress, with buttons running up the front from your ankles all the way to here," he said, placing one finger on her collarbone. December lay back and closed her eyes.

"On your feet, the most delicate gray suede boots that lace up just to the ankle," he whispered, unbuckling her platform sandals and taking off her striped cotton socks. He unzipped her jeans and pulled them off in one smooth motion. "White silk stockings, seams up the back." He lifted her up by the hips to remove her underwear, and then by the shoulders to take off her shirt. "An ivory satin camisole trimmed with lace. Satin shorts as smooth as your skin."

He kept talking in a low voice as he stood up and began to take off his own clothes. "You're lying on a deep feather bed, on cool white feather pillows." December heard a snap unsnapping and a zipper being undone and the soft fall of more clothing against the carpet. "Outside it is nearly dawn. It is very quiet, very still." He was lying next to her, holding her head in one hand. She turned to him, her eyes still closed, and he kissed her softly, their lips barely brushing, over and over. Her breath was coming faster now, but when she tried to pull him closer he held her back.

"Shhhh," he whispered. "Everything will happen very slowly. You have been waiting for me a very long time." With one hand he was stroking her hair, with the other he drew slow circles across her cheeks, down her neck, around her breasts, each circle a little lower, a little closer, as December felt him stiffen against her thigh.

"Everything will happen very slowly," he repeated, and she felt his fingers inside her, still moving in circles.

"As if in a dream," he said, and then he was quiet, and the only sound was their own breath and the soft bass of the music pounding up through the floor. His fingers were wet with her now, and she lost count of how many times he had massaged and flicked and teased her to the edge of coming and then stopped, suddenly, until she grew calmer and he began it all again. The part of her that had always remained conscious during even the wildest sex—the part that calculated if a rhythm was too fast or too slow, that looked for the moment when perhaps she should roll to a different position or do something unexpected with her hands—this part was all gone now, and Alex was in total control. She was nothing now, nothing except what he made of her, and just when she felt they might go on like this forever, he pushed her up so that she was sitting astride him, bracing her hips with his hands.

Now it was December's turn. She opened her eyes and she began to move around him, first slowly in circles, then faster, pressing, until she could see from the sweat beading up on his smooth chest and the tension in his throat that he was about to come. Then she would stop and sit quite still until his breath deepened and he relaxed a little inside her. And then she would start again, barely moving at first, taking just the tip of him inside her, and they went on this way until she felt her legs begin to quiver from fatigue. He drew her down to him and rolled over on top of her and when he kissed her on the mouth she knew that now, at last, they would not have to hold back. They rocked together and came together with the low long hums of people who have spent every final bit of energy to get to this precise perfect place.

"Well," was all Alex seemed to be able to say. "Well, well, well."

December said nothing. She never did. She smiled, and kissed him on the nose.

"You are the most perfect creature," he said, and then he went to sleep.

December woke first. It was cold on the floor, and the afternoon sun had brightened the room through the thin gauze curtains. She got dressed, and did the dishes, and washed her face with soap that smelled of cinnamon, and brushed her teeth with some mint-flavored paste she had squeezed onto her index finger.

She made herself some coffee and watched Alex sleep. He looked different by daylight: his body seemed more boyishly unmuscular, but his face looked harder, with the tiny creases around the eyes that the palest redheads develop at a very early age. She didn't want to wake him up—he must have been very tired, after all, and as long as he was asleep she could stay in this wonderful apartment filled with glorious expensive things.

There were some ceramic bowls that looked so delicate she was afraid to pick them up or even touch them. A carved wooden music box played Schubert when she opened it. She ran a hand across a shelf filled with expensive books in glossy dust covers. There were books in December's house, but they were mostly paperbacks or cheap club editions of best sellers that came in the mail, war histories and spy thrillers for her stepfather, novels of chaste romance for her mother.

December took out an oversized book of photographs and looked at the pictures of garden vegetables and rushing water. Another book was filled with fashion models, painted and corseted to suit the tastes of various decades. A history of gruesome crimes began with an introduction by a famous psychiatrist on the nature-versus-nurture debate: whether psychopaths were born to kill or formed by early adverse circumstances.

December turned the pages. There were Bonnie and Clyde leaning against a wall, Bonnie surprisingly unattractive compared to Faye Dunaway in the movie. The Boston Strangler looked like four or five boys in her senior class. Richard Speck was pale and blurry, and there was no mention of what had become of the nurse who had saved herself by hiding under a bed.

She flipped back through the book until she found what she was looking for. There were two full pages devoted to him, with little photographs of the twelve elderly people he had stabbed to death during a seven-month spree, all of them alone in their farmhouses at night, some of them without telephones. One couple didn't even have running water. That was how they traced him, finally; he hadn't been able to wash the blood off his clothes before he got back in his car.

The biggest picture was the famous one of him smiling at reporters the day before he went to the electric chair. His chiseled good looks, pale blond hair, and innocent blue eyes had earned him the nickname of the Choirboy Killer.

Harrison "Sonny" Kidwell, the caption said, 1937–1959.

"Good morning, love," Alex said, raising himself up on his elbows. "Or should I say good evening."

December quickly replaced the books, dropping the one on fashion models.

"That's all right," Alex said, "my cousin wouldn't mind. You can borrow whatever you want. Come over here and give me a kiss."

"I was just looking."

"Really, it's all right."

"Well, thanks, maybe I'll borrow this one," she said, picking up the book on models. Her hands were shaking.

"You know, you could be a model if you wanted to. You're tall enough. I suppose you've heard that before. You just need a little instruction, about makeup and clothing and how to walk. It's nice money."

December began to cry.

Alex got up and pulled on his pants. "I didn't mean to depress you. You must stop, I'm helpless with teary women. Come here, I'll give you a hug. Whatever is the matter. Shhh, come on, what have I done."

"Nothing, it's just me, nothing's the matter," December whispered. "I'm just happy. I'm just really happy right now."

3

Katie Lee Hopewell   Rosaline Van Schott
                    and
Marinda Vincent   December Dunne

request the dubious honor of your presence
at their first annual Christmas Party
Saturday, December 15, at 9 P.M.
Fielding 42

Répondez or else

"Or else what?" Alex asked, signaling the waiter for the check.

"Beats me," December said. "I hate giving parties. I told them I couldn't afford to kick in any money, and I told them there wasn't really anyone I wanted to invite, and I told them I hated cleaning up other people's messes, and they still insisted on putting my name on the invitation because they said it would have looked weird to have the three of them on there and not me."

"You'll forgive me if I don't attend. I'm leaving for London on the tenth."

"When do you get back?"

"First week of January." Just like that, December thought. No mention of Christmas. No mention of New Year's Eve, her birthday. Damn it, she said to herself, I knew this steady boyfriend business was going to turn into a huge drag. December had strayed only twice in the two months since she'd met Alex (once over Thanksgiving with the captain of her high school soccer team and once in the third-floor men's room at Hilles Library with a friend of Bobby Vincent's who'd given her his Shakespeare lecture notes).

"Well," she said, "it'll probably be a terrible party. It's all Katie Lee's idea. She's making this whole big deal over the guest list, and the dance tape, and what we're all going to wear."

"And what are you going to wear?" Alex asked, leaving a five-dollar bill on the table and getting out of his seat.

December shrugged.

"You wouldn't mind letting me play Santa Claus for a few hours, would you?" he said. "No, I thought not. Come along, there's this little shop on Arrow Street where my cousin shops. It's time we got you some decent clothes."

Alex took her by the arm and steered her down the narrow brick sidewalk. Though they had been seeing each other several times a week since the night of Bobby's party, this was only the second or third time they'd gone out together in public. Usually December went to Alex's apartment after her last afternoon class; he cooked her dinner and then they stayed in bed until late the next morning.

He had been to her room only once—she'd had to drag him there, her roommates had insisted on it—and he always begged off with a previous engagement if December mentioned a party she'd been invited to. December was used to men who liked to show her off. She suspected Alex had objections—to her clothes, her accent, she wasn't sure what—but she never questioned their arrangement. Alex could be very charming, but he could also be very moody and difficult, and December was relieved not to have to worry that he might be rude to her friends.

"Here we are," Alex said, opening the door to a long, narrow room with one whole wall covered with mirrors. "Hello, Maggie," he said to the woman sitting behind an antique walnut desk. "I've brought you another victim. December, Maggie; Maggie, December. The works, Maggie—clothes, shoes, hats, underwear—we're starting from scratch. Keep everything very tight because under that sweatshirt there's a quite spectacular body. I want a sort of twenties feel to it—a little decadent, muted colors, show some skin."

December stood on a Chinese carpet in the middle of the shop as Maggie pulled down the blinds, locked the shop door, and began to circle her wordlessly. Maggie was about forty, December guessed, with gray hair pulled back in a braid and exaggerated black eyeliner. She was wearing layers of bulky clothing over what looked to be a very large body, and, like other fat women December had seen, wore heaps of jangly and ostentatious jewelry: large dangling earrings, strands of beads, several bracelets on each arm, antique brooches here and there.

As Alex sat in a rocking chair smoking a cigarette Maggie sized up her prey. She lifted December's hair and held it up to the light. She turned December's face first to one side, then to the other. She pulled back December's shoulders, circled her waist with her hands, tested her thighs for firmness, and measured her every length, width, and circumference with a clear plastic tape measure.

In a thick eastern European accent she said to Alex, "She is a very nice one, darling, you will see what a wonderful thing, yes, I know just what to do."

And then, to December: "Take off that shit."

December stripped, and Maggie kicked her clothing under an antique armoire. Then the work began, no one talking, just the sound of Mahler coming over the speakers as Alex indicated with a nod of the head whether a certain item met with his approval. There were no price tags on any of the garments; Maggie simply made an entry in a little leather notebook, and Alex initialed the bottom of each page. December stood as still as a mannequin, watching each transformation in the long mirror.

In a mauve panne velvet dress with a sweetheart neckline and a flared skirt, and green suede boots that laced all the way up to her knees, December felt like the mistress of some very famous old French painter. In a blue satin camisole worn over matching blue velveteen trousers she was a California movie star holding an intimate dinner party for her hundred or so best friends. With every outfit—in the end there were ten of them, chalked and pinned and ready for Maggie's tailor—December lived another fantasy: cabaret singer, tango dancer, double agent, runway model.

"Wonderful, Maggie," Alex said when she was done. "We just need one thing, a signature piece, something she can wear with all of it." He reached up to a hat rack, pulled down an antique ivory aviator scarf, and wrapped it around December's neck. "This you can wear home. Maggie, send the rest of it to my place."

"Alex, I don't know what to say," December whispered. "It's gorgeous, all of it. I don't know when and where I'll be able to wear it, but it's all so beautiful. Thank you."

Alex frowned. "Well, you'll wear it every day of course, beginning in January when I get back. In the meantime you will have your little party and your Christmas vacation and you can wear your jeans and T-shirts and peasant blouses and have all the fun in them you want, because when I get back they are going into boxes under your bed."

"I don't get it."

"You will. That's another thing, I'd like to find you a good voice coach, to get rid of that awful accent. Thank God for those ballet lessons, at least you know how to walk."

"I didn't realize how, uh, imperfect I was."

"You are perfect, sweetheart, and now you are going to be perfecter. How would you like to be the most beautiful, famous, sought-after actress in the world?"

"Are you kidding me?"

"Please stop using those middle-class expressions. Simply answer me yes or no."

"Gee, Alex, I love these clothes, but you know, let's not get carried away or anything."

"Just answer me yes or no."

December looked into the mirror and saw what she was: in jeans and sweatshirt and Scandinavian clogs worn down at the heels she was a very pretty young girl, getting herself a very nice education at a place where she might find a perfectly nice husband. Then she remembered what she had been just a few minutes ago in the outfits Maggie had put together: a star.

"Okay," she said. "I mean yes. Yes."

Alex took her hands in his and kissed the top of her head.

"Then trust me, my darling, because it will be the smartest thing you've ever done. Because I'm the only one who really understands you. Because I have wonderful plans for you."

Every morning when Rosaline woke up the first thing she saw was the lavender shoe box, tied with a blue velvet ribbon, sitting on the windowsill next to her bed. The box held little mementos of her evenings with Schuyler. Though she knew its contents by heart, some days, like today, she stayed in bed a little longer and went through it item by item, each dried flower or restaurant matchbook proof that romance was really happening to her, as though she were taking an inventory of love.

There was the cork from the bottle of wine they'd shared on their first date. Rosaline had slipped it into her pocket when Schuyler wasn't looking, and now, as she closed her eyes and pressed it to her nose and breathed in the last faint traces of a rich Burgundy, she remembered how it had felt the first time he held her hand, right on top of the table for everyone to see.

There was the pale-yellow strip of paper that read "Surprises only happen when you do not look for them," the fortune she'd found in her cookie the evening Schuyler took her to Chinatown. Schuyler hadn't shown her his fortune, he'd just smiled and folded it up, telling her that if you really wanted your wish to come true you mustn't ever say it out loud. I'm wishing for you, she had said to herself, blowing out the candle on their table.

There was the ticket stub from the night they'd gone to see *Singing in the Rain* in an old vaudeville house you had to enter from a back alley. When they had left the theater it was raining, though the weather report hadn't predicted it. Rosaline jumped in puddles and Schuyler swung round lampposts and by the time they got to the Yard they were thoroughly wet. He pulled her close for a goodnight kiss and she could smell the wet suede of his jacket and the scent of his shampoo in his damp hair. When he kissed her she felt her knees go a little soft, she thought she might just sink to the sidewalk if he hadn't been holding her, one hand around her neck and the other against the small of her back. Later, when she got home and hung up her corduroy coat, she could see the imprint of his hand in the wet nap of the fabric.

Their first kiss. Rosaline remembered every kiss, because every kiss was so special, she thought, or perhaps because there weren't that many to remember. *Yet*, she said to herself, tying up the blue ribbon and getting out of bed.

Out in the main room December was ironing a long white scarf.

"Hey, Rosaline," she said. "You're up early."

"Katie Lee wants to drive out to a supermarket in Arlington to pick up some things for the party."

"They don't have supermarkets in Cambridge?"

Rosaline shrugged. "Katie Lee says they're too expensive. Nice scarf," she said. "Should you really be pressing it?"

"Not really. The more heat, the less it lasts. But I shouldn't look a gift horse in the mouth, right?"

Rosaline sat on the edge of December's bed and rested her chin in her hands. "Alex has certainly been generous lately."

December put down the iron. "You disapprove. So does Marinda. She gave me a little lecture when I told her about all the clothes. She says it's like paying for sex, like I'm his mistress or a call girl, accepting all this stuff. You have to admit it's gorgeous stuff. The man has taste."

"No, I don't disapprove. You'll look wonderful when you get dressed up to go out with Alex. It must be nice to"—here Rosaline paused, with the self-consciousness of a very rich girl speaking to a very poor girl about money—"it must be nice to be able to carry off such dramatic clothing. I wish I could."

December lit a cigarette. "Thanks, I think. Alex cares so much about appearances, it drives me crazy sometimes. But I have to be honest about it, appearances are what drew us to each other."

"Oh, well, maybe at first, but now that you know each other better, I'm sure it doesn't matter at all," Rosaline said.

Her innocence is a constant surprise, December thought, the way it is between Rosaline and Schuyler, that's how Rosaline thinks it is for the rest of us. December found herself feeling jealous for the first time in her life, not of Schuyler himself but of the way he treated her friend. No one will ever think of me that way, she sighed, I gave that up a long time ago. And what did I gain, she wondered. Enough knowledge about men to fill a history book about the war between the sexes. This crazy ambition that will never be satisfied. A lovely decadent Englishman who whistles "Ruby Tuesday" in the shower. A pair of green suede boots.

"So when will you get back from New York?" December asked.

"Right after New Year's," Rosaline said. "Schuyler and I were thinking of going away for the weekend, somewhere quiet where we can get some studying done, because I have so much reading before exams. Maybe the Berkshires."

So he has it all planned out, December thought. The country-inn-snowball-fights-brandy-by-the-fire-canopy-bed routine.

"But I don't know what I'll tell my mother."

"You mean if she calls while you're away?" December asked.

"And she will call."

"Don't worry. I'll cover for you."

"Oh, thank you so much. I've never done this before."

"Lied to your mother, you mean?"

"Well, yes, for one thing. Oh, December, you *know* what I mean."

"Why don't you just say what you mean?"

"*You know.* I've never gone away with anyone before."

"That's not what you mean, sweetie."

"I've never gone away with a boy, I mean with a man, before."

"That's still not what you mean. Just spit it out, Rosaline. Say what you feel."

Rosaline sat down on December's bed and pulled a pillow onto her lap. "All right," she said, blushing a bright pink, pulling at her sweater cuffs. "I think Schuyler wants to, no that's not it, I *know* we both want to—I know we're *going* to—could I have a drag of that cigarette? Thanks. All right. So. I'm going away to sleep with this man and you know I'm a virgin, December, it's more than that, I've never done *anything* really, and it's sort of scary, I love Schuyler but it's still scary, could I have another drag? It's making me dizzy, the cigarettes, everything, please don't tell Katie Lee, and you know I can't talk to Marinda about anything really, and so, the point is. Is this. I'm absolutely terrified."

December sat down at the other end of the bed and lit a cigarette for Rosaline. "And that's absolutely normal. Everyone is."

"Even you?"

"Well, not anymore. I'm sure you can trust Schuyler. He's crazy about you and he's a terrific guy and—" December stopped herself before she said what she was thinking: and I can tell he's dynamite in the sack, I can spot them a mile away. "And you just relax and let him take care of everything. You can trust him."

"Everything? December, I read books and go to the movies just like everyone else but, well, you have to understand that I went to this *convent* school, and they didn't really tell us very much. About certain things."

"Just let him take care of everything, Rosaline. When you get back from the weekend I'll go with you to find a good doctor, and then you can make some decisions if you want. Is that what you're asking?"

"That's part of it. I just want everything to be perfect."

"Well, sometimes it isn't at first, sweetie, sometimes it takes a while. Don't put too much pressure on yourself, or on him."

"What was it like for you the first time?"

"It was romantic, I guess," December said. She'd been fifteen, and his name was Jack. She'd met him at a party at someone's beach house in Belmar. They'd toasted with her first bottle of champagne and later, long after midnight, they'd driven north on the Turnpike all the way up to the Palisades. They'd parked on the edge of the cliff, and he held her by the belt loops of her blue jeans while she leaned over the railing and looked at the lights of Manhattan in the distance and then down at the river below. It was a straight rocky drop of two hundred feet. They could hear Jerry Lee Lewis rising up from the boats at the marina. This is it, December had said to herself, my life is beginning now, at this very moment. They drove back down to the beach in time to catch the sun rise over the ocean and had a board-walk breakfast of lemonade and fried chicken.

"It was a long time ago," December said. "I couldn't tell you where he is now. But he was really sweet—that's the most important thing, Rosaline. I was lucky. And you're lucky to have Schuyler. And he's lucky to have you."

"So we're all lucky," Rosaline said. "How can you keep smoking these things? I feel like I'm drunk."

"You get used to it," December said. "It wears off after a while. Just like everything else. You can get used to anything till you hardly notice it at all."

Marinda sat alone on a long wooden bench in South Station watching the crowd come off the train, waiting for the familiar bright-red scarf and brown leather bomber jacket. It was always like this: she spent all week longing to see Peter, and then in the last few moments, in the train station here in Boston or down in New Haven, her stomach contracted into a hard knot and a wave of dread came out of nowhere and washed over her and she found herself wishing he wouldn't appear. Maybe he'd missed his train. Maybe he'd gotten sick and hadn't had a chance to call her. Maybe he wouldn't show up, for no reason at all, and she could have a perfectly normal weekend, like Rosaline or Katie Lee or December, going shopping and studying in the library and hanging out at parties making silly jokes with other girls and dancing around with drunken boys who complained about their high school girlfriends.

But there he was, a full head taller than most of the crowd even with his lazy slouch, his long reddish brown hair pulled back into a neat ponytail. Aviator sunglasses hid his deep-set hazel eyes. He has such perfect bone structure, Marinda thought, such a strong nose and jaw, he'll age so well. He'll cut his hair eventually, of course, and the red will be streaked with gray, just like his father's.

She was always doing this with Peter—imagining what he would be like, what the two of them would be like in some distant future. Peter wearing a conservatively cut dinner jacket that hung loosely over his boyishly thin frame and she in a long satin evening dress.

Peter leaning against the railing of their sailboat, his bare narrow feet pushing through the broken seams of a favorite old pair of deck shoes, his cheeks burned red by the wind, as Marinda brought him a brandy from the galley below. Peter had potential that he didn't realize—potential that no one realizes except me, Marinda thought—and he would be capable of anything once he put his mind to it, once he figured out what he wanted to do, once he got through this phase. It happened to a lot of boys at his age. Marinda would be patient. She would wait for Peter to grow up into something wonderful, and she would be rewarded for waiting; she was sure of that.

Her family didn't understand a thing about boys like Peter. They were still practically immigrants after all, and they were so busy getting ahead, expanding the family businesses, making the right connections, working, pushing, never stopping to question the value of anything they did. Her father couldn't comprehend why Peter (whose family had been established politically and financially since before the Civil War even) just coasted along, living off his allowance, instead of making plans for the business or government career that could so easily be his. Look at Peter's father, Mr. Vincent would say to Marinda—Princeton, Rhodes Scholar, his own investment house —all he has to do is ask and the party will hand him the Senate nomination on a sterling silver platter. Look at his grandfather, they still called him The Ambassador, and his great-grandfather, one of the best governors the state had ever seen. Imagine what one of my sons could do with those advantages, Mr. Vincent would say. What a waste.

No one really understands him except me, Marinda thought, waving to Peter over the crowd. He tossed his army knapsack onto the bench beside her and pulled her close for the hello hug that always ended a second too soon and the hello kiss that always progressed to tongue wrestling a second too fast.

"Merry Christmas, almost," he said, mussing her hair. "Did you come in Katie Lee's car?"

"No, I took the subway. Katie Lee needed the car to pick up stuff for the party." They walked out of the terminal into a harsh breeze blowing off the water. "We left everything for the last minute."

"Party, party, I hate parties. No, just kidding, I'm sure it will be a terrific party. Is Bobby coming?"

"Bobby and Company, they'll all be there. Bobby and Katie Lee are carrying on some kind of completely demented flirtation. I can't stand to watch them. He actually holds doors open for her, and she has all these military nicknames for him. I mean, I think she wants to marry him or something. She kept hinting around about not wanting to go to Kentucky for Christmas, and at first I thought she was just trying to wrangle an invitation out of Rosaline, but then I started thinking she wanted to come down so, you know, she could see Bobby." Marinda put her hand in the pocket of Peter's jacket.

"Well, we've talked about this, right? She's another very manipulative girl. Don't let yourself be manipulated," Peter said, putting his free hand on Marinda's shoulder. "I could really use a little smoke right now. The problem with this energy crisis is the trains are so crowded, you can't get into the bathrooms for a smoke. People were standing all the way from New York."

"We'll be home in half an hour."

"Oh, man, let's take a cab."

"The subway isn't so awful."

"I can't do it. Really, it was a rough ride. I'll pay for it," he said, hailing a taxi. They didn't talk for the half hour it took to make their way through traffic to Harvard Square; they didn't talk at all until they were in Marinda's room, with the door closed and the stereo playing "Low Spark of High Heeled Boys" and the soda and potato chips they'd bought spread out on Marinda's desk and Peter inhaling thick smoke from the clear blue plastic bong Marinda kept for him in her closet behind her rainboots.

"So, did you bring any work with you?" Marinda asked.

"Not much. I figured there wasn't really any point, with the party and all." They were lying next to each other on the narrow bed.

"You all set for your exams next week?"

"Yes and no. A couple of courses I know I'll pass easily—the history course is mostly stuff we did senior year. I might even get a B in math. French is a definite flunk. I just didn't put in the time, I guess."

"There's a language lab here I could sneak you into. They have these tapes you can listen to really intensively for hours a day, and they say it really works. I mean you might at least pass it, you know, get the credit for it." Marinda pulled off his heavy boots and then kicked off her own.

"What's the point. It's too late now. Anyway, I came here to forget about all that."

"Well, I'll need to do a little studying tomorrow."

"Your exams aren't for another month. Loosen up."

"I can't do everything over Christmas."

Peter took another long drag and turned up the stereo. "You never change," he said, unbuttoning her flannel shirt.

"They'll be back any minute," Marinda said. "We have all week-end."

"I was thinking about you all week," he said as he undressed her. "Here, help me off with this sweater. It was such a terrible week. Come get warm under the covers. Just put your head on my shoulder and close your eyes. It's all going terribly, Marinda, not anything like I thought it would," he whispered in her ear.

"Oh, baby, it will get better, it always does. What can I do," she whispered back.

"Just hold me. Just talk to me."

"I miss you all the time, Peter. Sometimes I notice something, and I know if you were here I'd point it out to you and you'd say something funny, but you're not here and there's no one else who understands. Sometimes at night I have trouble falling asleep and I wish you were here, I wish we were together." She curled up against him. She could feel his shallow breath on the back of her neck. "Do you know what I mean? Sometimes I feel like I'm just killing time between when we see each other. I think that's why I study so hard. I really do. It's not just the grades, though that's important, I can't pretend it's not. But it's also like, when I'm in the library reading some article or book, I can close off the rest of the world. It's such an escape. Peter? Do you know what I mean?"

He was asleep. Marinda stared out the window as the record came to an end. Why, she wondered, when he was in New Haven did she feel like they were the best friends in the world and now, when they were together, she felt such a distance. The drugs were part of it, she was sure of that: the drugs took Peter to a place where he was all alone, where she couldn't follow him unless she got as high as he did, which she hated to do. It made her feel so sick afterwards. School was part of it too: she'd always done better than he had, if only because she worked so much harder, and he made her feel like such a little grind because of it. Outside the first snow had started to fall, and Marinda drifted into sleep.

She woke up to the touch of Peter's cool hand on her breast. It was already afternoon; they'd missed lunch, and she could hear her roommates moving furniture around in the main room.

"We have to get up," she said. "I should be helping them out."

"In a little while," Peter said. "It's so nice in here now." He started the turntable, the side of the record they'd already heard.

She could tell from how he was breathing, from the firmness of his touch, what he wanted. She felt so tired now, and there was the taste of sleep in her mouth; all she wanted to do was get up and brush her teeth and take a shower and start moving around, rolling up the rug for the party. If they did it now she knew what it would be like: quick and lazy and not much fun.

And if they didn't, she knew what that would be like too: Peter would pretend he didn't mind, but he would hold it against her, he would keep his resentment inside and then he would punish her later. He'd misbehave at the party, say something cutting in front of her friends, flirt with someone else maybe, get all coked up with Bobby.

He was stroking her, and she reached down to hold him. He was so soft. It would take forever.

"Peter," she said, "Peter, look—"

"Sssh, baby, don't say anything. You're so beautiful now. I thought about you all week. It was such a dreadful week. They're going to put me on notice next semester. My parents are going to flip when they see my grades. It's like everything is falling apart, and I just can't stop it from happening. Every day I wake up and say, Today I won't get high, I'll get my shit together and get some good work done. And then, I don't know what happens, I just lose it. That feels so good. You feel so nice."

He was still soft. Marinda didn't know what would be worse: if they didn't try to do it or if they tried and he couldn't get it up.

"You don't know what it's like, baby," he said, running a finger across her lips. "It's so easy for you." He pushed her head down gently, further down his chest. She stifled a sigh and then she began, holding him in her mouth until he was hard, circling the tip of him with her tongue until she could hear him breathing faster. His heart wasn't in it; this would take forever; he was trying to prove something to her but she couldn't figure out what it was.

She could go on like this forever, she thought, sucking mechanically while her mind wandered elsewhere. Her boyfriend before Peter had liked to play with her breasts as she sucked him off, but Peter just liked to lie there, perfectly still, watching her. Peter was the first boy she had swallowed come for. Was that a kind of virginity? Maybe virginity had different levels, different things you began doing as you went along. A lot of times Peter acted this way, sort of pathetic, almost, before she went down on him. No more sympathy blow jobs, she said to herself, it just gives them positive reinforcement for feeling bad. She felt his chest for the cool sweat that signaled the end was near, and then he came, in one short spurt, and she rested her head on his stomach.

There was a knock at the door.

"Marinda?" Rosaline said. "Are you in there? We were thinking of hooking up all the speakers to Katie Lee's amp. Am I interrupting?"

Peter sat up and pulled on his T-shirt.

"I'm starved," he said, tearing open a bag of barbecue-flavored potato chips.

"We'll be out in a minute," Marinda said. Now she wouldn't be able to brush her teeth right away; Peter got insulted if she did. "Peter's here," she said. "We sort of fell asleep."

Peter was wide awake now, pacing back and forth as he got dressed. "Let's go get some burgers," he said.

"I have to help them set up."

"How long will that take."

"I don't know. A couple of hours, I guess," Marinda said, remembering how Schuyler and Teddy had come by the night before to help them move the heaviest pieces of furniture. If she asked Peter to stay and help, he would. But she wouldn't ask, and she knew he wouldn't offer. He asked her roommates if they wanted anything from the Square and seemed a little surprised when Katie Lee gave him five dollars and requested heavy-duty trash bags from the five-and-dime.

"I think the bar should be in the back," Katie Lee said after he left, "or maybe even in one of the bedrooms. It will force people to circulate. I hate it when everyone hangs around by the bar and the rest of the place is empty. And then we'd have the whole main room free for dancing."

"We only have a couple of hours of music on tape," December said. "It took so much longer than I thought."

"We could just tape entire sides of records," Rosaline said. "Marinda has some great records."

"Absolutely not," Katie Lee said. "Bobby said he'd bring by some of his tapes."

But Bobby never lends out his tapes, Marinda thought, I wonder how she got him to agree to that. Katie Lee is up to something, that was for sure: this party was just part of a larger scheme. Katie Lee always had a plan—Marinda knew that by now—and Marinda had to give her this much credit: her plans always seemed to work.

"That's the sickest thing I've ever heard of," Carter said to Katie Lee as she handed him a shot of bourbon with soda over ice. "You can't be serious."

"I've planned it all out, Carter, and if you think about it, everyone gets what they want. Bobby. Me. And you too of course. It's rather brilliant, you have to admit that," she said, tapping his chest with a pink lacquered fingernail.

"My mother warned me about girls like you."

"Well, sir, I'll have to meet your mother some time. She sounds like a very clever lady. Do we have a deal?"

"Why not. I've got nothing to lose. Bobby's certainly got nothing to lose. It would seem that you're the only person who has something to lose," Carter said.

Katie Lee smiled. "There's a difference between losing something and giving it away. And there's a difference between giving something away and—well, don't worry about me. Hello, Bobby," she said, "I'm glad you finally made it."

"I put the tapes by the stereo," he said. "Hello, Carter. What are you drinking?"

"Bourbon and soda."

"Sounds good."

"Here you are," Katie Lee said, handing him a glass.

"You anticipate my every need," Bobby said.

"Aw shucks, mister, we aim to please," she replied, giving him a small smile that showed no teeth, that drew up her cheeks just enough to show off the tiny dimples that she accented with a gel rouge underneath her foundation.

"Every need except a swizzle stick, that is."

"No problem," Katie Lee said, stirring his drink with her index finger and then cleaning off her finger between two perfectly glossed lips. "Do excuse me, it's time to change the tape."

"She's fucking incredible," Carter said, watching her walk away. "You wouldn't believe what we were just talking about."

"Try me."

"She says she's going to marry you."

Bobby's face remained expressionless. "What else?"

"She says you'll be engaged before graduation, and she'll be a virgin
till her wedding night. She has this whole plan worked out. She
wants us all to work in Washington this summer—"

"Who's *us?*"

"You and me, Bobby. She has a job working for a lobbyist who
represents the hotel business, and she says her father can get us in-
ternships with congressmen, agencies, anything we want. With one
phone call. It's amazing."

"And what do we do in exchange?" Bobby asked.

"Beats me. Hang out with her in Washington. Take her to Clyde's
for drinks. Escort her to parties. Who the hell knows."

"Who the hell needs it," Bobby said.

"I need it, man, I need it. You know how it works—all you need is
one of those jobs one summer and you're all set, jobs, recommenda-
tions, law school, maybe a campaign job, you know how it works.
Who cares about the pay."

"So *you* go to Washington."

"She doesn't want me, friend. It's a package deal. You have to come
along. It's not like you have anything better to do. It's not like you're
king of the boardwalk down there."

"Why should I go down to D.C. to let some girl lead me around by
the nose when I can stay in Jersey and have a good time?"

"You can have a good time in D.C. You heard Woody's stories from
last summer. I bet you'd have more fun in D.C. than if you stayed
with your family."

"You bet? How much do you bet?"

"I wasn't talking about money."

"Well I'm talking about money," Bobby said, freshening Carter's
drink. "How much money do you want to bet?"

"Bet on what?"

"Bet that I will have more fun in Washington. With Katie Lee.
Come on, how much."

"That's a sucker bet, Bobby, I couldn't do that."

"Come on. How much money. That we go down to Washington
and I make it with Katie Lee."

"Okay. A hundred dollars."

"No, Carter, I'm talking about real money. You're the one who's on
financial aid and talking about fancy law schools. You're the one
who's always telling me about taking risks."

"All right. Five thousand dollars."

Bobby's eyes widened. "Where are you going to get five thousand dollars?"

"My uncle left me a little bit of money. But it doesn't matter, you'll be the one paying me."

"Sounds like a good deal for you, right, Carter? Fancy job, nice pay, and a five-thousand-dollar bonus at the end of the summer, is that how you figure it? And the fun of watching me follow this tease around the capital of our great nation?"

"Sounds just fine. Where do I sign up?"

"You just did," Bobby said, looking over Carter's shoulder to the dark corner where Peter was sitting by himself, smoking a joint. "Excuse me, I think I see a friend from out of town."

Carter stood by himself at the bar for a few minutes watching the dancers. Five thousand dollars: more money than he'd had in his entire life. The inheritance from his uncle had turned out to be a complete joke, some high technology stocks that he'd sold for a grand total of $436.28, and the title to a '67 Buick that got ten miles to the gallon, and that was on a good day. Five thousand dollars would take him a long way. And best of all, it was an absolutely sure thing.

"Oh, Schuyler, you know I'm a dreadful dancer," Rosaline said, staring at the black patent leather pumps her mother had sent up from New York just for the party. "You know this isn't my kind of music."

"Next party you'll have to put some waltzes on the dance tape. You do know how to waltz?" he asked, sitting down next to her.

Rosaline rolled her eyes. "Years of lessons. Dancing with other girls, mostly, though since I'm so short at least I hardly ever had to lead. But I'm lost with rock and roll. Look at December, though, she's fantastic, isn't she?"

Schuyler watched December dancing in the middle of the floor. She dances like a black girl, he thought, moving her hips and shoulders effortlessly to the fast, steady beat. A lot of men were watching December, Schuyler noticed; they all knew that Alex was out of town and December never left a party alone. When she twirled around, her platinum hair swung out in a circle and exposed her back, bare in a low-cut tank top. It wasn't just her beauty that attracted men to her, and it wasn't just something sexual. It was fantasy that she offered, Schuyler thought, the promise that your fantasy could come true, if only for one night.

Schuyler sighed. What fantasies made people do. December, for example, moving from man to man, acting like none of it mattered, all the time hoping that one of these nighttime encounters might turn out to be her dream come true. Schuyler understood December, he had been there himself. He had dreamed of a girl—a girl like December, strong and fearless and wild and beautiful, and yes, also like December, with long pale hair and wide blue eyes that sparkled with secrets. He would be riding over the hills of Montana and he would dream of how he would come upon her, just around the bend: she'd be sitting on a rock at the edge of a creek, her pale horse tied to a nearby tree. She'd look up, and smile, and he'd know right away. They would never have to talk about it. Everything would be understood.

He'd ridden every day after school and sometimes all day on the weekends, and he had only run into weatherbeaten hunters and the occasional neighbor fishing for trout. Well, that's what growing up is all about, he thought, realizing your fantasies are just that and getting on with your life. Rosaline, for example. She was wonderful, and he loved her with a tenderness he hadn't thought he had, and she loved him back in a way that made him feel they could do anything together. If he hadn't met Rosaline he'd probably be just like December right now, drinking a little too much and cruising a party on a Saturday night, looking for a way to make it through to Sunday morning.

"Let's get some fresh air," he said, taking Rosaline by the hand.

"I can't leave, it's my party," Rosaline protested.

"Just for a little while. No one will notice. The party will go on without you."

"It already is," Rosaline said. "I hardly know who any of these people are."

Outside they could hear music coming from open windows, from parties on all sides of the lawn just dusted with the season's first snow.

"It nearly feels like Christmas," Rosaline said. "There won't be any snow in New York. I guess you always get snow in Montana."

"You can count on Montana for that," Schuyler said, taking her hand. "I'd like to show you Montana. Sometime. Soon."

Rosaline felt her face blush warm against the winter wind. "I'd like that. And I'd like to show you New York. I guess you've already seen New York. Everyone has seen New York."

"I'd like to see it with you," Schuyler said, brushing the snow off the collar of her coat. "What will you be doing on Christmas?"

"Oh, well, the usual. Trim the tree. Eat a big dinner. Everything is done in the family colors, this sort of slate blue and bright red."

"Your family has colors? Like school colors?" Schuyler asked.

"Well, sort of. The colors for the silks the jockeys wear when they ride and the blankets for the horses, things like that. There's this special color that no one else uses, it's called blue smoke, and the jockeys wear everything in blue smoke, except for a bright-red pompon on top of their caps. It's sort of silly, but it's the tradition, and the farm is called Blue Smoke—the fences are painted in the colors too—and we race under the name Blue Smoke Stable. It started as a sort of joke, really. The farm in Virginia burned down during the Civil War, and legend has it the smoke was sort of blue, so when they rebuilt the farm they named it Blue Smoke."

"I didn't know your family was from Virginia."

"Oh, they're not, really, I mean, *we're* not. It's just the farm," Rosaline said, a little nervous. She didn't like to talk about all the houses—the farm in Virginia, the apartment in New York, the beach places in Newport and Florida, the hotel suites kept in London (where her father bought art) and Paris (where her mother bought clothes). "We should be getting back," she said.

"First, I have something for you. For Christmas," he said, reaching into his pocket.

"Oh, but I didn't get you anything! I didn't forget, of course I wouldn't forget, but I thought I'd get you something in New York, that was so silly of me. Of course I should have gotten you something for Christmas." She looked at the small gift-wrapped box he had placed in the palm of her hand. "Oh, I can't open it now. Sky, let's wait till after. Let's wait till we go away. We'll have a second special Christmas, just us."

"You don't have to open it now. You can open it on Christmas or in a few weeks when we're together or whenever you want. But I want to give it to you now." He closed her fingers around the box and leaned down to kiss her. They stood there for a minute, alone in the Yard, in a small pool of light cast by a street lamp, the snow falling all around them. How lucky I am, Rosaline thought, how lucky I am to be kissed by the most wonderful boy in the world.

• • •

Mr. and Mrs. Wonderful, make me puke, Marinda thought, looking out the window at Schuyler and Rosaline. Peter and Bobby were in her bedroom cutting lines behind closed doors.

"Ah, the happy couple," December said, coming up next to her. "Sweet young love, you remember that, don't you Marinda?"

"Better than you do, I'm sure," Marinda replied. "I didn't think you'd still be here. Could it be you're staying to help clean up? Or is it that no one asks to walk you home when the party is right in your bedroom?"

"Hey, sorry I asked," December said, stepping back. "Just because Peter's totally zombied out you don't have to take it out on me."

"Oh fuck off, why don't you," Marinda said. "I saw how you were wiggling your ass in front of Schuyler and practically every other man in the room. Imagine how Rosaline felt."

"Why don't you ask Rosaline how she feels," December said, pointing out the window. "Why don't you just stop projecting your own insecurities onto everyone else. That's it, isn't it, Marinda? Just because you're unhappy with Peter doesn't mean the rest of the world is as unhappy as you are."

"I'm happy," Marinda said through gritted teeth. "I'm so happy I could spit," she said, stomping off to her room.

So jealous is more like it, December thought. She's madly in love with Schuyler—December recognized the signs. The way Marinda stayed on the telephone just a minute too long when Schuyler called for Rosaline. The way she'd asked him what courses he was taking next semester and then pretended she'd been planning to take a couple of the very same ones. Of course she won't admit it to me, December thought, but at least she could admit it to herself. Schuyler must look like a pretty good deal when you're stuck with a loser like Peter.

Shit, Schuyler would look like a pretty good deal from just about any angle. He was like a dream come true, except dreams never come true, December reminded herself. Dreams are just what keep you sane, keep you in one piece, when the real world gets crazy and is about to defeat you.

December had dreamed about meeting the perfect man as long as she could remember. She'd be walking on the hard rocks of the sea wall and she'd think, Some day he'll just come walking toward me, I'll just be walking up the beach and there he'll be. He'll be tall and tan and hard but there'll be something soft about him, around his eyes, something in the way he'll smile. We'll just know. We won't have to talk about it.

Talking can ruin everything, she thought, catching the glance of a senior on the swim team who'd come with Bobby Vincent. No dream boy but fun enough for a night or two. We'd better leave soon, December thought, before the party thins out and it's time to clean up.

"Oh, there will be plenty to clean up tomorrow," Katie Lee said as December put on her coat and said good night. "Don't worry about it. Really."

"Well, great, thanks. See you then."

"Sleep tight, sweetie," Katie Lee crooned. "Rosaline, what happened to Schuyler?" she asked.

"He has an early plane tomorrow," Rosaline said. "If they don't cancel the flight because of the snow. This is a great party, don't you think? I mean, it *was* a great party. I can't believe how late everyone stayed. Did you have a chance to dance at all? You weren't too busy to have fun, I hope?"

"Fun?" Katie Lee said, pouring plastic glasses full of liquor, cigarette butts, and crushed napkins into a large rubber trash bucket. "Fun? Rosaline, fun is the point of *other* people's parties. Your own parties are for something else."

"Such as?"

"That depends, doesn't it, on what you give the party for. Could you get that, please, I don't want to chip a nail, I won't have time for another manicure before I go to Kentucky. This party was definitely a huge success. Thanks, and I think I saw someone toss a bottle behind the couch. Everything went just as planned. See, the mess isn't so bad once you get the glasses out of the way. It was the best party anyone's given in a while, don't you think? Everyone came."

"You mean Bobby, don't you," Rosaline said.

"Why Rosaline, Bobby and I are just good friends. You know that. Have you heard anything else?"

"Well, no. I just meant that I know you like him, you talk about him so much, and I'm sure he really likes you. I'm sure he'd ask you out if you wanted him to."

"Rosaline, and this is just between us chickens, boys can be made to do just about anything if you want them to. Schuyler would do anything for you, I'm sure of that."

"Well, we love each other."

"Of course you do, dear heart. The point is, now that he's totally crazy in love with you, what do you want him to do?"

"You mean, do I want him to ask me to marry him?"

"Do you want to marry him, Rosaline? Men are good for lots of things besides marriage. We'll have to get a vacuum cleaner in here tomorrow. Don't you want to do anything besides get married? Isn't there anything else you'd like to do?"

"I have three years to figure that out."

"Do you? You'll never get those three years back. Look at me, I know exactly what I want to do in the hotel business, and I've already started doing it."

"You have?"

"Didn't I tell you? I'm looking for a site, right here in Cambridge. I'm not going to waste three years waiting until I graduate."

"I thought we were talking about love and marriage, not careers."

Katie Lee looked at Rosaline. What a hopeless case. I'm leaving for Kentucky in three days, Katie Lee thought, and I still haven't managed to get an invitation to New York for New Year's Eve. Love and marriage. Careers. Wouldn't Rosaline ever figure it out? Love and marriage and careers. Family and money. It was all the same thing.

The last thing Rosaline did before she went to sleep every night for the next three weeks was to put the little gift box under her pillow. And every night she dreamed of Schuyler as she lay there, curled up like a kitten, with one hand clutching the feather quilt up to her chin and one hand under the pillow, wrapped around the tiny box.

The holidays hadn't turned out to be nearly as awful as she'd thought they would be. Her mother had dragged her around to dinners and parties as usual, and her father had drunk himself into a stupor nearly every day by late afternoon, also as usual, but it didn't seem to matter so much now that she had Schuyler.

And now here she was, back in Cambridge, packing her one small suitcase for the trip she and Schuyler were taking up to New Hampshire. Sturdy boots, in case they wanted to take a walk in the countryside, and long underwear, in case there was a cold snap. The biography of Charles Dickens she had to read for a final exam. A new toothbrush. Two Christmas presents: a pink cashmere cardigan (from her mother) and a narrow gold bracelet (from her father).

And at the top of the suitcase, packed between layers of lavender tissue paper so it wouldn't wrinkle, the first item of clothing she had ever bought entirely on her own: a long white lace nightgown that came down just to her ankles, with sleeves trimmed in pale-yellow satin ribbon and a neckline that was gathered with the same pale ribbon, tied at the throat into a small bow. She'd gotten it at a Madison Avenue shop that specialized in Victoriana and had kept it among the Christmas gifts she'd bought for her parents, where she knew Charlotte wouldn't look.

Tucked inside the carefully folded nightgown, like a secret amulet that imparted magic to everything that touched it, was her Christmas present to Schuyler. She had spent days looking for it, strolling up and down the wide avenues and narrow side streets, wandering in and out of the softly lit antique shops that smelled of lemon oil, the rare book stores that were so quiet Rosaline could barely summon up the nerve to ask the dealers if they had what she was looking for, and the tiny gift shops that carried everything from sterling souvenir spoons to cut-crystal bowls filled with cinnamon and rose potpourri. That was where she finally found it, in a small store in the basement of a brownstone in the east eighties. She was so excited she forgot to ask the price; she just gave the clerk a fifty-dollar bill and pocketed the change without checking to see how much it was.

On the ride north she and Schuyler discussed everything except what was really on their minds. Schuyler talked about a paper he had to write and described every last ornament on his family's Christmas tree. Rosaline repeated all the holiday gossip she'd heard from Katie Lee: how Alex had sent December a dozen white roses on Christmas Eve, how Peter had nearly OD'd on Quaaludes and Marinda had ended up spending New Year's Eve in a hospital emergency room, how one of Katie Lee's high school beaux had drunkenly proposed marriage and then passed out before Katie Lee had a chance to break his heart for the second time.

"So Katie Lee just left him there, right in the middle of her front lawn, and he stayed there all night and when the gardener found him the next day he called the police," Rosaline said. "The snow stays so white up here. Look, a real covered bridge, I've never seen one before, could you slow down just for a minute?"

Schuyler stopped the car so Rosaline could look out at the bridge and the creek frozen beneath it. She'd been doing this for about half an hour, asking him to slow down or stop whenever they passed something of interest. He knew she was trying to delay the moment when they arrived at the single room with the wide canopy bed they would share for the weekend. Schuyler had checked about a canopy bed in advance, the same way he'd checked about a fireplace and the skating pond and the stable nearby.

"Do you want to keep going?" he asked, stroking her cheek as she looked out the window. "It's okay if you want to go back. It's okay if you changed your mind over vacation. Rosaline?"

She turned to him. "No, I haven't changed my mind," she said. "I want to be with you, Schuyler. I just, well, I guess I'm just nervous. You know, traveling, exams, all that."

Schuyler smiled and headed back onto the road. She was so different from the other girls he had known. He could hardly believe someone like Rosaline could still exist. He remembered the first woman who'd taken him to bed; she was older than he, nearly thirty he had guessed, and had moved to Montana after divorcing a professor who'd written one of the books Schuyler had just been assigned in a history course. Schuyler was fourteen and couldn't quite figure out what this wise and sophisticated easterner had seen in him. He was a skinny, long-legged virgin boy who felt more comfortable with cattle than with girls.

A virgin, Rosaline was a virgin. Schuyler had never taken a girl's virginity (was that the right word, he thought, "taken"?), and it seemed such a frightening responsibility. It was going to be the one time she never forgot, not one detail, that's how it went, that's how people were, he thought, they never forgot anything: the day of the week, the time of day, the weather, the color of the bed linens. He was going to be the one she always remembered.

They passed a small fieldstone church and a red-brick schoolhouse with rows of children lined up in front of an old yellow school bus.

"Oh, look at that house," Rosaline said, pointing just ahead. "Can we just stop for a minute? Look at all the chimneys, there must be at least twenty! And the way the driveway is lined with pines, they must be at least a hundred years old."

"Let's get a closer look," Schuyler said, and he turned down the private road and stopped the car a few yards from the house, which was painted all white except for the front door, which was bright red and decorated with a wreath made of pine cones.

"Sometimes when I see a place I like to imagine who would live there," Rosaline said. "Is it a big happy family that all lives together? Is there just one old man who keeps all the fires lit in all the chimneys just so he doesn't get lonely? It's so absolutely quiet," she said, not realizing that Schuyler had shut off the motor. "The tables are set in the dining room even though it's only three o'clock. Maybe they're giving a party tonight. This is a happy house, I can tell. Happy things happen here," she said, leaning her head on Schuyler's shoulder.

"This is it, Rosie," Schuyler said, taking her hand. "This is the place. See that room on the top floor, all the way to the right?"

"With the bay window?" Rosaline asked.

"They're holding it for us," Schuyler said.

"Oh, Sky," she said in a whisper so quiet he could barely hear her. "It's perfect. It's perfect."

Rosaline and Schuyler were sitting in front of the fire sipping brandy from the single snifter Schuyler had brought up from Cambridge. Rosaline sat up very straight and pulled her nightgown over her small bare feet.

"Open yours first," she said.

"Let's open them at the same time," Schuyler said. He was wearing only a white T-shirt (an undershirt, really, Rosaline thought) and faded jeans. Rosaline couldn't stop staring at his feet. I've never even seen his feet, she said to herself, I've hardly ever seen his elbows, even. It made her dizzy to think of the rest of him.

Rosaline unwrapped her gift, careful not to tear the paper, and then opened the dark-blue velvet box to find a gold locket in the shape of a heart on a delicate gold chain.

"Oh," she said, and she couldn't think of what to say next. "Well. Put it on for me?"

"There's something inside the locket," Schuyler said.

She opened the locket with her thumbnail and took out a tiny strip of paper: it was Schuyler's fortune from the Chinese restaurant, the one he hadn't shown her. "Be careful when you give your heart away," it said, "because you may never get it back." She rested her head on Schuyler's knee as he lifted her heavy red hair off the back of her neck and fastened the clasp of the necklace.

"Now you," she said, stretching out her legs and propping herself up on one elbow.

"Shakespeare's sonnets," he said, running his hand over the smooth leather binding. "It's beautiful, Rosie."

"I know you know them all by heart, practically, but I couldn't resist. Read me one?"

He stretched out next to her and read. She closed her eyes and listened. His open Montana accent slipped away as he recited the lines. It's like he wrote them for me, she thought, when he reads the lines it sounds like it's all just occurring to him for the first time.

"Now you read to me," he said.

Rosaline leaned back on a pillow and held the book straight up over her head. Perhaps Schuyler had been reciting from memory—it was hard to make out the fine print in the dim light thrown by the little white candles they'd placed in ashtrays and saucers all over the room.

As Rosaline read she could feel Schuyler's fingers threading through her hair. "Number eighteen," she said, feeling his breath in her ear. "Number eighteen," she repeated, and then she set down the book and closed her eyes. "How does it go?"

Schuyler traced her lips with his finger and drew a line straight down to the hollow of her throat where her nightgown was gathered onto the thin yellow ribbon. " 'Shall I compare thee to a summer's day,'" he said. "I can't remember the rest." He pulled the ribbon loose and drew the nightgown down around her shoulders.

"Rosie," he said. "Rosie—"

"Sssh," she said. "You gave me your heart. Now I give you mine." She pulled him to her for a soft, chaste kiss, and then he gathered her up in his arms and carried her to the bed.

Schuyler undressed, and then he kissed her again, still these gentle innocent kisses, and then he pulled the nightgown farther down, freeing her arms, down to her waist, and he covered her everywhere with little kisses. She felt so safe, with these million gentle kisses and just the hint of his tongue, just for a moment here and there, on her neck, across her breasts, on her shoulders. And then he kissed her harder, on the mouth, and she could feel fabric against her skin as he pulled the hem of the nightgown up past her knees, and she could feel his breath deepening and her own breath deepening. He wrapped one long hand around the inside of her thigh just above the knee. She was nearly naked now, the nightgown was just a loose confusion of lace around her waist.

Rosaline felt herself melting, like a candle, into something soft and warm and shapeless. She was kissing Schuyler back with a strength that was entirely new to her, and she found herself willing his hand farther up her thigh, willing it all the way up and there it was. She was dry, that wasn't exactly right, was it, and then he brought up his hand for her to cover with wet kisses and then he touched her again, and she felt as if her brain had flown out of her head, she couldn't think at all, she was just this quivering thing in his arms.

Schuyler placed a pillow beneath her and moved her legs apart. I want to remember everything about this, Rosaline said to herself, and for one second she opened her eyes and drank it all in. She saw the tan muscle of Schuyler's shoulder against her own white skin. Everything was white: the snow falling against the window, the high canopy of the bed, the sheets and the pillows and the quilt and her nightgown and the dozen rose-scented candles flickering against the white walls and her own skin. She closed her eyes, and in that moment she gave herself completely over to him.

There was a little pain, more surprise than pain, really, and after a while she not only got used to it but started to like it, started to wonder if there wasn't something she should be doing. Some way she should be moving. Schuyler had one hand on her hip, guiding her back and forth, and she discovered it felt better if she relaxed and went with him.

It's like music, she realized. This is the rhythm. And there must be melody, and harmony too. She tried moving a little differently, and she listened to Schuyler's breathing; he made a noise like a little grunt, that must mean he likes it. It's like a symphony, she thought, with everything building on this rhythm. A trill, a chord, an arpeggio, major keys, minor keys, everything repeating itself except each time a little different until it builds to the crescendo. Suddenly he was pushing into her harder and faster, she thought he might crush her entirely, and he was saying "Rosie, Rosie, Rosie" over and over, and he pulled her tightly against him.

It was quiet again. When she opened her eyes he was staring at her and there were tears on his face. He wiped a tear off her face, though she didn't remember crying at all.

He is mine and I am his and I love him and he loves me and isn't the world a wonderful place, she thought. I am the happiest girl in the world. We are the two happiest people in the world. Schuyler and Rosaline, Rosie and Sky.

4

W ell, that's one more old saying that can't be true, Katie Lee thought to herself, because I'm sure I look exactly the same. Same eyes. Same mouth. Same hair (with the extra highlights she had put in last Saturday, an annual Labor Day weekend ritual; she'd actually had to provide references before the hairdresser, a favorite of embassy wives and congressmen's girlfriends, had agreed to take her). Same skin (with the light tan she'd acquired over the summer in twice weekly visits to the health club; it was safer that way, and you didn't get any horrible tan lines).

Maybe it's in the walk, Katie Lee thought, approaching the full-length mirror and then backing away. Or maybe it's in the hips. She held a hand mirror so she could see what she looked like from the back and watched herself walk. It simply wasn't true: there was absolutely no way to tell if a girl had lost her virginity.

Unless the boy talked of course, but she had a feeling Bobby Vincent was going to keep this one to himself. She knew he'd tell Carter —they'd talked about that, how everyone was allowed to confide in his one best friend—but other than that she felt pretty safe. She'd told him, afterwards, about what her uncle had done when someone took advantage of her cousin Sally, and about how her father was a million times worse than her uncle, and then she'd thrown in some tears for good measure. She had Bobby where she wanted him. He was already in it a lot deeper than he'd planned.

But then, so was she. It just wasn't possible, she realized, to get a boy like Bobby Vincent to propose before he'd slept with you, so she'd had to make some adjustments in her plan. That's what Daddy always said: stay flexible, reevaluate your situation as you go along, don't be afraid to make changes if they're necessary. It had been necessary. By Thanksgiving of her senior year she would have the ring.

71

Christmas at the latest. That gave Bobby two more years to sow the last of his wild oats and two years for Katie Lee to get her own business started in her own name. Plenty of time.

There hadn't been anyone for Katie Lee to talk to after it happened. She considered calling Rosaline, who was up in Saratoga with her family for the racing season. But Rosaline understood only about True Love—she wouldn't understand the agreement Katie Lee and Bobby had made, to act as if nothing had changed when they got back to school in the fall.

It hadn't turned out to be such a big deal after all. You made out just like you always did, using the traditional rule of three: say no the first two times they try something and then give in on the third. You let him take off your clothes only after he'd turned out the lights. You checked the condom wrapper to make sure it hadn't been sitting in his sock drawer for the last four years. Then he did it—if you used tampons you sort of knew what it would feel like anyway—and then after a while he did it again. The second time took longer than the first. He'd wanted to stay over, but Katie Lee knew he'd want to do it again in the morning, so she made him leave.

The first thing she did when she woke up the next day was take a long hot bath. Then she went to Saks and bought entirely new fall and winter wardrobes. She pretended that Charlotte Van Schott had come along with her; she could imagine Charlotte vetoing the heather tweed skirt in favor of a more traditional Scottish kilt, and selecting muted beige, peach, and ivory instead of the bright greens, pinks, and reds Katie Lee was always drawn to. She'd feel like a drab wallflower wearing these clothes in Kentucky, but in the Northeast this was obviously how it was done.

Katie Lee called the airline to make sure her flight back to Boston was still on schedule. The shuttle had turned out to be a terrible idea; they didn't offer first class, and now there were hardly any flights left that did. She'd be glad to leave Washington. It was hot and dangerous, and you saw the same people at the same old parties every single night. The most tedious people had managed to get themselves into office last November, and they expected you to be nice to them just because they'd won some stupid election or held some joke of an appointment. Fund-raising for the senator had been fun—you really found out all kinds of information about who had how much money and where they'd gotten it from—but it still was working for somebody else. Katie Lee swore she would never try that again.

She had one last detail to take care of before she flew back. She dialed the number, let the phone ring twice, and then hung up.

It rang back in less than a minute.

"Katie Lee?" he said. "Are you still leaving today?"

"Hello. Yes. I'd like to take care of this before I go."

"Sure. How are you doing, anyway?" he asked.

"I'm perfectly fine, why wouldn't I be."

"No reason, no reason. I'm sort of relieved this is over, if you want to know," he said.

But it isn't over at all, Katie Lee thought. Once you're in it, you're in it for good. "Could you come by in about an hour?" she asked.

"Sure thing. Bobby's already gone."

"I know that, Carter," she snapped, and then she hung up.

Marinda turned her lawn chair to face the pond.

"There's an extra order of French fries left in the bag," she said. "And a can of Coke. If you want them later."

Peter shrugged. "The fries will be cold and the Coke will be warm. Anyway, the food here is just fine, as I keep telling you. You didn't have to bring me dinner. I mean, thanks and all, but it wasn't necessary."

I wasn't doing it for you, I was doing it for me, Marinda wanted to say. So we could eat out here alone. So I wouldn't have to have dinner with—with "the rest of them," that was how she thought of the other patients.

"You're missing the great sunset, turning your chair to the east like that," Peter said, snapping the gum he had begun chewing nonstop, as many as three packs a day, ever since he'd gotten here.

"I don't want the sun in my eyes," Marinda said, pulling her sweater over her shoulders.

"You just don't want to look at the loverly loony bin," Peter said.

"It's not a loony bin, stop calling it that," she said, but she kept her chair turned away just the same. He was right: she didn't want to look at the large gray fieldstone house where Peter lived with fifty other patients, a dozen nurses and counselors, and three resident physicians. She didn't want to see the old wooden stable, converted into a gym and poolhouse, or the carriage house that had been subdivided into an art studio and a darkroom, or the tennis courts, or the formal garden with its prize-winning roses and wrought-iron gazebo. If you were just driving down the main road and didn't know any better you might mistake the complex for an expensive private school or a country club. But Marinda knew better: this was a mental hospital that charged nearly two thousand dollars a week to wean its carefully screened patients off drug and alcohol dependencies.

It was amazing that Peter had even been accepted here, she thought. Most of the patients had much more serious problems than his. They had lost their jobs, they had made a mess of their personal lives, and a few of them got violent from time to time. And Peter didn't meet the most important criterion of all: deep down in his heart of hearts he did not want to get better.

Marinda sighed. When Peter's parents had forced him to check himself in at the beginning of the summer she was sure he'd be out in time for the fall semester. He and a friend had been busted trying to score cocaine off an undercover cop; a legal technicality had prevented prosecution. Big deal, Peter had said at first, it happens all the time, no one like me (white and wealthy and well connected) goes to jail for this. A week later Peter had passed out while at the wheel of the family Audi and crashed the car into a telephone pole. That was June. Now it was September, and he was still here.

"I played Scrabble with Billy the Kid last night," Peter told her, using their pet name for the patient whose record company had insisted he come here to straighten out before his winter tour. "His brain is truly fried. Couldn't come up with a word that had more than five letters in it. He promised me a backstage pass when they get to Boston."

"Has he played at all?"

"Are you kidding?" Peter said. "He's totally blissed out. He can barely get it together to tune his guitar. He says he's found God."

"There seems to be a lot of that around here."

"Yeah, well, this place kind of puts you in touch with the eternal verities. I talked to Dr. Zorba about it," he said, using their name for his Viennese-born psychiatrist, whose pronunciation of "Kvaludes" and "mari-chuana" Peter was fond of imitating. "The good doctor said to me, 'Yes, I admit that religion is a crutch, but who says you don't have a limp?'"

"Very funny," Marinda said. "You haven't forgotten that I have to go back tomorrow."

"I haven't forgotten. I have *not* forgotten. Who me, forget? Are you accusing *moi* of short-term memory loss?"

Marinda reminded herself of what Peter's counselors had told her, that a lot of the anger and aggression he felt toward his family and the world at large was going to be directed at her. He couldn't help it. It wasn't his fault. She had to put up with it.

"I'll be able to get back down for Columbus Day weekend," she said.

"A lovely holiday," Peter said. "Do you know there's a nasty rumor going around that Columbus was Jewish?"

"And then I'll be back for Thanksgiving," she continued, ignoring him. "My parents are thinking of opening up the beach house for Thanksgiving. Do you think you could come? Do you have to ask your folks?"

"I shall have to ask Dr. Zorba," he said.

"But Thanksgiving is practically three months away," Marinda said before she could stop herself. "I can't believe you'll still have to be here by then."

"I don't *have* to be here, Marindalita. I checked myself in, re-member, I can leave at any time. Any time at all. As soon as I remove the invisible electronic dog collar they've stapled to my neck. Ha, ha, get it, it was a joke, we're still allowed to joke about this, right Mar-inda Sue? Marinda Jane? Thanksgiving sounds just peachy. I can barely contain myself with glee."

Marinda put the remains of their fast-food dinner into the bag and stood up to leave.

"Walk me to the car?" she said. When he stood up she saw how thin he still was. His clothes had been washed but not pressed.

"Think Batman's fans are still hanging around the driveway?" Peter said, using their nickname for the soap-opera actor who had checked in the day after his character fell into a long and possibly irreversible coma.

"I thought you said he was leaving last week," Marinda said, toss-ing the bag in the backseat and fastening her seat belt.

"He was, he was, but then his wife told him she was filing for divorce, so he's here for another month at least. His lawyers say it makes her look bad, giving him the heave while he's in such a weak position. I shall be very sorry to see him go," Peter said, resting his hands on the roof of the car and leaning into the window. He smells like fabric bleach, Marinda thought.

"What a strange place to make a new friend," she said.

"Friend?" Peter said, pushing himself away from the car and walk-ing backwards. "Friend?" he repeated, shuffling his feet like a vaudeville comedian. "I'll miss him, Marindabelle, because he's my connection."

She thought she might not have heard him correctly over the clanking of the car's engine.

"Batman is the fatman," he said, holding his hands in front of his eyes like a mask. "He brings me goodies from the bat cave. He hides them in his bat utility belt. Great stuff from Gotham City. That's right, Miss Phi Beta Kappa, he's my dealer," Peter said, and then he smiled, and took a deep bow, and retreated into the high stone house.

WHAT I PROMISED ALEX I'D DO OVER THE SUMMER:

Lose seven pounds
Practice walking in high heels (platforms don't count!)
Memorize Nora; read Ibsen biography; check out lit crit
Practice kissing in mirror—lips only, no lines around mouth!
Get ends trimmed at least once a month
Wear sun block every day and no ocean swimming
NO: cigarettes, nailbiting, hard liquor, coffee, tea, dark sodas
Get teeth cleaned at end of summer

December turned over the heavy parchment paper and looked at what Alex had written three months ago.

WHAT I VOW TO DO IF DECEMBER IS A GOOD GIRL THIS SUMMER:

Buy her a decent winter coat
Stop wearing sunglasses at parties
Teach her about wine
Take her to New York to find a modeling agency (7 lbs., love)

I've done everything he asked and more, she thought, remembering the two extra pounds she'd dieted, jogged, and jumping-jacked off as insurance against a last-minute binge or unpredictable water weight. She was almost too thin, but Alex said the camera demanded it.

Memorizing the play had been the most fun; December would take her script to the beach and get the lifeguards to read opposite her during their breaks. She had thought she would try out for a small part in a minor production for her maiden attempt at acting, but

Alex had insisted that if she worked hard she had a good chance to land the lead role in the first major student production of the new semester.

She had tried to explain it all to Rosaline that morning as they compared notes about their summer vacations and chose their rooms in their new suite. (December took the only one with decent closet space just to see how Katie Lee would react when she arrived after dinner). No one got to be famous without working for it, and you couldn't know where to begin your work unless you had a plan, and if you didn't have a plan—the way Katie Lee did—the next best thing was to hook up with someone who did. Like Alex. She would learn about acting at school, and in the meantime she could do modeling in New York and in Boston. Then by the time she had graduated, everyone in New York and California would know who she was and she'd get some decent auditions. Alex seemed to know how everything worked, or at least knew whom to ask to find out.

Alex had taught her this little psychological trick to get her going. When it was a gorgeous day and all you wanted to do was take a drive down the coast in an open convertible, instead you were supposed to focus on what it would be like, for example, to be all dressed up and going to the Academy Awards. Imagine the dress: something very slinky but very simple too of course, with a few sequins to pick up the flash of the camera. Imagine being directed through the crowd to your seat—near the aisle of course, because of your nomination—and everyone turning around to see how you'd done your hair. Everyone clapping for you, listening to your speech, congratulating you afterwards at the party thrown just in your honor.

Maybe it was silly, but it kept her off the highway and in her room, drinking club soda and reading a biography of Henrik Ibsen, because Alex believed that the best acting had a firm intellectual foundation. What December could never figure out was what Alex dreamed of. Where did he fit into this fantasy? Was that Alex, helping her out of the car, sitting next to her in the theater, bringing her a glass of champagne in a long-stemmed tulip glass at the party he was giving in his Hollywood Hills ranch house? Was he her lover, her manager, her producer, her mentor, all of the above?

Rosaline hadn't really understood any of it. No surprise there, December thought; it even sounds a little foolish, a little arrogant, to me when I talk about it with anyone other than Alex. But oh, when Alex and I are together, everything seems possible. Anything and everything can happen. Not that I'm really so special at all, it's just that I know what I want and I've figured out how to get it. Alex could have pulled this off with any number of pretty girls, there are certainly enough of them around, but he had chosen *her*. And she was going to do everything he said. Because he always could do exactly that, couldn't he, find someone else to dress up and take out and— here was the word she still didn't feel comfortable saying—make into a *star*.

She certainly didn't use this word to Rosaline as she tacked up her gift-shop poster of Katharine Hepburn over her desk.

"Modeling is the first step to becoming an actress," she said, waving her hands for emphasis. "You wouldn't believe how many famous actresses used to model to make money before they got decent parts. You can't expect me to wait tables if I can possibly avoid it. Not after all those years working at McDonald's. I never want to see a kitchen again!"

Rosaline giggled. "I baked my first batch of cookies yesterday. It wasn't so hard as I thought. As long as you're careful with the measurements—the cook showed me how to level off the measuring spoon with a knife."

"You baked cookies?"

"Oh, well, I was all packed and there was nothing to do. They're for Schuyler. I wanted to make him something myself, not just go out and buy something in a store. Do you want to try one?"

December grimaced. "Diet," she said.

"I don't believe it."

"Dr. Alex's orders. The camera adds ten pounds. But I'm sure they're delicious."

"They're pretty incredibly fantastic, if I do say so myself."

"Rosaline, I just can't picture you in an apron with flour all over your hands," December said. What she wanted to ask was, who cleaned up? Did you take all those sticky battery bowls and sponge them off yourself? Did you wear those rubber gloves that leave your hands smelling like the inside of a dishwasher? No, of course not, Rosaline had left everything in neat piles in the sink and some servant had taken care of it all. December would have a servant some day, a housekeeper was how she thought of it, someone who performed all those dismal, disgusting chores that filled Gloria Dunne's days. A career and a housekeeper and a few hundred thousand dollars in the bank: that's what December needed to keep from turning into someone like her mother.

"And when is this audition," Rosaline asked, "the one where you're going to kick everyone out of their seats?"

"It's *knock* everyone out of their seats. In two weeks. Alex gets back in a few days, and then I start practicing with him."

"We're like war brides," Rosaline said, "waiting for these boys to come home. Come help me move the bed out from the wall? I haven't seen Schuyler in months. Look at these new sheets I bought, aren't they pretty? Three months and two days, to be exact. Only these endless telephone conversations."

How nice that you can afford it, December thought, not that Alex, who was after all deliciously rich, had called her very much.

"And how was Schuyler's summer?" December asked.

"He was an utter cowboy. He even started calling me 'ma'am.' Do you want to hear something funny? He's begun a correspondence with Marinda."

"He doesn't seem like the pen-pal type."

"Well, first she just sent him a postcard, and then there was a long letter about Peter. You were right about Peter, he's hopeless, but Marinda still thinks it's just this phase she has to get through. That was how she put it to Schuyler. He read me the letter, it was so sad, so then he wrote her back, kind of a pep talk, and they kept on writing."

"Are you jealous?"

"Oh, of course not, Schuyler would never do anything like that."

"Well, you know, he's still a guy, like a lot of other guys." With the most incredible bedroom eyes, December thought. "Sometimes I get so jealous about Alex I can't see straight. But Schuyler is different, I'll give you that."

"We love each other."

"Of course you do."

"It's really special, December. Do you remember when we had that talk, before we—you know, last winter? I never really thanked you for it."

"You don't have to. I didn't say anything you didn't already know, deep down."

"I guess," Rosaline said, smoothing out the blanket. It made her feel sentimental to be making her own bed again. She couldn't tell December what she was really thinking, that over the summer she had imagined herself becoming a virgin again, that somehow she would forget everything that had happened between her and Schuyler and they would have to start all over again.

But that's what happened when you started sleeping with someone, Rosaline had realized: you couldn't really talk about them with your friends as you had before. You couldn't say whatever popped into your head, ask any question you wanted, it would be a betrayal of your loved one somehow. You certainly couldn't talk about *it*, no matter what.

Even if you did have a question or two that couldn't be answered just from reading the sexy parts of novels or listening to late-night radio. The question Rosaline had was this: the way that men feel when they come, all that sweat and groaning and sudden movement, was it exactly that same way for women? Or was it different, sort of like a soft, warm tingling, which Rosaline felt most of the time when she was with Schuyler—well, at least half the time. There were a few things he did just to please her, and they did of course, they felt just fine, but sometimes she got the feeling that he wasn't going to stop unless she did something dramatic. Moan, or arch her back, the way he did. Something to signal to him that it was okay to stop. Was that faking an orgasm, which she had heard on the radio you weren't really supposed to do? Rosaline didn't really think of it as faking, she thought of it more as exaggerating. Like when you told someone she looked beautiful in her new dress when really she only looked well groomed and maybe the dress was the wrong length. Was that faking, lying, being polite, being kind, or was it just following the rules? She was just trying to make him happy, it made him so happy, they both were so happy, afterwards, all curled up in each other's arms.

Anyway, it couldn't be Schuyler's fault, because he'd had lots of girlfriends before her. Maybe there was something else she should be doing, something December could tell her about if only she didn't feel that talking about sex with December would be an act of treason against her beloved.

Rosaline smoothed out the quilted bedspread and gave December a quick smile. "You could have one cookie, just to let me know they're all right before I give them to Sky. I promise I won't let you eat any more than one."

"You've obviously never been on a diet, Rosaline," December replied. "It's sort of like being a nun. It's all about absolutes. The only way you can keep going is if you maintain this total chastity. You have to pretend that your body has been purified: of sweets, of oils, of meat, of butter, of just about anything that tastes good. If I have even one cookie I'll lose the momentum."

"Well I hope Alex appreciates all this."

"If he doesn't I'll slug him," December said, not joining Rosaline when she giggled. "You and I can go to Baskin-Robbins and order four quarts of German chocolate cake ice cream."

"With Snickers bars for dessert," Rosaline said.

"Oh God, I'm fantasizing about food," December said. "This is pathetic. It better be worth it." She hiked up her jeans, now loose around the waist. The diet had become easier with time, actually; after a few weeks she'd just lost her interest in food. The strange thing was, she'd also lost some of her interest in sex. Look at Rosaline, all excited about seeing Schuyler again, December said to herself, and look at me—more nerves than lust, really.

He's just another boy, she reminded herself, *don't get so worked up over him.* But she knew it wasn't true. Alex was more than her boyfriend. He was her hope and salvation. He was going to rescue her from her past. He was her ticket out.

5

"*My* sweet darling December," Alex said after they had finished and she was lying curled up against him with her hair spread out over his smooth chest. "I was beginning to think I'd imagined you."

December ran her ring finger across his lower lip. "And I you," she said. The evening hadn't gone the way she'd pictured it, but she couldn't figure out exactly what was wrong. Alex had filled his apartment with flowers, as though he were apologizing for something, but December didn't know for what. He'd switched colognes over the summer—what did that mean? And the sex, the first sex they'd shared in months—something funny was going on there too. After all that time he'd taken her from behind, just about the least romantic position December could think of. Maybe he was just as nervous as she was. Maybe.

"You're going to breeze through that audition," he said.

"I wish I had your confidence."

"You have to be confident, love, confidence is more than half the game. Think about the wonderful party we're going to have on opening night. I've already asked some friends up from New York. They can't wait to meet you."

December had met very few of Alex's friends. "What did you tell them about me?" she asked.

"That you were absolutely perfect in every way and that if they were extremely nice to you now, you might deign to grace them with your presence when you become incredibly rich and famous." Alex took a hank of her hair and examined it for split ends.

And if I don't get this part, or if I go on a binge and gain twenty pounds, or if I cut off all my hair and start wearing overalls tomorrow, what then, December thought, and she knew the answer. Farewell,

adios, ciao baby, take your Stevie Wonder records and lock the door
behind you.

And then finally the day arrived. The cast list would be posted
inside the back door of the theater at four P.M. sharp. December
skipped her morning classes, napped through lunch, and spent most
of the afternoon soaking in lemon-scented bubbles. Alex had sent
over a blue mohair sweater for her to wear to their celebratory dinner—he'd been that confident after she'd described how well her audition had gone—and Katie Lee had lent her a string of lapis beads in
the same deep blue as the sweater.

At 3:30 she called Alex.

"Child residence" an unfamiliar British accent answered.

"Hi. This is December. Is Alex there?"

"Alex is sleeping. He doesn't want to be disturbed until after four.
May I take a message?"

"Are you sure he can't talk to me? Could you tell him it's me on
the phone?"

"He gets rather cranky when his sleep is interrupted."

You don't have to tell me, December said to herself. "I guess I can
wait an hour. Who's this?" she asked.

"I'm Bruno, I just got in from New York this morning. I look forward to meeting you tonight. Alex has told me a lot about you. I
understand you'll have some good news for us," he said. His accent
was almost identical to Alex's, as though they'd grown up in the
same place and had gone to all the same schools, December thought.

"I sure hope so. Well, just tell him I called. Until tonight, then,"
she said.

"Ciao," Bruno said, and then he hung up.

December walked as slowly as possible over to the theater, but still
she arrived five minutes early. A couple sat together, cross-legged on
the hard tile floor, their knees touching. The boy had wrapped a
muffler around his head and was pretending to be a palm reader.

"This is your life line," he said in an eastern European accent that
belonged to no country, that belonged only to television sitcoms
and nightclub comedians. "This is your love line. And this is your
clothesline. It runs long and deep. Your life will be filled with
many wonderful expensive outfits. Beware of light-colored furs and
synthetic fibers."

"Oh, Joel," the girl giggled, withdrawing her hand and giving his face a soft slap, "stop trying to make me laugh. I'll get wrinkles." She tied her long red braids into a knot under her chin and looked up at December.

"Hi," she said. "Are you waiting for the cast list?"

"Yes," December said, "am I in the right place?"

"This is most definitely the place," the girl said. "I'm Vicki Gold, and this is the Amazing Joel of Rumanovakia."

The boy got up and bowed from the waist. "That's Czechomania. I'm at your service."

"December Dunne. Pleased to meet you."

"Yes, I know who you are," Vicki said, standing up and unfolding her braids. "You read for Nora, right?"

December nodded. "And you?"

"I read for a couple of parts. Nora was one of them. I'll take anything, though, really. It's going to be a really special production."

"She says that about every play," Joel said, drawing his knees up to his chest. "A typical actress. Full of enthusiasm. Full of shit."

"Oh Joel, just shut up."

"Miss Vicki, you are cruel," he said in a southern accent. They were friendly and straightforward, but December disliked them all the same. She recognized Vicki's type: the kind of girl who repeated what you told her in confidence, who borrowed your lipstick and returned it all mashed up into the tube, who just couldn't be trusted on any count.

"You don't like me," Vicki said. "I can always tell."

"I just met you," December said, stepping back. A thin Chinese boy in a Vassar sweatshirt was tacking the cast list onto the bulletin board. "How can I like you or not?"

"No, you definitely don't like me," Vicki said, leaning her back against the list so December couldn't read it. "Women never do. Luckily all the directors around here are men."

"Excuse me," December said, standing as straight as she could, hoping her height would count for something, "could you please just move so I can see the cast list."

Vicki shrugged. "Why bother. You didn't get the part, honey. You should have tried out for something smaller first. You can't just expect to come in here and get a lead on your first try."

"Don't pay any attention to her," Joel said, "she's always like this until rehearsals start. Then she gets even worse. She's a total bitch."

"That I am, that I am," she said in an excellent British accent. She stepped to one side, her back still toward the wall, and beckoned December closer. "Read it to me, honey," she continued, now in a Mississippi drawl. "The top line. Where it says 'Nora.'"

December stepped up closer. She could smell Vicki's perfume— something heavy, full of musk.

"'Vicki Gold,'" she said, stepping quickly back. "Well. Congratulations."

"Why thank you, darling," Vicky said as December stepped farther back, away from the two of them, down the hall, toward the sign for the fire exit. "See you opening night."

December backed out the door, setting off the alarm bell. They were laughing at her, Joel swinging his scarf in the air like a chorus girl with a feather boa, Vicki throwing her head back so her braids swung back and forth. December turned and ran, in no particular direction, she just ran for blocks until she could no longer hear the alarm, until she had left the campus and found herself on narrow streets in a strange neighborhood, until she was so tired she could no longer walk without feeling the pain shoot up along her side, and she curled up on the bank of the river and held her head in her hands and wept.

She sat there, folding her arms against the chill of early fall, until the sky began to fade and the pink street lamps blinked on across the river. She found a telephone booth, examined her face in the glass door for signs of puffiness, and dialed Alex's number. It was busy; she counted to ten and tried again and it was still busy; she sang the first two verses of "Let It Be" and tried again and still it was busy. Alex was probably trying to call her at her room. Perhaps he had already heard that she hadn't gotten the part. She walked to his apartment, checking carefully for oncoming cars at every narrow street she crossed. It was more than just an unlucky day; December felt that any awful thing could and would happen. Suddenly the world was full of menace. A truck might come barreling out of nowhere and knock her down. Gray metal air conditioners would come hurtling off their shaky bolts onto her head. A family dog had caught rabies from the river rats and would leap over tornado fencing to plant his teeth deep into her leg. Someone had told her that bats nested in these high wooden Victorian houses.

There were only ten blocks left to Alex's house, she was going to die, she was sure of it, five blocks left, two blocks left, her hands were shaking so hard she could barely press the buzzer. No answer.

She couldn't go home—it would start to rain, she'd be struck by lightening. She would wait in Alex's apartment until he came back.

Why hadn't Alex ever given her a key to his apartment? Rosaline had a key to Schuyler's place, so she could lock up after herself if she slept later than he did. December took her student ID out of her back pocket. The smiling face on the laminated plastic, no more than one inch square, was unrecognizable. Was it only two weeks ago that she had looked so happy, so pretty, so young? She slipped the card between the door and the jamb and slid it down on a diagonal until the catch released.

Inside it was dark. A small tan suitcase lay open on the carpet. December could hear a Wilson Pickett song and Alex singing along in the bedroom in his fake black accent. She picked up an empty brandy bottle that had fallen onto the velvet sofa. The telephone handset, removed from its cradle and dangling against a table leg, beeped in time to the music.

"Alex?" December called, waiting just outside the half-closed bedroom door. "I buzzed and knocked but I guess you didn't hear me." There was no reply. "Alex? Hello?"

He came to the door wearing only his jeans, which were zipped but not buttoned.

"I must have fallen asleep," he said. "What time is it? We've a reservation at eight. Just sit down and I'll be out in a minute."

"I didn't get it. I didn't get Nora."

"What? Oh. Well. You can tell me all about it in the restaurant."

"Look at me, Alex, I can't go out like this, I've been walking around Cambridge all afternoon, I'm a mess." She burst into tears. "I didn't get the part because I didn't deserve it, I'm a terrible actress and I always will be, I can't ever face those people again." She leaned against his chest, waiting for him to put his arms around her. "I don't know why I even tried. I don't know why I let you talk me into this. I didn't even want to be an actress until I met you."

"What utter nonsense," he said, taking her shoulders in his hands and holding her away from him. "You're tired and you're hungry and you should just sit down like a good girl before you say something you'll regret. We'll go to that little place on the corner and I'll get some lasagna and red wine into you and you'll feel one hundred percent better. Just give me five minutes."

December pushed past him and spun around to face him. "You're always telling me what to do," she said. "I can't take this anymore."

She looked beyond Alex to the living room in all its disarray: the telephone off the hook, the brandy glasses and the ashtray heaped full of cigarette butts, the clothing strewn on the carpet. "You aren't the one who's been completely humiliated. You've been lying around all afternoon drinking and—will you look at me?—you don't even care, not really," she sobbed, but she felt as if she were talking to herself. He was looking beyond her, into the bedroom, and she turned around to see what he was staring at.

Propped up on the pillows, arms folded behind a head covered with thick black curls, naked save for the bedsheet wrapped around his hips, a cigarette held between smiling lips, lay a tan and handsome boy.

Alex did not move. "December, Bruno. Bruno, December," he said.

Bruno leaned forward on the bed and extended his arm as if for a handshake.

"At last we meet," he said. "The pleasure is all mine."

How she managed to walk past Alex and back out onto the street December could not remember. She had just done it without thinking, the way a hand retracts from touching a hot kettle, and here she was again, alone in the dark.

When she got back to the room there was Katie Lee, snipping the price tags off a pile of woolen socks.

"Hello, December," she said. "Whoever invented these little plastic tag holders ought to be held responsible for half the dental problems in the country. You look perfectly awful."

"Thanks."

"Well you do," Katie Lee said, shrugging. "Is everything all right?"

"No. Is Marinda on the phone?"

"Clever guess. Peter got kicked out of that country club of a mental hospital, and he's refusing to see a psychiatrist. As they say in Vienna, another day, another trauma."

"Where's Rosaline?"

"She's supposed to be taking the last shuttle to New York. She's having dinner at Schuyler's, and then he's taking her to Logan. Apparently her father went on another binge, and her mother called her down for a family conference. Honestly, sometimes I think I'm the only normal person left around here. You really do look terrible. I guess you didn't get the part."

"Good guess. Look, I'm going to try and track down Rosaline. If

Alex calls—never mind, if anyone calls, just say you don't know where I am." She headed for the door.

"December, wait a minute," Katie Lee said, coming toward her with a pair of scissors in one hand and a bright-red sock in the other. "If there's anything I can do—well, I suppose there's nothing I can do. I'm sorry about the part, I really am. I liked the idea of having an actress as a friend, it made me feel a little glamorous. The director is a complete fool, I'm sure—the girl who got the part couldn't be nearly as pretty as you."

"Katie Lee, they just don't give the part to the prettiest girl. It doesn't work that way."

"I know that. Do you want to go get a drink someplace? I can be very understanding, nearly sympathetic actually, as long as you promise not to tell anybody," she said, laughing.

December believed that Katie Lee, for the first time since they'd met, was trying to be her friend. "I could really use a drink," she said.

"Well, I'm supposed to meet some people on Dunster Street, why don't you just tag along? I'm sure they won't mind."

"I don't know. Maybe a drink is a bad idea. And I would like to see Rosaline before she leaves. See you tomorrow," December said, walking down the stairs.

Katie Lee stood in the hallway and watched her go. What a shame, she thought, one disappointment and that girl just crumbles. In the end everyone gets what she deserves. This is just what she gets for sleeping around, for trying to pretend she's someone she isn't, for thinking she can get away with anything just because she's prettier than the rest of us.

Katie Lee looked at the pile of socks and underwear on the floor. Once a year she replaced drawerfuls of the stuff. he just threw the old things away—you couldn't take underwear to the Salvation Army, and besides, it was creepy to think of some weird poor person wearing her things. Clothing is just like men, Katie Lee said to herself, pleased with the comparison, taking a mental memo to use it cleverly in conversation. Clothing is just like people: when Katie Lee is finished with them they have no earthly use at all.

"She wanted to leave town before the storm hit," Schuyler said, hoping December wouldn't burst into tears right there in his hallway. "She took an earlier flight."

"I hope she gets home okay," December said, the panic of the afternoon still with her. A plane could crash. A taxi could careen right off the highway. In New York City, she'd heard, people got mugged walking from the curb to the door.

"I'm sure she'll be fine," Schuyler replied. "It's you I'm worried about. There's a fresh pot of coffee if you'd like some."

"Coffee sounds great." December had never been to Schuyler's apartment, and she looked around as he busied himself in the kitchen. The one long room was nearly bare. In the middle, two oak rocking chairs faced a battered couch covered with a patchwork quilt over a woven Navajo rug. At one end of the room an unfinished wooden plank rested on beat-up gray file cabinets, creating a desk that looked out the window onto a schoolyard. At the other end, above the bed covered simply with a striped Hudson's Bay blanket, was the only piece of artwork Schuyler had put up on the plain white walls: a huge photograph of a desert somewhere in the Southwest, with mountains rising up in the background. It seemed the very opposite of Alex's place—austere, quiet, soothing.

"There's some whiskey in this," Schuyler said, setting an earthenware mug on the floor beside her. December waited for him to ask her questions: what happened? why didn't you get the part, and who did? why aren't you with Alex or Marinda or Katie Lee? But he said nothing, and they sat there together in silence for a while, listening to the first claps of thunder and hard rain falling on the pavement below.

December stared at the patterns of the wood grain in the floor. Every so often she lifted her eyes to his, and every time she did there he was looking right at her, unwavering. She began to feel that if he stared at her long enough he'd be able to read all her thoughts and she wouldn't have to tell him how she felt, he would just understand, he would just know about every painful thing that had happened. Occasionally he got up and refilled their mugs, each time the ratio of whiskey to coffee increasing, each bitter mugful getting easier to drain.

Schuyler watched her rocking back and forth in the chair. He could guess enough of what had happened. She hadn't gotten her part and Alex had been a shit about it. He remembered how he had felt a year ago when a piece he'd worked on for months about his home state was rejected by five magazines in quick succession. He had been sure that the piece would not only launch his career but would be recognized as the most brilliant voice ever to emerge from the American

wilderness. When it came back in the mail for what was to be the
last time, it wasn't just his own ability that Schuyler had begun to
question but everything he was and had ever wanted to be.

He didn't know how to tell December how special he knew she
was. He had no vocabulary for it. Words like beauty and talent and
generosity just didn't apply. There was a strength of spirit in her,
something noble that ached toward freedom, and he recognized it
because he was filled with that spirit himself. Having her so near
him in the quiet room he felt the rest of the world fall away. All that
remained was the two of them, and his sense that somehow they
were psychic twins, traveling the same road, inching toward the
same horizon. Everything else was gone: the house, the street, the
city, and all the people who filled it.

He leaned over and gently touched her knee as if to make sure that
she actually existed here, in this room, with him. She took his hand,
and there they sat, still silent. It was as if he had touched his fingers
to a live wire. He could feel a heat up along his arm, down his spine,
branching out into every part of his body like an electrified chart of
the nervous system.

When they kissed he could feel this current racing back and forth
between them. There was no passive or aggressive, no leader or fol-
lower, no urgent message to hurry nor a tender plea to wait, no right
or wrong. There were just Schuyler and December. She held the back
of his head with one hand and with the other unbuttoned his soft
corduroy shirt. She bent down to kiss his chest, and he lifted her shirt
over her head, watching the soft light catch in her hair as it fell back
around her shoulders.

December felt herself being renewed, as if her blood had been filled
with poisons and was now being cleansed, oxygenated, as her heart
pumped it to an ever faster beat. His touch—on her shoulders, down
her back, across her breasts, around her waist—was more powerful
than any words she had ever heard. Somehow he knew all about her.
She knew all about him. She knew what he would want her to do and
what he would want to do for her. It was so simple, at last, to love
and be loved. This man—his hair and lips and teeth and flesh and
bones—he was her fate.

She felt a sudden darkness in the room, as when a cloud passes in
front of the summer sun, and she lifted her head from Schuyler's
neck.

Standing in front of the one bright lamp, outlined in a halo of light like the moon during eclipse, Rosaline held her suitcase against her chest. She was soaking wet.

"My flight was canceled," she said, looking at a point just above their heads. December picked her shirt off the floor and covered herself. No one spoke for a few minutes and then, after a few stammers, Rosaline sailed into an embarrassed explanation, speaking softly, as though she were the one who owed the apology.

"First it was delayed, and they let us on the plane, but then the weather got so bad they had to cancel everything, so they let us off, but all the phones were being used, and of course there wasn't a taxi to be found, so everyone headed for the subway, which took forever, and of course the minute I left the station it began to rain even harder." A puddle had formed around her thin suede shoes. The front of her raincoat was stained from the dark red leather of her suitcase.

"Rosaline," Schuyler said, stepping toward her. "Listen."

Rosaline held up her hand like a traffic cop: stop, come no farther, be quiet. "I let myself in because I thought you'd be asleep already. I'm sorry," she said, pushing her wet hair off her face. "I'm very sorry," she whispered.

"It's my fault," December said.

"I don't want to hear it," Rosaline said, shuffling back toward the door. "I don't want to hear anything. I'm going to go home now. I'm going to forget this ever happened. Because I'm going to forget that the two of you ever existed, that I was ever foolish enough to consider you my friends. I never want to see you or talk to you ever again. Both of you."

She isn't going to scream or cry or anything, Schuyler thought. Because she's already gone. It's already over.

Rosaline hesitated for a moment when she reached the door. With shaking hands she reached inside her coat, unclasped the gold chain that held the locket, and left it in the enamel bowl where Schuyler kept his car keys and unanswered mail. The heart looked inconsequential, a tiny glittering thing, among the unpaid bills and the loose change Schuyler had emptied from his pockets earlier in the day.

"What I gave you can't be returned," she said in a voice as calm and hard as glass, and then she left.

6

*O*ver and over, December had talked herself through her episode with Schuyler. That's how she had come to think of it: an episode, one night dropped into her life like a stone into a pond, creating a brief confusion until it sank, down to the bottom, and the surface was smooth again.

Had Schuyler and Rosaline been having problems, had December just been caught between the two of them, their break-up inevitable? Was he simply drunk, too loose to rein himself in from whatever she had offered? Had he been fooling around for months, knowing Rosaline was too naïve to catch on? Or was it something worse—was he one of those men who could not refuse a damsel in distress, who was turned on by the tearful, the needy, the weak? A sympathy fuck. December had been on the other side of that exchange often enough. She had sat there, pathetic, a sexual charity case, desperate for the touch that would restore her self-esteem. It was as low as you could go. The bargain subbasement of love. The scene came back to her at random moments—when she crossed the street against the light, when she brushed her teeth in the morning—and it was enough to spiral her down into a depression for the rest of the day.

But none of it mattered now. Not Schuyler, not Rosaline, not Alex, not any of her friends from that first year in Cambridge. For the past ten months school had just been a place she visited twice a week on the Eastern shuttle from New York. She attended her classes, all neatly scheduled on Tuesdays and Thursdays, she checked her books out of the library, she handed in her papers, and she cabbed back to the airport well before the evening rush hour.

From the appearance of her modern L-shaped studio, in an east twenties high-rise that boasted two round-the-clock doormen and electronic intrusion alarms in every apartment, one would never know that she was a student. A bookshelf and typewriter were hidden away in her walk-in closet behind the plastic bags that held her out-of-season clothes. The leather and chrome furnishings, bought nearly new from a flight attendant neighbor transferred to Atlanta on short notice, wouldn't provide a single clue to the identity of the occupant.

There was plenty to distract her when she wasn't studying. Exercise classes uptown, swimming at the local health club, endless go-sees, the shoots where for a few hours' work she could make enough money to pay her rent for a whole month. And the parties, half business and half pleasure, New York was full of parties where they could always use another pretty face. Sometimes she knew the host. Sometimes she went with a friend. Sometimes she just got a call from her agent saying the invitation would arrive by messenger and giving her the names of three or four people she should be sure to be nice to, who might be able to throw some lucrative work her way.

At first, when Alex had called her with the name of his photographer friend who had contacts at all the best agencies, she'd wanted no part of the business. It had been Alex's plan all along, and now that he was out of the picture she would rather find something else to do. She could go to graduate school or get into computer programming or take the civil service exam.

Then the photographer began telephoning her. Alex had told him all about her, he said, they were looking for faces like hers, there was going to be a backlash against all these sensuous, ethnic faces and she could be a profitable part of it. Just one session, he said, I'll fly you down here for one session, and if you don't like the pictures, that's the end of that.

She had nothing to lose. She'd end up with the most glamorous passport photos the State Department had ever set eyes on. She could do some Christmas shopping in New York before the stores got impossible. She flew down one Saturday afternoon, wearing her baggiest, most unflattering clothes, without a trace of makeup.

Terry smiled when he answered the door. "You've been staying out of the sun, I see," he said. "That's very good. This is my friend Becky, she's going to do your face and hair. You washed it this morning? Very good, very good. We've got a dress here for you and a raccoon coat I'd like to try on you and a bathing suit—you don't mind? Very good.

Drink? Smoke? You really shouldn't, you know, but I keep it around to relax the girls. Nothing, very good. I'll be back in half an hour. Then we'll begin."

She felt like Dorothy in the Emerald City as Becky fussed around her, painting her face, spraying her hair. Terry returned and put some loud music on the stereo.

"What do you think of this disco thing? Very hot, very hot." He played with the lights as Becky stood behind him, frowning, her arms folded across her chest. "You should see these new clubs. Absolutely amazing. Lights, dancing, crazy people, all kinds of crazy things going on. Totally new, totally hot. It's just a camera, December, not a ray gun. It won't hurt you. Think of something very nice. Think of someone you like very much."

December could think of no one.

"Where are you from? The ocean, pretend you are at the beach on the hottest day of the year, it is too hot to move, very good, they are going to like this a lot. The blond girls usually look silly when they put on their sultry faces but I can tell this is going to come out very good. Move your shoulders, that's what the music is for. Becky, get some lift back into her hair."

He worked for an hour. This was easier than acting class—you only had to hold your emotion for the few seconds it took for the camera to whir through a half dozen exposures.

"Almost finished, just almost," Terry said as Becky changed the backdrop from white to violet. "Now for the *pièce de résistance*. I want you to think about the most wonderful man in the world. The top. Primo. Numero uno. I want your eyes to fill with love for this man. Look at me, no, not good, come on now, concentrate, show me how much you can love. Pretend I am this most wonderful man in the world."

December pictured a series of handsome men. Just last week she'd met a fantastic German at a party for a visiting professor, very funny and interesting and of all things a stockbroker, she might be able to fall in love with him. He'd sent her a dozen long-stemmed roses with a note saying he'd call when he got back from Munich.

"You are not concentrating," Terry said. "I need more from you. Give me everything."

December ran through the catalogue: a high school boyfriend, the stroke on varsity crew, Alex briefly, a lifeguard from last summer, even Paul McCartney, whom she had mentally married and had several little Beatles with after "Rubber Soul" was released.

A new song came on with a fierce synthesized beat. A woman was moaning and wailing about a man who had left her, about a love that was gone, about the rain beating against her window. And there he was, his face floating before her, his eyes creased in the saddest smile. Schuyler. He was leaning over to touch her knee. He was about to kiss her. Her lips parted. Her head tilted slightly to the left.

"Very good," Terry said, setting down his camera and motioning Becky to turn off the lights. "More than very good. The best. The absolutely best."

The pictures arrived in Cambridge two weeks later via air courier. Marinda had woken her up, holding the red striped envelope by two fingers as if she might catch something from it.

"Looks like this guy was for real," she said snippily. December supposed she should be grateful that Marinda and Katie Lee were still even speaking to her. Rosaline had left—it had taken less than a day to move all her things to her new apartment off Brattle Street—and December's roommates returned from their visits to Rosaline with the most unrevealing of news briefs. "Nice furniture. Sent from her mother." "New haircut, kinda on the short side." "Cold pasta salad. Better than it sounds." Yes, December wanted to say, but how is she? Depressed, angry, does she hate me, does she hate Schuyler, what is she feeling? It seemed she would never find out. December wanted to send some kind of message to Rosaline, something she couldn't entrust to Marinda or Katie Lee, something she hadn't yet quite formed into words. Something more than *I miss you* (it was Alex she missed) and something less than *I'm sorry* (she had never apologized for anything where men were concerned).

"I hope you didn't let him talk you into taking your clothes off," Katie Lee said, grabbing the envelope from Marinda. "You will rue the day, rue the day. They have a way of surfacing later, you know, just when you're about to be appointed ambassador to the Vatican."

December got out of bed and pulled on a sweatshirt. "I don't think they'll be taking my application for that job."

"It was just an example," Katie Lee said.

"Because I don't know Italian," December smiled. "Otherwise I'm the perfect candidate." She knew what they were thinking, they were always polite, but the disapproval just curled out of them like smoke from a fire. She would have to get away from them as soon as she could. Smart Rosaline.

"Look at this," Katie Lee cried. "December, these are unbelievable. You're gorgeous."

"Thank you. Let me see."

Marinda bent over to take a look. "You should have figured out a way to keep the coat. Do models get to keep everything they wear? It's amazing what a little bit of makeup can do."

"It was tons of makeup," December said. "And hairspray. Ugh."

"Look at you in this dress," Katie Lee said. "You could be on the cover of any magazine, honey, I know what I'm talking about. God bless Alex wherever he is—I don't suppose you know, but he was right. You could make piles of money. Huge piles of money. Piles of money as high as the Empire State Building. It makes me dizzy just to think of it."

"Well, I haven't agreed to do anything."

"Of course you're going to let him show these to agencies. December, this is your big chance," Katie Lee said. "As my daddy says, opportunities like this are as rare as hen's teeth, and that's a pretty old hen."

"I guess it can't hurt."

"December Dunne, you listen to me. You just get rid of this 'so-what-it-can't-hurt-why-not' attitude. You'll never amount to anything that way. You want this—and you're the biggest fool I ever met if you don't—you go out and get it. You just set out to be the biggest damn model that ever was."

"Maybe it's not what she wants to do," Marinda said. "She will have a Harvard degree, you know, she's not some kid from the sticks without any other choices. Being a model is sort of, you know, well, the kind of girls that do it, I'm not saying that they're all dumb bimbos, it's just—"

"It's just what, Marinda?" December broke in. "It's a good way to make money and meet people and travel and get noticed. I'm not about to drop out of school."

"That's not what I meant."

"It's certainly good enough for me, if that's what you meant." December held up a photograph that had a small card clipped to it saying "This is the best one—this one will make you a star. XOX Terry." It was the last shot he'd taken.

"I'm going to do it," she said, gathering up the photographs and tossing them onto her bed. "I'm going to go to New York."

• • •

And it was in New York that she finally ran into Rosaline at, of all places, a party given by some Harvard boys who were celebrating their graduation from Columbia's business school. December had gone into the bedroom to stash her bag and leather jacket under the bed, and there was Rosaline, sitting by the window, hanging up the telephone.

"Rosaline," she said, dropping her belongings on the floor. "At last."

Rosaline turned and held up her hand as if she were protecting her face from a flying object. "I didn't know you'd be here," she said. "I'm just in town for the weekend, for a christening. Actually I was just trying to call a cab. I'm on my way out."

"Can't we talk for a minute," December said, "just for a minute. Then you can go."

Rosaline looked down at her lap and shook her head. "There's nothing to say. Really. I hear you're doing well and I wish you all the luck in the world, I honestly do. But it's too hard to talk," she said, her voice beginning to crack.

"Then just listen for a minute."

Rosaline stood up. "Please don't. Don't."

"It's making me crazy, Rosaline. You have to at least let me explain what happened. After you hear me out, you can walk out that door and I'll never say another word to you again. But at least give me a chance."

"I can't. I'm sorry, but I just can't. I can't ever be your friend again, so what's the point. You want to explain whatever it is you think you have to explain so you can feel better about what you did. I don't care a fig about anything you have to say, and I don't care whether you feel better, well actually, I do care. If you feel rotten, you should, you know, you deserve it. It's the price you pay for—for being bad," Rosaline said, clutching her hands in her lap.

December felt her legs collapsing beneath her, and she leaned against the wall, sliding her back down until she was sitting, knees hunched against her chest, on the cold wood floor. "You're making me crazy," she said, "and you know what, I think you're making yourself crazy too. By not letting it go. Great, fine, you don't want to talk about it because you think that's some way of punishing me, and I guess it is, but you're punishing yourself as well."

"Maybe I am," Rosaline whispered, sniffling into a paper tissue she'd unrolled from her pocket. "But I don't want to hear it. Not now, anyway."

December rested her chin on her knees. "It's worse for you, isn't it. You don't want to let me off the hook, fine, okay, I understand that, but you know I'm not the kind of person who sits around feeling guilty and suffering."

"I don't believe that," Rosaline said. "That's just your pose. I never believed that. You know, you've always acted as if you're in total control, as if you could handle anything, as if you're the bravest girl in the world. But sometimes I think you're the most frightened of all of us. It's as if you're hiding something, I don't know, or running from something."

December and Rosaline stared at each other for a few moments and then December had to look away. I'll have to let her have the last word, December said to herself, I'll just have to swallow on this one until Rosaline is ready to hear what I have to say.

"I hate parties," Rosaline said.

"You used to love them."

"I did? Are you sure? Just the thought of walking back out into that room fills me with panic. All those noisy, drunken people trying to have a good time."

"Some of them actually are having a good time. Or their idea of it. You notice no one's come in here for the last few minutes. They're all probably out there wondering if we're tearing each other's eyes out."

"I could mess up my hair a little," Rosaline said, giggling. "That would give them something to talk about."

"Come on. If we aren't friends, at least we can put on a good appearance. I'll walk you out, and let's have one drink together so you aren't gossiped about for the next billion years, and then I'll see you into a cab."

Rosaline thought for a minute. "All right," she said with a sigh, appearances being what she had been brought up to value above all else.

Out in the room an overweight boy in a plaid madras jacket was gatoring to a minor Motown hit.

"He once asked me out," Rosaline confided.

"How incredibly disgusting," December replied, handing Rosaline an iceless Coke. "Of course you refused him."

"Of course," Rosaline said. She had refused nearly everybody, always coming up with some reason why the relationship wouldn't work out, why it was pointless to even have dinner with a boy if there wasn't at least the possibility of something serious, like marriage, developing.

A tall boy from Eliot House ambled up to Rosaline, his black wool dinner jacket barely reaching the hem of his Day-Glo flowered Hawaiian shorts.

"Care to dance," he said to the opening beats of an old Buddy Holly song.

"Thank you, no," she said, and he pivoted and disappeared back into the crowd.

"What was the matter with him?" December asked. Despite appearances, the gentleman in question was a Phi Beta Kappa philosophy major who spent his free time cataloguing his grandfather's amateur butterfly collection.

"Nothing at all. He's sort of cute, actually," Rosaline said. "But I hardly know him. I mean, I know who he is, but we haven't been formally introduced."

"Jesus, Rosaline, all he asked for was a dance. You dance with the guy, make a little eye contact, exchange names, have a conversation, it's no big deal. It's how you meet people at parties."

"I couldn't dance with someone I didn't know. Imagine if—" if the music slowed and he tried to hold my hand and put his arm around me, *if he tried to touch me.* "I don't know. I'm much shyer than you, I guess," Rosaline said, and she began to giggle again at her understatement.

December shrugged as someone came up behind her, grabbed her around the waist, and spun her around into the middle of the dance floor. December smiled and joined her partner in a drunken lindy.

She looks like she's having fun, Rosaline thought. She probably is having fun. So this is what life is like in New York, she thought, going to parties and dancing with strange boys and hoping one of them likes you enough to get your telephone number and ask you out. She would never be able to do it. She was going to graduate from college and move back to New York and—what was her mother's expression?—wither on the proverbial vine. She wanted to go home, but she was afraid to walk out onto the street unescorted. The east seventies were relatively safe, but still, it was nearly midnight, and she had heard all sorts of stories. Maybe the doorman would get a taxi for her.

She watched as December was twirled around the room, her hair flying out in all directions. Rosaline recalled the power of that hair, how when she used to walk down a street with December, men who passed them would twist around to see if the face lived up to the thick platinum hair. She remembered the way the men pretended to be looking back beyond December up at a building or out into traffic with expressions that expected disappointment, almost wished for it, as if December's frontal failure to live up to her hair would cause the men to turn to each other in smug congratulation. Rosaline used to watch the double take, the look of finding a new dollar bill or a single gold earring in the middle of the sidewalk, and she would feel herself sharing some small part of December's victory, the victory of the underestimated won by such surprise. Rosaline watched December dance in circles, and she watched the men watching December, and she felt very tired. December never seemed to get dizzy or lose the beat. Her partner appeared to be moving back in time, re-creating the history of popular dance in reverse, from the bump to the tighten-up to the jerk to the twist. December shook a finger at him and silently mouthed "You naughty boy."

When the song was over, December dipped in a parody of a curtsy and headed off the dance floor. She felt exhilarated from the exertion of dancing, from feeling the eyes of the room admiringly upon her, from knowing that Rosaline didn't hate her at all, that there was some hope, it seemed, for some kind of reconciliation.

She would make a date to have lunch with Rosaline before she left town. They would go somewhere quiet on Madison Avenue and then maybe they could take a walk in the park or go shopping. They could gossip about Katie Lee and Marinda, just like old times.

December walked the perimeter of the living room, scouted both bedrooms, checked the bathroom, and then returned to the living room, where she found a crumpled pink tissue next to an untouched plastic cupful of warm Coke. Rosaline was gone.

December stretched under the covers and pulled a pillow over her face. New York was driving her crazy. Maybe there were nice, relaxed, ordinary people in the city—the kind of people who called in the middle of the afternoon to say they were in the neighborhood and could they stop by, the kind of people who brought you groceries when you were sick—but she'd be damned if she knew where they were. Queens, probably.

Today was one of what December had come to think of as her weekly mental health breaks. Her calendar was clear. Joey, the unemployed actor who ran her answering service, had been told that she'd be out of town until the following morning. She put on an old flannel shirt and a pair of corduroy jeans and went downstairs to pick up the secondhand VW beetle she'd bought last summer.

"Kinda cold for October," the attendant said, holding open the door.

"It's only going to get worse," she replied, releasing the brake and heading out into the sparse midday traffic. She drove west through the shopping and garment districts, through the tunnel under the river and across the swamps to the Turnpike. Past the generating stations, past Newark Bay, where landing passenger planes swooped just a few yards over the roadway, past the refineries whose industrial stink was as familiar and reassuring as her own sweat, December cruised at a comfortable ten miles over the speed limit until she hit the Parkway.

It was here that she crossed an imaginary border and began, for the first time in a week, to relax. She rolled down the windows and turned up the radio. Off the highway and through the little towns whose names she recited like a benediction—Little Silver, Red Bank, Sea Bright, Highlands—she drove along the coast, as the waves, swollen by wind and tide, crashed over the high stone seawall and splashed across her car.

The bar was filled with fishermen who had knocked off for the day and a construction crew that had been sent home early when the strong gusts made their work too dangerous. There were a few women in the bar—some wives and girlfriends, mostly staff from the nearby hospital whose shifts either began at four in the afternoon or ended at eight in the morning—but mostly there were men, tossing darts and holding the halfhearted political conversations that tided them over from the end of the World Series to the first round of football playoffs.

"Can I get you a beer, honey," one man offered. Here it cost only a dollar to play the part of a gentleman.

December shook her head. "Just a Coke, thanks." She joined the table, where they were heatedly discussing the merits and drawbacks of various types of insulation.

"It's messy but it works and it's cheap so what can you do," said the man who'd bought her the soda. His name was Chip and he was about her age. "Know what I mean?" he said to December, raising one eyebrow.

"Sure," she said. Chip lived at home with his parents and three sisters; he put all his money into his car, a late-model Thunderbird, and into a savings account he was hoping would bankroll his own business some day. He had been raised by women, and it showed in his easy smile and almost formal manners. He stood up whenever a woman joined or left the table, and he monitored his language in their presence. She could trust him.

"As I see it," December continued, "this is a very serious philosophical issue. Like, are you keeping the heat in? Or are you keeping the cold out?"

"Right, right," Chip said, chuckling into his beer. "Like, is this glass half empty or half full? The bartender is Greek, let's ask him. George, is this glass half empty or half full?"

George placed a fresh bottle of beer on the counter without replying.

"I guess it was half empty," Chip said. "So, you like philosophy?"

December shrugged. "Sometimes," she said.

"I hate this bar," he continued. "Doesn't stop me from coming here every damn day, though. You feel like getting dinner someplace?"

"Seafood, I'd love some seafood," she replied. She knew this itinerary by heart, because she had been following it weekly since she'd moved to New York nearly a year ago. Dinner at an inexpensive restaurant where December would order the catch of the day. More drinks at a seaside bar where, if they stayed late enough, they'd dance to cover versions of last month's top-forty hits. Then on to the man's apartment or house or, if he still lived at home (and so many of them did until they got married), the kind of motel that didn't take credit cards.

December would be back in New York well before dawn. She'd hit the pool just after her health club opened, swimming ten extra laps as if that would cleanse her of whatever had happened the night before. She would take a long hot shower, scrubbing every inch of her body with the rough brown sponge a dermatologist had recommended, she would call Joey to pick up her messages, she would check with the agency for any last-minute appointments, and then she would get on with her day.

7

"After a while all stories are the same story," she said, picking a raw oyster off Schuyler's plate. "You'll find out for yourself soon enough. After a while it's just a job."

"Maybe so," Schuyler said, leaning back in his chair, trying to figure out why Pamela seemed suddenly different tonight. He'd met her three weeks ago on his first official day at the paper. His co-workers on the news staff had taken him out to a bar that filled up with reporters after hours. As one of the first women in the city to cover major league sports, she was much gossiped about, and as the new boy on the block, Schuyler had heard no fewer than a dozen Pamela Brown stories in less than twenty-four hours. Just minutes after a pennant game Pamela Brown had barged into the losing team's locker room, thrust a microphone into the naked relief pitcher's face, and grilled him about the controversial umpire's call that had cost his team the game. During spring training in Florida, the day after a mischievous team manager had hired a male prostitute to lie in wait in the room she'd rented at a local Holiday Inn, Pamela Brown had sent a Miami cultural institution known as Chesty Rodgers down onto the field to perform a strip tease during the seventh inning stretch.

When Schuyler first met her she was wearing a wrinkled man's oxford cloth shirt, baggy corduroy jeans, a single long reddish brown braid down her back and not a trace of makeup. It was hard to believe this was the same Pamela Brown who took players' wives out for drinks and asked them about their off-season sex lives. But sitting across the table from him now was the Pamela Brown he'd heard so many rumors about. Her long auburn hair fell around her shoulders in gravity-defying curls. She wore high-heeled gray suede pumps and a pair of gray velvet jeans that showed her to be in as good physical shape as any athlete she wrote about. Her peach-colored silk blouse caught the light whenever she moved, which was constantly: to light a cigarette, to push back her hair, to shrug her shoulders in such a way that the fabric lifted up and tightened around her breasts, which were packed into the kind of no-nonsense sturdy undergarment that Schuyler had only experienced in the pages of an old Sears catalogue. The sort of bra that had wires in it someplace and required not just the one simple fastener that Schuyler had learned over the years to undo deftly with one hand (he was ambidextrous in this department and proud of it), but at least three hooks to do its job, which was to prevent the wearer's breasts from moving even a millimeter in any direction. The implication was this: that the harnessing of Pamela Brown's breasts was serious business and demanded the best and strongest equipment. The further implication was this: that the equipment prevented the male onlooker from making an educated guess as to what Pamela Brown looked like in the nude, or rather, that Pamela Brown knew that men tried to make such guesses all the time, and that she took some sort of comfort in thwarting this particular aim.

Oh God, I've forgotten what she's talking about, Schuyler thought. The oysters were all gone, and the salads had arrived.

"So every good interview is really like a seduction," she was saying, waving away the waiter's long peppermill before he'd had a chance to offer it. "You know what you want them to say and they know what they want you to write. You're both there talking and joking like you're the best of buddies, but each of you is really out after only one thing, and they know what it is you want, and you know what it is they want, but you pretend everything is happening on this friendly, spontaneous basis. I call it Interview Flirtation."

"I've never been that great at interviews," Schuyler said. "I'm a good listener, so if they're good talkers, the interview comes off all right, but I'm really much better on the investigative end of things."

"Ah," she said, removing an olive pit from between her lips and laying it on the side of her plate, "a cynic. They make terrible interviewers. The subject can tell you don't really believe what they're saying."

"Maybe. Maybe I'm just bad at Interview Flirtation."

"And other forms of flirtation?" she asked.

"Bad at that too," Schuyler said, laughing. It was true, though: he'd come to New York after graduation with the hope of a fresh start but instead he'd found nothing but disaster, a series of tense party conversations and awkward dates that had led nowhere. Not only hadn't he slept with anyone in months, not only hadn't he met anyone he really wanted to sleep with in months, he hadn't even *thought* much about sex since—since what he had come to think of as The Scene. The night with December and Rosaline. That was how he thought of it, as a scene. And it was easiest to think of it that way: like something you saw characters act out in a bad soap opera. And when he ran the scene back mentally, that was exactly how he saw it: from the outside, as a detached observer, watching an actor play the part of Schuyler, the misbehaving boyfriend.

Each time he replayed the scene he wondered if there were any way it could have come out different. December had gotten dressed and, after sheepishly explaining that she couldn't go to Alex's and that she couldn't go home either, asked if she could stay the night. When he lent her the money for a hotel room she started to cry and said she'd use it to buy a train ticket back to New Jersey. She had some things to sort out, and she made him promise to wait until she got in touch with him. Which she never did. Which was fine with him, really. She represented the worst, most dishonorable thing he had ever done, and he didn't want to be reminded of it. He was a wreck for a while. Every time he had to date a check or letter "December" his hand shook; it was silly and melodramatic in a way he despised. He heard from Teddy that she'd moved to New York, but he never ran into her.

After she'd left his apartment that night he tried to follow Rosaline home, but she refused to see him. Marinda had answered the door with that look of disapproval women get, the look that says "you men are all the same and deserve to die," the look that tells you that women have been bearing the burden of unworthy men since the beginning of time and that they're all simply pretending that they don't mind a bit. Rosaline wouldn't take his calls or answer his letters. This was the childlike and innocent part of her, the part that couldn't compromise, the part that believed one should live life exactly the way life should be lived, the part that believed in absolute right and absolute wrong. *Forgive me*, Schuyler kept writing her. *I may not deserve it, but I love you, I need you, I want you back, I'll do anything.* But forgiveness was something Rosaline had not yet learned. And even if she could forgive his kissing December, she could never forgive him for not being perfect. For that was what she had been in love with all along, he came to believe. She hadn't really loved him, Schuyler, this boy learning how to be a man; rather, she had been in love with this idea of perfect, flawless love. If she couldn't have it with Schuyler she would have to break it off with him and find someone else. She couldn't believe that perfect love simply didn't exist, that life didn't work that way, that happily-ever-after only happened in fairy tales.

"Not so bad, I think," Pamela was saying, eyeing the grilled chicken he had ordered. "Oh, Jesus, here it comes again. I have this terrible malady known as Restaurant Envy. No matter what I order, once the food arrives I always wish I had gotten what the other person has." She stared down at her veal scallopini. "This is my favorite food, but I'm just incurable."

Schuyler smiled. "You just have to order the same thing the other person does. That way you'll want what you have. Not so bad at what?"

"At flirting, you're not so bad, or at least you wouldn't be so bad if your mind didn't keep wandering. Have a hard day?"

"No, just tired, I guess."

"Well, I'll have to remember about ordering whatever the other person does. Except what if it's pigs' knuckles in cream sauce?"

"Mmm, my favorite. It's not on the menu here—I checked." He switched their plates. "There you are."

She raised her eyebrows. "Well. Thank you. Though it doesn't exactly work that way. It's not just wanting what the other person has. It's *not* wanting what you yourself have simply because you have it. Or rather, wanting something precisely because you can't get it."

"Are we still talking about food?" he asked.

"I hope not. Anyway, maybe you've just been flirting with the wrong people."

"That's definitely true," he said with a sigh. The veal was excellent.

"A lot of women flirt meaninglessly, you know, they just like to flirt."

"There's a word for that."

"Yes, 'tease,' I know, but it's really more complicated than that."

"How so?" he asked. He wondered if underwires showed up when women walked through airport metal detectors.

"Well, the analogy is anorexics. Here are women who have a love-hate relationship with food. They crave it, but they deny themselves the pleasure of eating it. This denial is how they maintain the illusion of control. Control over themselves, control over the thing they love, control over the world at large. It makes them feel powerful. It's the same with sex."

"You're saying women flirt but don't have sex so they can pretend they have control over their sex lives," he said.

"Sort of. Which no one does, right, since sex is all about the loss of control, right?"

Schuyler stared at her. "Sure," he said, realizing with both pleasure and dread that Pamela Brown was not the person at this table who was beginning to lose control of the situation. She was seducing him, most expertly, and he decided to order another glass of wine and relax back into it. Perhaps this was what he had needed: someone older and sophisticated and aggressive, someone who would take the weight of decisions and maneuverings off his weary shoulders. She was going to figure everything out—she probably had already figured everything out, hours before he walked into the restaurant—how they'd share a cab, whether they'd go to his place or hers, it was all figured out for him. It was so easy this way, so wonderfully fun and easy, letting her guide him along into the night.

"You can take the analogy even further," she said, signaling for the waiter to bring them more wine. "Anorexics, who never eat, who are all disgustingly rail-thin, think they know more about food then anyone. They know exactly how many calories are in a slice of Kraft American cheese. They've got loads of cookbooks in their apartments and they know how to make Hollandaise on the most humid day of summer. They know about what has vitamins and what has fiber and all that kind of stuff."

"And sexorexics?" he asked.

"The same thing. They think they understand a lot about sex, even though they don't have very much of it. The Exics Theory can be expanded to all sorts of things. For example, Tanorexics. The same way anorexics start losing weight and keep losing weight and reach this point where they have no idea how thin they really are—you know, they look in the mirror, but they still see an overweight person—well, it's the same thing with compulsive sun worshipers. They don't realize how dark they are. They keep looking in the mirror and seeing unhealthy, pale reflections. They keep hitting the beach."

"Well, I can tell you, I don't understand a thing," Schuyler said. God, I'm getting drunk, he thought. "It's all a mystery to me, ma'am," he continued in his best country-boy drawl.

"Tanning or food or women?" she said.

"All three," he replied. "I hate veal. You would too if you ever saw how the calves were treated."

She pushed her plate toward the center of the table. "And I hate chicken." The waiter appeared with the check; Pamela signed it, and he disappeared with a nod of the head. "I have an account here."

"How convenient. You must let me—"

"I must let you buy me dinner some time?" she said, laughing.

"Pigs' knuckles, on me."

"Well, I like things convenient. For example, my apartment, which is just across the street. Were you ever a boy scout, Schuyler?"

"No, that was the great tragedy of my youth. Our town was too small to have a troop. I always coveted the badges and the uniforms. Five points for learning how to tie the English Drunken Sailor Knot. The whole idea that everyone agreed on what good deeds were and how much each was worth and that you could learn how to do them, and then do them, and then get rewarded for them. And impress girl scouts, of course.

"Well here's your big chance," she said, standing up and offering him her arm, and she laughed again when she saw the startled expression on his face.

"I meant your big chance to walk an old lady across the street," she said.

"Not so old, I think," he said as they left the restaurant.

She got out her keychain. A tiny gold baseball dangled from one end.

"And not so young, I think," she said. "I was a girl scout, actually, if you can believe it."

"You?"

"I was the queen of the girl scouts, actually. I performed good deeds on a daily basis. I've got badges for doing things you didn't even know existed."

"I'm impressed."

"I still have my sash." She pressed the elevator button for the fifth floor. "Would you like to see it?"

"I'd be delighted," he said.

"Wouldn't you just," she said, smiling, "wouldn't you just."

• • •

Here they were, dancing in small circles around Pamela's living room, listening to Dionne Warwick wonder softly just what it was all about. A lover who had left and changed his name, a lover who was asked to walk on by, a lover who made promises he couldn't keep—the message seemed absolutely clear to Schuyler: love didn't work out but Pamela Brown was here, tonight, offering something that was less than love but more than friendship.

Like the valuable secretary who anticipates the need for a letter, drafts and types it and leaves it on her employer's desk awaiting final signature, so she had initiated each new phase of the evening and was now waiting for this one gesture from him: the first kiss. It seemed that these days women could do nearly everything—call men up, ask men out, invite them up for drinks, ask them to dance, slip hotel room keys into their pockets—everything except the one thing that demanded the most bravery, that left them open to the one kind of rejection it was impossible to ignore or laugh away. Perhaps this was just her way of allowing him to think that he was the one making a pass.

He did want to kiss her, and badly. No soft brushing of lips and nuzzling of ears, necks, cheeks, hair, as they got used to the smell and taste and feel of each other. He wanted to open her wide and run his tongue along her back teeth. It was as though he were driving an expensive and exotic sports car that performed well only at high velocity. He wanted to release the throttle and hear the roar of the engine, to rev up and speed down a dark straightaway, to feel in his hands the hum of a machine being tested, of a barrier being broken. He wanted to take her.

He leaned over and kissed her and heard her inhale through her nose, a long even breath that signaled preparation and concentration, like a champion swimmer about to take the first long dive underwater. Her tongue fluttered quickly, swirling around his, and he wondered what it would be like to feel that tongue scurrying across and around every part of his body, and he felt himself stiffen as she pressed her hip between his legs.

She caressed his mouth with a finger and he took nearly her entire hand in his mouth, gently pressing his teeth against the soft flesh of her palm. She withdrew her hand and reached around his belt buckle and pulled the fabric of his trousers and shorts away from his body. His erection straightened out and up against the backs of her fingers, which, wet with his own spit, played with the tip of him, as if testing to see how hard he was, how ready he was, how soon she could proceed to whatever it was she next had in mind.

"I'll be just a minute," she said, and when he opened his eyes she was already halfway to the bedroom. He stood there, listening to the lonely sound of his own short breath as a single drop of sweat released itself down the front of his shirt, feeling for his slowing pulse like a long-distance runner. He usually hated this part, the flow of seduction interrupted by contraceptive maneuvers, the fragile balloon of romance punctured by thoughts of industrial rubber and chemical jellies, the soundtrack of soft music broken by a flushing toilet, a squeaky faucet, a slammed bathroom door.

But tonight it excited him. He pictured her in some halfway state of undress, kicking off her heels and pulling down her jeans, propping a foot on the edge of the bathtub and a hand against the wall for balance, or maybe crouching down like an animal—women never let you watch. She was feeling inside herself, her fingers were up inside her, she was sliding the thing into her, feeling her own warmth and wetness and readiness, and suddenly he wanted to know exactly how it was done.

He knocked on the bathroom door, and when there was no reply he pushed it open and peered into the darkness.

"I'm in here," she called from the bedroom. And there she was, lying in what Schuyler believed was his first actual sighting of what could only be called a peignoir, a peach confection of satin and lace held together at the bodice by a single drawstring.

"You're amazing," he said.

"Come find out just how amazing," she said.

"I feel sort of silly with all these clothes on," he replied.

"We can't have that," she said, watching with a smile on her face as he undressed in the doorway. "No, stay where you are for a minute," she said. "I want to drink it all in." Her eyes traced upward from his long, narrow feet, past the pronounced cut of his calf muscles, his knees bowed from early riding and scarred from countless scrapes and falls, the endless ellipse of his thighs, his hips seeming narrow and fragile in comparison, an erection, a marvelously huge erection pointing straight at her like a shotgun or a command, the pale hairless flat stomach, his sweat-gleamed chest with its small boyish nipples, the thin and muscular arms, up to those shoulders, those broad, hard shoulders, the second thing she'd noticed about him, up past the slightly too prominent jaw, his sandy hair, mussed by the pulling off of his undershirt, falling forward nearly onto his cheekbones, up to the first thing she'd noticed about him: his eyes. Was it sun that had given him those premature creases, that leathery, weather-beaten look or was it something else, some kind of knowledge that usually came with age and experience, some wisdom, some understanding that had left its mark on his wonderfully bony face. His eyes, a smoky gray against the browns and beiges of her living room, now burned bright blue as if they were lit from within. She smiled, and he smiled back, and she patted the bed beside her.

He kissed her again, and she was as hungry as before, and when he opened his eyes she was staring back at him with something slightly more than hunger in her eyes. Something closer to greed, something that said that here, in the slightly too bright lamplight of her bedroom, on the bed where she had clearly entertained men before, perhaps in just this way, to just this music, wearing this same peach silk negligee, she knew exactly what she wanted and was going to make very sure she got it.

Schuyler felt something lurch inside him, like the subtle slip of a gear just a fraction off kilter, as the evening moved from promise to performance. It would have been nice, perhaps, to hold her close and kiss her softly a bit. He would have enjoyed, most definitely, undressing her bit by bit, unbuttoning each tiny mother-of-pearl button on her blouse, releasing her breasts from her bra and feeling them fall against his hands, against his mouth. But now there didn't seem to be any way to go back, to slow things down after they'd traveled so fast. He was losing it, he realized, and the realization made him lose it even more, and the sweat on his chest seemed scented for the first time with a hint of panic.

She licked her fingers and reached around to grab him and he watched her eyelashes lift a fraction of an inch with the surprise of his softness. She began to massage him, up and down, her thumb flicking back and forth across the long ridge, and he stiffened again. A little. Not nearly enough.

"Tell me what you want," she said.

"More of the same," he replied, not sure of what he wanted. Not sure at all, for this had never happened before, but of course he couldn't tell her that, she'd never believe him.

She curled over and took him in her mouth, her lips moving in synchronization with her hands. It felt great, it felt absolutely wonderful, but somehow he couldn't lose himself in it, couldn't bridge that mind-body split, some part of him remained detached, watching, wondering, *worrying*. He couldn't seem to focus. All sorts of weird thoughts came to him: why was this happening now, with her? what was she thinking of him? how long would she continue with this expert licking and sucking and massaging until she gave up on him? just when was the last time things had gone well for him—was that it, had it been too long between women? What if he finally got hard enough to enter her and then lost it again in the middle of things? What if he came too fast? That had never happened before either, but who knew, in this evening of disaster, anything might happen at all.

Disaster. She lifted her head and raised her eyebrows in question. "Tell me what you really want. Tell me something you want to do that you've never done before," she said, her voice a low growl, a near parody of sexual movie dialogue. Her hand kept moving slowly up and down.

"I want to fuck your brains out," he growled back, regretting instantly the fake bravado of his tone, his sorry attempt to infuse some sort of macho drama into the scene.

She gave him a long, slow suck and lifted her head again. "Tell me. Is that too much pressure? Not enough?"

"Come here," he said, pulling her up by the hair and placing her head against his chest. "I think I need a little break. You get an A for effort, Miss Queen of the Girl Scouts."

"You musn't make fun." Pamela sighed. "I used to perform good deeds on a daily basis."

"And now you perform them on a nightly basis?"

"Not quite. I'm really a good girl at heart."

"At heart and everywhere else," he said, untying the drawstring and pulling her peignoir down over her breasts. He played with her, first one breast and then the other, with no particular plan of giving her pleasure. He toyed with her, almost absentmindedly, watching her nipples stiffen against his fingers.

He felt that clutch again when she closed her eyes and her breath deepened and she arched her back against his hands. He had wanted to lie like this for hours, aimless, playful, friendly, unhurried. He hoped some conversation, some silly joking, a *double entendre* or two, might distract her.

"I'm sorry," was all he could think to say. "It's not you, I want you to know that." Very original, Mr. Aspiring Writer. Just exactly what everyone else says in the same situation.

"It happens to everyone at one time or another. Don't worry about it," she said. Score two, he thought, for originality.

"You're incredible. You really are," he said. "I've been thinking about you for weeks." How easy it was, he realized, once you told one lie, to tell another and then another. "You're gorgeous," he continued, giving her breast a squeeze. "You look—you look—"

"Good enough to eat?" she asked, removing his hand and placing it between her legs. She was dripping wet. It's a thin line, he thought, between flirtation and vulgarity, as thin as the fabric she was wearing, which he now realized was not silk but some synthetic that could endure repeated launderings in a washing machine, as thin as a single strand of the long red hair that lay across his chest, so thin she had crossed it in a second.

He slid a finger inside her and felt her contract against him. He nibbled his way across her chest and down her belly and, parting her with two fingers, licked around her in circles. She was moaning. Thank God, he thought, she would come quickly, and after a polite interval he could go home. She smelled terrific, her own scent mixing muskily with whatever perfume she must have dabbed right into her red pubic hair. He was sucking on her, and she took his free hand and gave it a squeeze, and he stuck two fingers back inside her, bending them against her, beckoning her as if to say, Come to me, come on Pamela, come on, and she was squeezing against his fingers, God, she had incredible muscles, her cunt was moving around his hand in all sorts of ways, and he felt himself growing hard again. He quickly lifted himself up and entered her; she was lifting her hips and sliding a pillow underneath herself when suddenly he came, just like that. He reached down between them and finished her off with his hand. She made a sound halfway between a moan and a sigh, and the force of her orgasm expelled him, slowly, and he came to a rest against her damp thigh, and when she opened her eyes her gaze was filled not so much with satisfaction as with relief.

"I'm sorry," he said.

"Don't be. I feel great," she said.

"I mean I'm not sorry it happened, I mean I'm sorry because—"

"Sssh. Don't say another word," she said, giving him the first soft friendly kiss of the evening. And he didn't, he didn't say a word as she lay there in his arms, he didn't say a word as she fell asleep and rolled away from him, as he watched the sun come up behind the school across the street, and silently left her bed, slipped back into his clothes, and left her apartment.

He would call her later, or maybe he would send her flowers. Yes, that was it, he would send her flowers. It was a thoughtful gesture. Women always loved getting flowers. He would send something friendly and expensive and exotic, something in yellows and pinks and purples (was she the sort of girl who liked irises?) or maybe oranges, tiger lilies to match her hair. Something that said he appreciated her, something cheerful and sophisticated but not too delicate or romantic or feminine. Nothing that promised another date; whatever happened, he didn't want to go out with Pamela again. Tiger lilies, that was it. And some yellow mums. White gladioli. Some purple Peruvian lilies. He'd tell the florist the bouquet was for someone in his office. He'd be very specific. Nothing romantic. Nothing in red. And definitely no roses.

8

*T*he alarm clock clicked on at five A.M., and within half an hour Rosaline was washed, dressed, and watching the first rays of the November sun wash over the treetops in Central Park. This was her favorite time of the visits to her parents in New York, the mornings when she accompanied her father to the family stable out at Belmont Park. She'd been coming down to New York nearly every weekend since the "incident" with Schuyler and December. That's how she had come to think of it, as an "incident," the sort of tawdry event that nice people didn't discuss. Her parents, God bless them, hadn't inquired after the grisly details, they simply sent her a check to cover her monthly rent and living expenses.

Charlotte made it clear, and Rosaline couldn't help but agree, that perhaps she'd be better off conducting her social life in New York, with nice boys whose parents were friends of her parents and who wouldn't dare misbehave, as that Smith boy had. Rosaline had missed out on a formal debut, but Charlotte would make up for that with a vengeance, dragging her daughter to benefits and openings, securing attractive escorts from only the very best families. Charlotte was active in the organizations that gave the most spectacular fund-raising parties for various good causes, mostly art museums and fatal diseases. If only there were a Museum of Diseases, Rosaline often thought, what a party Charlotte would throw then.

Just last night she had gone out on a real live date with one of these escorts, Trevor Goodwood (the very name made her wince), a distant cousin who was in the training program at Morgan. Rosaline had been out on exactly two dates since her breakup with Schuyler, and she had behaved badly on both of them. I just don't know how to date, she had told herself. I don't know how to make small talk, how to ask them about their schoolwork or jobs, how to draw them out.

Each evening had ended with Rosaline staring silently at the table-cloth and the embarrassed boy offering his father's credit card to the gracious waiter, whose polite inquiries about the quality of their meal could not take the awkward edge off a total social disaster. Neither boy had called again.

Considering the circumstances, Trevor was surprisingly gallant. He took Rosaline to a small restaurant in the east fifties and unlike her other dates, who had shown off their prep school French in the most obvious ways, he let her order whatever she wanted. He asked her opinion in choosing the wine and didn't make the obvious dumb jokes about her looking underage. He spoke intelligently about music and some rather exotic places in Asia he had visited in the year after he graduated from Yale. Still, there were plenty of awkward silences when neither of them had anything to say. Rosaline played with her wine glass. She could feel Trevor staring at her, and she knew what he was thinking: how did I ever let myself get talked into this mess?

Who could blame him? Trevor was tall and strong and clearly used to better-looking companions. His mother had probably roped him into this, forcing him to cancel other more promising plans, in the hope that Charlotte would reward her with a prime table at the cancer benefit the following week. Rosaline began to wither under his stare. She couldn't think of a thing to say that wasn't utterly stupid. She didn't ski or sail or do any of the things that would interest him. To her utter horror, she began to cry.

Without saying a word Trevor signaled for the check, paid in cash, and steered Rosaline out of the restaurant and onto Park Avenue, where a light snow was just beginning to cover the sidewalks.

"I'll see you home," Trevor said, waving for a taxi.

"Oh, thanks, you don't have to," Rosaline said in a shaky voice.

"No, I insist. It's not as safe as it looks." A cab pulled up and Trevor opened the door for her. Snowflakes were sticking to Trevor's thick yellow hair and to the high collar of Rosaline's dark wool coat. She could feel her tears returning.

"Really, I'm okay," she said as she got in the car and began to pull the door closed behind her. "We have a doorman. You don't have to worry."

"Where to?" the driver asked, pulling away from the curb before the door was completely shut.

"Ten forty-two Fifth Avenue," Rosaline said. She hoped she wouldn't have to face her parents when she got home. Charlotte would ask how the evening had gone, and Rosaline wouldn't know how to answer.

You didn't have to be a dating expert to recognize what a hopeless case she was. Trevor was probably glad of the chance to ditch her early and go on alone to the half dozen parties a young Ivy League graduate was sure of being invited to on any given Saturday night. Rosaline suspected that he had planned this all along and that perhaps he had even arranged to meet his real date later on; it was only ten, and things were just getting started. She could imagine what he was thinking about her: what a waste of time she had been. She knew he was swearing the same as she that it was the last dumb date their parents would ever be allowed to arrange.

If she had looked out the back of the taxi as it drove up Park Avenue, she would have seen a young man standing on a dark street corner with his hands in his pockets and an expression on his face that a more experienced woman could have interpreted with ease. Trevor Goodwood was oblivious to the cold November wind and the chatter and laughter of the crowded sidewalk. He was cursing himself for his rudeness, for not being able to put Rosaline at ease, for choosing the absolutely wrong restaurant, for being so stiff and standoffish that she had slammed the cab door in his face without saying good night. It would be useless to telephone her tomorrow and apologize for how things had gone. The evening had been a disaster, and yet somehow his spirit felt uplifted, because he had just fallen wildly in love with the most beautiful girl in the world.

By seven A.M. Rosaline and her father were leaning against the railing at Belmont Park watching the horses being led out for the first set of daily exercise. Joseph Van Schott surveyed his horses with pleasure. He had inherited Blue Smoke from his father, along with the apartment on Fifth Avenue, a tobacco farm in North Carolina, a four-story Victorian house in Saratoga Springs, and investments that generated enough income to maintain all four in the manner to which they were accustomed.

Blue Smoke's horses were trained by George Parker, a forty-year-old Kentuckian best known for his success with younger fillies and his habit of matching his bow ties to his socks. Parker enjoyed Van Schott's visits to the track. Joseph was one of the few owners who knew a lot about horses but gave his trainer a free hand in deciding when and where the horses ran.

Rosaline listened as Parker gave a progress report on each of her father's horses as they were led out onto the track. A two-year-old colt bred from two champions was failing to live up to his regal pedigree. A small gutsy filly was coming back after an injury, and Parker wanted to be sure he didn't rush her. This one might run better on grass than on dirt; another might improve in the sprint races that, at distances of less than a mile, took a little over one minute to complete.

Rosaline noticed the flash of a yellow windbreaker across the track, belonging to the rider of a small black colt that was running by an older, larger horse with remarkable speed.

"Who is that?" she asked.

"Not one of ours, I'm sorry to say," Parker answered. "One of Hopkin's two-year-olds, they're shipping him down to Hialeah next week. Nicely bred but nothing in the bloodlines to indicate so much talent. If he stays in one piece, nothing will get near him."

"When will they run him?"

"Maybe April. They're aiming him for Saratoga and the big fall races. The colt's been here less than three weeks and already he's the worst-kept secret on the track."

Rosaline watched the bright-yellow windbreaker come down the stretch and then followed a few steps behind as Parker and Van Schott walked back to the barn discussing Kentucky Derby prospects and gossiping about various trainers and owners. When the two men went into Parker's office she waited outside, watching the horses being led up and down the length of the barns to cool them off after their morning workout.

She leaned against her father's car and nervously fingered one of her small pearl earrings, the only jewelry her mother allowed her to wear during the day. She was watching a young filly nuzzle at her groom's arm when she felt the tiny gold fastener pop off the back of one earring.

Rosaline knelt down to retrieve the piece of gold; it was too small to be felt among the pebbles and clumps of grass. She moved her head from side to side, as if listening to the slow movement of a symphony, hoping the sunlight would reflect off the metal.

She heard the scrape of leather on stone behind her. She turned on her knees and as she stood up she saw a pair of dusty brown boots, jeans that were less faded than worn thin, suggesting heavy use and little washing, a wide strap of leather made into a belt by the addition of two large steel rings, a nylon windbreaker the color of daffodils, and a set of perfect white teeth in a small dark face.

"You looking?" The voice was Spanish. The eyes were bright green.

"No. Thank you." Rosaline was not sure what was being offered.

The rider looked confused, perhaps by Rosaline, perhaps because of a lack of English. He moved his boot toward Rosaline's shoe, into the dirt.

"Not looking?" he said.

"Oh. Yes." Her eyes were precisely level with his. They were the same height and of the same fine build; if not for his broad, square shoulders and the muscles that came from riding daily, they would have been the same weight.

"I lost part of an earring."

He continued to stare, and Rosaline decided that he did not understand her English. He's standing too close to me, she thought, I wonder what he wants.

"Hey, Frankie!" someone called from across the road. "Come on!"

Rosaline stepped back, and as she did the rider bent down and picked out the lost bit of metal from behind a smooth white pebble and held it up in the sun.

"Thank you," Rosaline said.

"You're welcome. You're welcome who?" he asked.

"Rosaline."

"Rosaline," he repeated, pronouncing it perfectly on the first try, unlike the majority of people who called her Roz-lynn until Charlotte corrected them.

"Thank you—thank you, Frankie." She held out her hand for the gold. He closed his hand over hers. She could feel the sharp edge of the metal pressed between their palms. His fingers were rough with calluses. His bones were as delicate as hers—it was like holding your own hand.

"Not 'Frankie,'" he said in a disdainful imitation of a suburban Long Island accent. "Francisco," he said with an exaggerated roll of the r. He released her hand and crossed the road just as her father came into view.

"Parker says you're turning into quite a good-looking young lady," he said, opening the car door for her.

"He may be a better judge of horseflesh than of women," she said.

"I certainly hope so," Van Schott said with a laugh. Parker was three times divorced and spent millions of Van Schott dollars at yearling auctions every year. "Let's see now, we got up at five this morning, which is four hours earlier than usual. So it's now, on our body clocks, just about noon. Would you like to join me in a lunchtime cocktail?" He pulled a silver flask out of the carved walnut cupboard that was bolted to the floor of the back compartment and took a sip without waiting for Rosaline's reply.

It was useless to suggest that he wait. Van Schott was nowhere near the world's richest man (the original eighteenth-century fortune had been divided, through an intricate and unbreakable trust, over several branches of the family), but he was without a doubt the world's richest drunk.

"I could use a drink, actually," Rosaline said. "No, just kidding."

"Feeling down?" he asked. "Guess your date didn't go so well?"

"Bingo."

"It was just a date."

"I don't feel like talking about it."

"Well. You know, part of the reason I asked you to come along to the works with me this morning was that I'd have a chance to talk to you alone. We hardly ever do that, you know."

"I noticed."

"I'm sorry. Sometimes I think I've abdicated my responsibility. Maybe given Charlotte too much of a free hand. She's always so sure of what's best for you. I hardly ever am."

"Well, I guess I turned out okay. Haven't disgraced the family name yet. Not that I'd even know how."

"Sugar, I think you've turned out wonderfully. Partly because of your mother but, I suspect, just as much in spite of her."

Rosaline looked out the window at the people in the cars around them. A young black man was nodding his head to a song on the radio, and Rosaline tried to imagine whether he was driving home from the night shift or into the city for a day job. A couple drove by quickly in a bright-red Oldsmobile, and Rosaline wondered, seeing their animated gestures, whether they were having a fight or a discussion about their children. "Thanks," she said.

"Sometimes it's easier to sit back and let her call the shots," Joseph continued. "She's desperate to get you married off, you know."

"I'm barely twenty-one, and I won't graduate for a year and a half. I don't see the rush."

"It's not as though you have a big career ahead of you, sugar. Nothing would make Charlotte happier than to have you married the week after graduation. By her timetable that means an engagement by Thanksgiving of next year. Which gives you twelve months to meet, charm, and ensnare the appropriate candidate."

"Were you ensnared?" she asked.

Joseph laughed. "Looking back, I suppose that I was."

"I just wish she wouldn't put so much pressure on me," Rosaline said. "She tries to control nearly every aspect of my life—she's still buying my underwear, if you can believe it—and I just don't have the strength to fight back. I just let her run all over me, and then I hate myself for it."

"That's a trick you probably learned from me," Joseph said, sighing. "You realize that she'll never let up, not until you're in the care of a socially acceptable husband. She has no intention of letting up on you, she simply intends to hand the reins over to a worthy successor. Probably a handpicked one."

Rosaline echoed his sigh. They were back in front of their building. "And I thought the meek were supposed to inherit the earth," she said as they got on the elevator.

The apartment smelled of fresh coffee and the rose-scented oil the cleaning man dabbed on the light bulbs once a week.

"Phone for you," Charlotte sang out from the library. She held the receiver toward Rosaline. "A young man" she mouthed silently, her face a portrait of surprise. Rosaline took the phone and waited while Charlotte stood there until the message sank in that she was supposed to leave the room.

"Hello?" Rosaline said.

"Hello, it's Trevor. Goodwood."

"Hello."

"Hello. Well. I just wanted to call and tell you that I enjoyed last night. Really. I know I was a bit of a bore, well, it's been an insane week here with the market the way it is. But I would like to see you again—Thursday night? If you're still in town."

"I'm going back up tonight. I don't know when I'll be back in New York." Rosaline wrapped the telephone wire around her wrist like a bracelet.

"Will you be back before the Christmas break?" he asked.

"I don't know." She unwrapped the wire and let it dangle against her leg.

"Well, if you don't want to see me, just say so. I won't fall apart, you know."

"No, of course I'd like to see you. I was tired too." She picked up the wire and coiled it around the fourth finger of her left hand, where no ring had ever been. "I think I probably will come down next weekend. It gets so quiet after midterms."

"Yes, I remember. Saturday night?"

"Saturday night would be terrific."

"We can do something a little more casual if you'd like. Stay in the neighborhood, maybe see a movie."

"That sounds just fine," she said, tightening the coil around her finger.

"I'll telephone you Saturday morning. Have a good week, then," he said, and they exchanged goodbyes.

Rosaline hung up and sat down on the red leather chair her father used when he studied bloodstock records. Her finger was growing numb and discolored from lack of fresh blood. Trevor Goodwood. Mrs. Trevor Goodwood, née Rosaline Van Schott. Mr. and Mrs. Trevor Goodwood request the honor of your presence at an informal luncheon in honor of the Duke and Duchess of Excruciating First Dates. Mr. and Mrs. Trevor Goodwood are pleased to announce the birth of their son, Travis "Mother-are-you-happy-now" Goodwood. In lieu of gifts, donations may be made to the Fund for Overprivileged Children.

Time to grow up, she thought, steeling herself to meet her mother's inquiring glance. He may not be wearing a suit of armor and he may not be riding a white horse, but all the same, this perfectly nice young man has just been selected to rescue me. We'll live happily ever after of course—Trevor is so wonderfully nice and smart and handsome and stable, so how could it be otherwise? With a man like Trevor, a man bred and trained from birth to marry a girl like her, how could anything go wrong?

9

With a hot August breeze blowing across her neck and a cool vodka tonic in her hand, Rosaline believed the world to be a pretty, congenial place. It wasn't just the racetrack, with its gracefully proportioned old wooden beams and historic elms set in a lawn made lush by a summerful of rain. It wasn't being here with Katie Lee and Marinda, the three of them having a happy last fling at irresponsibility before the beginning of their senior year and the time, after graduation, that they had come to think of as "real life." It wasn't just Trevor, who sat beaming with them in the Van Schott box, the perfect seersucker picture of a young man in love, though he was certainly part of it. It was something deeper that filled Rosaline with this feeling of contentment: it was knowing that against all odds, in spite of every awful obstacle that had been thrown in her path, she had somehow gotten her life back on track. For the first time in her life she woke up secure in the knowledge that the day would be filled with happiness. The old feeling that some terrible surprise was about to be sprung on her had vanished. Disaster no longer lay just around the corner—it had been banished to another country entirely, a place that Rosaline never intended to travel to again.

"Now Trevor," Katie Lee cooed, slapping his knee with her racing program, "just because you picked one winner doesn't make you an instant expert. I want to know what Rosaline thinks."

"Oh, they're maidens," she said, referring to the next race, in which none of the runners had ever finished first. "It's practically a lottery."

"Don't hold out on me, darling," Katie Lee said. "I think I turned into a compulsive gambler over the weekend. If I don't bet at least five dollars, it won't be any fun at all."

"Well," Rosaline said, looking at the odds displayed on the tote board, "the three horse, his trainer always keeps a few aces up his sleeve for Saratoga. But he's the favorite, you'll hardly make any money."

"Oh, pooh, who cares about money," Katie Lee replied. "Did I say that? Don't quote me, but you know, the thrill of victory and all that. I just want a winner."

"I don't think I can take your screaming in my ear one more time," Marinda said, laughing. "Can I pay you five dollars not to bet?" Peter and her family seemed a million miles away. There was nothing to do in Saratoga except eat, drink, go to the races, and attend parties. No wonder Rosaline's father had never taken a job. You'd have to be a fool to give this up.

Marinda had just left her first full-time job, doing paralegal work at her uncle's law firm. It had been five days a week of total drudgery, interrupted by two days of complete torture at the hands of this boy she kept reminding herself she loved. At least they were having sex again—thank God they'd taken him off the medication that made him seem like one of the walking dead—but it had become so mechanical, she could predict everything he would do ahead of time. She had begun pretending that she was in bed with someone else— movie actors, rock musicians, the cuter associates at the firm—anything to get the passion rolling.

She hoped that Peter wouldn't notice that he seemed to be in bed with a different woman every weekend. Over the July Fourth holiday, visions of an actor noted for his wild ways had her whispering wicked instructions into Peter's ear. Seven days later, imagining herself with a long-limbed folk singer whose chronicle of heartbreak had just made it to number one, she cuddled against Peter like a kitten and baby-talked through the night. Just last week she had moaned her way through one of the longest, deepest orgasms she had ever experienced. Funny thing was, she hadn't even been thinking about anyone incredibly sexy or handsome or famous. It had just been Schuyler Smith.

She had tried talking about it with Bobby, but he just laughed at her. "You women always want the big bang," he said. "Just cool out and enjoy sex for what it is." Then he asked her to do some of the research work he'd been assigned so he and Carter could spend the afternoon at the beach. He probably got someone else to do his work for him at law school too. It was difficult to imagine Bobby taking anything seriously.

"And how is Bobby," Katie Lee asked. "There's a horse in this race called Get Em Bobby. Worth two dollars, don't you think?" She hadn't seen Bobby since early July, when they'd spent the night together after the wedding of mutual friends. July, August, September —it would be October, then, that she would next allow him the pleasure of her sexual favors. He was practically hooked. It drove him crazy the way she gave in just when he was about to call it quits out of frustration. "But Bobby, honey," she would say, "I know you have other girls to satisfy your needs. Don't act so pathetic. It doesn't look attractive. Let's just be friends for a while." She had him figured down to the last millimeter. There had been only one girl who had presented any kind of real threat, someone she was afraid Bobby might even propose to if she didn't do something about it. But Carter helped her put a stop to that; he told the girl that Bobby had been sleeping with a secretary in his office (a complete lie but a necessary one, Katie Lee thought) and that anyway he was already practically engaged to Katie Lee (not a lie, really, more like an exaggeration, she decided, it would be true soon enough). Carter would do anything she asked, absolutely anything. She'd made sure of that two summers ago in Washington.

"Bobby's okay. He broke up with Celia," Marinda said.

"Oh, too bad, why is that?" Katie Lee asked.

"Who knows. Because his parents were crazy about her, probably. Let's go bet before the lines get too long." Marinda and Katie Lee left the box for the crowd of the clubhouse.

"They're not driving you crazy?" Rosaline asked, taking Trevor's hand.

"They're wonderful," Trevor replied. "What a threesome you must make."

We used to be a foursome, Rosaline thought. "We're going to be roommates again this year. We have the most beautiful suite, you can see the river from it. You'll have to come up and visit."

"I'd like that very much," Trevor said, a bit surprised. He'd never visited her in Cambridge before—in fact they'd never spent an entire night together. They'd begun seeing each other last winter, an old-fashioned New York courtship filled with parties and day trips to the country and family dinners. It wasn't until May that he'd had the nerve to cook her dinner in his little brownstone apartment and afterwards, when they were both a little drunk from the champagne, try to seduce her. It was such an old-fashioned word, "seduce," and it didn't quite sum up what had happened at all—she hadn't been a virgin, he could tell—but it fit Trevor's old-fashioned view of things. Of course she couldn't stay overnight in his apartment—how would things look.

Even now—Jesus, it was 1975, who cared about these things anymore—Trevor had politely refused Charlotte's offer of guest quarters in their rambling house on Caroline Street and had reserved a room in a nearby hotel. But something about Rosaline told him to proceed with caution. She had been hurt before, it was obvious when they'd met, and he didn't want to rush her, he certainly didn't want to be part of any rebound romance. He was going to do things right because he wanted this one to last, but mostly because he was simply the sort of person who thought things should be done right for the sake of doing them right. The same way he carefully selected his summer suits of the most conservative cut and finest cotton, the same way he knew exactly which wine would be most welcome at dinner, the same way he knew precisely which words would sail a conversation smoothly away from an awkward moment, so he knew how to make Rosaline happy.

She couldn't stop smiling at him; it was true, people were gossiping about how Trevor Goodwood had finally been nabbed by Charlotte's daughter, of all people. If it wasn't in her face it must be in the genes. Rosaline could remember the exact moment when she'd fallen in love with Trevor. It had been on New Year's Eve. They were at a noisy party given by one of Trevor's old roommates at Yale. They had all been members of some secret society that they weren't allowed to discuss, even with their wives. At midnight they were all going to sing a dirty song in Latin and perform a dance that had been first choreographed on the night Grover Cleveland died.

"Is this too loathesome?" Trevor had asked her. "They're terrific guys, really, they just need to let off a little steam now and then."

"Oh, no, this is fun," she had lied.

"You're a terrible fibber," Trevor said. "Come on, get your coat, let's sneak out somewhere we can be alone." He took her up a back staircase and onto the roof. "The people who have the penthouse go to Mexico for the holidays. It's just us up here."

He held Rosaline around the waist as she leaned over the railing and looked down Park Avenue to the lights of the skyscrapers. The Empire State Building was still lit up in Christmas red and green.

"It was a stuffy party, wasn't it," he said.

"Not really. Well, yes, I guess it was."

"You're a little like me, I think," Trevor said.

"And how is that?"

"Oh, you do all the proper things, go to all the proper places, come from this proper family, but there's this other side of you. A little, not rebellious really, more like mischievous. It's the side of you that comes up to rooftops on freezing New Year's Eves with dangerous young men."

"Trevor," she said, giggling, "you're not dangerous."

"Aren't I?" He sighed. "Not even a little?"

"Well, maybe a little, if you want to be," she said. "You're more— mysterious than dangerous."

"I like that. Mysterious. Trevor Goodwood, Master of Mystery." He squeezed her around the waist. "You are different, you know. I can tell."

"And how is that?"

"Because I'm different too. Underneath, I mean."

"Scheming stockbroker by day, man of mystery by night."

"Something like that. You mustn't ever lose that part of you, Rosaline, as people tend to do when they get older. You have to hold on to it like life itself. Because it's the very best part of you," he said, kissing the top of her ear.

"And how do you know that, Mystery Man?" she whispered.

"Because it's the part of you I'm falling in love with. If you don't mind, that is."

She turned to face him, the lights behind her. "I don't mind at all," she said. "I think I'm falling a little in love with you back."

"Just a little?" he said.

"For now," she said.

"You wouldn't be getting my hopes up now and then smashing them later? Broken hearts can get very messy."

"Don't I know it," she said, putting her arms around him. "I would never ever break your heart. Promise."

"Promise noted," he said, and there they shared their first real kiss, there at the stroke of midnight, while down below them taxi horns honked and people opened their windows to sing into the street.

• • •

"It's only the seventh race and I'm already up nearly two hundred dollars," Katie Lee said, her wallet bursting with the creased ten-dollar bills she'd been collecting from the parimutuel clerks all afternoon. "Rosaline, I've got fifty dollars on that little red horse, how does he look to you?"

"The color is called chestnut. He looks very good to me."

"His rider looks even better," Marinda said. "I saw him going out to the paddock. If there are more like him in Puerto Rico, I'm hopping on the next plane."

Rosaline looked at her program. The lone chestnut was named Bold Question and the rider was listed as Francisco Gomez, 112 pounds. "He's Panamanian, actually," she said. "A lot of the top jockeys are."

"Whatever, he's gorgeous. I'm going to put two dollars on him. Are you betting on this one?" Marinda asked.

"Oh, no," Rosaline replied. "I'll just root for you and Katie Lee."

"Rosaline, are you getting a commission on their winnings?" Trevor asked. "In my business there's no such thing as free advice."

"We'll make Katie Lee buy us dinner," Rosaline said. "At the most expensive restaurant we can find."

"Absolutely," Katie Lee said. "I hope your parents can join us. They've been great about letting us use their box all week."

"My mother hardly ever gets to the track," Rosaline said. Charlotte put in an appearance only on big stakes days or when a particularly talented Blue Smoke horse made its racing debut. To her the races were merely a pretext for the luncheons and dinners that filled her calendar; she needed to attend them for only a few hours a week to remind people that she had married a Van Schott and had thereby gained membership in the exclusive inner circle of the best and oldest racing families. Besides, it was so dreadfully hot and humid here in August, all the hairspray in the world couldn't prevent her carefully constructed platinum helmet from wilting around her ears.

"If I bet as much as you, Katie Lee," Marinda said, reaching into her pocket for two dollars, her maximum bet, "I'd be a nervous wreck."

"Caution never made anybody rich," Katie Lee replied, "at the track or in business. And there's nothing like a little risk to get your blood pumping."

"The key word there," Trevor said, "is 'little.'"

"Ah, the voice of the true conservative," Katie Lee said.

"'Conservative' is just another word for 'sensible.'"

"Are you trying to tell me something about the hotel deal I spoke to you about?" she asked. Katie Lee had spent the better part of breakfast describing to Trevor the complicated network of partnerships and holding companies she was putting together to finance the Hopewell Inn she hoped to build in Cambridge. She had found the perfect site for her first independent venture: a supermarket connected to a string of storefronts, half vacant, in a part of the city that had been earmarked for the expanding computer and technological support industry. There was a huge office complex under construction just a few blocks away, and a California consulting firm had purchased an option on adjoining acreage for their first East Coast headquarters. New kinds of people were going to be coming to Cambridge with a new kind of money, and Katie Lee was going to provide them with a place to stay.

She'd presented her proposal to her father early in the summer, showing him the architect's rendering she'd commissioned and a demographic survey a friend of hers at the Business School had done without charge.

"Seems promising," Henry had said, leaning back in his high leather chair. "Let me run these figures by the boys downstairs. Though it looks like a definite go-ahead. I've been studying that area for a while now, you know."

"Why, Daddy, you should have told me," Katie Lee said. "I've started thinking of it as my home territory." She looked at the collection of gilt-framed family photographs arranged on a teak credenza behind her father's desk. There was a picture of her oldest brother, Henry junior, about to tee off on the championship green of Augusta, Georgia. Charlie, the next in line, stood dripping wet at the side of a pool with his fist raised in victory, having just received a nearly perfect score as the star member of his college diving team. Her younger brother, Tommy, exhibited flawless form in immaculate tennis whites as he raced over the court at the local country club.

Behind her sons Mrs. Hopewell sat primly, legs crossed at the ankle, in the formal garden she'd had copied out of a book. Next to her was a picture of Katie Lee holding the keys to her very first car, a bright-red secondhand Oldsmobile convertible.

"This is good work, Missy, I'm proud of the way you've taken an interest in the family business," Henry said, cleaning his thumbnail with an antique silver letter opener. "You're one little acorn that hasn't fallen far from the old oak tree. Now, your brothers, I just can't seem to light a fire under them. They think the whole world is just going to be handed to them like a plate of fried fish. Never would have figured my sweet baby girl would be the one with the initiative."

"I just want to make you happy, Daddy," she said, smiling.

"We might be able to use you on this project after you graduate." He ran the letter opener along the sleeve of his light-brown suit. "If we can get the land sale closed quickly. KDH Associates, we'll have to find out more about them, see how desperate they are for cash."

"What exactly did you have in mind for me?" Katie Lee asked.

"This is an excellent learning opportunity for you. See a project through from start to finish. I'm sure Casey could use an assistant."

"So you think I should work for Casey?" she asked.

"He's the best project manager we have."

Katie Lee leaned back in her chair and mirrored her father's pose: hands folded behind her head, chin tilted down against her neck. "I'd love to see Casey on this project. But I don't want to work for him."

"Opportunities like this are as rare as hen's teeth, and that hen's been eating a lot of sugar."

"Exactly. That's why I want Casey to work for me."

Henry laughed and reached across his desk to tweak his daughter's nose. "You do have the family spunk. Casey working for you. Someday, if you play your cards right, I guess he will. But you don't need eyeglasses to see it's an old-fashioned business, these aren't luxury hotels we're building, this has always been a man's game."

"I hope I can change your mind about that," she said. It was sickening how everyone just assumed her oldest brother would eventually be handed the reins to the company just because he had the proper equipment between his legs and happened to be born first. She just wasn't going to sit back and let that happen. Daddy would see that she was the only one who understood how to run the company.

"You *are* changing my mind, bit by bit," Henry said, scratching just above his right ear and then holding his finger there for an extra moment, as though he were pointing to the specific area of his brain that controlled his opinion of Katie Lee. "Spend a year with Casey and there may be a spot for you here in the home office."

"Daddy, I don't think you understand. I *am* KDH Associates. I bought the land. It's my proposal. The numbers say this hotel is going to show a profit within eighteen months after opening. Sooner, if we reach eighty percent occupancy through group sales. It's a perfect deal for Hopewell. I don't want to work for you, Daddy. I'm asking you to come in as my partner."

Henry took off his glasses and rubbed the top of his nose. "And where did you get the money for all this?"

"I bought the land for ten percent down with money from the trust fund. Two days after my twenty-first birthday."

"And what kind of partnership did you have in mind?"

"Fifty-fifty, I wouldn't be greedy where my own family is involved. I've got the land. You control the franchises. I'm putting the time into this. You've got the staff with the experience I need."

"And what if I say no? You're stuck with a supermarketful of outdated fixtures and a parking lot the size of Rhode Island."

"Hardly," she said. "The Ramada people would jump at this, and you know it. Anyway, you won't say no."

"Is that what you think, I can't turn you down just because you're my daughter?"

"You can't turn me down because you don't know how to say no to this kind of profit. You never have and you never will. Do we have a deal?"

Henry laughed and extended his hand. "We have a deal, Missy," he said, and suddenly he stopped smiling. "I underestimated you. I want you to know that's the only reason you're getting away with this. And I want you to know that there's no way I'll make the same mistake again. You want to play hardball, I can play hardball." He stood up to let her know he considered their meeting over.

Somehow she had thought he'd be happier, tell her how proud he was of her, give her a kiss instead of a handshake. She'd expected to win this battle but hadn't quite realized her father might take it as a declaration of war.

"I can handle this," she said from the door. "You watch me."

"I'll always be watching you." He picked up the telephone and dialed his secretary. "Very carefully, you can count on it. Tell your mother I'll be home by eight. By the way, what does KDH Associates stand for?"

"Katie's Dream Hotel, of course," she replied. Keep Daddy Happy, she thought, Keep Daddy Happy.

"He's going off at eight-to-one!" Katie Lee cried. "Trevor, how much will I get back?"

"If he loses, nothing."

"He'll win. I just know it. Marinda, you were right, that boy is c-u-t-e. Eight times fifty—that's four hundred dollars. Marinda, how much did you bet?"

"Two dollars to show."

Rosaline and Trevor exchanged glances. She knew that he had been betting all day, quietly getting up and going to cash his tickets alone. Trevor rarely discussed money away from work, and he never let his friends know exactly how much money he had made or lost at the track. Trevor had explained to Rosaline how you could tell the vintage of a family's money by how little they spoke of it. The older it was, the less you heard. Katie Lee had watched her father build his company from one roadside motel and two gas stations into one of the largest hotel chains in the world, and it showed. He had kinder words for Marinda. You would never guess she was Italian, he'd said, wondering aloud just where along the line the family name had been Anglicized to Vincent.

Marinda picked up her binoculars as the horses were led into the starting gate, which was positioned almost directly in front of their box. She could see the sweat breaking out on Bold Question's back and the tension in Francisco's jaw as he snapped his chewing gum.

The bell rang and the horses burst across the track. Francisco held back on the reins, letting the rest of the horses crowd ahead of him, guiding Bold Question to the favorable path along the inside rail. By the time they had reached the backstretch the early leaders were already beginning to tire. "Go, go," Marinda whispered, but still Francisco held Bold Question back behind the others. You fool, she thought, the front runners have been winning all week, you stupid fool. She put down the field glasses. She seemed to have a talent for picking losers.

But Katie Lee was jumping up and down and tugging on Marinda's sleeve.

"Here he comes now! He's using the whip!" she said. The horse was gradually gaining ground as he swooped around the far turn. There were only five horses in front of him now.

"Too late, I'm afraid," Trevor said. "No one is going to come from behind today."

"He's going to win," Rosaline said as Bold Question raced into third place, "look at how much horse he's got left." Marinda and Katie Lee exchanged glances. Rosaline never contradicted Trevor in public.

Bold Question surged into second, gaining on the leader with every step, and when the two horses passed the finish line no one could be sure who had finished first. They waited while the stewards examined the photographs and, out of politeness to Trevor, tried to subdue their excitement when Bold Question was announced as the winner by a nose.

Marinda and Katie Lee got up to cash their tickets and Trevor joined them—he'd put ten dollars to place on the horse that had finished second.

Rosaline leaned her elbows on the railing of the box and leaned over to watch Bold Question being led into the winner's circle. A late afternoon chill had set in, and she rummaged around in her bag for the small square of flowered silk she'd brought to tie around her neck. Everyone was shaking hands and smiling for the track camera—their horse had done well and was unlikely to go off at such a high price again. The owner's wife extended her hand to Francisco for a congratulatory shake, and he lifted it up to his lips and bestowed a courtly kiss. He threw a kiss to an exercise girl who was cheering from the rail and then he blew a kiss to the box just behind Rosaline.

She turned to look, but the box was empty, and as she shifted back in her seat a sudden breeze lifted the scarf off the railing. It floated high over the crowd into the winner's circle, where Francisco reached up and clutched it in his fist.

Damn, my favorite scarf, she pouted, remembering how she'd happened upon it one day while shopping for her father's birthday present. Its border was filled with daisies, and if you looked closely you would see that the pattern had been broken in one corner and a tiny white heart had been painted by hand. She didn't know what irked her more—that she had lost her favorite scarf or that it now belonged to a complete stranger, this Francisco Gomez (had she met him before? she didn't think so), someone who wouldn't appreciate its delicate pattern, who would never see the small white heart that reminded Rosaline so very much of her own.

10

"And the exercise room goes right back in here," Katie Lee said, pointing to the location on the blueprints she'd spread out over her bed. "Unless we decide to enclose the pool, in which case it gets moved over here. What do you think?"

"Sounds great," Carter said. "I don't really know much about this stuff." It had been a mistake, coming to see Katie Lee when Marinda was around. Word might get back to Bobby.

"Well, it all has to do with what I explained to you last week. We're trying to emphasize our special weekday packages for businessmen. People are getting more and more concerned about staying in shape. If they stay with us they can maintain whatever kind of fitness program they do at home. We're even going to mark out a jogging path for them on the local streets if I can get the city to approve the signs. The computer room, though, that's going to be the main drawing card, especially for all the M.I.T. and Route 128 types. We'll have terminals and modems and even some software available so they can work right out of the hotel. It sounds crazy now, I know, and it's costing me a fortune, but you wait and see, in ten years every decent hotel in the country is going to follow my lead."

"Makes perfect sense," Carter said. I don't give a flying fuck about any of this, he thought, I'm sick to death of your stupid projects, let's get down to business already.

"Of course it does," she said. "But enough about me. How is Bobby doing?"

"Compared to last year, law school is a breeze. He's been seeing this nursing student in Boston, but I don't think it's anything to worry about."

"Is she very pretty?"

135

"Pretty enough. Tall, long brown hair, sort of a wholesome, out-doorsy type. Wants to be a midwife."

"Ugh. How many times a week?"

"Just Saturday nights mostly, sometimes something midweek. She calls nearly every day."

"Does he stay over the whole night?"

"Fifty-fifty."

"Well. You'll let me know if anything changes," she said, rolling up the plans and putting them back in their long eardboard tubes. "And how are you doing?"

"Well, not so good, actually. School's no problem, but things are a little tight in terms of money." He watched her face, but her expression didn't change. Damn, he hated this part of it, the way she made him beg for it. "Big bill coming up after Christmas. I'm a little short."

"What happened to the two thousand I gave you in October?" she said, looking at the ledger she kept under her desk blotter. "It can't all be gone already."

"I told you I was going to Colorado with Bobby over Thanksgiving. I thought you wanted me to go, I mean, I don't even ski, I spent half the time sitting around the lodge listening to broken-bone stories."

"Poor Carter. I almost feel sorry for you. What a tough life you must have. Let's see. I think I can get you three thousand dollars by the second week of January. But I'm going to have to cut back. I'm putting nearly everything I've got into this hotel project. You wouldn't believe the expenses."

"Three thousand. I was counting on five."

"It's just not there, sweetie, though things may change in March." She didn't want him to think she was an easy touch. She still needed him, though, she needed the information he gave her about Bobby. And he needed the money, not just for his school expenses but in order to keep up with the kind of life Bobby led: the traveling, the dinners in expensive restaurants, the drugs bought to ease the way with women for whom the Vincent name was not enough.

Everyone knew that Carter was hoping to ride Bobby's coattails down to Washington. Every political family had this kind of devoted second lieutenant hanging around on the edge of things, the boys who could be counted on to clean up the messes and keep their mouths shut. The friendships usually began in prep school or college; you served your apprenticeship by procuring women, drugs, copies of exams in advance, whatever was needed to make the golden boys happy. Later on you worked on their campaigns, wrote their speeches, and escorted their unmarried sisters and cousins to various public events.

Still, she'd bankrolled Carter to the tune of nearly twenty thousand dollars so far, and she was getting tired of it. That didn't even include the first ten thousand dollars, five thousand of which Carter had given to Bobby to pay off the bet he'd made that Bobby wouldn't be able to land Katie Lee in the sack, five thousand of which he'd kept for himself as a reward for setting Bobby up, for convincing Bobby that seducing Katie Lee was the ultimate challenge. She'd known even then that the one thing Bobby couldn't walk away from was a dare of any kind.

"Well, here you are," she said, handing him a stack of hundred-dollar bills in a small manila envelope.

Someone was banging on the front door. It was Bobby, yelling for someone to open up.

"He can't see me here," Carter said, jumping up in panic, opening the window that led out onto the fire escape and stepping out on it.

Katie Lee locked the window behind him and answered the door.

"Well, Bobby, what a wonderful surprise. Would you like a drink?" she asked. He looked as if he needed one. His shirt was half unbuttoned and his hair lay flat along one side of his head as though he'd just jumped out of bed.

"Where's Marinda? Do you realize your phone has been busy for the past two hours?" he shouted, shoving past her.

"Don't blame me," Katie Lee said. "You know how much time it takes planning a wedding. Invitations, caterers, hotel arrangements —it's amazing Rosaline has any time left for classes. Last month her calls to New York came to over eighty dollars, can you believe it, and it's only going to get worse."

Bobby burst in on Marinda, who was running a pink highlighter across the pages of her history notebook.

"Bobby, what's the matter?" she said, reaching up to straighten his hair.

He put his hands on her shoulders. "Something terrible has happened. We've been trying to get hold of you all morning."

Marinda's hand froze. "We?" she asked quietly.

"Your mother called me when she couldn't get through here."

"Is it Daddy?" she asked weakly. "It's not Daddy, is it?"

"No, Marinda—look, let's sit down. It's Peter. He got hold of some bad stuff, we don't know how yet, the doctors aren't sure what happened."

"Oh, Bobby, the way you came in here I thought something really awful had happened." She started highlighting her notes again, running the pink felt tip evenly along the page. "He'll be fine, you'll see. Did they have to pump his stomach this time?"

"It was too late for that. Marinda, look at me."

"I have a lot of work to do, cousin," she said. He looked over her shoulder. She was scrawling down the inside of her left arm the letter *P* over and over again in shaky block letters. "I'll call him later. Are they going to send him back to the halfway house?" she said in a singsong voice.

"No. Not this time."

"So it can't be that bad, can it," she said. She began drawing bright-pink teardrops on her cheeks. "Peter just does this every so often. He just does it for the attention. He just does it to make me cry. Peter likes to make Marinda cry." She put down the pen and covered her face with her palms, smudging the ink until her face and hands and neck were streaked with the fluorescent ink.

"He's dead, isn't he," she whispered.

"I'm sorry, baby," Bobby said, folding his arms around her. "I'm so sorry, there wasn't anything anyone could do, it just happened."

"It doesn't matter," she said, "it really doesn't."

Bobby was holding her tightly, crying into her hair.

She pushed him away. "You don't have to be sad, Bobby," she said in a low, calm voice. "It wasn't Peter who died. It was someone else. The doctors will be able to tell. It was just someone who looked like Peter."

"They don't make mistakes like that," Bobby said. He tried to wipe off the ink with a tissue.

"Oh yes they do," Marinda said, smiling at him. "Everyone was fooled except me. I could tell, though. I always knew."

"Baby, you're upset, you're not making sense. Listen to me. Peter took an overdose. He died last night. Just before midnight."

"Oh Bobby, that couldn't possibly have happened," she said, still smiling. "That was just someone else. The first time in the hospital is when they made the switch. It was never the real Peter after that."

"Look, I've brought a little Valium, you have to get control of yourself. We have to drive down to New Jersey this afternoon."

"Bobby, can't you figure it out?" she said. "We don't have to go anywhere. Peter died a long time ago. He's been dead for years." She looked at the photograph she'd hung over her bed: a shot of Peter at the beach, taken just after he'd graduated from high school. He had sculpted a mermaid out of the fine white sand and had lain down alongside of her, cupping one breast in his hand.

"Years and years and years ago," Marinda said. "Years and years."

"I've become my own grandmother," Marinda said to Bobby, leaning over her seat belt, clutching her hands in front of her so that the long loose sleeves of her black turtleneck dress fell down to her elbows. "*Cookie! Cookie!*" she said in a heavy Italian accent. "God, even Peter's mother didn't wear black to the funeral. His family looked like they were all going off to some job interview together. You're driving too fast."

Bobby took his foot off the gas. "They're pretty awful, aren't they," he said.

"I always said."

"Didn't sink in till I saw them for myself," Bobby said, tossing the end of the joint out the car window. Peter's father had thanked Bobby for the basket of fruit, cheese, and imported salami that Marinda's parents had sent, *What a nice tradition you have,* he'd said, though the food was nowhere to be seen among the sterling platters of bland sandwiches cut into narrow, crustless strips. Peter's mother had asked Bobby how Marinda was holding up, *She looks so dreadfully pale, but perhaps it's just the black. We hope you'll help her forget this awful time, It's been a pleasure knowing her,* she said, making it clear to Bobby that they would like nothing better than to pretend Marinda didn't exist, though Peter's father's secretary might send her engraved Christmas cards for a couple of years. In the trunk of Bobby's car was a shoeboxful of pictures of Peter, happy pictures mostly, that Marinda thought his family might like to have. Bobby had stayed up late last night with Marinda as she went through them, stopping over each one to tell a story about what clever thing Peter had said or done on that particular day, until Bobby had pleaded with her to stop, they were going to have to get up at six to make the three-hour drive from Jersey to Washington.

Bobby had left the photographs in his car, believing that Peter's parents neither wanted nor deserved them. At Harvard he'd met lots of kids with parents like Peter's, parents who raised families as if their children were simply rough drafts of their own adult successes, mere pencil sketches, to be inked in when they proved their worthiness. Peter had proved a failure and was being erased.

Pressure, pressure, he'd had enough of it himself. Both his father and Marinda's had made it clear to him from an early age that he wasn't being raised so much as groomed. Marinda had it easy—all she had to do was get married and have a few sons. Sometimes he wished he could change places with Marinda, that she would have to ace her way through law school (she could do it in a snap, he knew she was a better student than he was) and take over the family firm, and he could find himself a pretty girl and settle down and play the proud papa.

"Do you blame them for what happened," Bobby asked.

Marinda shrugged. Some days she had blamed Peter, and it was Peter who blamed his parents, and his parents who blamed the drugs. Some days Peter had cursed her, and she had cursed the drugs, and his parents cursed the doctors. But today she felt as if everything were her own fault.

"It wasn't your fault," Bobby said, thinking some small part of the fault might be his own, for how many times had he and Peter pooled cash and ingenuity in search of better dope, cheaper pills, purer cocaine?

"I guess," Marinda said. "Are you driving back to Boston tomorrow?" she asked.

"I guess," Bobby said. "Want a lift?"

"I guess," Marinda said, though she hadn't the strength for one more sorrowful conversation with anyone besides family.

Friends from high school had telephoned Marinda in tears, some of them were talking about organizing some kind of scholarship fund, though most of them hadn't seen Peter in over a year, and Marinda knew that at least three of them had stopped returning Peter's calls when the drugs had gotten out of hand. December called to say there was nothing at all to say. No one from Yale called at all.

Katie Lee had been the worst, offering to accompany Marinda down for the funeral, though Marinda suspected that Katie Lee's offer to support her in a time of trouble was nothing more than a desire to be near Bobby dressed up in a cloak of generosity and selflessness. *Did he make a will?* Katie Lee had asked. *Don't stare at me like that, he was over eighteen. I've made three wills since then, and you*

*should think about one too, sweetie—you never know, we could all
go at any minute.*

Rosaline had been sickeningly solicitous, bringing Marinda dinner
and helping her pack, talking vaguely religious nonsense about how
Peter had found peace at last and that people don't really die, their
spirits live on in those who remember them, and did Marinda want
Rosaline to come to Mass with her? Peter loved you so, Rosaline had
said, and when Marinda heard Rosaline say it, she knew it was not
true.

"Don't worry about it, Marinda, my mother bought lots of extra
fabric," Rosaline said as Marinda finished off her third croissant. She
must have gained more than thirty pounds since Peter's death and
showed no signs of slowing down. "Maybe we can just let out the
seams a little."

"It's still only March," Marinda said. "If I go on a diet next week
I'll have plenty of time to take off the weight." Coming down to New
York with Rosaline for the weekend had been a mistake. She really
couldn't stand hearing every little detail about the wedding. She and
Rosaline were supposed to go out with Trevor and a friend of his from
work tonight; Trevor hadn't seen her since last August, and she
doubted that Rosaline had told him how fat she'd become. She could
imagine Trevor pulling his friend aside, whispering an apology, sorry
chum, she wasn't like this when I knew her, she used to be a really
pretty girl.

"Well, you don't have to do it just for me," Rosaline said. "They
say diets only work if you're doing it for yourself."

Like you have any way of knowing, Marinda thought. "Katie Lee is
going to look great in this dress," she said. And I'll be waddling down
the aisle beside her, a tub of lard teetering forward on hot-pink high-
heeled shoes. She would have to go on a diet as soon as she got back
to Cambridge, the dress was one thing, but it was just too embarrassing to explain to Rosaline that she'd need a new pair of larger, wider
shoes. Size 8D, wasn't it perfect how they awarded shoe sizes like
grades for good eating habits: A—bravo, you skinny thing. B—nice
work, keep it up. C—acceptable, but we think you can do better.
D—what's a nice girl like you doing in a fat-lady store like this?

"When do you hear about law school?" Rosaline asked.

"Some time next month."

"Well, I hope you get into Columbia or N.Y.U. I'd love to have you here in New York with me."

"From what I hear about the first year of law school, there isn't too much time left over for socializing," Marinda said. Which was just how she wanted it: a pile of work so huge she could bury herself under it and not have to deal with anything else. She couldn't imagine herself as a lawyer, actually, doing the job of her father and uncles, but three years of law school was a neat way to postpone the inevitable decision about just what she was going to do with her life.

"And what about you," Marinda asked. "Any plans for after graduation?"

"Well, we're going to Europe for July, and then I'm going up to Saratoga for August, Trevor will drive up on the weekends. Then we have to find an apartment, and it will take me a few months to get that all set up, and then, who knows?" Rosaline said, but she knew exactly, because she and Trevor had talked about it before they'd gotten engaged. They both wanted children, lots of them, and everyone knew how much easier it was when you were young. Later on, when all her thirty-plus friends were making appointments for amnios and being told by their doctors to spend their last three months of term in bed with their feet up, Rosaline's children would all be in school and she could find something interesting to get her out of the house during the day.

"Did Katie Lee get her zoning approval yet?" Rosaline asked.

"She won't know for sure until the summer. I think she misjudged how powerful the community groups are in Cambridge. In the South the real estate people run everything, they can get away with anything they want, just about. I don't think Katie Lee had any idea that the neighborhood would put up such a fuss. I can see both sides, though. I mean, some of those families have lived there for generations, and they're scared that if the neighborhood gets too expensive they'll have no place else to go."

"Katie Lee will figure out a way to pull it off," Rosaline said.

"Maybe, maybe not. It's an election year, that's the real hitch. Katie Lee has one vote, and the people who oppose her add up to a couple of thousand. Jesus, look at the time, I have to run," Marinda said. She'd told Rosaline the night before that she was having lunch with December, but she still felt awkward about leaving.

"Say hello for me, will you?" Rosaline said. "It's funny, you know, but now that I'm getting married it doesn't seem so important anymore—what happened with December. I really do wish her well. Will you let her know?"

"I'll tell her hello," Marinda said, putting on the khaki man's trenchcoat that made her feel like a pup tent in motion.

Charlotte came in after Marinda had left and frowned at the empty croissant platter. Even the little glazed crumbs were gone; Marinda had licked her thumb and run it over the plate, collecting every last buttery morsel.

"Did you tell her?" Charlotte asked.

"She said she was going on a diet. Even if she doesn't, we can always let out the dress."

"I won't have a fat bridesmaid at my daughter's wedding. What if she doesn't lose the weight? We can't just kick her out of the wedding party at the last minute. The sooner you do this, the easier it will be. Why didn't you just tell her we'd decided to cut back?"

"She would have seen right through that, Mother. Anyway, I don't care, she's my friend, she's one of my best friends, and I want her to be a bridesmaid. I don't care what people think."

"But sweetie," Charlotte said, "I was just thinking of what's best for Marinda. Look at it from her point of view. Think how uncomfortable she'll be. Think of the embarrassment you're saving her. Imagine how she'll feel standing next to four girls who look absolutely perfect in this dress. If you really care about her you won't put her through it. Promise me you'll think about it some more."

"Just wait a month. She'll lose weight. I'll help her."

"Of course you will," Charlotte said, taking Rosaline's hand. "That's what best friends are for."

"I don't know how you pulled it off," Marinda said, looking around December's apartment. It looked like a department store model room—perfect detailing but no personality. Anyone could live here. There were no family photographs, no sentimental knickknacks or kitschy souvenirs, not a single clue to what made December tick. "Isn't there some rule about students having to live in Cambridge?" Marinda said, running her finger around the rim of a smooth crystal ashtray. "Didn't anyone ever figure it out?"

"I paid this woman twenty dollars a month to let me use her address. If anyone ever called she just said I was away for a few days."

"Are you coming up for graduation?"

"No way, José. They can mail the diploma to my mother, she can hang it up next to her husband's honorary degree from McDonald's Hamburger University. How's Rosaline doing?"

"All right. She can't think about anything except the wedding, and it's sort of a bore actually, but we're all putting up with it. Um, so, do you want to have lunch here or is there someplace nearby we can go? I'm starving. They hardly feed you over there, true WASP hospitality."

"Jeepers, lunch, I completely forgot," December said, getting up and heading for the kitchen. "Let's see, I hardly ever cook, but I think we can throw something together. Here's some soup, and there's some yoghurt—oh, forget the yoghurt, it expired yesterday—how about some frozen pizza? Mushroom and pepperoni."

"Maybe we should go out."

"I guess."

"No wonder you stay so thin," Marinda said with a sigh. "I wish I had your discipline."

"You mean you wish you had my friend the medical student," December said, giggling. "You don't think we all stay so thin by jogging around the park and nibbling at lettuce do you?"

"Don't you?"

"Give me a break," December said, pulling a vial of pills out of a drawer next to the stove. "Appetite suppressants. We used to call it speed when we took it for fun. One of these in the morning and you're a good girl all day long."

Marinda laughed. "God, you don't know how great it makes me feel, knowing you're not perfectly naturally thin."

December laughed too. "I know, don't you hate them? Look, do you want some? I've got a refillable prescription on file at the pharmacy downstairs."

Marinda looked at the little capsules. How easy it would be, how desperate she had become. Peter had gone through a speed phase before he found more interesting things to do.

"No, thanks," she said. "Me and drugs don't mix." She'd figure out a way to get the weight off by June, and if she didn't, so what? Hadn't she really been a fat person all along, hadn't she been a chubby baby, weren't her thin years just a phase, like the rest of adolescence, something you grew out of? There was something comfortable and reassuring in growing up and accepting who you really were. Her fat was part of her, she was going to turn into one of those beaming

Italian matriarchs just like her mother and aunts, the fat kept her happy and warm and protected her from—what exactly did it protect her from? Marinda looked at December: you could almost count her ribs through her tight T-shirt. Whatever my fat protects me from, Marinda thought, it's something December sure isn't afraid of.

"This looks like underwear from outer space," Marinda said, waving the dress shield over her head. "Do I really have to put them on? How do I put them on, anyway?"

"Yes, you have to, and here, I'll show you," Katie Lee said, knocking over a vase of daisies as she leaned toward Marinda. "That's the problem with these old historic churches, they never have decent dressing rooms. Have you been to see Rosaline yet? I swear, they've stuck her in a broom closet. She does look pretty, though, don't you think? I personally would have gone for something with a little more lace, that's what wedding dresses are all about, aren't they, but it fits her personality."

Marinda sucked in her breath as Katie Lee fastened the back of her dress. "It was her grandmother's dress. I think the dress was sort of slinky and daring back then."

"Well, when I get married you can be sure I'm getting a brand new dress made just for me, and it's going to have tons and tons of lace all over it," Katie Lee said.

Of course you'll get a brand new dress, Marinda thought, your grandmother probably got married in a burlap bag. "And who's the lucky man?" she asked.

"Oh, don't think I don't have someone in mind," Katie Lee said. Marinda had been absolutely no help where Bobby was concerned, and Katie Lee was getting fed up. An invitation for a weekend at the family beach house, was that too much to expect from her roommate and best friend? A last-minute we're-all-going-out-for-pizza-want-to-come-along, was that asking too much? Marinda is just a self-centered person, Katie Lee thought. She only thinks about herself, Marinda this, Marinda that, it was just amazing how absolutely selfish some people could be.

Something old: that was her grandmother's wedding gown, taken in at the seams so the ivory bias-cut satin would fall softly over Rosaline's slender figure. The bodice and sleeves were embroidered with hundreds of tiny seed pearls and the long velvet sash fell nearly to the ground. It was a dress for a princess, a fairy-tale princess, and that's just how Rosaline felt.

Something new: that was the veil, which Charlotte had ordered from Paris. When Trevor lifted it up off her face it was as if he were raising the curtain for the first act of this play that would be their life together. Everything up till now had been an overture, a preparation; everything that mattered lay ahead, in the family they would start together. Their own family.

Something borrowed: that was the pair of emerald earrings her father's sister had lent her, and their sparkle brought out the brilliant green of her eyes. She'd been afraid she might start crying in front of all these people or, even worse, have a fit of stage-fright giggles, but it seemed so easy now, with Trevor beaming down at her, to say the words she felt she'd been rehearsing from the day she was born.

Something blue: that was the garter, which at some point later on, she couldn't remember exactly when, got tossed into the crowd. The bouquet would be thrown into the crowd too, and she and Katie Lee had choreographed how it would happen. Today Rosaline wanted to share everything with the people around her, not just the garter and the bouquet and the champagne and the music but this happiness she felt just bubbling up out of her. Had every married couple in the church felt this same way on their wedding day? Had her parents? She felt as if she and Trevor were bathed in a pure golden light, a light that radiated out from them and was reflected in the faces of everyone in the room.

Once upon a time, thought Rosaline Van Schott, a fair maiden lay sleeping in the woods, until a lad named Trevor came galloping along.

"I do," she said, lifting her face for the softest, sweetest kiss.

And we'll live happily ever after, Mrs. Trevor Goodwood thought, forever and ever until the day we die.

11

She thought about him all day long, every day, it never stopped.

When she ate her solitary breakfast in her narrow railroad apartment in the east nineties she pretended he was sitting there opposite her; he was asking about her classes and she was pouring him a second cup of coffee as they traded sections of the daily paper, news for sports, business for entertainment.

When she shopped for clothes in the boutique of a local department store where they played current disco hits over the sound system, she pretended they were dancing together at a party in a club downtown; he was cutting in, pulling her in close and whispering something in her ear, then twirling her out and sending her a smile as he squeezed her hand.

When she went to bed at night she pretended he was there beside her, playing with the long strands of her hair spread out over the pillow, slowly unfastening the top buttons of her nightgown, sliding the fabric over her knees, up around her hips. He was telling her he loved her, he was telling her how long he had waited for her, he was describing all the things he wanted to do to her, he was telling her to lie perfectly still as he began to make love to her, slowly, in time to the music that played softly from another room.

Each night she pretended, over and over; it was always the same and it was always perfect. After a while she would raise her knees and slip her hand under the covers, imagining it to be his hand, his tongue, his cock, bringing her to an orgasm so intense she would lie there for minutes afterwards, pleased with herself and also a little frightened because the best sex she had ever had was with a man she had never even kissed.

But I know exactly what his kisses will be like, she was telling herself now as she walked past the building where he lived in an apartment she had never seen. He wasn't home yet—she knew that because she had telephoned him a few minutes ago and gotten the answering machine. She called him several times a week, just to hear his voice. As soon as he said hello she always hung up. *Girls don't call boys*, she reminded herself. *You have to wait for him to call you.*

But Schuyler hadn't called Marinda in the two months since she'd moved to New York to go to law school. It was a sublime form of self-torture, walking five blocks out of her way twice a day just in case she might run into him as he left his house. Buying her groceries (just a few items at a time, never everything she needed, necessitating frequent trips) at his neighborhood deli just in case he might be there too, picking up a sandwich or a six-pack of beer.

She was in no rush. She had loved him a long time, she realized now, probably since the first time she had seen him. She just couldn't admit it to herself while Peter was alive, she thought. And she was going to love him for a long time to come. Eventually he would be hers. In the meantime she could dream, and pray that he didn't get serious about someone else, and try to lose some of this weight she had gained. In her fantasies she was always thin; she was beginning to believe that becoming thin was the way to make her fantasies come true.

She had tried a few of the diets she had read about in glossy women's magazines, and she had even plunked down two hundred dollars for the pleasure of having a doctor run a series of painful metabolic tests and then inform her that there was absolutely nothing wrong with her metabolism. She was simply someone who ate too much and didn't get enough exercise, polite euphemisms for "fat" and "lazy."

She had considered jogging until she read an article that said it could ruin her knees. Swimming meant having to buy a bathing suit, something that had driven Marinda to the fringes of depression even when she had been in excellent shape. Tennis, squash, and racquetball involved some other person who got to watch her heave her weight around, someone who would have to pretend not to notice how she broke out in a heavy sweat after the slightest bit of warm-up running in place. Exercise was a Catch 22: the only people who felt good about doing it were the very people who needed it least.

Someone in her torts class had lent her a diet book that recommended extended daily walks and meals of chick peas, unsalted whole wheat wafers, and raw spinach. Stepping over an ice cream cone that someone had dropped on the sidewalk, Marinda tried to complete the mathematical calculations in her head. If she walked three miles per hour at her present weight (something she knew only approximately—her scale seemed to have broken last month and she didn't feel like spending twenty dollars on a new one) she would be burning up about five calories a minute. Times sixty, makes 300 calories an hour. Three hundred into that magic mystical number 3500— the number of calories you needed to burn off a single irksome pound—she would need to walk nearly twelve hours to burn off one pound. She would need to walk 36 miles, so if 20 blocks equaled one mile, that would mean 720 blocks. If she walked from her apartment on East 90th Street all the way down to Houston Street and back four times, that would do it.

Of course, if she decided to walk at the rate of *four* miles per hour, she'd be burning seven calories a minute, or 420 calories per hour, which meant she'd need to walk for only eight and a half hours. A distance of 34 miles, or 680 blocks. If she walked downtown and back four times, she'd be able to turn around as soon as she reached East Fifth Street.

Was that Schuyler up ahead, turning into the stationery store? It looked like him. It couldn't be. It had to be. She sprayed some Chanel on her neck and followed him in.

There he was, next to the register, trying different widths of Japanese felt-tip pens on the sheet of blank white paper provided by the store. She picked up an item from the rack nearest the door—a package of refrigerator magnets shaped like circus animals—and brought it to the cashier.

"Marinda," he said, looking up from the large circle he'd sketched in varying shades of blue, "what a nice surprise."

"Schuyler, hello, how are you?"

"Fine, thanks. You?"

"Fine, I guess. How's the job going?"

"It's going," he replied, picking up a dark-red fine-point. "This color reminds me of school. I used to be addicted to these when I was a kid."

"I remember when they first came out," she said, drawing a triangle in bold purple, "we called them Magic Markers. Gosh, it makes me feel old, reminiscing about some invention. Next I'll be starting my sentences with 'The kids today.'"

Schuyler laughed. "My mother used to tell stories about the first package of margarine that arrived in my hometown. The mayor's wife gave a luncheon party to show it off." He filled the triangle with bright-green polka dots. "Do those colors go together?"

"They look great together. You could design—I don't know, ties for rock stars?"

"Have rock stars begun wearing ties again?"

"You're asking the wrong person," she said. "I don't have time to notice anything except law school."

"I remember the first time Mick Jagger appeared on Ed Sullivan he was wearing a wristwatch. How is law school, anyway?"

"A million times more work than they said it would be, which was a million times more work than I've ever done in my life. I hardly have time for anything else."

Schuyler lifted one eyebrow. "Such as?"

Marinda blushed. "Whatever it is people do in their first year in New York." She took a deep breath. "I was just on my way to get a quick burger, do you want to join me?"

"No, thanks, I just ate," he said. "I have to get this piece done tonight. I thought if I bought some new pens it would give me the necessary energy."

"Well. Anyway. I'll tell them what a good worker you are, not stealing pens from the office."

"We work on computer terminals. You can't slip them in your coat pocket on your way out the door."

"Unless you've got a really big pocket," she said. He stared at her. In all her imaginings of him she'd forgotten about those eyes, bright gray, like polished metal. "Uh, that was a joke. Sorry."

He picked up a pink pen and drew a perfectly straight line across the page. "And how is the rest of the gang?" he asked.

"Pretty good. I had dinner with Rosaline and Trevor last week."

"And how are they?"

"Pregnant. Actually it's only Rosaline who's pregnant, but it seems to be the way people talk these days, saying they're both pregnant as a couple."

"That's terrific news," he said, drawing a parallel line. "Please send her my best. And to Trevor too."

"Do you know him?"

"We've never met," Schuyler said.

"You probably wouldn't like him," Marinda said, wishing instantly tht she could take it back. "I mean, he isn't what you'd expect at all, or rather, he's *exactly* what you'd expect. I don't know what I mean, really. He's sort of predictable."

"Maybe he has inner resources," Schuyler said. He'd noticed this before, the way a group of women tends to disapprove of the first marriage within their set. Had Marinda gained more weight since the last time he'd seen her or had he just forgotten how fat she'd become? She seemed to have crossed the border between overweight and obese. The line that men didn't cross. Peter had been dead a long time now, he thought, she should have rebounded by now. "I'm sure Rosaline chose well," he said.

"Oh, I'm sure too."

"And Katie Lee?" he asked, staring at her still, his hand moving lazily over the page.

"The final hearing on her hotel is coming up next week. She's sweating bricks." She couldn't think of a thing to say next. He was staring at her with an expression both stern and encouraging, as if he had asked her a question that he knew to be very difficult and that he was hoping she would answer carefully and correctly. "So. Anyway," she said, handing the cashier five dollars. "Maybe I'll see you around. I have to get back to work."

"I thought you were going out to eat."

"Right. And then back to work," she said, collecting her change. "Why don't you call me sometime and talk me into a study break?" She wrote down her telephone number, ripped the paper from the pad and offered it to him. "I'm not listed. Daddy's rules."

"Are men allowed to change their minds or is that just a female prerogative? I could get some coffee and dessert while you get dinner. If the offer's still open."

"Sure, that would be great," she said. "There's a place around the corner with a terrific jukebox."

"I know it," he said. "Let me just pick up a few things first. It'll just be a minute."

"I'll meet you outside," she said, and she waited on the sidewalk. It's happening, it's happening, she said to herself. She was still holding the paper. I'll give him my number over dinner, she told herself, he'll have to ask for it at some point. This piece of paper would be the very first memento of their time together. She would keep it in the same box that held some clippings of his better newspaper pieces and a photograph of him that Katie Lee had taken once when they'd all gone to a football game together.

And purple and green would be her new favorite colors. She took a last look at the scrap of paper before folding it into her pocket.

Inside a wide blue circle, between the triangle and the parallel lines, he had made some random marks, just meaningless chicken scratches he'd drawn as they talked. Something that could have been a tiny crooked heart. And a curlicue that looked to Marinda like an ocean wave. And something else, obviously it was nothing at all, obviously it was anything at all, anything but a letter, the capital letter *D*.

The next day Marinda spent nearly a hundred dollars at the local record store buying albums by every singer Schuyler had selected on the jukebox during dinner. The Dylan she already owned, but she was going to have to give herself a crash course in Chuck Berry, Tom Waits, and early Kinks.

It was just a dinner, she kept reminding herself. She had barely been able to finish half the cheeseburger special she'd ordered. She didn't seem to have any appetite the next day either; she tried to work her way through a green apple sliced into a cup of yoghurt (a meal that usually left her famished) but she hadn't been able to do it.

They hadn't discussed anything very important, but still she remembered everything he'd said. He'd talked mostly about his job and how competitive it was: there were reporters on the paper who at age fifty were still waiting for their big break, and people were telling him his career would move a lot faster if he left the city and went to work on a small local paper outside of the Northeast. The thought that he might leave the city terrified her.

He'd seen her home, and she'd waited inside by the elevator as he walked back down her street. Then she'd left her building, raced a back way around the block and waited on his corner until she saw the lights come on in his apartment. Now she knew exactly which set of windows was his, and she'd be able to tell whether or not he was home without calling him up.

He'd circled around the subject of December all through dinner without ever bringing her up directly. Though she hadn't heard from December in weeks, Marinda gave him what little news she had.

Before she went to bed she called December and set up a dinner for the following week.

She picked up a bottle of cheap Italian white and arrived at December's apartment five minutes early.

"Your hair looks great that way," December said as she let Marinda in.

"It's easier to keep it up and off my back while I study," Marinda replied. Ever since she'd gained weight she'd received endless compliments about how she wore her hair, which was still as long as it had been in high school. Hair, makeup, and earrings: they were all part of the unspoken safe zone above the neck, where thin people were allowed to pay not-so-thin people compliments without fear of treading on sensitive territory.

"Actually I've lost five pounds in the last week," Marinda said, "without even really trying. It just sort of happened."

"Well, keep up the good work," December said, uncorking the wine. "Is this a new diet I should know about?"

The Schuyler Diet, and I'll kill you if you even think about trying it, Marinda thought. "I guess I'm just too busy studying to think much about food. Have you lost weight too or is it just that I haven't seen you in a while?"

"I'm about the same," December said, sniffling. "I can't seem to kick this cold."

"Are you taking anything for it? I mean, should you be drinking wine?"

December smiled. "No, it's okay, I'm not on antibiotics or anything, though I've got some around in case my skin breaks out, you know, the swimming and the chlorine and all that, and of course the air is so polluted here in New York it's amazing I can breathe." She sniffled again. "You know I keep getting these colds, and I've always had such good resistance, but the air quality is so bad it really kills my sinuses. You're lucky not to have that problem."

"I guess."

"So, law school, how's law school. Oh, you always say the same thing, it's boring and a ton of work, but you knew that before you went in, right? School, you couldn't get me to go back to school for a million dollars." She giggled and wiped her nose. "Well, maybe for a million dollars, who knows. I don't mean to be putting it down, it's right for you but it just isn't right for me, I'd probably be a terrible lawyer anyway. I mean, what if my client were wrong, you know what I mean, I don't think I'd be able to defend him properly, but of course they teach you how to do that, I was dating a lawyer last month and he explained to me all about it but I don't know, I mean what if you absolutely knew that your client had committed murder but you still had to defend him?"

"I'm not going into criminal law," Marinda said, "so I don't think I'll ever be in that situation."

"Well, whatever, murder, it doesn't have to be murder, it could be something else, white-collar crime I guess, who knows." December rolled the cork between her palms and tapped her foot. "Do you want to hear some music? I just got a new stereo, don't ask me why, I was just walking by the store and I'd gotten a new credit card and I figured what the hell, I'll pay for it eventually. I have no self-control. So what do you want to hear? I have the new Stones album, which pretty much sucks, but it's still the Mick and Keith show, you know, and also I just got this synthesizer kind of stuff, it's sort of fast, but it doesn't have any words so it's good to talk to, what do you think?"

Marinda crossed her arms. "I guess it depends on whether or not you're going to do another line."

"Oh," December said, making a fist around the cork. "That obvious, hunh?"

"Sort of."

"Well, I think this stuff I got is stronger than usual, so I guess I overdid it," she said, pulling the small plastic vial out of her jeans pocket. "A friend of mine's daughter is three years old and for Christmas I'm going to use these to make a spice rack for her dollhouse. Her mother will have a fit." She lifted the small silver spoon up to her nose and inhaled, then offered a scoopful across the cocktail table.

"No, thanks," Marinda said. "I've got an early class tomorrow. You go right ahead though, I don't mind." She was tired of this kind of evening—she'd had too many of them with Bobby and his friends, sitting there listening to someone babble on about some topic he knew next to nothing about. So that's how December kept so thin. "How much are you doing these days?"

"Oh, not that much, I just got this great job to do a shoot in Arizona, so I guess I'm celebrating."

Sure you are, Marinda thought. She knew from experience that the people who didn't get specific were the ones who bought at least weekly, several grams at a time.

"Does celebrating still include dinner?" Marinda asked.

"Well, sure, if you want some, are you hungry?"

"Not especially," Marinda said.

"You know, there's this party downtown we can go to, some people I met through work. They've got a great loft and they always have great food, we could go there."

"I'm not really dressed for it," Marinda said.

"Oh, you look fine, no one will notice," December said. "I mean, it's the kind of thing where some people come in black tie and some people come in blue jeans and T-shirts and no one cares about that kind of thing. But I guess we should talk some and catch up, I haven't seen you in ages, how long has it been? Have I missed any great gossip?"

"Rosaline is pregnant. Due in the spring."

"Wow, that's great, she always wanted a zillion kids."

"I think three or four would make her happy. Katie Lee didn't get the zoning for her hotel. Election year and all that."

"I'd hate to see what she's like as a loser."

"Not a pretty sight," Marinda said, remembering the late-night call from Katie Lee in Cambridge. "She's lost a lot of money, and she's having some kind of summit meeting with her father next week about the Future of Her Career in the Hotel Industry. It's sort of like in some weird way he's happy she failed, you know? Like he expected it all along?"

"He sounds like a real shit."

"A real rich shit. Stay tuned for further bulletins. Anyway, she might be moving down to New York. They want to do some kind of luxury hotel midtown to catch the convention business."

December examined her nails. "So we'd all be in New York again." She looked up at Marinda. "Just think, this is where I first came to get away from everyone, and now everyone has ended up here."

"It just sort of happened."

"Right." December looked out the window. "Seen anyone else I know recently?"

"Just Rosaline and Katie Lee," Marinda replied, "and a couple of people at law school. No one you really knew at all. Do you really want to go to this party? I'm feeling kind of restless. As long as you don't mind if I leave a little early—I really do have to get some studying in tonight."

December leaped off the couch and finished her glass of wine. "Let's go. It'll be fun. I'm just going to put on a clean sweater."

"Let me go fix my face first," Marinda said. "Do you have any lipstick and blush I can borrow?"

December pointed to the bathroom. "Help yourself. To whatever you want."

The bathroom was done in green and white, with additional lighting fixtures over the medicine cabinet and two round magnifying mirrors that swung out from the wall. On a small table next to the oversize bathtub was an ice bucket, two clean champagne glasses, imported bubble bath, a tall black candle stuck in a crystal holder, and an assortment of magazines and some mail. The pages of one of the magazines had curled up from being dropped in the bath. A MasterCharge bill showed December to be a few dollars shy of a three-thousand-dollar credit limit. Peeking out from beneath the bill was the corner of a note written in fine blue ink; only the date was showing—just last week—but Marinda recognized the handwriting immediately.

She locked the door to the bathroom and slipped out the note.

December,

Yes, yet another note, forgive me for being so thick in the head and not getting the message, so perfectly clear I guess since you never write back, that you don't want to hear from me.

I can't help feeling we have some unfinished business and I'd like to get together, for lunch or a walk in the park or whatever you're comfortable with, just to talk things through. It's strange us both being in the same city this way. I know you're doing well, or rather I hear you're doing well but you can't blame a man for wanting to see for himself.

I think about you, more than I should. More than you'd want me to, I suppose. I want you to know that I'm proud of your success and whatever happens, I'll always be on your side.

Enough late night drunken rambling from an old friend.

You know where to find me,
Schuyler

Marinda slid the letter back under the bill and sat down on the edge of the tub. He didn't really come right out and say anything, she thought, he didn't even end the letter "love," which everyone does even just for regular old friends. People do and say all kinds of things they don't mean when they're drunk.

She took some blush off a rack and brushed it over her cheeks, examining her reflection in the mirror. How much weight would she have to lose, she wondered, before it would start showing in her face.

"It shows in your face, you know," the man in the Western-cut shirt was saying to Marinda in an Oklahoma accent, "you're a very serious person. I can tell just from looking at you."

"You say 'serious' like it's a bad thing to be," Marinda said, looking for December, whom she'd lost in the noisy crowd soon after they'd come to the party. The man was a record producer, or at least he claimed to be one, and he was flirting with her in a way that was charming only because it was so unembarrassedly straightforward.

"No, I've got my serious side too," he said, frowning into a bottle of Coors he held slightly out from his body, the pose of a high school actor handed his first skull and script of *Hamlet*. "I think about death. All the time."

Marinda shifted away from him. He was cute enough. He could be doing better. Maybe he thought she would be easy because she was fat.

"Well, we're all going to die," she said. "Sooner or later."

He took a step toward her and stared at the space between her eyes. "You're very wise. I see you've thought about this too. We have something in common."

"Well, not too much. I mean I don't think about death that much. It just happens."

"Most people don't truly realize it," he said, taking another step closer. "Deep down they think they'll live forever." His breath smelled of cigarettes and barbecue sauce. "I try to fit as much in every day as I can, because we only go to the rodeo once, if you know what I mean. I believe you know what I mean."

"Well, it's been nice talking to you, but I have to go now," Marinda said, looking for December's platinum hair in the mass of dancers.

"The rodeo is a metaphor for life," he continued, swaying toward her, spilling some beer onto the bleached wooden floor. "If you know what I mean."

"The young lady is allergic to horses," said a British accent coming up behind her and placing a protective arm around her waist.

"Alex," she said, turning and smiling, "I can't believe—"

"Yes," Alex continued, smiling at the Oklahoman, "it's tragic. She's allergic to all kinds of animals. Horses, dogs, cats, fur coats. The doctors think it's psychosomatic, but I disagree."

Marinda started to giggle. Alex put on a serious face and whispered behind a cupped hand.

"Because she's only become allergic since the breakdown, you see. Before that she worked in a pet shop. Training snakes."

The Oklahoman backed away and made a little bow. "Well, it's been a real pleasure meeting you."

Marinda giggled, and Alex shook his head.

"It's the antidepressants that make her keep giggling," he called out as the man retreated, walking backwards into the crowd.

"Thanks," Marinda said. "He was awful."

"The worst thing about this sudden popularity of American country music is that all these creatures who used to stay in Nashville have been let loose on the rest of us. He's harmless."

"Thanks for rescuing me just the same. I had no idea you were in New York."

"I guess we haven't been moving in the same circles," he said. His hair was shorter and he was wearing an additional earring in his left ear, but otherwise Alex seemed unchanged. The thin stooping frame and European clothing that had made him seem so outlandish and decadent in Cambridge seemed perfectly in place in this expensively decorated loft filled with abstract paintings and oversized modern furniture.

"You've come with December?" he asked.

Marinda nodded. "Are you guys in touch?"

"We go to a lot of the same parties. She acts very kissy-kissy, but I think she's still a little annoyed with me," he said, sighing.

"That was a long time ago," Marinda said.

"Was it. I'm still a bad boy in December's book."

"You are who you are. You can't be blamed for that."

"You are very wise, my pet," he said.

Marinda tossed back her head and grabbed him by the elbow. "Oh, please don't, that's what the cowboy said. Where are you living now?"

"I'm based in L.A. now. Writing movies that never get made. Which

I could do in London if it weren't for the damn tax situation."

"Sounds glamorous."

"You'd be disappointed if it weren't. Our December looks rather lovely tonight, don't you think? Where do you American girls learn to move your hips like that?"

"From *les noirs*. She always looks lovely, it's her job."

Alex shook her head. "And I got her into it."

"I'm sure she's grateful."

"Is she. I'm not sure I'd do it again if I had the chance."

"Why not?" Marinda asked.

Alex rested a hand on Marinda's shoulder and leaned into her ear. "I don't like feeling responsible. I'm not the heartless chap you all thought I was. I did truly care about her, in my fashion."

"She's rich and famous and successful and goes out with any man she wants. I'm supposed to feel sorry for her?" Marinda said.

"She's successful because she slept her way onto the cover of *Sports Illustrated*, she's famous because of a poster that hangs on the bedroom walls of half the teenage boys in America, and she won't be rich for long," Alex whispered. "She won't have any of it for long."

"You're frightening me. Stop beating around the bush."

Alex shook his head. "A loathesome expression which I forgive you for for only because you're a dear, sweet old chum. I thought the two of you were so close, but I see I was wrong. She'll hate me for saying anything to you."

"Is she sick? What's wrong?"

"Nothing's wrong. Nothing at all. Your friend December just happens to be the most marvelously fantastically outrageously beautiful cocaine addict in New York."

Marinda gasped. "I don't believe you," she said. Of course he was right. She had been an idiot not to see it.

"Would that I were wrong, darling. I see my escort getting nervous by the bar. Whistle if you see an oncoming lasso."

Marinda thanked the host, who didn't remember who she was but did recall that December had left a few minutes earlier through the back entrance, and she went outside to find a taxi. It's the same thing all over again, she said to herself, first Peter, now December.

I really fucked up the first time around, she thought as the car sped through yellow lights all the way up Third Avenue, I can't let it happen again.

• • •

"Great apartment," the man said, tossing an English tweed jacket over the back of a chair. His name was John and he was a photojournalist who spent most of his time in countries where the villagers took target practice on anything that looked even remotely American. He chain-smoked with great affectation, moving his cigarette between his fingers to emphasize stories of risk and danger, waving his cupped hand from his wrist like a child throwing shadow animals in the blank white light of a film projector.

December thought he was kind of cute, at least cute enough to take home for a late-night brandy. Journalists and photographers returning from states of siege tended to be all edge and no center; when they could get it up (which wasn't too often) they were intense and talky and they always left well before dawn. She had an early call the next day.

"I don't spend that much time here," she said, dismissing the room with a wave.

"How many rooms are there?" he asked, a sudden student of architecture.

"Three. Would you like a guided tour?"

"Maybe later," John said, sitting down and lighting a cigarette. He'd just flown into Kennedy that morning, he explained, and was already itching to leave. Holding the cigarette between clenched teeth, he began rubbing the back of his neck with both hands.

"Why don't you let me do that for you," December said, standing behind him and massaging his shoulders. "Jesus, you really are a wreck."

"Thanks so much," he said, squinting his eyes against the smoke.

"Full of knots," she said. "I know just the thing. Be back in a minute."

He looked around the room while she banged cabinets in the bathroom. When he'd first met her at the party he'd been charmed and surprised by her intelligence, but now he was having second thoughts. Sometimes it was easier when they had no idea who you were or what you did or where you'd been. When there was no pressure at all, and if you failed them you could forget about them the moment you got back out on the sidewalk.

"Time for your tour," she said, lifting the bottle of brandy in one hand and pulling him up by the wrist with the other.

In the bathroom, by the light of a single black candle, they sat on the edge of the tub, talking about international debt and watching the pine-scented bubbles rise up out of the hot water.

"They won't extend the loan until after the election," he said, leaning his elbows on his knees as she kneaded the back of his neck.

"Ours or theirs?" December asked. She rested her lips against his neck, the lightest suggestion of a kiss, and began unbuttoning his shirt.

"Theirs," he said, tossing his cigarette in the toilet and closing his eyes. "Though everyone knows in advance what the outcome will be. It's all just for show."

She pulled his shirt out of his trousers and down around his shoulders. "So why do they keep pretending it could go either way?" she asked, dipping her fingers into the warm water and tracing circles across his back.

He sighed. He knew she knew. "I think I'm all talked out," he said.

"I think you're a very tired man," she said.

"That I am," he whispered, breathing deeply as she undressed him.

"Why don't you just let me take care of things for a while," she said, standing up and dropping her clothes to the floor. She turned off the faucets, dipped a black washcloth into the water and rubbed it over his shoulders. She lifted his feet over the edge of the tub and watched them disappear into the foam.

"This is fantastic," he said when they were both submerged in the water. They were sitting together, her back against his chest, her knees pressing against his, his arms folded over her breasts, like a couple waiting for the roller coaster ride to begin.

"Sssh," she said, twisting her head around and kissing his chest. "Just be quiet now and let me take care of you." She twisted her hair into a single braid and fastened it with a clip, and then she took the washcloth and ran it slowly, slowly, up and down the outside of first his left and then his right thigh. She pressed her ear to his chest and listened for his heartbeat, just a little quicker now, and she moved the washcloth to the inside of his thighs. He ran a finger over her lips and she took it between her teeth in the softest bite. When he didn't tense up or withdraw his hand she knew that at last he was relaxed, and trustful, and that she could begin.

She let go of the washcloth and he dropped his knees against the sides of the tub. She felt for him with her hand—he was still soft, and she played with him under the water, fluttering her fingers around him from every direction until he stiffened against her touch.

She pulled him down into the water, propped his feet up on the far end of the tub, and lifted his hips up where the water met the foam; it was easy to hold him here, he was practically floating in the warm pine water, and she took him into her mouth. First she moved her mouth up and down around him and then, when he'd caught the rhythm of it and she was confident of her ability to move him as she wanted, she held her mouth still and with a hand on each cheek lifted him up and down, tonguing him back and forth. It was so quiet here. The soft early morning light glowed through the narrow translucent window, and the traffic had slowed on the city streets below. He was absolutely silent, not even the smallest groan escaped his lips. The only sound was the slapping of water against porcelain echoing faintly against the hard tile walls. She held him to this easy cadence, pulling him back when he tried to hurry it along; she wanted everything to be as calm and quiet and inevitable as tide lapping in before dawn.

When he came, slow and steady, he arched up into her and then dropped down, pulling her back with him. He tugged her head up by her braid and held her head to his shoulder.

"My mermaid," he said, swirling her hair in the water. After a few minutes he reached down and played with her, lazily, not really paying attention, one hand fingering her and the other tickling her breast. It was perfunctory—the evening was already over for him, she knew he was already thinking about leaving—but she didn't care, she was ready and she came quickly. It was light out and she could hear trucks rumbling up the avenue. She was starting to crash. She wanted him to leave.

With her foot she pushed down the lever that opened the drain and felt the chill of the cool air against her damp skin as the water receded around them. He shivered against her and got up to dress. It was taking him forever. She hoped he didn't ask her to breakfast. She wanted to be alone. She needed to get in a few lines before work.

12

Rosaline turned sideways in front of the full-length mirror. She barely showed at all, even now when she was practically five months pregnant. The bright-red velvet jumper trimmed in kelly green piping (a gift from Trevor she would probably wear only once a year, on Christmas Eve) hung loosely from her shoulders.

No one would ever suspect that she was going to have a baby, except for the way Trevor had begun acting like a complete fool whenever an infant was in the vicinity. Just yesterday they'd been walking together down Lexington Avenue doing some last-minute shopping for stocking stuffers, and Trevor had practically accosted a woman pushing a stroller in the opposite direction. The mother had looked up in alarm to see just who this strange man was, this man who, without asking, began jangling the plastic keys that hung from the top of the stroller. When she took in the short, careful haircut, the cashmere topcoat, and the perfectly polished loafers, she smiled at Rosaline, who hung back, a little embarrassed at her husband's display.

"One on the way?" the woman asked. Rosaline nodded.

Trevor knelt on the sidewalk and babbled nonsense to the child, all wrapped up in a quilt against the cold.

"You can hardly tell. First one?" the woman said.

Rosaline smiled. "Due in May," she replied. "I hope you don't mind," she continued, waving toward Trevor.

"What a beautiful, perfect child," he said, "what incredibly blue eyes."

"His father's," the woman said. "He takes after Daddy in every way." She pushed the stroller back and forth.

"Eight months old?" Trevor asked.

"Six. Big for his age."

Trevor batted the keys with his index finger and resumed his nonsense talk. Rosaline rolled her eyes.

The woman giggled. "They all get this way the first time around. When I was pregnant with the first one my husband turned to total mush every time he was around kids. Just passing by window displays of kids' clothing, he melted into a puddle. Just wait till after the baby's born. Then you'll really see it."

"See what?" Rosaline said.

"It's like you don't even exist," the mother said. Trevor stood up and took Rosaline's arm. "It's like you don't exist at all," the woman said, giving Rosaline a sad smile before she pushed on past them.

"That was a pretty baby," Rosaline said as they walked on down the avenue.

"Ours will be prettier. And smarter. And bigger. And better. And richer of course."

Rosaline leaned her head against his shoulder. "Super Baby," she sighed.

"It's in the genes," Trevor said, pausing in front of a window filled with tiny antique silver picture frames. "We can't fail. What about those?"

"Cute," Rosaline said. "We could pick up one for everybody. They're so small. What would people put in them?"

Trevor held open the door and waved her inside. "Baby pictures of course. They're perfect for baby pictures."

"Any particular baby you had in mind?" Inside the store the saleswoman interrupted a conversation with another customer and walked toward Trevor. He always got immediate and courteous service, even in stores during the height of the Christmas rush or in restaurants where others waited endlessly for tables. Rosaline was amazed at how taxis seemed to materialize out of nowhere whenever Trevor stepped off the curb and how even in the most crowded airports skycaps appeared magically at their side to whisk their luggage out the door.

"I'm going to be one of those total bores who takes a million baby pictures and insists on showing them to everyone he meets," he said. "Would it be too terribly vulgar to buy one of those new video cameras? I hear they're really easy to use."

"Darling, get a grip on yourself," Rosaline said, pointing out frames to the saleswoman, who wrapped each one in a dozen layers of white tissue paper.

"I've totally lost control, haven't I," he said. "It's only going to get worse, you know."

"I know, sweetheart, I know," she whispered as he laid his credit card on the counter. They never bothered to call in his card number for authorization, she had noticed.

"I think I've decided how many children we should have," he said when they were back on the street.

"That's nice," she said. "When do I find out?"

"Try to guess. A number between one and a million."

"Four?" she ventured. Two boys and two girls, she thought, in no particular order.

"Close," he said. "Four hundred. I think it can be done. We're lucky to be starting early."

She giggled and squeezed his hand. "I think you're overestimating my capabilities," she said.

"Not at all, not at all," he said, making a mock frown. "You can do anything you set your mind to. And if you have twins it will only be two hundred times around the track."

"And if I have triplets?"

"One hundred thirty-three and a third pregnancies," he said. "The last one would only have to be for three months."

"That means I'd be pregnant for—how long? What's the arithmetic?"

"Nine hundred months and three hundred months—twelve hundred months all together," he replied.

"I'd be pregnant for a hundred years. A full century."

"I guess that sounds rather awful," he said. "Maybe I'll have to reevaluate my projections."

"No, not at all," she said, smiling up into his face. "It sounds absolutely wonderful. As absolutely wonderful as can be."

It filled her with a perfect pleasure, walking down the narrow sidewalk with her handsome husband. She curled her toes against the thick fleece that lined her new winter boots, bought a size too large in case her feet swelled up, as she had been told they would. But none of the horrible things she'd been warned about had happened: she hadn't been sick or tired or bloated, and though she still had months to go, she felt confident that she would sail through her pregnancy like a sturdy little boat across a smooth lake on a sunny day.

She and Trevor had gone to dinner with another couple last week —the husband worked at Trevor's firm and the wife, on leave from an auction gallery, had just had her second child. After the meal Philip took Trevor into the basement of the brownstone to show him the climate-controlled wine cellar he'd had built, and Grace led Rosaline upstairs to see if she had any maternity clothes Rosaline might want to borrow.

Rosaline reckoned that in the past several months she had spent more time with Grace than with any other woman close to her age and yet she couldn't believe she would ever truly consider Grace her friend. Grace was like Maria (whose husband had gone to prep school with Trevor) or like Rachel (who lived with Trevor's fishing companion, an architect who specialized in renovating country estates) or like Sylvie (who had married Trevor's favorite cousin and best man, an attorney who had devoted the last five years of his life to a single lawsuit against the company that had invented instant cameras): she was generous and loyal and could always be counted on to keep a secret or do a last-minute favor, but there was still this unspoken understanding that the friendship would have been extended to whomever Trevor had chosen to be his wife.

Sometimes Rosaline felt that she was standing in a maze of interconnecting tunnels that these men had built during years of schooling and fishing and hunting and dating and traveling and working together. The bouquet of fresh herbs that Grace sent over after a weekend at their farm in Connecticut; the family gossip that Sylvie punctuated with sarcasms said with a giggle in French; the party invitations that Maria mailed coded either "AMA" (Absolute Must Attend), "IBNE" (Interesting But Not Essential), or "GCBP" (Good Cause, Boring People); the weekday evening openings that Rachel brought her to, careful to point out which artists' works were likely to appreciate short-term—it was as if all these offerings reached Rosaline only after traveling through these tunnels of male bonding.

They were all wonderful women. Trevor had occasionally expressed a personal pride in how well he and his friends had chosen their mates, as though marriage were a collective class endeavor and each individual decision reflected on the whole. But by the time things reached Rosaline, curving here for a summer the men had spent together in Europe, twisting there for a drunken binge the week after college graduation, the warmth of friendship had dissipated, been lost to the cool air like a fine meal wheeled through the hallways of a drafty old hotel.

Perhaps it would have been nice to have a sister. Maybe now that

Katie Lee was back in New York they could spend more time to-gether. Rosaline made a mental note to bring Katie Lee to a party for the new wing at the hospital next week; Katie Lee never turned down an invitation to a benefit, and they needed an extra woman at the table.

They passed a shop window filled with handmade Scandinavian sweaters. I should pick one up for Marinda, Rosaline thought, I haven't seen her in weeks. She knew Marinda had been spending more and more time with December, and she felt Marinda to be shifting away from her somehow. A month ago she would have bought the sweater without a second thought, but now the purchase seemed complicated with hidden meanings that Rosaline did not care to examine. Trevor discouraged her from spending too much money on her friends—they would feel awkward or guilty or inade-quate, he had said, if she gave them expensive gifts when they were in no position to reciprocate.

It hadn't been that way in college, Rosaline had tried to argue, telling Trevor that they'd never kept track of who picked up checks in restaurants or paid for the long distance telephone calls. Anyway, Marinda had plenty of money. And everyone knew how crazy the first year of law school was; it was selfish of Rosaline only to think of herself when Marinda was under so much pressure.

A Valentine's Day dinner, that would be the thing. Their apartment was nearly finished. Trevor had been saying that it was time for them to entertain at home, to return some of the invitations they owed before things got too hectic with the baby. Rosaline could picture a perfect row of place settings, a single red rose in a slender crystal vase in front of each plate, and the English china she'd gotten with roses painted around the rim, and for party favors monogrammed lace handkerchiefs for the women and something silly—red silk bow ties?—for the men. Grace and Philip, Sylvie and George, Rachel and Richard, Maria and Lewis. And Katie Lee. And Marinda, and she could ask Marinda to bring Bobby and Carter. Bobby had dated Lewis' younger sister years ago, and Carter knew Rachel from a couple of summers on Long Island.

Being pregnant had filled her with a maternal benevolence. She felt herself possessed of unusual and temporary powers: the power to pic-ture her friends as children, years before she'd met them; the power to comprehend the emotions, if not the entire life histories, of the people she barely knew; the power to see the goodness in everyone, for hadn't everyone once been a child, innocent and loving, as sweet and helpless as the child she was carrying now?

Pregnancy was her drug, and its hallucinogenic vision was forgiveness. Of her father, for his alcoholism, which was medically proven to be an actual incurable disease. Of her mother, who was one link in a long chain that would continue through Rosaline and her children, a chain of daughters turning into mothers.

She passed a bag lady screaming into a parking meter and forgave her for whatever wrong turn she had taken, and then she forgave whatever errant husband or unloving family had sent her out into the street. She forgave the president for underestimating the deviousness of various foreign governments; he was a good and thoughtful man facing difficult times. She forgave the nun who had been especially strict with her in Switzerland; she had been a misguided and troubled woman who believed herself to be acting in Rosaline's best interests.

She forgave Katie Lee her greed and ambition; it was not fair for Rosaline, brought up in the security of privilege, to judge those who had done without. She forgave Marinda her bitterness; Marinda was hard on people, but she was even harder on herself, and what had happened with Peter had been so very awful. She even forgave Schuyler—he had been young and foolish, just as she had been so young and foolish to believe herself truly in love with him. Perhaps in some strange way he'd been testing her love for him, to see if it would survive, if it was strong enough to bend under the weight of that night with December. Instead it had just snapped in two, like the fragile twig it was. Besides, if she hadn't broken off with Schuyler she might never have gotten together with Trevor, she might never have arrived at this precise and wonderful moment in her life at all.

And then, turning a corner and walking down a street lined with sycamores, the delicate branches twined with hundreds of tiny white Christmas lights, she forgave December. Who was beautiful, a free spirit, a strange and wonderful gift of a girl, set apart somehow from the rest of them. Rosaline believed herself in possession of a special secret, one she and December shared. The secret was this: that goodness was absolute—either one tries all the time or one doesn't bother at all. Goodness was a constant pursuit, it was both draining and exhilarating, like running a marathon or dancing in a ballet. It took everything from you and gave everything back.

Rosaline felt thin sheets of ice collapse with each step she took as Trevor instinctively tightened his hold on her elbow. That was it, that was it, she thought, watching her breath puff out into the cold night air, and December knew it too, knew it every time she'd made the choice not to be good. December's beauty was her shield, her protection, like the special powers the gods granted to the Greek warriors they would send into the worst of the battle.

Rosaline would find a way to make it up with December, and with Schuyler, and she'd find a way to make sure Marinda didn't slip away. People are so precious, she thought, so fragile, so easily hurt. You could give all the love you had to your baby and still it might not be enough. So many things happened. People got damaged young—look at Joseph, look at Charlotte—and they might never set themselves right. She wanted to share all this with Trevor but couldn't find the words.

But Trevor is good without even thinking about it, she was sure of that, as they turned under the wide gray canopy of their building and nodded to the two sets of doormen who were changing shifts. The tree in the lobby was decorated with glass ornaments that Rosaline remembered from her childhood, when her head barely reached the lowermost branches. Here nothing changed from year to year, and why should things ever change, Rosaline thought. She couldn't think of a single reason why they would.

Rosaline watched the rum swirl down into the rich eggnog as her mother twisted the sterling serving spoon with a firm hand. The dinner guests (Charlotte's cousins down from Connecticut for the holidays, Joseph's widower brother and his three sons on vacation from prep school in New Hampshire, Trevor's younger sister and her Argentinian boyfriend) would be arriving at eight. Joseph had asked Trevor into the library to tell him one of the family lawyers would be calling him next week concerning financial arrangements for their unborn child. Conversations about family money never took place in mixed company. While Joseph outlined briefly why certain papers needed to be signed prior to the birth (leaving the actual details to the lawyers, who had known each other for years and had initially discussed provisions for Rosaline and Trevor's children in the weeks after their engagement was announced), Charlotte reviewed the situation with her daughter.

"So the only thing you have to keep in mind, really, is that the child gets a lump sum from the Goodwood Trust when he or she is eighteen but has to wait for the Van Schott funds until the earlier of his twenty-fifth birthday or his wedding day," Charlotte said, sprinkling nutmeg across the bowl. Trevor had repeated to Rosaline the gossip that Charlotte had delayed her wedding to Joseph until after his twenty-fifth birthday in order to prevent any rumors that Joseph was marrying simply to gain control of the several millions that became his as the oldest of three brothers. There were all sorts of stories about her parents that Rosaline, sequestered in Switzerland, had never heard until she met Trevor, or rather, until after she and Trevor were engaged.

For example, her father's drinking, which Rosaline had always assumed to be her private shame, was a matter of public record. One August, when Blue Smoke yearlings were fetching record prices at auction, he had embarked on a four-day binge during which he sent bottles of champagne to every box in the clubhouse. When the yearlings he'd sold reached the racetrack the next year as two-year-olds, among them was a filly named Bringonthebubbly and a colt by Northern Dancer out of Hat Shop named Lampshade. Charlotte had pretended not to notice.

He'd been pretty good recently, which Charlotte ascribed to the winding down of late middle age and Trevor credited to the calming joy of impending grandfatherhood. Only Rosaline was nervous. She believed her father was drinking heavily on the sly. He had spent two weeks in Paris earlier in December, supposedly on business, but Rosaline suspected the real reason was so that he could do some old-fashioned acting up away from Charlotte's disapproving eye.

"It's still more money than anyone could ever figure out how to spend in one lifetime," Rosaline said, looking at the single cup of eggnog that had been set aside for her before the rum was added. She hadn't truly realized how much money she had until the last few months, when Charlotte had taken her around to antique dealers and decorator showrooms in the hope that Rosaline would be able to get her apartment organized before the baby was born. Rosaline couldn't believe that one little chair could cost three thousand dollars; Charlotte merely shook her head, requested again that Rosaline not discuss prices in front of the sales help—that's what decorators were for—and explained why furniture by this particular maker was so expensive. It had something to do with a war in a European province (though Charlotte couldn't remember exactly which war or precisely which province—something that may have been part of Germany or Austria once, it was so hard to keep track).

In the end Rosaline's apartment looked remarkably similar to her mother's—the same dark, delicate furniture covered in velvets and tapestries, arranged over faded patterned carpets. It was as if one had simply substituted another color scheme, with Charlotte's peaches and greens giving way to the dull roses and deep golds that Trevor preferred. Rosaline had done only one room entirely on her own. Trevor called it her dayroom, but she liked to think of it as her office, though she had no idea as yet just what she would be doing there, among the Impressionist paintings and French Provincial furniture that she found romantic but her mother thought a little vulgar, suitable only for a room that no one would see except Rosaline herself.

"And what does Dr. Alsop have to say?" Charlotte asked, Dr. Alsop being the senior associate of Rosaline's obstetrician and the man who had overseen Charlotte's heavily anesthetized delivery.

"Well, I hardly ever see him," Rosaline said. "But Dr. Larkin says I'm doing just fine. We finally talked him into letting Trevor into the delivery room."

"A disgusting idea," Charlotte said. "Fashionable but disgusting. I can't imagine why you'd want your husband to see you—to see you in such a state."

"Trevor wants to be there. I think it's kind of nice. It's sort of scary, but it won't be so scary if he's there. I hope."

"Sweetie, you really ought to give some more thought to this. They give you this shot that makes you feel absolutely lovely, and then afterwards you don't remember a thing. I wouldn't have done it any other way. I don't know what it is you and Trevor are trying to prove."

"It's better for the baby, Mother," Rosaline said, her voice weakening the way it always did when Charlotte questioned her. "Trevor can explain it to you better," she said as the men came into the dining room to join them.

"Explain what?" Trevor asked, putting his arm around where his wife's waist used to be.

"It doesn't matter," Charlotte replied, believing childbirth to be the least appropriate topic of conversation between a menopausal former debutante and her handsome son-in-law.

"Well, I've got an announcement to make," Joseph said, ladling out eggnog for Charlotte and Trevor. "A Christmas present for all of us. Before the guests arrive."

"Darling," Charlotte said, "I hope this isn't another one of your dramatic gestures."

"It is, it is. I shall give you a hint," he said, and then he stood silently, staring into his cup, trying to think of a hint. "Did you remember the rum, darling?" he asked. "This smells just like vanilla ice cream."

"Yes, darling, there's plenty of rum," Charlotte said.

"Did you bring something back from France?" Trevor asked.

"Yes. That was my first hint."

"A painting?" Rosaline asked. "It's a painting."

"No, not a painting," Joseph said. "Let me think of another clue."

"Is it bigger than a bread box?" Trevor asked.

"Just how big is a bread box?" Rosaline said.

"I have no idea," Trevor said. "I suppose it depends on how big the bread is. Do people still use bread boxes?"

"There are two in your kitchen," Charlotte said, having supervised the purchase and installation of their appliances, equipment, and custom oak cabinets, "next to the refrigerator."

"Trevor never goes into the kitchen," Rosaline said, giggling.

"I'd just be in the way," he said. "I know all about refrigerators, though. That's where the ice and limes are. So, is it bigger than a refrigerator?"

"Well, now," Joseph said, refilling his glass, "it certainly is. Very big."

"Exactly how big," Charlotte said. "Would you measure it in inches, yards, or—goodness, you wouldn't measure it in acres, would you?"

"You would measure it in hands," Joseph said.

"A horse!" Rosaline cried. "A mare?" she ventured. Blue Smoke was noted for its broodmare band, which year after year yielded nicely pedigreed foals that fetched handsome prices at auction. Racing thoroughbreds was an expensive and glamorous endeavor; in less than two minutes a horse could carry your name and colors across the finish line and on to the winner's circle. Standing stallions involved an all-your-eggs-in-one-basket gamble that could pay huge dividends over the years, if your horse sired a champion or two. But Blue Smoke's reputation had been built on its cautious and well-researched acquisition of prime mares; beginning with Joseph's grandfather, each successive master of Blue Smoke had made his first priority maintaining the high standards of their breeding stock.

Out of each year's crop the best fillies were kept for future breeding purposes, and a handful of colts were kept for their racing potential, but the majority of the foals were sold at auction, with the proceeds reinvested in the farm itself and in the purchase of new mares, often from England or France. In the past few years Joseph had occasionally bought a share of a syndicated stallion, but for the most part he had continued the thoughtful if unexciting program set down generations before. No Blue Smoke horse had ever won the Kentucky Derby, the Preakness, or the Belmont. Indeed, it had been years since Joseph had even won a graded stakes race. But the offspring of Blue Smoke mares had won nearly every important race in the United States and abroad, and both Rosaline and Trevor could recite the bloodlines of Joseph's mares several generations back, for it would eventually be their duty to carry on with the carefulness and conservatism that had made Blue Smoke what it was.

"Not a mare. I've bought Agamemnon," Joseph said, giving his wife a tight smile.

Rosaline gasped and grabbed her husband's elbow. It seemed unbelievable. That fall Agamemnon had become the most famous, or rather infamous, colt in France. His owners, whose principal fortune derived from their family vineyards, had touted him as the fastest horse of the decade. Before he had run his first race, even before his first public workout, his name had been whispered by those who knew as the heir apparent to Northern Dancer, the most successful and valuable stallion of all time. His breeding was impeccable. His confirmation was perfect. His running style, even as an inexperienced two-year-old, was smooth and flawless.

His owners had kept him close by on their farm and scheduled unannounced workouts at dawn, seen only by the horse's trainer, owner, groom, and various stable hands, all of whom were sworn to secrecy as to the exact times the horse ran. The owners rejected several handsome offers to buy part interests in the horse, including one from a Greek shipping magnate who was said to have brought five million dollars in cash packed in matching Vuitton luggage.

Finally his owners announced that Agamemnon would make his racing debut—not in an easy maiden race or in a minor stakes but in what was considered the toughest race in Europe: the Arc de Triomphe. It was the equivalent of entering an unraced horse in the Kentucky Derby—an unprecedented and even foolish move but one so utterly confident and dramatic that when the racing world converged in Paris that October it was with the strong sense that they were about to see history being made.

And it was. Agamemnon broke well and was kept back along the rail, his energies conserved for the final difficult stretch drive. The crowd, many of whom had wagered heavily on him with the hope that they would be able to tell their grandchildren that they had cashed a ticket on the race of the century, cheered loudly when he began to make his move toward the front of the pack. And then Agamemnon simply gave up, despite the heavy whipping of his rider, and the cheers of the crowd turned first to angry hooting and then to wild laughter. The race of the century had turned into the joke of the century. Agamemnon finished last, and his owners shipped him back to the farm in the middle of the night to avoid the humiliating inquiries of the press.

The next day it was announced that Agamemnon had suffered a mysterious injury and would be retired to stud. He was, after all, a son of Northern Dancer and therefore valuable no matter what his racing record. The owners said they were entertaining offers to syndicate the colt, but no deals ever materialized. The Greek, his mistress, and his suitcases filled with carefully counted green were driven south to a waiting yacht. The British tabloids turned their attention to the romantic follies of a young prince. The owners returned their attention to the family vineyards, which they said were in better shape than ever.

Rosaline felt her knees grow weak, and Trevor helped her into a chair. It was more than unbelievable, it was scandalous. Agamemnon had no value as a racehorse, and his bloodlines were so close to those of the Blue Smoke stock that she couldn't think of more than three or four mares they could possibly breed him to. Joseph had violated the entire premise upon which the Blue Smoke fortune had been built.

"How much did you pay," Charlotte asked, fingering her wedding band. "It couldn't have been much, considering the circumstances."

Rosaline did a quick calculation in her head as to what Agamemnon might be worth. Three hundred thousand dollars, maybe three fifty at most. It would be a full-time job getting him bred to the right mares, convincing other breeders to take a chance with this unproven, untested colt. The top mares would still go to Northern Dancer or to his champion son Nijinsky. A stallion was only as good as the mares he was bred to: that was something her father had taught her at an early age, something he had told her never to forget. Still, if they could get Agamemnon to some decent mares this spring, and if the foals turned out nicely and brought respectable prices at auction, three hundred thousand dollars could be a decent investment.

"Four million dollars," Joseph said, and Rosaline watched her mother's face grow pale and tense.

"But that's everything," Charlotte said in a whisper. "That's all our income for the year. It's impossible."

"Four million dollars," Joseph repeated. "The papers are all signed and the money was wired last night."

"All of it?" Trevor asked. Perhaps Joseph had arranged to pay out the money in installments. The Goodwood Trust was arranged in such a way as to prevent withdrawals against capital; if Joseph had indeed wired four million dollars to France, he and Charlotte wouldn't even be able to pay their electricity bills until the next annual income check arrived on the first of July. "I don't quite understand," Trevor said, fearing the worst.

"I understand perfectly," Charlotte said. "You were drunk. You must have been drunk. Four million dollars is nearly every available cent we have."

"Don't be a spoilsport, sweetheart," Joseph said. He was beginning to break out in a sweat. Things weren't going at all the way he'd imagined. "We can live conservatively for a few months, it's only until next July. Trevor can spot us if necessary," he said, turning to his son-in-law.

"Of course we can," Rosaline said. "But four million dollars. It's so much money. All at once."

"Nothing ventured, nothing gained," Joseph said. "Isn't that how the saying goes?"

"A fool and his money," Charlotte said, "that's how the saying goes. Who else knows about this?"

"Everyone will know soon enough," Trevor said.

"They'll be laughing at us," Charlotte said. "You rotten, filthy drunk. You've blown everything on a horse that can't run. Well, I won't let you get away with it. I'll stop this somehow. I won't have people laughing at me. I won't have people laughing at my family." She turned and left the room.

"My loving, supportive helpmeet," Joseph said, wiping his sweaty brow. "Rosie, love, I know you know I did the right thing?" he said, imploring more than asking.

"It's just a lot to absorb right now," she said.

"Oh, but you'll see," Joseph said. "Everyone will see. When Agamemnon's colts start to run, then everyone will see. History will prove me right. They may laugh at first, but in a few years they'll be lining up at our front door."

There was a soft chime from the front hallway, as if Joseph had commanded right then and there a heavenly intervention to prove him right. He needed nothing less right now, so monstrous was his folly.

"I'll see who it is," Trevor said, wondering how they were going to get through the elaborate Christmas Eve dinner Charlotte had arranged. Rosaline was left alone with her father, who sat down next to her and held her hands in his.

"Rosie, love, I know I can count on you," he said, his speech slurred by alcohol. Though she hadn't been sick in the months since she conceived, she felt the room growing warm and stuffy, and her stomach began to turn. He smells like a drunk, she said to herself. He smells like he's dying.

"Tell me I did the right thing," he said, releasing her hands, leaning his head on the table. His hair had thinned so—when had that started to happen, why hadn't she noticed—and the skin of his neck fell in folds over his shirt collar. In the last few minutes he seemed to have crossed some line, the line between middle and old age. She could barely hear him speak. She held him by the shoulders and felt him begin to sob.

"You did the right thing," she whispered into his ear.

"Your mother hates me for this. She's always hated me."

"Oh, no, she loves you very much. We all love you. You have to pull yourself together now. We've got guests in the living room." Rosaline stroked his hair, and strands of silver came away between her fingers.

"We can pull it off, you and I," Joseph said. "They'll never say it again if you help me."

"Say what, Father?" Rosaline asked, leaning her head on his shoulder.

"What they said in the papers. In England. They read it to me over the phone this morning. Poor Charlotte. She hates to be talked about like this."

"What did they say?"

He murmured something she could not make out and seemed to be falling asleep. She shook him softly, and he stirred and smiled up into her face, the dumb trusting smile of a young child or an animal that doesn't know it's about to be hit, and she saw how his gums were receding from his teeth, and how his skin was spotted with age.

"Blue Joke Farm," he said, and he passed out in her arms, his chest collapsing against the edge of the table, the embroidered linen table-cloth stained with his sweat, and the scent of his drunkenness filling her with a dread and a nausea unlike anything she had been warned of, unlike anything she had read about, a terror and a sickness that had no remedy.

13

*K*atie Lee unpacked the bags she'd brought back from her Christmas visit to Lexington as Rosaline paced in front of the bedroom bookshelves, curling her hands into little fists whenever she reached a particularly dramatic point in her story. She tossed her soiled clothes into two piles: a small one, to be picked up by the Chinese launderer down the block on Second Avenue, and a larger one, to be picked up by the dry cleaners around the corner. She returned her unused clothing to the two bedroom closets, the set of drawers in the dresser that matched her antique carved four poster bed, or the large Victorian armoire she'd bought in North Carolina (there was no such thing, she had learned, as a New York apartment with sufficient closet space). Nearly everything she'd brought back had been untouched during her week-long trip home for the holidays; as usual Katie Lee had packed four times what she would need, bringing all sorts of "just in case" items—two long satin dresses, a heavy tweed suit, high-heeled suede boots, a few silk day dresses, a couple of cashmere sweaters, a new pair of sneakers, an extra pair of jeans, there was simply no way to predict the last-minute invitations that might arrive during her visit—and some of them would be sent to the dry cleaners anyway, to be properly pressed.

"So my mother called the lawyers on Christmas day, if you can believe it, she couldn't waste a second. When she telephoned Davis —she actually called him at his *mother's* house in Greenwich—he was in the middle of carving the turkey, and of course he just dropped everything and came back to the city to meet with Mother. On Christmas, Katie Lee, while we were all opening presents and stuffing ourselves silly, she's on the telephone scheming and—my goodness, you packed all that just for one week?" Rosaline asked, waving at the clothing piled on Katie Lee's bed. A red silk polka dot dress, its

178

sleeves stuffed with tissue paper and propped up against the pillows, looked as if it might wave back.

"Oh no," Katie Lee said, picking up a velvet skirt that she was sure Rosaline had never seen before. "I had all this stuff in storage in Lexington and I thought this would be a good time to bring some of it up here. Though where I'll find the room for it, who can say. I thought about getting another armoire, but I don't know where I'd put that either."

"You should put your out-of-season things in storage. It's all insured, you know," Rosaline said.

"That's an idea," Katie Lee said, not wanting Rosaline to know that half her clothing already was in storage. The tenant next door was giving up the lease on her studio; Katie Lee had considered renting the apartment, for nearly six hundred dollars a month, simply to have a place for all her clothes.

"So what is it exactly that they want you sign, honey?" Katie Lee asked.

"Apparently there's a provision in the trust having to do with incompetence. Everything my father now has control of will get divided up, with people supposedly acting on his behalf. My mother will get control of the annual income and will make the day-to-day decisions about the apartments and the houses and things like that. Then they want to appoint Trevor to sit in for my father at board meetings about long-range planning and investments. That part makes sense at least—Trevor's so smart about these things, I know he'll do the right thing." Rosaline sipped the tea Katie Lee had prepared for her; it had grown cold, and flecks of pale brown leaves had settled at the bottom of the cup.

"Then there are the charitable foundations, which my uncles have been involved with all along, so they'll probably appoint one of their wives, which is fine, really, we all pretty much agree on what the right causes are. My father will get some kind of allowance, which for the first year or so will go toward covering the expenses at this— they call it a farm."

"Somehow I don't get the impression he'll be planting corn and milking cows," Katie Lee said.

"He'll be drinking vitamin-rich fruit shakes and reading murder mysteries up in New Hampshire. I've been told they have an excellent counseling program, hardly anyone goes back to drinking once they get out, but really the whole point is to hide the embarrassing family member from the inquisitive public. They don't even have telephones in the rooms. It's awful."

"So what does your father's lawyer say?" Katie Lee said, pressing a blue velvet evening jacket to her face and breathing in. Though perfectly clean, it stank of cigarette smoke and was tossed on the heap for dry cleaning. "This isn't actually going to get to court or anything, is it?"

"Oh, no, Trevor would never let that happen. This is the strange thing: Davis *is* my father's lawyer. He's represented the Van Schotts for years. That's a great color blue, what would you call it? It's too dark for royal blue, isn't it. My mother's somehow managed to get everyone on her side, and my father's in no shape to fight back or try to find himself a good lawyer. I suppose I could find a lawyer for him. Maybe Marinda would know of someone." Rosaline picked the jacket off the floor and began smoothing the nap all in one direction.

"Cobalt or ultramarine, there's some painterly name for it. There's a crayon name too, but I can't remember. Don't even bother about the lawyer," Katie Lee said. Though Rosaline's hands were perfectly clean and the jacket was destined for the cleaners, it still bothered her somehow, seeing her friend handle her clothing in just this intimate way. She had to stop herself from snatching the jacket out of Rosaline's fingers. "If Davis is preparing the papers, your father hasn't got a chance."

"There are lots of good lawyers, Katie Lee," Rosaline said. "I never had that kind of crayon, the ones everyone else had. December once made some joke about goldenrod and carnation pink, and I had no idea what she was talking about."

"Look at it from Davis' point of view," Katie Lee began. "Your father's been his client for years. The Van Schott account is worth big bucks to his firm. Your mother calls him, outlines the situation, tells him what she wants to do, probably throws in a few horror stories about your father's past behavior just to let Davis know what kind of ammunition she's got." Katie Lee watched Rosaline draw stripes against the plush grain of the fabric.

"Let's pretend," she continued, "Davis hears all this, still thinks there's a chance Charlotte can't pull it off. If he backs up your father, she probably won't get her way. He's done his duty of protecting the precious Van Schott heirs from conniving and greedy wives." She watched as Rosaline smoothed the nap back in one direction. She hated when people touched her clothes. She never let Bobby undress her; she always slipped off to the bathroom, taking the time to hang up and fold her clothing before she reemerged in one of the three full-length dressing gowns she kept hanging on the back of the bathroom door.

"Clearly this is not what's going on," Katie Lee said, pacing back and forth like an impatient professor lecturing first year students. "So. Let's pretend Davis hears all this and realizes that Charlotte has a great case and it's just a matter of time before Joseph gets shipped off to dry out in the hills of New Hampshire. Davis is a businessman. He wants to keep your family as a client. So he sides with Charlotte and probably talks your uncles into doing the same. For the sake of the family of course. The 'We want to avoid publicity' speech, with some 'Let's stand together as a family' and 'for the good of the Van Schott name' thrown in. Your father doesn't have a chance."

"I hadn't thought of it that way," Rosaline said.

Of course not, Katie Lee said to herself, you've never had to think about anything at all in your entire life. "So what do you get out of all this?" she asked.

"Well, if I sign everything, they offered me control of the farm and the stable."

"How generous of them, leaving you the Agamemnon mess to clean up."

"Trevor thinks it's too much for me, though, what with the baby and all. I won't have the time for it."

"Men are always doing that," Katie Lee said.

"Doing what?"

"Finding a way to take power from women and convincing them it's all in their best interests."

"Trevor isn't like that, Katie Lee."

"Of course he isn't. Listen, I've got to meet an architect at the hotel in about an hour. Why don't you come along, and then we can have lunch afterwards?"

"I'd love that," Rosaline said. "I'm sorry for ranting and raving so. I want to hear all about this glamorous new hotel you're building." She stood up and dropped the jacket to the floor.

"Midnight blue," Katie Lee said.

"What?"

"Midnight blue, that's the name of that particular crayon."

"Even though by midnight the sky is nearly black," Rosaline said. "Did they have a color named midnight black?"

"No, just plain black. That was the crayon that always broke first," Katie Lee said, unbolting the last of the three locks on her front door.

"And what broke second?" Rosaline asked.

Katie Lee had to think for a minute. Her crayons had always been replaced as soon as they wore down or broke. She could barely remember herself as a child, carefully shading in between the lines of the coloring books her father brought back after each business trip.

"I think it was red," she replied, and suddenly she pictured herself sitting in a particular spot on the carpeted floor of her playroom where the sun shone in the late afternoon, coloring in a flower or a wheelbarrow or an umbrella, waiting for her father to come home. The one that broke second was called rose red.

Rosaline adjusted the strap of the hard hat Katie Lee had lent her for this visit, a dome of clean white plastic that contrasted noticeably with the worn and dirty hats of the construction workers around her and marked her as a friend of the Hopewells. She felt awkward in the throng of muscled, sloppily dressed men who had stopped their conversations in mid-sentence when they saw Katie Lee approach.

"This will be the main ballroom," Katie Lee said, waving her arm to indicate the vast open space around them. "Future home to the very best parties in New York. We'll be able to section it off to accommodate smaller events, and the balconies can be closed off and used as temporary office areas."

For all that Rosaline had heard Katie Lee talk of her career over the past few years, she had never actually seen her at work. Rosaline suspected that Henry Hopewell had assigned his daughter to oversee the development of their first luxury hotel here in New York as some sort of punishment for her failure in Cambridge, but Katie Lee would never admit to either punishment or failure. The New York project was her reward for showing such strong interest and initiative in the family business; the Cambridge project hadn't failed, really, it had just been a matter of being in the right place at the wrong time. Katie Lee still owned her property in Cambridge, and eventually things would change. There'd be a new mayor or a tax deficit that needed to be made up by commercial revenues. Though she'd lost a great deal of money and had been humiliated in the press, Katie Lee seemed to Rosaline to be physically incapable of admitting defeat. She was like the general manager of a baseball team ten games out of first place with only eleven games left in the season. There was still the possibility of victory, and where there was hope there was pride.

Now Rosaline was facing that pride as if for the very first time, as Katie Lee explained exactly where she would hang the crystal chandeliers they'd special-ordered from Ireland, and how food would arrive on a hermetically sealed, fiberglass insulated, electronically operated unmanned elevator from the kitchens in the basements, and why a specific synthetic fabric, when stapled across the walls, would provide the optimum acoustic environment for the kind of small brassy orchestras that were usually hired for fund-raising events.

"Do you mind if I sit down for a minute," Rosaline asked, though there wasn't a chair in sight. Katie Lee spread a dropcloth over a small steel drum and motioned for Rosaline to sit.

"Are you tired?" she asked. "We can do this some other time."

"Oh, no," Rosaline lied. "It's just that my feet doth protest too much."

"Well. You see the first few parties are the most important, because they establish the tone of the hotel. The very first party, the one for the opening, that's the one that's really key. If we can get some traditional high profile charity to hook up with us for a benefit, we'll get the kind of publicity you just can't buy, and then everyone else will follow suit. We're talking cancer or heart disease, you know, something fatal and expensive," Katie Lee continued. "Publicity is so important. We've got to be the right kind of hotel—"

"—for the right kind of people," Rosaline finished for her. "You should ask my mother about it."

Katie Lee winked and flashed a centimeter of a smile. "I already have, sweet pea. I didn't think you'd mind."

"Oh no, of course not. I'm sure she was flattered."

That woman is incapable of being flattered, Katie Lee thought, because even the most exaggerated praise could not approximate Charlotte's own vision of her ultimate importance on the New York social scene. "She had some excellent suggestions," Katie Lee said. "And the next week I got five invitations to fund-raising luncheons. You know, you have to give to everybody's pet charity before they'll even consider giving to yours."

"I'm sure they're all great causes," Rosaline said. She was sure that Katie Lee would accept each and every invitation.

"If you installed a library for unwed girl scout decorators in the Bronx Zoo you'd be covering all the bases. I think I'm on every list in New York now. But it's all in the budget."

"You budgeted for parties?" Rosaline asked.

"Of course, sweetie. I'm representing the family interests here in New York now, and I've got to do it in a very special way. Did you catch me in the tabloids last week?" she asked.

"I've hardly any time for the newspapers anymore," Rosaline said, wondering if Katie Lee had retained a public relations firm to get her name and picture in the very pages, the ones filled with news of beauty pageant runners-up and weight lifters and aging television actors, that the well-established families tried so hard to avoid.

"Oh, I'll send you the clip," Katie Lee cooed. "I was the second item, right after the kitty litter heiress who wrote the exercise book. It was about how the cleaners accidentally switched my stuff and Mimi Taylor's—we have the exact same Chanel suit except mine's one size smaller—so I thought I'd lost all this weight, and she thought she'd bulked out nearly overnight. She actually made reservations for the Maine Chance before it all got straightened out."

Perhaps Katie Lee doesn't have a publicist, Rosaline thought. The story could have been called in by Mimi Taylor (her husband was thinking of running for Congress) or by the people at the spa or even by the dry cleaners. Even publicists have publicists now, she had heard one of Trevor's friends joking last week at dinner.

"Let's go see a typical room," Katie Lee said, and Rosaline followed her up to the twentieth floor, where the view to the east included the Brooklyn Bridge, and to the west took in Central Park. As Katie Lee reeled off million-dollar figures and five-year occupancy projections, Rosaline felt herself dwindling like Alice in Wonderland, and the baby inside her shrink to the size of a garden flower, so small were her ambitions next to those of her friend.

What makes some people want to go out and conquer the world, Rosaline wondered, and what makes the rest of us sit by the fire, contentedly knitting baby clothes and needlepointing pillows? Sitting at home with Trevor, with dinner finished and a favorite Dickens novel open on her lap, she felt raising a family to be the happiest and most fulfilling endeavor she would ever know. But now, standing on the swirled concrete floor with the rooftops of New York facing her at eye level, she questioned if that would really be enough. It didn't seem to be for any of her friends, for any other women her age.

"I'm a woman obsessed," Katie Lee said. "I'll talk your little ear off if you let me. So we never really finished—I mean, just what are you going to do about your father?"

"Oh, it's too nice out to think about that," Rosaline said. "I'll think about it tomorrow."

"Oh *please*, that's my most unfavorite saying in the whole wide world," Katie Lee said. "I promise you in real life Scarlett O'Hara never did any such thing or she never would have gotten so rich and had all those men swooning after her."

Rosaline smiled. How like Katie Lee to think that somehow Scarlett O'Hara had existed in real life.

"You're going to take over Blue Smoke," Katie Lee continued, "I just know you are. Because you can do a better job than anyone of bringing it around. Better than Trevor even, if you'll forgive me a little Baptist blasphemy."

"It's so much work," Rosaline protested. "It may be beyond rescue."

"No such thing as a project beyond rescue, honey," Katie Lee said. "If you've got all these incredible superstar mares hanging around, how can it be beyond rescue?"

"Because none of them has got exactly the right pedigree to breed to Agamemnon. If they did, we could just keep Agamemnon on the farm and breed him to our own mares and sell or race the offspring. But Agamemnon is too closely related to most of our stock. We can send him to two or three mares at most, and at his age a colt can be bred about fifty times a year. Anyway, it's too late for this year, they start breeding next month and continue through June. Everything's already planned in advance. Some mares are booked for years ahead."

"They are?" Katie Lee's eyes widened. "Just how far in advance?"

"It depends. Sometimes people will make these complicated deals —for example, they'll agree to send a mare to a specific stallion for two years in a row, and whoever owns the mare gets the offspring one year, and whoever owns the stallion gets the offspring the next. We don't do too much of that, though, we like to see what happens from year to year and keep our options open. In case a stallion suddenly gets hot, for example."

"So your mares are booked for this year, but they're free after that?"

"For the most part," Rosaline replied.

"Well, honey, your problems are solved. Honestly, it's so obvious."

"It is?" Rosaline asked.

"Well, I don't know chopsticks about horses, really, but it seems to me you could make some terrific deals if you've got all these great mares sitting around."

"Horses don't sit."

"Whatever. Listen. What if you took your very best mare and offered her services three years in a row to whoever wanted her?"

"You can't really do that. A mare's value depends on the quality of her foals, which in turn depends on which stallion she's bred to."

"Oh, *please* try to be just a little bit more open-minded. Just because things have been done a certain way for the last zillion years doesn't mean you can't make a change or two. Or three. Or four. Just pretend for a minute. You've got your best mare, and you'll promise her to anyone for the next three seasons after this—1978, 1979, and 1980. What can you ask in return?"

Rosaline giggled. "The indentured service of first male sons. Just about anything I want. I'd be giving away the store."

"So you could ask, in exchange for these three seasons you're giving away, just one itty-bitty season, just 1978, with someone else's top mare? And breed her to Agamemnon?"

"I suppose."

"So there's your solution. Agamemnon will go to the top mares in 1978, and if he's half as good as your father thought he was, he'll sire a great crop and his reputation will be established."

"But it doesn't work that way, Katie Lee. If Agamemnon stands in 1978, the foals will drop in 1979, be sold as yearlings in 1980—probably not for great prices, considering his reputation—and they won't reach the racetrack until 1981 or 1982. In the meantime we'll barely be making back our feed bills, with all our mares committed three years in a row."

"Oh, stop being so conservative, it's so incredibly boring. If you can't sell the yearlings at auction, keep them and race them yourself. Just because Blue Smoke hasn't hardly raced at all in the past doesn't mean you can't start now. Find yourself an enterprising young trainer—how hard can that be? So you won't make piles of money for a few years, isn't it worth the gamble? Unless, of course— No, I won't say it."

"Say what?"

"Unless you agree with what everyone's saying about your father. That Agamemnon will be worthless at stud. Then it wouldn't be a gamble, it would be suicide. But if you do agree with him it's not such a bad risk. Not such a bad risk at all."

"I appreciate your trying to help," Rosaline said with a sigh, "but I get tired even thinking about all this. It really would be a full-time job—it means going to Kentucky, calling in old favors, endless days on the telephone, hours in the office looking up bloodlines. I've got a baby to think about."

Katie Lee turned her back to Rosaline and looked out on Central Park. "Well, of course you do, honey. Forgive me. Of course your baby is the most important thing right now. You've just got to devote all your time to your child if you want it to grow up right. Twenty-four hours a day. Three hundred and sixty-five days a year. For the first five years at least."

Rosaline closed her eyes. The way Katie Lee said it, it sounded like a prison term. We hereby sentence you, Rosaline Van Schott Good-wood, as punishment for being old-fashioned and loving your husband too much, to five years of hard work and confinement in your newly decorated apartment. With two weekends off each year for good behavior. Early parole dependent on finding a top-notch nursery school within walking distance of your home.

Katie Lee turned and faced Rosaline, folding her arms across her chest. "I do want you to know how happy I am for you. Jealous, almost. Seeing you like this makes me want to get married next week and start having babies myself. Though I don't know when I'd find the time."

"Oh, you'll find the time. The time finds you."

"Who knows when, with all this work to do."

"You could get help," Rosaline said. "You can afford really marvelous help. These young English girls make excellent governesses, and they're terrifically loyal. You know what they say: it's not the quantity of time, it's the quality of the time you spend with your child that counts. And children can sense when you're happy and when you're unhappy. You'd be so frustrated staying at home with a baby, changing diapers, feeding it, listening to it cry. Honestly, they sleep so much at the beginning, they hardly know whether you're there or not. You'd be frustrated and unhappy, and your baby would probably pick up on it. It wouldn't be healthy."

"But you don't really believe that," Katie Lee said, poking a two-by-four with a kidskin toe.

"It's just not right for me," Rosaline said. It was another phrase, she realized, that she'd picked up from her husband. It's just not right for us, Trevor always said, about everything from living together before marriage to buying frozen food. But it's perfectly all right for *them*, was the unspoken condescending message, *them* being not—what was the other phrase she'd just used for the first time?—not *the right kind of people*. Trevor said the true importance of money was that it bought you freedom and choice, but it seemed to Rosaline that the richer one was, the more rules one had to follow, the less opportunity she had to do whatever it was she wanted.

"Well, anyway, this is a typical room for typical people," Katie said. "Do you want to go all the way to the top? See the view from the penthouse?"

"I'd love to," Rosaline said.

"Follow me." Katie Lee opened the door for Rosaline and brushed aside a braid of ropes hanging from the ceiling.

"Forty-nine, please," she told the elevator operator, who nodded immediately and punched the button marked 50. Rosaline raised her eyebrows at Katie Lee. "There's officially no thirteenth floor," Katie Lee explained, "because hotel guests are so superstitious. So we call the thirteenth construction floor the fourteenth, and the fourteenth construction floor becomes the fifteenth, and so on up."

"But couldn't they figure it out and just refuse a room on the so-called fourteenth floor?" Rosaline asked, her stomach clutching as they sped upward.

"The fourteenth floor will be nothing but suites leased long-term to out-of-town corporations," Katie Lee said. "The people we negotiate the leases with never actually stay there—the rooms are for visiting businessmen and entertaining during conventions—so they're not too worried about being visited by the demons of the dead during the middle of the night."

They stepped off the elevator onto a concrete floor littered with wood shavings.

"This will all be carpeted," Katie Lee said. "That wall will be marble—we've picked out something sort of rosy that's being shipped from Italy next week—and over there, floor-to-ceiling mirrors. We're going to call it Club Fifty. We'll have a restaurant with the best wine list in New York and a health club for the guests and a few private party rooms. You won't believe the view," she said, directing Rosaline under a trellis of black and red electrical wires into a wide room filled with narrow copper pipes.

For a moment Rosaline, standing at the center of the room, could not be sure if she was looking at walls or windows: the sky at noon was unclouded, and they were so high up that, looking north and east, not a single building reached up into view. She walked over to one of the windows, afraid to stand right up against it despite everything Katie Lee had told her about the strength of the glass.

"Don't be scared," Katie Lee said, "it's a distant cousin to the kind of thing you drink water out of. You'd need a small truck to drive through it."

Rosaline walked along the border, looking down across the river and the warehouses of Queens and Brooklyn, up the residential grid of the East Side (there was her building and the museum and the armory), and out onto the park, some of it still covered in last week's snow. There was something about simply being up so high, about the pure height of the place, that filled her with a sense of power. From here you couldn't see the people on the sidewalks or hear the traffic of the street. All the rush and noise and complications of life in New York—all the things that made an errand as simple as buying a birthday present or picking up a new plant from the greenhouse into something that could consume an entire afternoon, leaving you drained and weary from the mere effort of leaving your apartment— all this slipped away.

Rosaline could see for miles in all directions. It was as though an intimacy had been revealed: in the same way that, once you catch someone sleeping, he will never look the same again when awake, so the city was somehow changing, rotating up to her at an angle, disclosing itself in the patterns of its rooftops and rivers.

Katie Lee was right: she was the only person who could salvage Blue Smoke, she didn't even have the choice to make. It was her obligation to give her best to continue the efforts of generations before her, to make sure that Blue Smoke persevered and prospered for generations to come. She was not going to let it all end with her. She was not going to sit with her child, going through boxes of old racing programs and explaining the glory of what had once been and the tragedy of how it had come to a drunken end.

All around her the number 49 had been scrawled by the construction crew, in rough chalk on concrete beams and in dripping spray paint on high slabs of Sheetrock, reminding her that she was, in real life, just a level below the place where she felt herself to be. Katie Lee had called for the elevator and was waving Rosaline back into the dusty corridor.

"What would you like for lunch?" Katie Lee asked. "There's a new seafood place down the block that makes the absolutely most divine shrimp salad."

Rosaline giggled and took Katie Lee's hand for balance as she stepped over a copper pipe. "You say it as though there were angels working in the kitchen."

"Coming up here always makes me hungry," Katie Lee replied. "It's the weirdest thing. Aren't you hungry?" she asked.

"We both are," Rosaline said, patting her stomach. "I haven't been this hungry in years."

14

*D*ecember looked at her watch: five more minutes on the treadmill and then she could call it quits. She'd be showered, dressed, and out of the club before the lunchtime rush at noon. Her next appointment wasn't until four—that gave her a few hours to kill, shopping or checking out a new photography exhibit downtown or even just cruising the streets. It was an unseasonably warm day in early February, the kind of warm weather that would have gone unnoticed in April or May but that now, after an excruciatingly cold winter, sent the entire city sailing out onto the sidewalks, dizzy with the promise of the spring ahead.

Whatever she did, December wanted to avoid her apartment, where Marinda had encamped herself, uninvited and unwelcome, nearly full time since last November. Marinda had simply appeared one night with a suitcase of clothing and a backpack of schoolwork, announcing her singular and surprising mission: to save December's life.

"I'm not going to sit back and watch you do this to yourself," Marinda had said, kicking off her boots and hanging up her down coat in the front closet.

December lit a cigarette and draped her legs over the back of the sofa. "Exactly what is it that I'm doing to myself. Besides having a good time and making a ton of money."

Marinda sat down opposite December and pushed her heavy hair off her face. "I know all about the drugs. I know you're too stupid or too proud to get the kind of help you need."

"Marinda, I'm not a drug addict, if that's what you mean. I take things for fun, and I don't do anything that interferes with my work. I work really hard to make the kind of money I do, and if I want to

191

spend a little of it on myself I don't see what business it is of yours."

Marinda unzipped her suitcase and took out a sterilizer for her contact lenses, a large brown bottle of antidandruff shampoo, and a half dozen tape cassettes. "In other words, you're in total control. You can stop any time you want."

"That's right. Unlike someone else you used to know." December looked over at the tapes: the Who, a couple of Zeppelins, David Bowie, the Kinks. Nothing that had been released in the last three years. Oh God, I hope she isn't going to make me listen to that stuff, December thought. Marinda must be lonelier than I realized. Maybe the first year of law school really does make people as crazy as they say. "How long were you planning to stay?" she asked.

"Until you straighten out," Marinda said, leaning back and applying eyedrops. "I can sleep on the couch."

"It doesn't fold out," December said.

"I can sleep on the floor."

December stood up and folded her arms across her chest. "I don't think this is such a great idea, Marinda. I haven't had a roommate in a couple of years, and I've gotten used to the privacy, to being able to come and go as I please."

"You always came and went as you pleased."

And you always found some way of letting me know how much you disapproved, December thought. The telephone rang and Marinda stiffened. December waited until the answering machine clicked on and then listened as her mother's voice came muffled from the other room.

"I've been meaning to get one of those," Marinda said.

"They're getting cheaper every day," December said. "Look, if you want to stay over through the weekend, that's fine, I haven't really got any plans. But no longer. I mean it."

"However long it takes," Marinda said, popping out a lens and dropping it into the plastic case.

"We'll talk about it in the morning. I'm incredibly beat, and I've got an important shoot tomorrow. There are extra linens in the hall closet. Make yourself at home," she said, and she went to bed.

Marinda unpacked her things, stacking piles of clothing in a neat row against the far wall. She arranged her books on a shelf and poured herself a beer. She waited until she saw the light go out under the bedroom door, until she was sure December had fallen asleep, and then she went to work.

• • •

Her eyes still gritted with sleep, her mouth still tasting of brandy and cigarettes, December sat up in bed with a start. Someone had been in her bedroom during the night. The vase of daffodils had been shifted on her dresser top and the closet door was slightly ajar. After a moment of panic she remembered: Marinda, Marinda was here.

Still half asleep, the bright morning sun stinging her eyes, she brushed her teeth with the special paste that claimed to prevent the unsightly stains that accumulated from tobacco and coffee, and then she opened the medicine cabinet for the floss that was supposed to keep her valuable grin intact all the way into her twilight years.

She reached up and felt the sharp sting of a razor against her fingers. I can't believe it, Marinda has rearranged everything, December said to herself, and then it hit her: the cabinet was nearly empty. The razor was where the floss used to be, and the floss was up on the vitamin shelf, and the vitamins had been moved to, to, *where were they.* Where were the Valium and the codeine-laced Tylenol and the diet pills and the Quaaludes she kept stashed inside a vial marked "tetracycline" and the large dark-green Placidyls she hadn't had a chance to try yet—someone had brought a handful as a little gift and she'd kept them wrapped in toilet paper behind an extra bar of pH-balanced eye-makeup remover.

She rummaged through the wicker trash basket and came up with a handful of empty plastic vials. *That bitch, she'll be out of here before breakfast,* she thought. She charged into the living room and gave Marinda a jab on the shoulder.

"Out," she barked. "Get dressed and get out."

Marinda turned over and gave her a sleepy smile. "What time is it?" she asked. "I haven't got a class until eleven today." She pulled the comforter over her head. "Five more minutes, then I'll get up."

December stormed back into the bedroom, banging drawers and doors open and shut. It didn't hit her until she unrolled a pair of white sweat socks she took from a dresser drawer that she hadn't heard the familiar rattle of plastic against wood. She opened the drawer again and reached back behind a pair of never-worn navy-blue argyles. *Marinda has stolen my stash.* She rushed over to the closet and felt down among the deep pockets of an old corduroy jacket: empty. She opened the porcelain jewelry box Katie Lee had brought back from a trip to Europe, knocking over the daffodils in her haste: all gone. All her cocaine was gone. Two thousand dollars' worth.

Marinda is insane, she thought. She would have to call Bobby and explain what had happened, see if he could come by and help her get Marinda out of here. She dialed his number in Cambridge, but the line was busy. She waited a few minutes and tried again: still busy. She heard the slam of the front door and went out to discover the comforter folded in a neat pile at one end of the couch and a pot of coffee brewing in the kitchen and a note taped to the stereo: *I've gone out for a few minutes to pick up groceries and breakfast and papers and have the keys copied on the corner. Back in a flash, M.* Suddenly December felt tired, so very tired, as though she hadn't slept in days. She knew she needed energy to deal with Marinda when she returned, but all she wanted to do was get back in bed and pull the blanket up over her head.

She fished around the bottom of the kitchen garbage can and came up with the stub end of a joint, a half inch of Columbian that two days earlier she hadn't deemed worth saving. She lit it and inhaled continuously until she felt the burn against her fingers.

She wondered if anyone else knew that Marinda was here. Had Marinda discussed her with—Katie Lee? Rosaline? Her friends at law school? Who else was worrying about her? Why couldn't people just leave her alone? Maybe they'd all gotten together for some kind of summit meeting and nominated Marinda to carry out this plan, this weird plan.

It wasn't just the drugs, the drugs were just an excuse. Marinda was spying on her. Marinda could be very dangerous. December curled up in the middle of the floor and pulled the comforter off the couch. Marinda was going to have to be dealt with very carefully. Marinda had made alliances with the others. They'd been planning this for weeks. Marinda was probably reporting back to them at this very instant from the pay phone outside the locksmith's.

December was going to have to pretend to cooperate. There was no point in putting up a fight: she was outnumbered and outmaneuvered. She could keep clean for a few weeks—she wouldn't even have to, really, it wasn't as though Marinda were going to follow her around every time she left the house.

Marinda came back carrying a bag of croissants from a new French bakery.

"The first rule is," she said, "eat breakfast every day. Smell this stuff, it's terrific, just out of the oven an hour ago." She held the bag up to December's nose.

December gagged. It was disgusting, all that chocolate and butter, Marinda's pudgy hand holding the greasy edge of the waxed paper, this fat person leaning over her, leering into her face.

"I'm not hungry," December said. "Maybe later."

"Well, I'm starved," Marinda said, reaching inside the bag and withdrawing a pastry covered with almonds and confectioner's sugar. "Sure you're not hungry?" she asked.

They could be putting stuff into my food, December thought. From now on, drink only tap water. Eat only from cans. Marinda doesn't look at all like a spy, not like the spies in movies at least, but that's probably why they chose her. They didn't think I'd catch on. They underestimated how clever I really am. How very very clever I really am. Spy/counterspy, December said to herself, having a sudden vision of the rat-faced cartoon characters from her younger brother's *MAD* magazines. She started to giggle, and Marinda laughed along with her.

"I'm glad you're keeping your sense of humor about this," Marinda said, wiping the crumbs off the front of her sweater. "Bobby was afraid you wouldn't cooperate."

"Bobby? When did you talk to Bobby?" December asked.

"I'm always talking to Bobby. He's my cousin, remember?"

"Right. Your cousin. Your father's brother's first-born son."

"That's the guy."

"That's the guy," December repeated. So Bobby was the one calling all the shots. So Marinda hadn't flushed the drugs down the toilet, as December had thought earlier, she'd probably just given everything to Bobby. Spies and thieves, all around her. And there was no one in New York who could come rescue her. She was trapped, completely trapped. Spies and thieves, thieves and spies.

By Christmas, December's system was nearly cleaned out, and Marinda felt secure enough to join her family for the weekend in New Jersey. Marinda had been following December nearly everywhere she went, toting her heavy law books along to shoots, sitting poolside memorizing case law as December did her daily laps, hanging out against walls at parties while December circulated among the crowd. December simply introduced her as "Nurse Ratched" and counted the days until her departure.

Though her early paranoia had abated and, drug-free, December actually felt happier and more energetic than she had in years, she still couldn't shake the gut instinct that Marinda had some kind of ulterior motives, was spying on her in some way. There was something reassuring about having this maternal presence in her home, this warm, round person who prepared elaborate healthy salads and concocted vitamin-enriched fruit shakes in what had been until now her unused kitchen. The funny thing was, Marinda seemed to be losing weight on their shared diet. She was actually on the edge of becoming pleasingly plump. It would be a shame to kick her out now, December thought, when she's making so much progress.

And that's how she began explaining Marinda's presence to her friends. "She's had a very bad time, her boyfriend committed suicide and she gained a hundred pounds," December would whisper, nodding to Marinda across the room. "So I invited her to move in with me until she straightened herself out. She's lost twenty pounds in the last month, and she's going to ace her law school exams." What a saint you are, came the replies, how generous, how caring, how kind. "That's what friends are for," December would say shrugging. "She'd do the same for me."

She spent her twenty-second birthday at a New Year's Eve party on the West Side, and the following week she binged out at the postholiday sales along Fifth Avenue and down Fifty-seventh Street. She hadn't realized how much money she'd been spending on drugs until she saw her checking account grow fatter by the week. In a fit of generosity she mailed five thousand dollars to her mother, whom she hadn't seen in nearly a year. *I know you know how incredibly busy I am up here, but I did want to send you a little something now that things are going so well. Buy something special for yourself, and stash a little away in the college fund.* This really isn't filial generosity, December thought as she wrote, it's more like—like she was buying something, but she wasn't sure what. The money would keep her mother away and out of sight back in New Jersey. The money would ensure that her mother kept quiet and stayed out of her life. She knew that her mother wanted to share in December's success, in what Gloria probably saw as their mutual success, and money was the only thing December felt like sharing.

And it was an investment in her future as well, because December's career was gearing up and lifting her off the covers of magazines and into the league of major endorsements and television work, the sort of exposure that landed you on gossip pages, that exposed you to the curiosity of the press. One day she was going to be very famous, and she was also going to be very, very sure that Gloria kept her mouth shut.

Rumors of an old drug problem—her publicist would be able to deal with that. A little bit of personal-triumph-over-difficult-times had never hurt anyone's career. Old gentlemen friends who kissed and told—well, it *was* the seventies, and no one really cared about that kind of thing anymore. But being the daughter of Sonny Kidwell was something else. Every day when she looked in the mirror and saw her father's reflection she was reminded of the secret that, if discovered, could bring the whole house of cards tumbling down.

She wasn't that naïve, she knew that eventually people would find out. But she was going to go as far as she could and get as rich as she could before the day that happened. She was going to have a big fat pile of money earning interest in her savings account and a handsome portfolio of blue chip stocks and a pile of expensive jewelry sitting in a safe deposit box.

Though there wasn't a clue in her apartment to give her away, it still made her nervous having Marinda around. There was something she couldn't put her finger on—the way Marinda seemed to eavesdrop on her telephone conversations, the way she sometimes picked up December's mail from the front desk ("I was just coming home as they were delivering it"). But Marinda would be gone soon enough. She had lost more weight and was even having some kind of perverse flirtation with a fellow law student named Jason—what was it? Something Jewish. A nice Jewish boy for Marinda, December thought, smiling to herself. Just what the doctor ordered.

December fluffed her hair, still wet from the shower, out into the weak February sun. She was heading into a vintage-clothing store when she heard a familiar voice call her name from down the block.

"Miss Dunne, you look as lovely as ever." It was Alex. "Damp but lovely."

December bounded over and gave him a hug. "Alex, you fool. How are you?"

"Please don't be so demonstrative in public, you shameless wench. You seem almost happy to see me."

"And why shouldn't I be?" she asked. After her dreary hours with Marinda she needed a strong dose of fun, and Alex was still one of the funnest people she'd ever known. It seemed ridiculous, that he'd think her angry with him after all this time. "Have you done something awful I don't know about?"

"Well, I've moved to Hollywood where I manage the famous and would-be famous. That's relatively awful."

"But extremely profitable?" December asked, taking his arm.

"In California they give their money away. They plead with you, they get down on their knees and beg you to relieve them of all this vulgar cash they've got lying around, who knows where it comes from. It seems the least I can do."

"Considerate Alex."

"As ever," he said. He had hardly changed, and his age had caught up with the lines in his face. In school he had seemed prematurely traveled and experienced, decadent and worldly wise; now he seemed boyish, impish even, a happy spirit dressed in the familiar velvet and tweeds. "So considerate, in fact, that I'm going to buy you lunch. To pay for my past sins, whatever they were, I can barely remember."

"Oh, well, if that's the deal, it'd better be some place incredibly expensive," December said, laughing.

"Some place French, with abysmally slow service? Is that what you had in mind?"

"Sounds good."

"The French—you Americans have this thing for the French. They are truly a filthy and barbaric people. You ought to see their kitchens. You'd never eat in another French restaurant as long as you lived," he said, leading the way down the steps of a narrow brownstone and back to a small secluded table that looked out onto a garden.

After the soup and endive salads and a few glasses of Pouilly Fuissé Alex asked about her personal life.

"There's really nothing to report," December said. "Marinda's been hanging around for months—she's moving out next week and I can't wait—but it's sort of put a damper on, uh, entertaining at home."

"I find this difficult to believe, my darling."

"Well, it's true. I've practically been a nun."

He shook his head. "A tragic waste of one of our most precious natural resources."

She giggled. "And you?" she asked. "Still with Bruno?"

"Oh dear, Bruno. My beloved Bruno. I haven't yet permitted him to come to Hollywood, and he sends these pathetic wires from London, but he can be a sort of unwelcome interference, as you well know, if you'll forgive my saying so, and I'd rather not have him around until I'm more settled. We'd gotten into a rather sorry rut, actually."

"Do tell," December said. He was a little drunk, and a nice person wouldn't have taken advantage of this opportunity to probe into his personal life. But there aren't any nice people at this table, December thought.

"He starting getting jealous when I went around with women, though I hardly ever took them to bed, but it's part of the business, you know, being seen with these devastatingly beautiful women. Clients, mostly."

"Hard job."

Alex shook his head. "I knew you'd understand, darling. Bruno threw absolute hissy fits. And then when I stayed home he was hardly any fun at all. We started watching bootleg blue movies on the Betamax and sordid things like that."

"Blue movies? You mean porn?" December laughed. "Are you kidding me?"

"There's some unbelievable stuff available from private collections. Bruno's favorite involved these two women—veritable heaps of silicone—it was like some sort of perverse double date, just try and picture it, these two amazons wrestling on the telly and Bruno and I curled up like some old married couple. I believe you've gotten me drunk and made me say all sorts of nasty things. You'll be punished for this," he said, refilling his glass.

"How is that?" she said as the main course arrived.

"Ah. Well. I have been following you from afar. I understand you are quite the hot property."

"Lukewarm at most," she replied.

"I understand as well that you took some acting classes in the Village last year with—what is her name? The widow. The famous widow."

"It was a joke," she said. "You know, crawl around on the floor and relive your birth trauma. Expose your innermost secrets to waitresses and moped messengers. Not my cup of tea."

"I wouldn't think so. But you still want to become an actress?"

"Oh, I don't know. Who can say. I've only got a few years of print work left. I don't feel the way I used to, that I could do anything in the world if I set my mind to it. I'm a pretty rotten actress, to tell the truth."

"Promise me you'll never say that again."

"To tell the truth?"

"That you're a rotten actress. Not that it matters. In television it's actually a severe impediment, any kind of intelligence or acting ability at all. Which brings me to my inferior, that is my ulterior motive."

"Yes sir."

"Come to California. Let me represent you. Let me make you a star."

"I've heard this tune before," December said.

"And I delivered before, didn't I. You were the one who walked out on our deal, not me. Not that I blame you, I understand perfectly, my darling, perfectly perfectly."

"And what is it exactly that you do?"

"Well, to be a star you've got to have all sorts of people working for you. An agent, for one thing, who gets you jobs. A lawyer to negotiate deals. An accountant to invest your money. A publicist. A shrink."

"And you, as manager, are all those things rolled up into one?"

"Dear Lord no, I'm none of those things. Those people do all the work and give you very good advice, and then I come in and advise you about their advice."

"Well, thanks, but I don't think so," she said as he signaled for the check. "I'm pretty happy where I am."

"I don't believe that for a minute," Alex said, leading her up onto the sidewalk. He handed her a card. "You may change your mind," he said, leaning over and giving her a kiss. "Stay in touch."

She took the card and stuck it in her back pocket. "Thanks for lunch," she said, giving him a goodbye wave.

"You'll call me," he said as he walked wobbling away, less a question than a command. Of course she would. What she hadn't told him was that she had been keeping track of him too, had heard how well he was doing out in California, had been trying to figure out how to get back in touch with him without it looking as if *she* were coming to *him*.

Of course she'd call him. Alex was the best.

15

*R*osaline leaned over to Philip, seated on her right, and gently tapped the cuff of his suit.

"It was so kind of Grace to lend me her mother's recipe for German apple torte. Trevor's been raving about it for years."

"Grace is like a C.I.A. agent about matters of the kitchen. She was thinking about writing a cookbook a few years back."

"Wouldn't that be a delicious project," Rosaline said. "Promise me you won't tell Trevor about the recipe. Dessert is supposed to be a surprise. I told him we were serving homemade ice cream."

"I promise. I didn't know you had an ice cream maker."

"Oh, we don't," Rosaline said, keeping her eye on Rachel's boyfriend, Gregory, who had had three drinks before dinner and was now loudly telling an off color joke at the far end of the long table. Katie Lee, seated to Gregory's right, shot Rosaline a wink that said, Don't worry, I'll take care of this one. "But Trevor doesn't know that. I could tell him we've got rare Chinese pandas mating in the kitchen cupboard and he wouldn't have the foggiest."

Philip laughed. He was surprised at how well Rosaline had taken on the role of society hostess; she had seemed so shy and unconfident when he'd first met her, the week before Trevor proposed. And now here she was, sitting at the foot of an exquisitely set table for fourteen she'd had done up in reds and pinks for Valentine's Day. Trevor had confided to Philip that Rosaline had been unsure about entertaining with all the legal troubles they were having with her father but that Trevor had convinced her that it was just at these times, when a family was under the gun, when it was most important to keep up a good appearance and open your house to friends.

The favors were a big hit—even Sylvie, who was competitive about entertaining to an extreme and who never professed much pleasure in any of her friend's menus or decorations, had cooed with delight when she unwrapped her monogrammed lace handkerchief.

"I think that means she likes it," said Maria, who was seated on Trevor's left just as her husband, Simon, was seated to Rosaline's left. "Oh, look at that," she cried as Gregory lifted a red silk bow tie from red-and-white striped tissue paper.

"What a terrific idea," Simon said and then lowered his voice slightly. "And I hear Hailey promised you two of his best mares next season for Agamemnon."

"Oregano and Lady Washtub," Rosaline replied.

"Quiet a coup, isn't it."

"They've been wanting a season with French Fire for years. They kept five shares in Silver Anger, you know, it's a smart match for them," she said. "It's just the beginning. With Agamemnon, I mean."

"I wish you all the luck," Simon said.

"Thank you. I may need it."

"You've all got to put on your ties," Sylvie announced. "You've all got to put them on right away."

And the men complied, though the two "extra" men invited from Trevor's firm, seated on either side of Marinda, who was exhibiting rare discipline and avoiding anything heavy or laced with cream, had to be shown how the knot was made.

"Allow me. I've got about fifty brothers back home so I can do this in my sleep," Marinda said. Rosaline had never seen Marinda being so flirtatious. She wondered if it had something to do with this boy she'd met in law school, Jason Feld, whom Marinda had steadfastly refused to bring around for Rosaline's inspection.

It was Marinda who had encouraged her to invite Schuyler tonight, and it turned out to have been the right thing to do. Rosaline had run into Schuyler on the street a few weeks ago and they'd gone into a coffee shop for a quick lunch. Last year I would have crossed the avenue if I'd seen him, she remembered saying to herself, and now here I am. Pregnancy was some kind of shield against old beaux; carrying another man's child, it would have seemed too disloyal to admit that any hurt remained at all.

She hadn't recognized him at first. She had gotten so used to it, now that she was obviously, hugely pregnant, to having strangers offer to hail cabs for her, carry packages for her, even hold umbrellas for her, that when he came up beside her and asked her if she needed any help she turned and gave him an automatic smile.

"No, thank you, they're not as heavy as they look," she said, and then she saw it was Schuyler, and the bags of groceries slipped and fell onto the sidewalk. She stood there, her arms limp at her sides, as he gathered up the plastic shopping bags filled with cans of diet orange soda, macadamia nuts, raspberry-flavored fruit strips, and half a dozen KitKat bars. A pint of lemon ice had rolled against a fire hydrant.

"They'll deliver if you ask them to," Schuyler said, straightening up, grinning, holding the bags in his left fist.

She blushed; she had planned to go home and finish everything off before Trevor got back from the office at six. I was hungry, she wanted to say, but it was one of those things her mother had trained her never to say—*I'm hungry, I want, I need, a lady never asks, Charlotte would say, a lady never complains*—so Rosaline just stood there, uncertain of what to do next. How long had it been, how many years and months, since she and Schuyler had, had, had been polite to each other, was how she thought of it. *A lady is always gracious, a lady is always polite, a lady always puts her guests at ease.* Rosaline extended her right hand and smiled again.

"Schuyler, it's wonderful to see you again," she said. That wasn't so hard, she thought. It wasn't such a difficult thing to say, because it was true: she was glad to see him.

He took her hand and held it. "You look terrific. I hear you married someone nearly as wonderful as you. Congratulations to you both."

"Thank you," she said, pulling her hand back and patting her stomach. "I'm going to have a baby," she continued. She couldn't think of anything to say. "I got married, and now I'm going to have a baby." Her knees felt weak.

"I believe that's the way it's done these days," Schuyler said. He looked into the shopping bags. "Have you had lunch?"

She nodded. "Two times today already."

"Want to make it three? I was just about to grab a burger at the local greasy spoon. Do you have time? I'll treat you to a milk shake." He took her arm and led her around the corner to a coffee shop that, in the early afternoon lull between lunch and the end of the school day, was nearly empty. She could barely slide in between the table and bench of the back booth he'd chosen.

"I'm so fat now," she said. "It's out of fashion, you know, all the other mothers in my class watch their weight and take these special exercise classes."

"You really do look great," he said.

"Well," she said, listening to the whir of the milk shake in its old-fashioned metal mixing cup. She had known that someday they would run into each other—it happened eventually with everyone who lived in New York—but this wasn't how she had pictured it at all. Somehow she had thought Schuyler would be embarrassed, apologetic, guilty, beseeching, and she would be collected, withholding, cool, remote. She knew she wasn't in love with him anymore, though now, looking at him sitting across from her against the red vinyl upholstery of the restaurant booth, she felt suddenly proud of herself for having at one time loved him so much and for his having loved her so strongly in return. She was beginning to cry, which she blamed on the hormones, on being so tired and puffy, she hated this aspect of pregnancy, how it made her so emotional all the time.

He took her hands across the table. "Are you all right?" he asked.

"Yes," she whispered. "I don't know. It's not you. It just comes on like this sometimes. Twelve more weeks and I'll be a normal person again, or so they promise me."

"Do you want me to go?" he said, turning his head away.

"Oh, no, please don't. I'll be fine in a minute." If he left she knew she'd collapse utterly. It was what he'd always done best, taking care of her. "Just keep talking. I'll be fine."

"All right. What about?"

"Tell me what you've been up to."

"Well, let's see. After school I got a job—"

"Wait, stop," she said. "Marinda gives me all the news about you. And vice versa, I guess. The résumé things, I mean. I don't know what I mean. I'm babbling, forgive me. You just keep talking." It was safer that way.

"Rosaline," he said, touching the tips of his fingers together. "There's a conversation we need to have, we've needed to have it for a long time, we need to get it out of the way at some point, but maybe now isn't the right time. But we have to talk about it some time."

She stared at him. He was still the handsomest man she'd ever seen. He was still so strong, so smart, so everything that she'd ever loved in him. Nothing about him had changed. He had never been good at small talk, and he clearly wasn't going to start now. Whatever it was she thought they were going to talk about—his job, her apartment, his apartment, her marriage, their mutual friends—she realized now that there just wasn't such a thing as a trivial conversation with Schuyler Smith. You could be absolutely silent, he wouldn't have minded if they just sat there, quietly, together in the booth. Or you could talk about what really mattered. But there was no middle ground. She closed her eyes and took a giant leap across all the chit-chat, the gossip, the anecdotes, the polite conversations that old lovers have when one of them, the one who did the leaving, has gotten married and the other, the one who was left, has not.

"I really hated you for a while," Rosaline said. And suddenly she felt better, stronger. The worst part was out of the way.

"You had every right to. I was ashamed of myself for a long, long time."

"Me too!" she exclaimed, almost girlishly, as though they'd just discovered they had a favorite old movie in common. "Of me, I mean, not of you. I don't know. It was the easiest thing to do, to hate you and December. To feel you've been so utterly, tragically *wronged*. There's this moral grace that attaches itself to whoever was wronged. Being good by default, being good only in contrast to someone else's evil. Oh, I'm sorry, I don't really mean *evil*, it's just that—"

"It's all right," Schuyler said. "The world needs more of it, I think. More people who believe in right and wrong, in good and evil."

Rosaline shook her head. "What I was trying to say is that the world is a more complicated place than I thought it was when—when I knew you. I know this sounds trite, but we're all only human. It's something you learn in marriage, I think, that no one is perfect. Though Trevor is frighteningly close. People make mistakes, I make mistakes, everyone makes mistakes, and everyone has to, everyone has to—" She broke off and stared at him.

"Everyone has to what?" he asked.

She looked up at the ceiling.

"Not everyone," she said. "Me. I have to."

"You have to what?"

"Schuyler," she said, realizing that they were still holding hands, giving his hands something short of a squeeze. "Schuyler. I forgive you."

He pulled back as though she'd slapped him. "There was a time when I wanted more than anything to hear you say that. Now that you have, I feel like shit."

"There's more. I need you to forgive me."

"For what?" he asked, taking out a cigarette.

"For a lot of things. Please don't—" she said, waving a hand in the air.

"Don't what?"

"Don't make me say them. And don't smoke, please."

He smiled. "You didn't do anything wrong," he said, blowing out the lit match.

"But I did," she said, "and I have to hear you say it. Because I want us to be friends, and we can't until we get all this unfinished business out of the way. If you want to."

"I do want to. Be friends."

"You'll have to come meet Trevor. Would you come over for drinks some time? I think you'll really like him." Their shakes had arrived. Schuyler accordioned the paper wrapper down to the end of his straw and blew into the other end; the paper flew over Rosaline's head into the booth behind them. Rosaline giggled.

"That sounds very grown up," Schuyler said. He was thinking that, in the years since she'd left him, he too had had time to get married, to settle down, to have a child. Hardly anyone he knew of his age had done so. "I think I can handle it."

Rosaline leaned over and sipped her shake, a red wave of hair falling across her eyes. To Schuyler she looked the same: a young girl's head attached to a matron's body. She was so fragile, with those delicate bones, he wondered how the rest of the pregnancy would go. Trevor was, from what he had heard, one of those strapping, athletic types who made big happy babies. *Happy,* that was the word, Rosaline was happy. She might have been the only person he knew who was doing exactly what she set out to do exactly when she'd set out to do it.

"You're the only old beau I have," Rosaline said, sending him a wink. "So you've got to show off when you come over. I've met some of Trevor's old girlfriends and they've all got blond hair and they're six feet tall and they shoot and ride and swim and one of them even has an Olympic medal. For archery, I think, I can't remember exactly."

"It's probably just a bronze," Schuyler said, laughing.

"Well, anyway, I didn't fit the pattern at all, so please be your most totally charming handsome self you can be so Trevor won't suspect what an easy thing it really was, to marry me," she said, giggling again. No matter how old she got, Schuyler thought, she'd always be able to carry off that innocent schoolgirl's giggle.

"Hey, I was sorry to hear about your father. How is he?"

"Not so good," Rosaline said. "He's living on this farm, sort of. He doesn't drink anymore, thank goodness. He still gets the *Racing Form* every day, and he still puts on his suit and tie every day just to go into the cafeteria with all the other—other patients."

"I heard about Agamemnon. It must have been hard on your mother."

"It was. But we've lined up some amazing mares for next year. Just wait and watch what happens at the yearling sales in 1980," she said. That was two and a half years away. Who knew what state Joseph would be in by then. They talked about horses and about Schuyler's job at the paper and then it was dark, and Rosaline said she had to hurry home. He walked her to her corner.

"Well, goodbye," she said. "I'm going to call you very soon and you must promise to come over."

"I will," he said. "And I do, you know."

She lifted her eyebrows in question.

"Forgive you," he said. "For breaking my heart." He handed over her bags.

"It was so long ago," she said.

"We were just kids," he replied. "It happens to everybody."

She shook her head. He was trying to make her feel better, but it was a lie. "No, it doesn't, not the way it happened with us. It was special. We can't pretend it wasn't."

"Well," he said, sucking in his breath and exhaling into the cold winter air. "I guess not."

"And now we can be special friends," she said, standing on her toes and giving him a kiss on the cheek.

"I guess so," he said, sticking his hands in his pockets. He said goodbye and turned and walked away into the wind blowing hard from across the park. She watched him walk off, cupping a matchbook in his hands to light the cigarette he'd been waiting for all afternoon. She looked inside her bags. The ice had melted and spilled all over, and she tossed everything into a wire barrel and slapped her hands together like a workman who has just completed a particularly messy task. And she realized, now that it was too late to say it, just what it was she'd been feeling about Schuyler for so long, what it was that she hadn't known until just now, now that she'd watched him walk downtown, against all the gentlemen in their cashmere and herringbone topcoats coming home from work. She'd missed him. It wasn't any more complicated than that. She'd missed her best friend.

Several days later he came by the house to meet Trevor over drinks, and Rosaline had been amazed at how well the two men got along. It all had to do with fishing and hunting and sports—there was some obscure baseball player, long dead and mostly forgotten, who had set some kind of batting record during their shared youth. Trevor, as it turned out, had once seen the man play, and he stood up to re-create the drama of each inning. Then Schuyler got up and demonstrated precisely what subtle dip of the shoulder had given the player such an amazingly strong swing, and when Trevor cried, "That's it, that's exactly it!" she knew that the entire matter was out of her hands. The two men had decided, for reasons that had nothing to do with her, to become friends.

And when Marinda had suggested that they invite Schuyler to dinner on Valentine's Day, it was Trevor who seconded her suggestion enthusiastically.

"It could have been worse," Trevor was saying now, adjusting his red bow tie. "She could have given us all lime-green leisure suits. Or designer jeans."

Schuyler put on his tie and turned to Katie Lee, seated on his left, for sartorial approval.

"You look the perfect southern gentleman," Katie Lee said, sipping her champagne. She knew for a fact that it was considered slightly vulgar to serve champagne with dinner, but she supposed the Goodwoods were allowed to get away with whatever they wanted just because they were whoever it was they were. "You look like Ashley Wilkes, you really do."

"Before or after the war?" Schuyler said, laughing.

"The first scene, the one where he sets Scarlett O'Hara's heart on fire." She batted her lashes in true belle style. "Do excuse me while I swoon," she said, faking a collapse against the back of her seat. It was only half exaggeration, really, for she'd forgotten how amazingly handsome this boy was. She knew for a fact that he wasn't seeing anyone, and now that she was living full time in New York it might be nice to have a man like Schuyler around, someone who could be counted on to escort her to these endless half-business half-social functions, someone who had been here long enough and had the right connections to take her to some interesting parties and introduce her around, someone to make Bobby a little jealous and, if she guessed

right, someone who would make few to no sexual demands. Katie
Lee detected that Schuyler had withdrawn somehow from the sexual
fray: it was something in the way he carried himself, in the way he
automatically leaned away whenever a woman stood just a bit too
close.

"But Scarlett O'Hara, as I remember," Gregory said, "ate like a
bird. And you've completely demolished your dinner."

Katie Lee allowed an expression of displeasure to cross her face for
just one second (*These people eat slower, she reminded herself, because for generations no one in their family has gone hungry*) before
she broke out into a smile.

"How true," she said, shaking her head at her plate. "My appetites
will undo me yet. I wish I had Marinda's discipline."

Marinda, seated across the table between what she had just decided
were the two most boring men in New York, wondered how the
flawlessly groomed Katie Lee would look with a gravy boat upturned
over her newly streaked head. If she doesn't stop flirting with
Schuyler I'll find out soon enough, she said to herself. God damn it,
he was invited here for *me*, and I'm sorry I ever talked Rosaline into
it.

Marinda knew, for reasons she could not admit even to Rosaline,
just how vulnerable Schuyler was to female attention these days. She
knew because for weeks, no, for months, she had been intercepting
the letters he sent and the telephone messages he left at December's
apartment. The letters had been easy; in December's so-called high
security building first-class mail was held hotel-style in cubbyholes
behind the second doorman's desk, and once Marinda had moved in
they offered it to her without comment whenever she entered the
building. Which she was sure to do as soon as the mail arrived—the
mailman's schedule was one of the first things she'd checked out.

The phone machine was a little harder, because when you erased a
message you also erased all those left after it, but then Schuyler had
called only a few times, and it didn't really matter if December
missed an appointment or two. People were always lying about leaving messages on your machine; December would never suspect the
truth.

Only once had he called while Marinda was in the apartment. She
had crept over to the answering machine and, turning up the volume,
held her breath as he spoke. Though she had learned, from reading

the instruction manual, that it was impossible for a caller to hear anyone screening calls, there was some part of her that was afraid, that craved stealth and silence. At the sound of his voice she'd broken out into a sweat, and as soon as he'd hung up she'd had to go to the bathroom, where she discovered that everything inside her had turned soft, and she felt quite ill.

She had hidden his letters, a half dozen of them, inside a sleeping bag back at her apartment. They were pure torture to read; Schuyler had somehow convinced himself that he was in love with December, who Marinda knew for a fact didn't care a fig about him. She was doing what was best for both of them.

After a while the calls and letters stopped (just a few days before she told December that it was getting to be time for her to move out), and Marinda knew what that meant: Schuyler had given up, if only temporarily, and was trying to get on with his life. She knew he hadn't actually found a girlfriend—she still telephoned him, always hanging up at the sound of his hello, and occasionally walked by his apartment—but it was only a matter of time. If only she'd begun her diet earlier, had been able to lose weight more quickly. And now here he was, making a fool of himself in front of everyone over Katie Lee. *Katie Lee.*

"And how exactly do you know Trevor and Rosaline?" the man to her right asked.

"My father is the superintendent of this building," Marinda snapped, watching the man's eyebrows lift in surprise and then drop in bewilderment. "My mother does Charlotte's laundry."

Trevor stood and silenced the room with the tap of a dessert spoon. "I'd like you to join me in a toast," he began. "All of you except my lovely, devoted wife, who is not allowed to drink, which makes parties such as these a triumph of, of—" He halted in mid-sentence.

"Good over evil?" offered Grace.

"Style over substance?" suggested Philip.

"All those things," Trevor said, leaning a hand against the back of his chair for balance. He gazed over four small arrangements of red roses and baby's breath down the long table at Rosaline, who hated more than anything to be the center of attention.

"To the new mistress of Blue Smoke Farm," he said, and Gregory stood up to call out a "hear, hear," and then Schuyler stood up, and the rest of the table followed, murmuring approval.

Rosaline lifted her glass of pure spring water.

"To friends and valentines," she said, and everyone touched glasses together, the sound of crystal against crystal like a soft musical percussion signaling the beginning of a new movement, the quiet middle part of the symphony, the part Rosaline always liked best.

16

"What you really need is a boyfriend," Alex said, rubbing the sun block across December's shoulders. "I'm going to have a case of this sent over to you first thing tomorrow morning. Though you'd be much better off if you just stayed out of the sun entirely."

"Can't," December said, pouring herself some more iced tea from the pitcher Alex had brought poolside.

"You beach bunnies never grow up," Alex sighed, handing December the tube of sun cream, watching as she applied another layer to her legs. "It's nothing to be proud of, you know."

"This stuff makes me smell like one big piña colada," she said. "It's totally gross."

"Please don't talk to me that way," he said, pulling a sprig of mint out of his tea and taking it between his teeth. "You've been here only a couple of weeks. You're already starting to sound like the local trash."

"We find our own level wherever we go," she replied. It was fun annoying Alex, or rather, he seemed to enjoy it when she annoyed him; it gave him the opportunity to chide her, to make parental pronouncements, to put himself once again in the position of the more knowledgeable and sophisticated insider who could show her the ropes. They both knew that this trip, arranged by Alex over the protests of her agent in New York, was pure seduction. He was showing her what the good life could be like here on the West Coast, taking her to parties and introducing her to some people who could introduce her to some other people who could get her started in movies.

"And I don't need a boyfriend," she said, leaning back into the canvas lounge chair and closing her eyes. "Boyfriends are a total bore. And as you may remember, I'm not very good at it."

"But sweetie, you must have a boyfriend. This isn't New York, where pretty girls get invited to more parties than they can keep track of. There are tons of pretty girls in California. We have to get you hooked up with someone interesting. Someone who will get you a little press, take you around, et cetera, et cetera."

"I like going around with you," December said, opening her eyes and gazing straight into his. "I really do. I always have."

Alex looked away; he hated anyone being friendly and honest before sundown, before liquor had loosened him to the point where he could accept an old friend's warmth and affection.

"I'm charmed. What about Robbie Kent? His divorce will be final in a few weeks, and his new series is going to be a terrifically big hit, and I know for a fact that he thinks you're deliciously cute."

"You've been pimping for me. No fair."

"*Moi?*" Alex said, spreading ten fingers across his hairless chest. "I was simply there for lunch, and there was simply an old issue of *Elle* open to that safari spread you did, and I simply mentioned that I knew you, and can I help it if he started drooling down the front of his Sea Island chemise? You could do worse."

"No actors," December said. "They're all morons."

"I see."

"In fact, no movie people at all. They're all loathsome, present company included."

"Thank you, darling. Since when have you gotten so picky."

"We're talking boyfriends here."

"How about Tommy Winston? He'll have high visibility when the campaign starts heating up."

"Bore me later," she said. The alarm of the travel clock began to buzz. December shut it off with the nudge of a big toe and turned over onto her back.

"How about a writer? What happened to that boy from Harvard—what was his name? The one who wanted to be your love slave? His career has been going aces since he went free-lance. They're making a movie of his piece on Olympic swimmers. He was through here last month making the rounds with a screenplay."

"You remember his name."

"At my age everyone starts to blend together."

"*Toi?*" December said, shifting against the canvas. "Schuyler Smith—there, you made me say it."

"So?"

"So? He and Katie Lee have been hot and heavy for six months now."

"That's never stopped you before."

December raised herself up on one elbow. "No fair, Alex. Anyway, he's old news. Boring, boring, boring." She leaned back again and closed her eyes; it was easier that way, she had learned, Alex still had the knack of catching her out even in her most harmless lies.

"Whatever you say," he replied. "Then you pick somebody."

"Anybody?" she asked.

"Anyone at all. Except the royal family, I can't procure the impossible. Come on. December goes on a dream date. There must be someone out there worthy of your continued attention."

No one who would have me, she thought to herself, for now, a month away from her twenty-third birthday, she was finding out that even in 1977 there was such a thing as a reputation, and December, never one for discretion, had the sort of reputation that made nervous dinner party hostesses seat her well away from their husbands and beaux.

Perhaps Alex was right: just the way he needed December as a beard for his exploits with pretty boys, so she needed some kind of cover, someone she could point to as the man in her life, someone to protect her from the kind of gossip that could hurt her career. She hadn't told Alex that she'd been out here last year to test for a role in a television movie and had been nixed by the producer's jealous third wife, a woman whose best friend and jogging partner had agreed to sing the theme song if someone other than December got the lead role. The producer had cast an eighteen-year-old sitcom princess who had recently been interviewed by a national talk show host on the subject of her virginity, and December's agent gave her a lecture about how it was time for her to start behaving in public.

Still, a steady boyfriend—what a drag. Someone who counted on you to be around. Someone who felt he had the right to know what you were doing, where you went, what you were thinking and feeling, twenty-four hours a day. Like you were his own private, personal property. It was the last thing she needed.

When the alarm buzzed again half an hour later, Alex insisted they get out of the sun and find themselves some lunch. The daily rhythm never changed here in California: there were no lines drawn between weekdays and weekends, people dressed at the same carefully casual level whether they were staying at home or going to a party, meeting old friends for lunch or having dinner with a new business connection. December was having trouble falling asleep at night, and at

other times, in the middle of the morning or while shopping downtown in the afternoon, she would find herself suddenly weary and
ready for a nap. Her metabolism was out of whack. The colors here
were too light and too bright—white wine, men in bleached denim
jeans, women in pastel cottons with nails lacquered fuchsia and
coral, all the drinks made with vodka or rum or tequila, expensive
cars polished to a shiny new white—like a Hawaiian print shirt before its first washing. It was beginning to hurt her eyes. She wanted
to be in a basement nightclub wearing dark stockings, drinking bourbon, watching the black boys dance with each other under the ultra-
violet strobe lights.

"Let's go for a cruise," she said, jangling the keys to her borrowed
'65 Mustang. "I must have red meat. Now. Cheeseburgers. On me."

They drove around for an hour, pulling off the expressway and onto
an older, local highway that was lined with fast-food restaurants,
auto body shops, a bowling alley as big as an airplane hangar, outdoor
furniture emporia, and a combination miniature golf course/all-you-
can-eat barbecue stand. December pulled up in front of a squat one-
story building, its rough stucco painted the bright yellow of a
fruit-gum wrapper, and ordered four cheeseburgers with everything
on them: one for Alex, three for her.

She was like a surly child coaxed into temporary cheer by a parent
exhausted into indulgence. Alex paid for food that he assured her
would make her sick later on; he bought her the stuffed pink flamingo toy that she swore would bring her good luck and that he was
sure she would leave behind her when she returned to New York; and
he protested only a little bit, just for the record, when she parked in
front of a wax museum and led him into the darkened vestibule
where an effigy of Humphrey Bogart, his shiny tan the color of peanut butter, beckoned them toward the cash register.

The tableaux grew more elaborate as they wandered through the
exhibits. Alex, being British, was at a slight disadvantage; though he
could easily identify Scarlett O'Hara draped in green velvet curtains,
he was having trouble with a teased peroxide blonde sitting astride
an expensive motorcycle.

"Nancy Sinatra," December said. "In her 'These Boots Were Made
for Walking' phase. Look, they've put a mirror on the floor. You can
see up her miniskirt."

"How accurate do you think they get underneath the panties?"
Alex said.

"They can do anything with wax," December replied. "Look, Fred and Ginger. I wonder if that's the actual dress she wore in the movie."

"I wonder if that's the actual Ginger Rogers."

December giggled. "Do you think people have to petition to get in here? Like getting their stars on the sidewalk?" Fame was the sole criterion here: if you could be recognized in wax, there you were, no larger than life, forever smiling in air-conditioned bliss.

"They're getting better as we go along," December said.

"They're probably saving the best for last," Alex said. "I suppose the president closes the show."

"No, it's always the same person at the end of every wax museum."

"And how many have you been to, darling?"

"Enough to know. Come on, guess."

"I wouldn't want to."

December shrugged. She knew who would be waiting for her around the very last corner, she knew before she heard the opening strains of "Love Me Tender," she even knew what he would be wearing: a bell-bottomed jumpsuit with a matching cape encrusted with fake gems and metal studs.

"Ah, your king," Alex said.

"I remember exactly where I was when I heard he died," December said. It had been a sunny day in the middle of August; she was crossing West Seventy-second Street against a crowd headed for opera in the park. It would turn out to be a summer full of deaths: first Elvis, two days later Groucho Marx, to be followed by Zero Mostel, Leopold Stokowski, Robert Lowell, and Maria Callas, all within a week of each other. The cultural icons were making a mass exit stage right, and December could almost picture them lined up, holding hands for their final bow: Joan Crawford next to Vladimir Nabokov next to Toots Shor next to Anaïs Nin next to Sir Anthony Eden. We're getting out of your way, seemed to be the message as December heard it, we're moving over and out, and just try to follow this act. Just try to come up with someone who can take Presley's place.

December and Alex bought postcards in the gift shop. Outside, the sun was still bright and the dark leather steering wheel burned against December's palms.

"Home, please," Alex said. The return trip seemed half as long as the ride out, and they discussed the changing aspects of time and distance like lazy philosophers of the road. Why driving back always seemed shorter than driving out. Why walking was the opposite: the return trip was endless, each step a misery.

December dropped Alex off at the foot of his driveway. "I'm still feeling restless," she said, tossing the flamingo up into his arms. "I'll see you later."

"Shall I count on you for dinner?" Alex asked.

"I'll try," December called back as she pulled away. She needed some time alone to think about this Boyfriend Problem. It was really more a business decision than an emotional one, and she tried to figure out what Katie Lee would do in her situation.

What was the technique Katie Lee had described to her last month? *Lateral thinking as a problem-solving technique,* that was it, that was the favored executive way. When someone presented you with a problem, sometimes the best thing to do wasn't to meet the problem head on; sometimes the best thing to do was to come at it sideways, take a lateral step, redefine the problem into something more easily solved.

What was the example Katie Lee had given her? In order to qualify for some sort of tax deduction, the hotel in New York had to open by the end of this year. The problem was, the hotel wouldn't be ready to receive guests until March of 1978. Everyone *thought* the problem was rushing the construction to get the rooms ready, and crews were working overtime plastering walls, laying down carpets, installing bathroom fixtures in the guest rooms. Katie Lee redefined her problem by researching what "opening date" really meant, and she discovered that if she held a New Year's Eve party for the construction workers on the very last day of the year and then let them stay over in the unfinished rooms so that no one would have to drive home drunk, her hotel would officially be considered to have opened in 1977. Katie Lee would get her tax deduction, the crews working overtime would get a swell weekend, and the press would be marvelous. Lateral thinking.

So what exactly is my problem? December said to herself as she drove aimlessly down the coast. I've been sleeping with too many people, or the wrong people, and word has been getting around, so I need to find some official steady boyfriend who will quiet these rumors and ease the fears of jealous women.

But sleeping with people isn't the real problem, she thought, turning left through a yellow light and heading down the main street of a sleepy suburb. Sleeping with people *who talk about it afterwards* is the trouble, and she felt herself taking that little lateral step: if I find someone who doesn't know movie people, who doesn't even know who I am, the problem of finding a boyfriend goes away.

Congratulating herself on her rational dissection of her life's dilemma and reminding herself that in times of crisis cool-headed logic is a girl's best friend, December looked down and noticed she was nearly out of gas. She pulled into the next gas station and there, a pack of Winstons rolled up in his plaid cotton shirt-sleeve and an oily blue rag hanging out of his back pocket like a sailing signal to a lost and weary voyager, was the absolutely positively most gorgeous man she had ever seen.

It was the kind of car that just begged to be checked out. Everyone had a story to tell about a '60s Mustang, a story that usually involved an all-night drive across state lines, or a beautiful woman in a halter top and water buffalo sandals, or a drug dealer nicknamed Professor or Doc who had evaded the draft by particularly clever means, or possibly all three. It was like Woodstock memorabilia: people told you, without being asked, how close they had gotten or how far away they were when they gave up or why they never even attempted the trip in the first place.

December cared about none of this. The weekend of Woodstock she and her friends had been working on their tans and gossiping about tryouts for the junior varsity cheerleading squad, which, about to enter the tenth grade, they were now eligible for. The car had been built and sold before her tenth birthday. When the manager of the gas station emerged from behind the plate glass of his office cubicle and asked if he could take a look at the engine, she got out of the car and told him to take his time.

The guy in the plaid shirt folded his dark aviator glasses into his front pocket as she walked by.

"Regular?" he asked.

December nodded. His eyes were a surprisingly dark brown. His sandy-brown hair—he had probably been blond as a child—was as straight and fine as a baby's, and hung around his ears and down the back of his neck in the sort of non-style December associated with people who got their hair cut only once a year. By October he'd be pulling it back into a ponytail, and next June he would lop it off again, in that old-fashioned center-part cut that demanded a great amount of cool to prevent the wearer from looking like Opie or, even worse, Alfalfa.

His two upper front teeth were slightly brighter than those he'd grown himself, and they disappeared altogether when he gave her a quick smile, his bottom lip coming up nearly to his nose, displaying a severe underbite. It was the jutting out of jaw that movie actors had affected for decades when playing tough-guy roles; a dentist would have described it as an eccentric occlusion, but to December it was just plain sexy, the dare and insouciance of it, this particular expression that was so thoroughly male. It gave a false heft to his face, which on closer examination was really quite delicate, as were his hands, surprisingly clean and well manicured for a grease monkey. He was just about her height, she guessed, lanky and thin, with the kind of naturally graceful and athletic body that would surprise him in a few years—she judged him to be in his late twenties—by demanding maintenance through diet and exercise. His stained khaki fatigue pants hung loosely from his waist and fell in soft folds around the high tops of his black basketball sneakers.

He had the sort of androgynous good looks of every twelve-year-old's first crush, the kind of boy girls naturally liked before they learned what they were *supposed* to like. Before they learned, from television and from fashion photography and from the rude discovery of the gap between what they wanted and what they could get, that this particular kind of cute was something you were supposed to outgrow.

Which December had never done, because she had never had to. She got a Fanta out of the soda machine and watched the two men leaning over the motor. The manager asked her something technical about the carburetor, and she confessed that she didn't know a thing about cars, she was just borrowing this while she was in town, and the two men exchanged knowing looks. December didn't like having to compete with a car for male attention. The guy in the plaid shirt hardly seemed to notice her at all.

"I'd love to see how she runs," he said, refastening the cap with his left hand. The meter read ten dollars even. "I just bought one of these, it's in pretty bad shape, and I'm trying to figure out what to do with it."

"I guess that could be arranged," December said, fishing a ten out of her pocket.

"Why don't you bring her back around seven," he said, waving away her money. A Plymouth station wagon had pulled up on the other side of the pumps. "We'll take her out for a spin."

"I guess that would be okay," December said.

He grinned at her, the grin of a man who is used to getting exactly what he wants, and asked her name.

"Deirdre," she said.

"Tom Roberts," he said, extending his hand.

"Deirdre Davis," she said, taking it.

"See you at seven," he said. As she turned around to leave she tripped over a length of hose and he grabbed her with one hand around either side of her waist and pulled her back up toward him. She could feel his breath on the back of her neck. He held on to her a little longer than necessary, just a few seconds more than it took for her to regain her balance, and in that moment she felt something catch inside her gut.

"Careful, Deirdre," he whispered into her ear, guiding her with his right hand resting gently on the small of her back, opening the car door with his left.

She started the engine, and as she pulled away did a quick calculation in her head: she had two hours to drive back to Alex's, shower, change, and get back to the station. She could pull it off if the rush hour traffic wasn't too bad. A car honked to her right, and she realized she had run a red light.

This guy was trouble, but December couldn't figure out exactly what kind of trouble. He wasn't dangerous or scary, she had seen that right away from the way he and the manager had been kidding around as they poked through the wires of the engine. And he certainly wasn't going to be aggressive, she could tell he was used to having women come to him, he'd hardly looked at her at all, and when she'd spoken to him he'd maintained unbroken eye contact— in fact she'd been the one who'd had to look away first.

The trouble was this: for the first time in a long time December was interested in a man she did not know how to control. Every flirtation was different, but in a sense every flirtation had been the same: she might be cajoled or teased or seduced or flattered, but up till now she had always felt that she was the one doing the ultimate manipulating, that she was the one who was pushing the buttons. She didn't know how it had happened, but in that brief moment when Tom Roberts had spread his fingers across her waist and pushed his thumbs up against her back some shift had taken place. Suddenly he had become the challenge, the mystery, the one who was calling the shots.

The real trouble was this: December loved it. She was sure that if a doctor took a blood sample right now he would find some rare and perhaps even unnamed chemical substance pumping through her veins, something Tom Roberts had released in her, something that was going to make her do whatever he wanted.

The trouble had a name: powerlessness. It was sick, it was old-fashioned, it was masochistic, it was neurotic. He was going to make her crazy, he was going to make her feel weak, he was going to make her feel and say and do a lot of things that an attractive, successful, self-aware woman wasn't supposed to feel and say and do in 1977.

And so fucking what, December said to herself as she pulled up into Alex's driveway. She might be powerless, she might be unsure, she might be confused and nervous and a few other things she didn't care to be around men.

But the one thing she wasn't: afraid.

"She handles great," Tom said, coming out of the curve at fifty miles an hour and pushing the car back up to eighty.

December nodded and handed back the can of beer she'd been holding between her knees, now grown nearly as warm as the breeze blowing off the ocean. It was just after sunset, and she had no idea where they were.

"So, Deirdre," he said, "what keeps you busy in L.A?"

"Not much," she replied. "I just got here, and I'm staying with friends while I figure out what to do." It was nearly the truth. He hadn't asked her too many questions, which she took as her cue to return the favor. This much she had found out: he had grown up on the beach somewhere south of here and was now living with his sister in Venice. His sister was a nurse and his brother-in-law had opened a surf shop when he got out of the army. They had three kids who drove Tom crazy, but it was a place to stay. He didn't officially work at the gas station; the manager was an old friend from high school, and sometimes Tom went over and helped out when one of the regulars didn't show, which seemed to be pretty often. Together they bought vintage cars, fixed them up, and resold them at a profit that didn't quite justify the time they'd put into them.

December didn't believe he was telling the truth, or rather, she had the feeling Tom was hiding something, an old drug problem or a bad marriage, some piece of information he didn't trust her with. He was testing her, that much she knew, looking over at her occasionally when he did something particularly risky on the road, waiting for her to show him she was frightened, to ask him to slow down.

But the more risks he took, the calmer she got. Any little thing could happen now: a truck could surprise them around the bend or a kid on a bicycle could wobble across the road or an oil slick could send them spinning over the edge of a cliff. December just leaned back and opened another beer. Bad things happened only to frightened people. That was the law of the road: fate protected those who put their faith in fate.

As they moved ahead, faster and faster, she felt them to be breaking some barrier, entering a new kind of space. They were just a man and a woman in a car going very, very fast. They were maybe the only man and woman on this planet right now, everything else had disappeared into the blur along the side of the highway: a dark-green wash of trees, the hard blue light of a drive-in, an oversize billboard that, had they been driving at the legal limit, Tom would have seen to be a twenty-foot rendering of December lying across a velvet couch smoking a dark-brown cigarette. When Tom pulled off onto a private road and drove them through the woods, past a *No Trespassing* sign, around a large dark house and back to a clearing overlooking a canyon, she didn't ask any questions.

"They're never home," he said, shutting off the engine and reaching across to open her door. "A friend of mine does their gardening. Movie people."

December got out of the car and stretched her legs. Somewhere along the canyon someone was giving a party—she could hear the shriek of a woman being pushed into a swimming pool, and the Rolling Stones drifting out of a loudspeaker.

Tom sat down on the grass and held up a beer to December. She sat down beside him and took a sip. When "Wild Horses" came on he lay back and played a perfectly synchronized air guitar, his face a grimace of concentration, his back arching up against the imaginary instrument. She giggled and lay down next to him.

"Some days I worship Keith Richards," she said, leaning her head against his shoulder.

"He's cool enough," Tom said, curving an arm under her shoulders and resting his hand on her bottom rib. She inhaled and smiled: so he had gone home and showered before she picked him up. She rubbed her nose in the nook between where his jaw ended and his ear began; she smelled baby shampoo and menthol shaving cream. His clean flannel shirt felt soft as an infant's blanket beneath her cheek. He had changed into black jeans and cowboy boots with squared-off toes.

He had slipped the elastic off the end of her long braid and was now slowly running his fingers through her hair, loosening the twist of it, pulling it across her shoulder and over her chest. The record was flipped over and another one began and ended and still they lay there, perfectly quiet, neither one willing to make the first move.

I'm just a girl he picked up at the gas station, December reminded herself, he has no idea who I am. She had dressed carefully, wearing nothing that might give away how much money she had or that she came from New York. She was wearing a blue-and-white-striped T-shirt over a skirt of matching fabric, its loose folds gathered into a cheap elastic waistband. The malls were full of stripes this year, horizontal mostly, it was a very bad season to be overweight. On her feet, thin white cotton anklets and bright-red high heels. It wasn't so hard, really, looking like the kind of girl who got picked up at gas stations. It was pretty much what she had been raised to be.

He lifted himself up a little to get a swallow of beer, and when he lay down again he shifted his hand just a little lower, and she felt his cool touch against her skin in the narrow gap where her shirt had fallen back from her waist. He moved his thumb lazily back and forth, like the halfhearted stroking given to a cat curled up and sleeping on its owner's lap.

She was waiting for him to move his hand up higher. He was going to make her wait. She thought about sliding down, just a fraction of an inch, and then she reconsidered: eagerness wasn't what was called for, not just yet. He thought about turning over and kissing her, and then he reconsidered: this time he wasn't going to rush. This time they had all night.

When his hand came up over her breast she heard herself sigh, and she heard him make a sound in his throat somewhere between a snicker and a moan. He was still pretending absentmindedness, his fingers playing her in a light repetitive rhythm, promising nothing, but she could tell from the way his breath was deepening, his chest rising harder against her head, that everything had already been decided, had probably been decided from the first time he set eyes on her. He rested his lips against the side of her mouth, a fraction short of a kiss, and they lay this way for a while longer. It was perfect torture, and it was perfect bliss.

When he kissed her, a deep open kiss, his tongue everywhere at once, she dropped her hands against her sides. She couldn't think of a single thing to do, except lie there perfectly still and be kissed. She cupped one hand around his shoulder—it was the least she could do, even thirteen-year-old girls knew enough to do this—and he took it and held it over her head, against the ground. It was as though he didn't want her to do anything that would get him more excited than he already was, anything that would get them where they were going more quickly. It was another rule of the road: the point of the trip wasn't your destination but the road itself, the process of getting there. She laced her fingers through his. This kiss was going to last a million years, long enough for everything she knew to fade away and disappear, so long that when it ended everything in the world would be different. Was it possible to come just from a kiss, she wondered. Was she about to find out.

When he placed a single finger against the back of her bare uplifted knee she felt something melt inside her. She felt something that she usually didn't feel with men until they were much further along, until they were nearly *there,* it was crazy, that he could make her feel more with the brief touch of one finger against her knee than she had ever felt before. She wasn't thinking about what he was thinking, she wasn't doing anything specific to give him pleasure and she wasn't doing anything special to receive it, she just *was,* and he just *was,* and they just *were,* it was enough for them just to be here, together. Like a concert pianist who after years of practice and memorization finally feels the masterwork flowing directly from his soul across the black and white keys, who finally forgets all the technique and theory and finesse and becomes at one with the music, so they lay there, unthinking and innocent.

When they undressed each other, spreading out their clothes like bed linens against the grass and pine needles, they exchanged a long smile, and she ran her hand across his mouth. He took it between his teeth and nibbled for a minute, and then they lay back down, perfectly still, prolonging the longing, only their toes touching. It was going to be very simple. She couldn't remember how to do it any other way.

When he ran his fingers up and down outside her, and she felt him pressing slightly against her hip, they kissed again. Their second kiss. His lips and tongue fluttered everywhere but for all the gymnastics were as soft as sleep. He began to move a finger inside her but she took him by the wrist and pulled him away: she was ready, and she wanted his cock to be the first thing she felt inside her, she wanted that first thrill of being entered, the pure contracting and expanding and rearranging herself around him, around *him*, not his fingers or his tongue but *him*, just him, purely him.

When he leaned over and entered her, one hand still entwined with hers over their heads, the other cupping her from behind, lifting her up around him, she heard the first sound of pleasure from him, a single "oh," what else was there to say. It was so slow, so slow, she felt herself coming around him, and he whispered into her ear: "of course," as though she had been trying to tell him something he already knew.

When he continued on, just slightly faster, she at last lifted her arms and held him. He was finally giving himself up to it, ceding the power he had taken from her, forgetting control, forgetting that there was such a thing as control. There was nothing fancy happening here, it was as simple as it got, each time he withdrew nearly to the tip of him, each time he entered her as deep as he could go, each time in a pure straight line, their arms wrapped around each other tightly as if to keep each other from flying off into space. She had forgotten how delicious it was to make love outdoors, with the earth hard beneath you and the night sky opening up above you, with nothing around you, no walls or furniture or objects, to remind you of who you were or who he wasn't. The wind blew chill against her bare thighs, streaked with his sweat.

When he came, he whispered again: "of course." Then he lifted himself on his elbows and they stared at each other. Beyond him she saw the tops of trees and a single cloud moving across the stars. Beneath the narrow crescent of the moon two planets sparkled; someone had told her this was a rare astronomical event, Mars and Venus aligned just so—but she had forgotten the rest of it, how to distinguish the planet of love from the planet of the warrior god. In his eyes she saw a little bit of the hardness gradually coming back, and then he smiled, to show her he was in control once more.

It didn't matter. She had passed the test. They got dressed in silence, and she drove him back to the gas station, where he'd left his car. There was nothing to say. He knew she'd be back, and she knew he'd be happy to see her. There was no question of it. They belonged together. They were a fact.

"You look like the cat who ate the canary. Or is it vice versa," Alex said, removing the crusts from his toast.

"Do I," December said, finishing off her second cup of coffee. She hadn't been able to eat any of the breakfast he'd prepared for her. She'd gotten only four hours of sleep. Every time she thought of Tom Roberts her gut did a little flip, as though it were trying to somersault upward toward her heart.

"Your afterglow is showing," Alex said. "You'll have to eat eventually, you know."

"I suppose," she said. She felt absolutely terrific. The world was a marvelous place. She was the most blessed girl in the universe. She could do anything she set her mind to. There were nothing but fantastic possibilities laid out before her. She was going to be a big, big star.

"What are you thinking about?" Alex asked.

Oh, just the usual, she said to herself. What I'll wear when I'm nominated for my first Oscar. How I'll handle it when Johnny Carson asks me the embarrassing questions. Which magazines I'll allow to interview me, what kind of commercial endorsements are lucrative without being tacky, whether I'll need to hire a private secretary.

"I'm trying to come up with a baby present for Rosaline," she said.

"How old is the little monster?" Alex asked.

"Five months, and he's hardly a monster," December said. "In fact when I saw him in September he was a perfect angel."

Alex sighed. "Of course. Rosaline isn't capable of anything else."

"You're in a lovely mood," December said, running her tongue along the inside of her lower lip. It was still there.

"Well, what do you expect?" Alex said, moving the butter out of the sun so it wouldn't soften. "You stay out all night doing God knows what with God knows who—"

"Jealous?"

"Don't insult me. You come home at dawn looking like you've just done ten trips on Space Mountain and then have the audacity not to come through with the gory details. Not nice."

December shrugged. "Some guy I met. No big deal."

"Anyone I know?"

"Nope."

"Anyone I wish I knew?"

"Nope."

"Anyone I've ever heard of?"

"Nope."

"Well, that's a relief. But mystery doesn't suit you, darling. You're too blond for that."

December looked over at Alex. California was agreeing with him. His hair, now shot through with strawberry-blond highlights and a sprinkling of gray, curled down nearly to his shoulders, and he'd lost some of his decadent pallor. He'd begun exercising a bit—were those actual triceps she detected?—and for all his bitchy talk he seemed more relaxed, more at ease with himself.

Perhaps California was just what she needed. The career move had been long overdue. There was a house just down the road for rent. She could keep her place in New York, just in case; she could still fly back for print work a few times a month. What was there tying her to New York, anyway? Rosaline, Marinda, Katie Lee, Schuyler: a scene she'd be happy to leave behind. It was time to move on.

"That house for rent," December said, "do you know if it's still available? Is it incredibly expensive?"

"Not too," Alex replied. "I'll check it out for you if you'd like. But they're only interested in someone long-term. You'll have to sign a lease for two years at least."

"I can handle that," December said.

"And my contracts are for three years. To start."

"I can handle that too," December said.

"And I'm serious about finding you a boyfriend. I hope I don't need to put that in writing."

"Whatever," December said, pushing back her chair and stretching her arms over her head.

"I'll have everything ready for signature by the end of the week," Alex said, and she left the table and walked across the stone terrace back to the house. When she got to the doorway she turned, as though she'd forgotten something.

"Oh, one more thing," she said. "The car. I've sort of gotten used to it. Do you think they can be talked into selling?"

"For the right price," Alex said, gathering up the dishes.

"Could you take care of that for me?"

"I'll take care of everything," Alex said, balancing two coffee cups on December's untouched plate. "It's a lovely heap of metal. A fantasy machine."

"It's just a car," December said, slipping a hand into her pocket. She could feel the jagged edge of the car keys pressing against her leg, reminding her, through the thin cotton lining of her jeans, of last night. Just another car. Just another guy. Like any other car. Like any other guy.

17

She had known, right away, exactly what he needed.

Even if he didn't. But then, men hardly ever did. He probably thought he was falling in love. Katie Lee found this vaguely amusing, that Schuyler Smith had somehow convinced himself that he was falling in love with her. He hadn't actually uttered those three little words, but sometimes, in the crackling pause of a long-distance telephone conversation or as they danced together to something slow and sentimental or after they had made love, she could feel that he was thinking it, that he was about to say it, that he was wondering what she would do, what her response would be if he said it. I love you.

And each time he was smart enough to keep quiet, and that was when she liked him best, in that moment of pure relief when she rested in his arms secure in the knowledge that his impulse had passed and the evening wasn't going to take an unpleasant detour. She wasn't going to have to talk about her feelings or her emotions. Which were none of his business, anyway, when you got right down to it. She was sleeping with him. That should be enough.

She had known right away, on their first real date together, exactly what he wanted. It had nothing to do with her, in fact it had nothing to do with women, but Schuyler would never have believed that.

In early March, just a few weeks after Rosaline's Valentine's Day party, Schuyler had called her up to invite her to an opening at a photography gallery. The pictures were mostly of construction sites, shot at unusual angles with distorting lenses so that the girders and beams and pipes became nearly unidentifiable elements of abstract compositions. He thought Katie Lee might enjoy the show, and afterwards they could have dinner together and do some catching up.

Over bay scallops and lime mousse Schuyler brought her up to date on his various projects. He'd left the paper to do free-lance work, and one of his articles was being made into a comeback vehicle for a movie actor who had publicly battled a serious drug problem. Schuyler had used the movie money to finance his travels to Central America, and he had just finished a piece on a particularly savage band of guerrillas, whose sophisticated arsenal of weaponry had been financed with the profits from a stadium tour by an aging California synthesizer band. Now he was doing the preliminary research for a long article on organized crime—"an old story," he said, "that just keeps getting better and better."

"But aren't you scared?" Katie Lee asked, swirling the pastel cream up onto her spoon.

Schuyler rolled up his shirt-sleeve and showed her a large round scar. "That bullet was paid for with your tax dollars. Yes, I'm scared shitless, and anyone who says he isn't is lying."

Katie Lee circled his scar with her index finger, gazed into his eyes, and sighed. "I think bravery is the quality I admire most in men. I know that sounds terribly old-fashioned."

"Maybe you're just an old-fashioned kind of girl," he said, rolling down his sleeve and buttoning the cuff.

"That I am," she said, giving him a wink. She knew what he was scared of most right now: women. She could spot the signs. The way he had gotten a little sloppy about his appearance, as though it were remotely possible for him to make himself less attractive, make himself less interesting to women. The way he was writing about subjects that took him into such completely male worlds—locker rooms and battlefields and oil rigs—as though he were in search of the lost formula for his own masculinity. The way he seemed to delight in facing down the dangerous—first Central America, now the mob—as though he were trying to prove he was a man.

Which Katie Lee knew he would be able to prove in only one place —a bedroom, and she was going to make sure it was hers. She had seen a lot of men like him since she'd come to New York, men who'd had one too many bad experiences with aggressive and demanding women, men who'd been raised to be one way and now were expected to be another, men who claimed to be confused about women when really they were only confused about themselves.

For all that she considered herself a daddy's girl, right now, sitting opposite Schuyler as the waiter brought the check, she thanked her lucky stars for the one thing her Kentucky mother had taught her: how to make a man feel as if he were the only man in the room, in the city, in the whole wide world that existed for her tonight. Though she had an account at this restaurant, Katie Lee didn't even make the customary halfhearted offer to pay half of the check. She waited for Schuyler to pull out her chair and help her on with her black gabardine blazer, and she rested one hand in the crook of his elbow as they left the restaurant.

Suddenly she couldn't seem to do anything by herself: open a door, cross a street, hail a cab.

"There was a really awful robbery in my building last month," she said, leaning against him in the back of the taxi. "This woman downstairs came home from work—in the middle of the week, and it was only around seven o'clock—and there were four men cleaning out her apartment. She walked in on them just as they were finishing up. Maybe you read about it?"

"I don't think so," Schuyler said, relaxing a little bit into her.

Of course he hadn't, because the robbery had involved only two men, and it was a couple who had walked in on them, and it had happened over a year ago, somewhere in Queens.

"Oh, well. They tied her up, and—well, you can imagine. I went to visit her in the hospital and she was completely covered with bandages. Just two holes for her eyes and one so she could drink stuff through a straw. She was the sweetest little girl, she had just moved to New York from Indiana, and as soon as she got out of the hospital she moved straight back." The cab pulled up in front of the canopied entrance to Katie Lee's building, attended by two uniformed doormen.

"Would you like me to see you inside?" Schuyler asked.

"Oh, please," she said, and she waited while he walked around the car, opened her door, and helped her up onto the curb. As they left the elevator and turned onto her hallway she tripped a little and fell against him. He caught her, and as he supported her she placed her arm around his waist.

"New shoes," she explained, lifting one leg in front of her and pointing her foot so as to expertly show off her brand new red patent leather high heels, the solid curve of her calf, a flash of thigh in sheer dark stockings as her side-slit skirt fell away from her leg.

"I like them," he said. "They remind me of the ruby slippers in

The Wizard of Oz. Maybe they have magic powers."

Katie Lee let him into her apartment and turned on a table lamp. "Such as?" she asked.

He shrugged and leaned against a wall. "Click your heels together and make a wish."

She closed her eyes, puckered her lips, clicked her heels three times, and then smiled. She knew he was expecting her to offer him a drink. Instead she held the door open and said, "Well, thanks so much for seeing me home. I feel so much safer having you around." She wasn't going to make a move, she wasn't even going to do anything that would let him know she wanted him to make a move. This was the way Katie Lee Hopewell intended to seduce Schuyler Smith: by reinventing herself into the most fragile, passive, uncritical, traditionally feminine creature imaginable. She didn't think she'd be able to keep it up for very long, but then again it wouldn't take very long to get what she wanted.

This was the way she planned to seduce him: by convincing him that *he* was seducing *her.* After a few weeks of nearly innocent dinners (kisses on the cheek turning to soft brushings of lips) and evenings of parties and dancing (the kisses getting deeper, making out in her doorway or on her living room couch before she backed away, sighing, whispering that he was moving a little too fast for her), she finally let him carry her one Saturday night across the deep carpet of her bedroom and allowed him to make love to her.

She had lain there, nearly quiet and still, as he undressed her and then himself. He was an expert lover, but the one element of sex that had always excited her most with Bobby Vincent, the push-and-pull of power and daring, was absent. She had once spent an entire weekend teaching herself how to fake coming (by masturbating with her fingers inside herself, and then by practicing the exact sequence of voluntary muscle contractions that most closely duplicated orgasm; sometimes, when she went months without sex, she kept her muscles in tone by practicing as she sat at her desk making telephone calls), and that night she faked three times.

In those first few weeks she told him over and over that he was the best lover she'd ever had. That he was the best writer she'd ever read. That he was the smartest man she'd ever met. That he could do anything he wanted, anything at all, if only he set his mind to it.

She never forgot what he needed, what he wanted, and she never forgot to give it to him. It wasn't sex. It wasn't affection. It wasn't understanding. It was only confidence, and it was easy: she had plenty extra to give away.

By November they had settled into a comfortable routine: weekends together at her apartment and one or two nights during the week at his. They had sex one, maybe two of those nights, and tonight was not going to be one of those nights. This Katie Lee had already decided, though it was not yet ten o'clock, and they would probably get home by midnight.

Katie Lee applied a new coat of lipstick and left a dollar for the bathroom attendant. All around her women in sequined and beaded evening dress were gossiping and raving over the Russian dancer who had just made his American debut and telling each other they looked absolutely marvelous. They were full of shit, Katie Lee thought; they were all wrinkling and sagging and softening into middle age, and there was nothing they could do about it. They reminded her of the little colonies of deposed European royalty she had met in the resort cities of the Riviera and the Mediterranean and the islands of the Caribbean, where faded ladies with minor titles from someplace vanished and unpronounceable were forever bound together by their fall from power, by their shared remembrance of a better time and their unwavering belief that someday they would be restored to their rightful places and the world would once again recognize their beauty, their brilliance, their positions.

These women casing each other during intermission, patrons of the ballet and the opera and the museums, had welcomed Katie Lee to the fold. The Hopewells had begun giving substantial amounts of money to the right causes, and Charlotte Van Schott had vouched for Katie Lee through a series of a half dozen intimate luncheons at an East Side restaurant where reservations were accepted three weeks in advance.

Katie Lee smiled at the woman who had invited her to this particular benefit performance and examined her reflection in the full-length mirror. She had no illusions: in a few months she'd be twenty-four years old, and she figured she had two, maybe three years left before everything started to show. She had already cut her long hair so that it just brushed her shoulders and fluffed into waves framing her face. Everyone would have to do that eventually to give their hair some lift as their faces started to drop. Katie Lee had noticed how many women, in the months before and after their thirtieth birthdays, underwent major transformations at their hairdressers. Better to get it out of the way now, she had figured, to be the first of her friends to give up their girlish collegiate haircuts. Later it would seem an obvious, desperate, hopeless attempt to hold on to youth.

Her thighs were already beginning to go. She had considered taking up jogging or swimming, but then she had calculated just how much each hour-long session of exercise would cost her by dividing her annual income by fifty (the weeks she worked each year) and then again by seventy (the hours she put in during an average week). It came to hundreds of dollars a week just to fight a losing battle. It hardly seemed worth it.

She turned sideways in the mirror. Her backless blue-sequined halter dress fell in a single swoop to the top of her dyed-to-match silk pumps. Earlier, at home, she had done jumping jacks in the mirror to make sure that no sudden movements would cause the dress to slip or slide. She wasn't going to be able to get away with backless dresses too much longer. Push-ups were the only exercise she had time for now (her breasts were her major vanity), but no matter how many she did, the pull of gravity was unstoppable. Two or three years, that was it. She'd be having lunch with Bobby the day after tomorrow. She had it all planned out. This time she would get what she wanted.

Out in the lobby Schuyler was leaning against the back of a velvet armchair, holding her drink. It was unfair, he was going to look great forever, Katie Lee thought with a sigh, his hair would always be thick and his body tough and lean.

"It's a zoo in there," she said, taking hold of her bourbon.

"They're about to start, so drink up," Schuyler said. She stood with her back to the crowd and downed her drink in four swallows.

"Thirsty girl," he said, taking her arm and leading her down the aisle to their seats in the tenth row. The lights went down, the curtain came up, a flute trilled over violins, and a row of dancers tourjetéd toward center stage.

I hate the ballet and I hate dancers, Katie Lee said to herself. They're so disgustingly thin and flexible and *dumb*, with those tiny heads perched on scrawny necks, how could it be otherwise? All these men pretending to be cultural, connoisseurs of the arts. She was sure they were all sitting rapt in private erotic fantasies involving women naked save for tutus made of pink netting and pink toe shoes with pink satin ribbons tied around their ankles, women who curled their legs up into impossible positions and never spoke.

Maybe she should start getting involved with the opera. They had much better sets and costumes, and the women were mostly overweight and looked like their eye makeup had been applied with a child's Magic Markers, their liner extending halfway to their ears. Schuyler hated the opera, but right now he would do just about anything she asked of him. Just about anything at all.

"What time is it?" Katie Lee asked when they got back to his apartment, though the digital alarm clock was easily seen from where she stood.

"A little before twelve," Schuyler said, loosening his tie.

"It feels later," she said. She undressed, hung her gown on the right side of his bedroom closet, carefully folded her underwear and stockings, got into bed, and pulled the covers up to her shoulders while Schuyler washed up and brushed his teeth in the bathroom. She read the early edition of the next day's paper, feigning total concentration behind her amber-framed schoolteacher's glasses, as he undressed and got into bed beside her. When he turned out the light she took off her glasses and curled herself into the crook of his arm.

"I wish I didn't have to go away," she said, though the prospect of seeing Bobby excited her so much she almost felt like having sex.

"Then don't," Schuyler said, playing with her hair.

"I have to. They just had a big shake-up at the bank in Chicago, and I need to make an appearance, stroke the new boys. Totally boring and totally necessary."

"Marinda says Bobby's in Chicago this week," he said, and there was a moment of silent assessment as he tried to gauge from her response whether she had already known this and she tried to figure out when he had seen or spoken to Marinda.

"God, I haven't seen Marinda in ages," she said. "How is she?"

"Nearly thin, with a very good-looking boyfriend."

"If you like that type," Katie Lee said.

"What type is that?"

"Um, you know, *ethnic*. Where did you see them?"

"At the liquor store. They were buying champagne, but they wouldn't tell me what they were celebrating."

"Well, I hope it works out," Katie Lee said, nearly meaning it. She knew Marinda was still madly in love with Schuyler, and she'd be able to have him soon enough, but in the meantime Katie Lee wanted Marinda out of her way. "She certainly deserves it, she's had such a hard time these last few years." She tried to think of something else nice to say, anything to stall and distract so that Schuyler didn't bring up Bobby's name again.

"Are you going to see Bobby in Chicago?" he asked. This always unnerved her, the way he just came out and asked direct questions.

"Not unless he's working as a bellboy in the Lakeshore Hopewell House."

"I'd like to get in touch with him, actually," Schuyler said, shifting his weight.

"What for?"

"This piece I'm working on. Just general background, nothing crucial. He might be able to help me out."

"Help you out with what?" Katie Lee asked, though she knew exactly what Schuyler was looking for. Last week, when he'd left her alone in his apartment for a few hours while he went out for drinks with his cousin Teddy, she'd gone through his notes for the organized crime piece. He'd hit a roadblock, was having some trouble figuring out the true ownerships of various shell corporations, and the Vincent name had surfaced on a few legal documents and registration forms. Schuyler believed that although Bobby wasn't involved in anything personally, he might make a phone call to his father or his uncle, who would arrange for Schuyler to interview people who might arrange for him to interview some other people who might tell him something interesting. Katie Lee believed differently: that Bobby, as heir apparent to the family holdings, was in up to his eyeteeth in the various cash-laundering operations that Schuyler was coming so close to uncovering.

Indeed, it was Bobby who had introduced her to the various concessionaires who had agreed, on ridiculously unprofitable terms, to manage certain cash operations in their Chicago hotel. Katie Lee had signed the contracts for the florist stand and gift shop in the lobby, for the adjacent multilevel parking garage and the basement beauty salon without asking questions. Though it seemed unlikely that any of these concessions would generate enough legitimate income to warrant the high rents she was charging, she knew why all the supposedly unrelated companies wanted the contracts: they could doctor their books and funnel the cash from illegal enterprises through their hotel businesses into the very bank whose officers she was supposed to meet with the next day. The Internal Revenue Service would have no way of knowing that only fifty cars had parked on the night the records showed eighty or that only five women had come in for manicures and facials on the day the books showed twenty or that the eleven orders of three dozen long-stemmed out-of-season red roses (paid for in cash, supposedly, in case a jealous wife went through her husband's credit card receipts) had never existed at all.

Schuyler was finding out more than she wanted him to know. It was time to end this conversation, and she began to nuzzle the back of his neck. They kissed each other lazily for a while, and as his kisses fell lower and lower, around and across her breasts and down to her stomach, she felt a familiar clutch. It was one thing to fake when he was inside her, carried away with his own excitement; it was something else entirely when, with eyes open and a clear head between her legs, he might detect her charade. She pulled him up by the hair and gave him a hug.

"It's that time," she said, though her period wasn't due for three days.

"I don't care," he said.

"I just don't feel like it," she said, hugging him tighter. "I'm going to miss you. A lot," she murmured, her mouth on his throat. She felt the bobble of his swallow against her lips as he squeezed her against him. He was about to say it. He was going to say it. She placed two fingers across his lips and raised herself up out of the embrace and they stared at each other, eyes wide open in the dark.

"Katie Lee," he said into her hand. "When you get back from Chicago, we have to talk."

"What about," she said, turning over and curling her back against him, pulling his free hand onto her breast.

"About this. About us. About where this thing is going."

"I like what we have right now," she said, softening her speech into the slur that comes just before sleep.

He kissed the back of her neck. "So do I. But nothing ever stays the same forever. It's like that law of physics. There's no such thing as standing still. You're either moving forward or falling back."

"I always hated physics."

He ran a finger across the soft baby hair that arrowed down her neck. It always ended like this, he thought, with her unspoken message: Don't get too close, don't ask too much, don't tell me you love me. At first he thought it was just some fear in her, some insecurity, some problem he could help her work through. But lately he had begun to realize that it was part of what had drawn him to her, that on some level she was offering him the unspoken emotional assurance that she would never ask of him more than he had to give. It was what he had wanted, what he had needed, in those days when he had thought of himself as a total mess: a woman who wouldn't make demands.

But things were different now. He felt her slipping away into sleep. He lay there wide awake and watched the dawn come up through the narrow slats of the vertical blinds. He was twenty-five years old: at this age his father had been settled, with a wife and a four-year-old son.

Katie Lee had taught him something, and for this he had come to love her in an odd kind of way. She had taught him the value of partnership, of two people who believed in each other and helped each other toward their dreams. They had spent hours and hours together analyzing her deals and his articles, Schuyler offering advice as Katie Lee talked through the frustrations of a particularly troublesome venture, Katie Lee reading his first drafts with her librarian's glasses slipping down her nose, making faces when his thinking got fuzzy and exclaiming with delight over each deft turn of phrase.

But for all her support and encouragement of his work, he knew she would never marry him. He wasn't nearly rich enough. He came from a "nice" family but not a powerful one. He was just a writer. She had picked him up when he was feeling down, and for that he would always be grateful. As the sunlight streaked a grid across the bedcovers, he could for the first time imagine their parting: amicable, adult, tearless, lunch in a sunny restaurant, a handshake and a hug on the sidewalk, two taxis pulling off in different directions.

"Adult," that was the word, mature and sophisticated and with no false illusions or romantic hopes about the bargains that men and women strike with each other. Everything that he and Katie Lee had together, and nothing that he had ever dreamed he would be.

Under the pink linen tablecloth Katie Lee tapped the toe of her navy-blue kidskin pump against her briefcase. It was still there. She felt as though she had a time bomb under the table. Was that a ticking she heard? Of course not, both she and Bobby wore watches made costly by negatives: soundless, faceless, narrow to the point of invisibility. She wondered if he'd noticed they were wearing the men's and women's versions of the same gold Swiss wristwatch. It was a sign of some sort, though she rarely thought about omens and fate in matters of romance.

"That boyfriend of yours is going to get us all in trouble," Bobby said, slicing into his steak. "I'm surprised you haven't warned him off by now."

Katie Lee leaned back and folded her arms across her chest. "Sometimes you're so dumb about people it amazes me. If I told him he was swimming in dangerous waters he'd just go after the story twice as hard. Anyway, he's hardly told me anything at all about what he's doing."

"And he never gets suspicious when you send him out on errands for weird flavors of ice cream or whatever it is you do to be alone in his apartment?"

"Oh, he's incredibly careful. He locks his file cabinet and keeps the key taped inside the lining of an old suitcase in the bottom of his closet, which is also locked. The key to the suitcase is taped to the ceiling of his oven. And he lays stuff under the tapes, like strands of hair, or one time a grain of rice, so he can tell if someone's been into his stuff."

"And how did you get around this elaborate security system?"

Katie Lee smiled. "Don't insult me. It was easy. Anyway, he thinks I know nothing, and he has no idea we're having lunch together."

"You're the worst. Or the best. I can't decide." He cut into his steak again and, hitting bone, laid down his knife and pushed the plate away. "You really have to fly back tonight?"

"I do. I told you, no messing around with this one."

Bobby leaned back and mirrored her pose. He was trying to figure out if there was enough time, before her evening flight reservation, to take her upstairs to his hotel room. He was trying to figure out just what it was that kept pulling him toward her over the years—maybe if he figured it out he'd be immune to it.

She looked terrific of course, she was one of the few women he knew who could carry an extra ten or fifteen pounds in just the right places. There was something about the way she was always so perfectly groomed—the immaculately manicured and enameled nails, the hair streaked and cut with scientific precision, the makeup flawless and always fresh—that made him want to peel away layer after perfect layer. The suit that never wrinkled, the shoes that never scuffed or wore down at the heels, stockings that never ran or bagged, the full slip and bra and briefs all perfectly matched, the lace stretched against skin made smooth with oils and fragrant with powders—he wanted to peel it all away, rip it all off until he found the place that wasn't perfect, correct, planned in its prettiness: the place that was human.

There was a lot not to like in Katie Lee, and he reeled off the shopping list: cold, calculating, manipulative, greedy, ambitious, deceitful, it went on and on. But how could he hate those things in her, in anyone? If he did, he'd have to hate them in himself.

She wasn't even a particularly good fuck, he had to remind himself. Sure, she had this great body, fantastic breasts, an honest-to-god waist, hips you could grab hold of, and sure, she had figured out all the right moves, even if she did them in a somewhat workmanlike manner, as if she were saying "This is my job, and I do it with pride and enthusiasm." Still, he'd had better, much better, and still, after all this time, he wanted Katie Lee. Because when it was all over with Katie Lee, and he was lying in bed watching her shower and dress and reapply her makeup and refasten her expensive jewelry, he knew something had happened that was more than physical. "Spiritual" was the wrong word, it was a word both of them would have laughed at. "Emotional" wasn't the right word either, it was a word both of them held in contempt. Katie Lee, who was the strongest, smartest, meanest girl he knew, who was the woman most like himself, made him feel as if he had conquered something. As if he had won a battle or a prize. It had nothing to do with pleasure, and everything to do with power. Like drugs, especially like this particular drug he had been doing a lot of lately. Cocaine and Katie Lee: the two things, these days, that made him feel good about himself.

"It's been an awfully long time," Bobby said. She was playing hard to get, and he knew that she knew that he knew it. Sex with Katie Lee was like poker: the game itself was nothing, it was the strategy and maneuvering, the bluffing and betting and selective showing of cards, that kept him at the table. She held a strong hand today, something royal, the kind of hand you wait for a long time.

"Nine months, two weeks, and three days," she said. "I do sort of miss you."

"Sort of?" he asked.

She sighed. "Oh, Schuyler is wonderful and all that, but it just isn't the same. It isn't what I really want."

"And what is that. What you really want."

"I think you know," she said. She had just flipped over the ten of spades. Four more cards to go.

"Well, you know the old song," Bobby said. "You can't always get what you want."

"I've never believed that," she said. Jack of spades. "Listen, though, about Schuyler. He's found out about the shell corporation your father set up in Delaware. He's going down there next week."

"Who is he meeting with?" Bobby asked.

Katie Lee rested her elbows on the table and cupped her chin in her hands. "How much is at stake here really? For you, I mean."

"Just answer me. Who's he meeting with."

"You answer me first. How much is at stake here."

"Nothing serious," Bobby said. "I'd just like to avoid a little embarrassment, especially during an election year, when everyone starts acting like the king of holiness. He's being a pain in the ass more than anything else."

Katie Lee said nothing.

"He can't cause any serious trouble. It'll make me look bad, more than anything else, because he's supposed to be a friend of mine from Harvard. Normally I wouldn't care at all."

Katie Lee still said nothing.

"And you know, once this piece comes out we'll have to discredit him somehow, which I'll hate to do, because Marinda will have a fit, and because of you of course."

"Of course," Katie Lee said. "You still haven't answered my question."

"And you haven't answered mine."

"You first."

"I told you. It's embarrassing, this kind of press."

"Bullshit."

"That's all there is to it."

"Bullshit," she said, looking at her watch. "I have to get going."

"Okay, okay. Everything."

"What?" she asked.

"Everything. Everything's at stake. Things I can't tell you about. Things they don't even want to tell me about," Bobby said, flushing. "I don't know how he gets all these people to talk to him. I don't even know who he's talking to. If I did, I could do something about it. Get to them first."

"What do you mean, get to them first?"

Bobby laughed. "Oh, it's not as creepy as it sounds. It's just money. People get awfully quiet when you offer to help out with their kids' college bills or their alimony payments. People start forgetting things."

"Schuyler's been so sweet to me," Katie Lee said, lowering her eyes. "And he's so excited about this story. It would be disloyal of me, don't you think, if I told you his sources."

So she knew who his sources were. Queen of spades. Bobby reached across the table and took her hand. "What do you want, Katie Lee?"

"You know what I want."

"Say it."

"You. I want you, Bobby. I always have."

"You've got me."

"No, I don't," she said, squeezing his hand. "Not the way I want you. Not the way it was meant to be."

"And how is that?"

"Partners. All the way, not just business. Don't you see how great it could be? We'd be invincible, the two of us, together." She raised her left hand, and spread out her fingers, and then slowly wagged her ring finger back and forth.

"Partners," she said.

"Do you want to marry me?" he said.

"Is that a proposal?"

"Jesus, Katie Lee, I can't marry you."

"But you can fuck me and use me and ask me to betray this man who happens to be in love with me. Who would marry me in a minute, if I wanted him to. Maybe I should marry Schuyler. After this story comes out and the movie is made he'll be pretty hot stuff. And you'll be—what will you be, Bobby, after this story comes out?" King of spades. Ace of spades. Royal flush.

"Look, Katie Lee, it's complicated. It's not like I can go off and marry anyone I want. For one thing, you're not Catholic."

Katie Lee rolled her eyes and stood up. "You're a fool. No, stay here, I want to remember you like this. Someday you'll realize what we could have been together—someday, when it's too late." She picked up her briefcase and pushed her hair back off her face. "I've wasted too many years on you, Bobby," she said, and she walked out.

When she got to the elevator she counted to ten: that's how long it would take him to leave money for the check and follow her out into the hallway.

"Wait," he said, coming up behind her and putting his hands on her shoulders. He spun her around. She held her briefcase against her chest like a shield.

"Wait," he repeated. He thought he saw tears in her eyes. Here she was, the strongest, smartest woman he knew, and she wanted him. She could get anyone she wanted, anything she wanted, and what she wanted was him. She had made him an offer: she could be his worst enemy or his best friend, but he knew there was nothing in between.

He pictured the wife he had always imagined for himself: the pretty middle daughter from a family not unlike his, a woman who would keep a happy home for him, who would bear his children and stay behind uncomplaining while he worked, while he traveled, while he had affairs—it was the traditional bargain and an awfully attractive one from his end. Someone like his mother, his aunts, his sisters, his cousins, someone who fit in.

And here was Katie Lee. He had a sudden vision of her in a white bride's dress, something with yards of lace, a long train, white satin scalloped into a sweetheart neckline. Everything about her was gold: the golden jewelry, the gold flecks in her eyes, her hair, her skin everywhere tanned to that even color. He pictured her lying there in his bed, their bed, every night for the rest of his life, this battle both wonderful and awful. He felt himself weakening before her. He felt tired. He wanted the thing that would make him feel strong again. She knew what that was. She would always know.

When the elevator arrived it was empty. She did not protest as he pushed her inside, took her up to his floor, and pulled her into his room.

"Marry me," he said, pushing her against a wall and holding her head in his hands.

"When," she said, setting down her briefcase.

"Whatever you want," he said, taking off her jacket and tossing it onto a chair.

"We'll tell our parents over Thanksgiving," she said, kicking off her shoes. He unzipped her skirt and pulled her skirt, pantyhose, and briefs to the floor.

"I want us to have Christmas together," she said. He had buried his face in her hair and was kissing her roughly up and down her neck. "We'll get married in June, in Kentucky. Marinda will be my maid of honor and I guess Carter should be best man."

"Whatever you want," Bobby said, lifting her up onto the leather-topped desk. He swept a paperweight and a pile of file folders to the floor. The top of the desk was hard and uncomfortable. She rested her head on a stack of computer printouts. Something was caught under her, something hurt, she arched her back and found a pocket calculator. He had taken off his jacket and trousers and, standing at the edge of the desk, pulled her against him, folding her legs around his waist. He shoved into her and came almost instantly. She raised herself up on her elbows, knocking over a pencil holder, and gave him a wide smile.

He smiled back, a smile without warmth or affection, and carried her over to the bed. He unbuttoned her blouse and unhooked her bra and threw them onto a pile with his shirt and socks, and began again. He was chewing on his lower lip, and his forehead was knitted into a frown. Katie Lee never liked it when they did it twice, because the second time always took so long, and she was starting to feel dry, she always got this way before her period. She began moving from right to left, squeezing him as hard as she could, anything to hurry him along, but when she finally faked it he hardly seemed to notice, he didn't give her the customary peck on the lips, he just kept on pumping. He hadn't felt this huge, this hard, since the first time they'd done it. He was pressing a finger—it took her a second to figure out just what he was doing, no one had ever touched her there, not even her doctor, it didn't feel good and it didn't feel bad, it just felt weird. He poked his finger in and hooked it against her and wiggled it first gently, then more insistently—this is totally disgusting, she thought, this is the most disgusting thing anyone could ever do. He was breathing hard into her ear. She stared at the ceiling. Maybe she was supposed to enjoy this, she thought, maybe other girls enjoyed this, maybe this was something special he was treating her to. Now that they were engaged.

She wanted to giggle, and she felt a little nauseated, but most of all she wanted him to stop. She pulled herself away from him and he opened his eyes and stared at her, his finger still inside her, his expression filled with anger and surprise. She hadn't meant for everything to stop, she had just needed a break, a breather, and she gave him a smile and spread her legs apart and with one hand tried to draw him back onto her. He shrugged away. His face was bright red. His chest was heaving. Suddenly he rolled her over, pulled her legs apart, and entered her from behind. Katie Lee gasped in pain, and each gasp seemed to excite him more and more, until finally she let out a scream, her cry muffled into the pillowcase, and he came again.

He collapsed against her and they were silent, his weight crushing her. She wanted to go into the bathroom and lock the door and take a long hot shower. She wanted to hide under the bedcovers and pretend she was something very small, something that didn't exist at all. He had punished her, he had *violated* her, with one act he had violated every unspoken agreement between a man and a woman. She hugged a pillow to her chest and curled around it. She stuffed a corner of the pillow slip into her mouth, she'd be damned if she'd let him hear her cry.

But Bobby heard nothing. His breath was deep and even. The future Mrs. Robert Vincent turned to face the man of her dreams and found him fast asleep.

18

Rosaline hung up the telephone and turned to her husband.

"The good news is," she said, laying down her pale-yellow knitting, "Katie Lee is getting married."

"The bad news?" Trevor asked, taking off the horned-rimmed glasses he had begun wearing in the evenings, just for reading, though eventually he'd have to wear them constantly, his vision was weakening so rapidly.

"She's marrying Bobby Vincent," Rosaline said, standing up and smoothing down her gray velvet jumper. In her final months of pregnancy it had at last become acceptable for her to wear the loose, girlish dresses and jumpers she had always favored. Though she had lost all the pregnancy weight, sometimes in the evenings, alone with her husband, she still wore her old maternity clothes. "I had no idea they were even in touch anymore."

The telephone rang again. Rosaline stiffened, and Trevor leaned over to answer it.

"Marinda," he said, giving her the handset.

"Hello," Rosaline said. "Yes. No, not a clue. No, thank you, that's wonderful of you, but we already have plans here for Thanksgiving. Of course, of course I will. I don't know where Schuyler is. Maybe he's out of town. Oh. Well, maybe he's not picking up the phone, considering the circumstances. I don't know, Marinda, this is as much of a surprise to me as it is to you."

Trevor folded his arms and frowned. He hated messy behavior, and as far as he could tell, listening to Rosaline's side of her phone conversations, they were in for a rash of messy behavior. Katie Lee had gotten herself engaged to Bobby Vincent while she was still officially going out with Schuyler Smith; after all the effort she'd made in the

246

last few years, Trevor thought, her true colors were showing. *White trash* is what he would have thought, but those words weren't even in his mental vocabulary. A good marriage, like a good business deal, was something you entered into carefully, thoughtfully, weighing the upside and the downside, listening to the advice of those older and more experienced than you. Isn't that why they called marriage a social contract? Katie Lee was making a mistake, not in *whom* she was marrying but in *how* she was marrying.

Trevor sighed as Rosaline told Marinda that it was her duty as Katie Lee's friend to offer Katie Lee support if the Vincent family was going to disapprove of this wedding as much as Marinda was predicting. Marinda was another one who went in for messy behavior. It was part of being a fat person (even though Marinda was quite thin now, in Trevor's mind all you had to do was be overweight once, and forevermore, no matter how thin you became, you were always a fat person who happened to be in a thin phase), fat people tended to lose control. If you couldn't control something as simple as the food you put in your mouth, how could you control your emotions, your life? He could tell from what Rosaline was saying that Marinda was nearly hysterical with glee. Perhaps it was because Marinda's family was giving her such a hard time about seeing a Jew, and now she'd be relieved to have some of the heat turned on her cousin for a change. Perhaps it was because Marinda had never liked Schuyler and Katie Lee being together—even Trevor had been able to figure out, during the many dinners he'd shared with Rosaline and Marinda, that Marinda's interest in Schuyler's love life was more than it should be.

It pleased Trevor that so many women seemed to fall to pieces over Schuyler Smith, whom he had come to think of over the last few months as one of his closest friends. He thought it was part of his personal vanity—that all his and Rosaline's female friends and relations were pretty and charming and excellent dancing partners, that all their male counterparts were good-looking and intelligent and successful and could pick out the best bottle of Bordeaux from the longest wine list. He thought he was merely taking the harmless, vicarious pleasure that married men took in seeing their single friends capture the hearts of women they themselves were no longer free to flirt with. It made Trevor feel as if he were part of a charmed circle of exceptional people.

Had he been more self-analytical—in other words, had he been someone else entirely—he would have realized quite early that the more desirable Schuyler appeared, the more desirable Rosaline appeared, and therefore the more desirable he himself was. It was like a chain letter of sexual attraction. Here was this man who seemed to be able to have anyone he wanted, anyone except Rosaline, the one woman who had left him (before they were married Rosaline had given Trevor a sanitized version of how she and Schuyler had broken up), the one woman who chose Trevor to be her mate for life, the father of her children.

Trevor's personal mythology depended on Rosaline's being the only woman who had ever turned Schuyler down, and so, in the instant after she had said goodbye to Marinda, he constructed an acceptable scenario that had led to Katie Lee's getting engaged to Bobby Vincent. He hardly ever did this—he usually assumed people did what they did exactly for the reasons they gave, he rarely tried to figure out the hidden layers of emotion and motive—and now, as he presented his theories to his wife, he prided himself on how sensitive he was being, how wise he had become in affairs of the heart.

"She was probably trying to get Schuyler to marry her, and when it became obvious that he never would, you can't blame her for taking the next best thing that came along," he said, pouring himself a fino. "Why buy the cow when you're getting all the milk you want for free?" he continued.

"Katie Lee is not a cow," Rosaline said, picking up her knitting and then tossing it aside.

"You know what I mean. If Schuyler had wanted to marry Katie Lee he wouldn't have been carrying on with her the way he's been. They're practically living together."

"Schuyler isn't like that."

"All men are like that," Trevor replied, meaning *All men I like are like me.* He had nearly convinced himself, without speaking to any of the parties directly involved, that he understood the situation completely. It was the best thing for Schuyler, it was exactly what Schuyler had wanted, that Katie Lee would run off and marry a mobster's son. Perhaps Schuyler had even planned it this way to avoid the mess of having a heartbroken Katie Lee running around town saying mean things about him, winning sympathy for herself. Rosaline would insist on staying friends with Katie Lee, Trevor knew, and he sighed to himself with disappointment. He liked the old-fashioned way of choosing sides, of society closing its ranks against the offender.

"I know she and Bobby have liked each other for a long time,"
Rosaline said, "and if they were meant to be together, and I'm sure
they are, then I'm happy for them. It's just so sudden. She came home
from a business trip last night and told Schuyler this morning she's
engaged to another man, and on Thursday she's going down to New
Jersey so they can tell his family over Thanksgiving dinner, for goodness sake."

"It's all for the best," Trevor said. "She and Schuyler just weren't
meant for each other."

It was true, Rosaline thought, and suddenly, for the first time in a
long time, she wondered what December was up to. December had
sent some lovely baby things from California. Rosaline had sent December a thank-you note, but now she felt like calling December up
and telling her the news.

Rosaline went into the nursery to check on Trevor Van Schott
Goodwood, who, at the tender age of six months, had not yet learned
to pronounce his own nickname, Scotty.

"My perfect boy," Rosaline whispered, resting her elbows on the
railing of the crib. The hand-carved oak crib had held three generations of Goodwoods, and Trevor had insisted they use it for Scotty,
even though Rosaline protested that the slats were too far apart for
today's safety standards. Trevor found a carpenter who constructed
new railings out of nearly matching oak, the slats close together as
Rosaline insisted, so that Scotty wouldn't be able to stick his head
between them and somehow harm himself. It was ridiculous, Trevor
thought, all the books Rosaline read, all the rules and guidelines and
health and safety tips she picked up from reading and television and
her friends. Nearly twenty little Goodwoods had slept in that crib,
and not one had ever done anything so stupid as choke himself on the
railing. It was the same with the window guards, which Rosaline had
asked the coop board to install and which ruined the view across
Central Park when you were sitting down. It was only ghetto children who did that sort of thing—find ways to choke themselves to
death, hurl themselves out of ten-story windows, set themselves on
fire with matchbooks advertising cut-rate lawyers and stamp collections from countries that didn't send representatives to the United
Nations. Trevor believed that the best way to raise Scotty was to
leave him pretty much on his own, to let genetics and a few carefully
selected nurses allow the boy to grow up into a younger version of
himself.

But Rosaline was full of ideas. She read to Scotty from an old book of nursery rhymes, from the story of a baby duck who could not learn how to swim, and from Homer in the original Greek. She talked to Scotty about the temperature of his formula, about the colors of the leaves turning in the park, about Agamemnon's bloodlines, about what she should wear to dinner with Charlotte, and now, leaning over his crib, about Katie Lee and Schuyler.

"The man who gave you Brunswick Bear, Brunswick Bear, over there," she sang in a melody she had just invented this evening. When Trevor tiptoed in and put his hands on her shoulders she straightened up and stiffened.

"You'll wake him," she said, though Trevor hadn't said a word. Trevor hadn't seemed to notice the way she snapped at him occasionally, or perhaps he had noticed, but he said nothing. A few times when he'd come home from work and tried to be helpful she'd nearly blown up at him. Part of her, weary from her day alone with Scotty (it didn't matter how much help you had, it drained you just to be in the same house with a baby, just to always have the main part of you listening, watching, concentrating on the baby), was glad to see Trevor, grateful for the relief. *It's your turn*, she almost said once, *my shift is over*. But another part of her resented him utterly from the moment he walked through the door, and it was this other part that hated answering his stupid questions about feedings and diapers and, for goodness sake, he had once even asked how to hold his own child. *If you don't know, don't bother*, was how she felt, *just leave us alone*. Because however much she once thought she loved Trevor (which was, she once thought, as much as any one human being is capable of loving another human being) she loved her child, their child, countless times more.

It was the greatest love affair of her life, if not of all time. Trevor had been demoted to number two. Did this happen to everyone, she wondered, reaching back and holding her husband's hand as mute apology for her behavior, was everyone just pretending that having children didn't utterly and irrevocably change a marriage? Why didn't Trevor understand her? Why didn't he understand anything at all?

When the telephone rang again Trevor left to answer it. The light blue teddy bear that Schuyler had given Scotty was leaning against a stuffed rabbit Katie Lee had sent. Rosaline lifted the bear and hugged it to her chest.

"It's Schuyler," Trevor said from the doorway. "Do you want to talk to him?"

"Yes, of course," Rosaline said, placing the bear on the far side of the crib, next to another stuffed bear (they must have gotten at least two dozen of them), the white fleece one December had sent from California.

Schuyler seemed to own only large earthenware mugs, which Trevor disapproved of (he'd asked Rosaline to return all the mugs they received as wedding gifts, and she had, exchanging them for napkin rings and placemats), so that now, as she lifted the teabag out of the steaming water, Rosaline was not quite sure what to do with it. The teabag twirled in the air between them, but Schuyler didn't notice, he hadn't noticed much of anything since Rosaline had arrived two hours ago, bundled up against the November cold. He hadn't even offered to hang up her coat, he had just begun talking immediately, repeating his conversation with Katie Lee nearly word for word, asking Rosaline questions about Bobby and Katie Lee but then never waiting to hear a reply.

Rosaline dropped the teabag into an ashtray. "I honestly had no idea, Schuyler," she said. "This is a great shock to everyone."

He leaned back and lit another cigarette as Rosaline looked around the room. This apartment seemed nearly identical to the one he'd had in college: same pale varnished floors broken up by an occasional woven carpet, a few pieces of utilitarian oak furniture, their lack of ornament belying their value as antiques, same photographs of the West hung in simple aluminum frames—although now there were more of them, Rosaline noticed, and now, after all the gallery evenings and museum benefits, she could identify the work of different photographers. The bedroom door was ajar, and she spotted the familiar striped corner of a Hudson's Bay blanket.

Rosaline sipped her tea. Though Schuyler had asked her to come rushing over in what she now considered the middle of the night (ten P.M.), once she arrived he was much less upset than she had expected. His voice was calm and his manner relaxed. He wore the expression not of a heartbroken young man but rather of a prizefighter who's taken an exceptionally hard punch: stunned, hurting, but neither surprised nor angry, for the blow he has taken is fair part of the game he has chosen to play.

"I always sort of expected something like this would happen,"

Schuyler said, stabbing out his cigarette. "Not exactly this thing, never Bobby, but that she'd be bad about leaving. Or that I'd leave first. I don't know. She was great in a lot of ways, but she was never the sort of person you wanted to count on."

Rosaline looked away. "Did you love her," she asked.

"Sometimes I thought so," he said. "That's not exactly right. Sometimes I thought I could fall in love with the person she could be. If she wanted to."

"That's different," Rosaline said.

"That's what Katie Lee said," Schuyler continued. "She said that she felt I was always expecting her to be someone she wasn't. She said that Bobby loves her for who she is. Whatever that is."

"I think you know," Rosaline said.

Schuyler sighed. "I guess I do. Look, could you do me a favor. She's got her stuff all over the place. In the closets, in drawers, in the bathroom. I want it all out."

Rosaline stood up and began to pack. She went through the closets and folded all of Katie Lee's things into piles on the living room couch. She opened drawers and, noting the labels, separated the identical Shetlands, button-down shirts, corduroy jeans. She took a brown shopping bag into the bathroom and filled it with half-used bottles of French shampoos and creme rinses, a stack of unwrapped complexion bars, a bright-green toothbrush, a boar-bristle hairbrush. It was easy to identify Katie Lee's things, for her tastes hadn't changed since freshman year. The expensive soaps and lotions had seemed inappropriate then, when everyone was sharing bathrooms and shopping for sundries at discount stores, but now the rest of them had caught up with Katie Lee. Even Rosaline had begun using moisturizer and hand cream.

"I think I've got everything," she said an hour later, pointing to the high stack that was nearly as large as Katie Lee and thoroughly smelled of her. "I'll send someone in the morning to pick it all up. If you can wait till then?"

"Yes, sure, thanks," Schuyler said. "Please tell Trevor I'm sorry for keeping you out so late."

"Oh, Trevor's fine. He said he wants you to come riding with him on Saturday—Philip keeps horses on Long Island—and then you're all supposed to stay over and get incredibly drunk, I think. Grace is going to come stay with me—they're having their floors redone, and they have to be out of the house overnight."

"That sounds terrific."

"I think it sounds awful," Rosaline said, "but what do I know? Trevor's already scheming to set you up with all his old girlfriends."

Schuyler laughed. "Didn't one of them win an Olympic medal?" he asked.

"For the breast stroke," Rosaline said, giggling. "Trevor didn't tell me for years because he didn't want to say *that word*. Well, anyway, I have to go. You seem to be holding up nicely, considering—considering that—"

"That I've just had my heart broken?" he said.

"I didn't say that."

"Well. I haven't."

"Well," she said, "good. You know who I thought of tonight?" she asked, buttoning up her coat. "December. Have you been in touch with her?"

Schuyler shut the door he'd been holding open for her. "No."

"She sent some lovely baby things. I was just wondering. She still spends a lot of time in New York, you know, I thought she might have called you. She asked me for your number once," Rosaline said, feeling herself start to babble, knowing she was unable to stop. "I've just been thinking about her all day and I don't know why."

Schuyler didn't say anything, because Rosaline had just spoken exactly what was on his mind: *I've been thinking about her all day and I don't know why*—except he was beginning to figure out why. In the same way that, when one is weakened by the flu or just the common cold, every other ailment is suddenly felt more keenly, a bad back or trick knee, a headache, a troublesome wisdom tooth, so Katie Lee's leaving had opened up old wounds for Schuyler. He'd be cured of Katie Lee within a week, he knew. He hadn't wanted to tell Rosaline, but he was already making a list of women who'd be happy to hear from him about New Year's Eve. Like the fever brought on by the flu, its cooling measured and predictable and assured, that's how Schuyler thought of this particular breakup. He just had to wait it out and take a few days off. It happened to everyone. It was going around.

But there was this other ache that would never go away. Was it December, he wondered, did he still love December, or was he just lamenting what they had all once been, young and romantic and full of impossible ideas about what love would bring? That was what he had been telling himself for a long time: that it wasn't the loss of

December that saddened him so, it was the loss of some part of himself, the part that everyone had to let go of as he grew older.

Except now, returning the wave Rosaline had sent him through the rear window of her Checker cab, he knew that nothing was lost, it was only misplaced or ignored or forgotten. It's still there, he said, walking past the elevator and taking the five flights of stairs up to his apartment two at a time. And I'm still here, he thought, picking up the telephone, dialing a number and waiting fifteen rings for the late-night operator to pick up.

"I'd like to make a reservation for one in coach from LaGuardia to Los Angeles," he said.

"Certainly," she said, asking him the departure date, asking him his preferred form of payment, asking him to hold as she checked what was available, and he held, and he held a little longer, until she came back on the line and asked him, one way or round trip?

19

"*H*aving a rich girlfriend certainly does agree with me," Jason said, turning up the radio of Marinda's father's Mercedes. "There was a girl in my high school I went out with for a while, she had this friend from summer camp who lived on Long Island, her father was a dentist, and they had this brown Mercedes, a sort of chocolate brown, and we used to drive it around. It was a great fucking car. Not as big as this one, though, I don't think."

"What was this girl's name?" Marinda asked, taking a last toke and throwing the roach out the window.

"Shari."

"*Shari?*" Marinda shrieked. "You went out with a girl named Shari? I love it. Did she have puppets?"

"No, the girl with the Mercedes was named Shari. The girl I went out with was named Debbie."

"Was this before or after Joanie?" Marinda asked. It was so hard to keep track of all of Jason's old girlfriends. There were so many of them, and before he got to Columbia Law, when he was going to high school in Bayside and college at N.Y.U., it seemed that he went out only with girls whose names ended in *ie* or *y*, though at some point in the late sixties several of them had changed this to simply *i*, an *i* often dotted, Marinda had found out from going through his old letters one day when she was alone in Jason's apartment, with large circles or hearts or daisies.

"So sometimes Shari and Debbie would drive over to pick me up after dinner," Jason continued. Jason had already explained to Marinda that none of the kids in his neighborhood drove cars. Most of their families didn't even own cars, and Jason had learned how to drive only two years ago. Marinda grabbed onto the side of her seat as he took a turn a little too fast.

"And my mother always made them park around the block and walk to the house," Jason said. Which he had explained to Marinda wasn't exactly a house, it was the left side of a two-story tan brick structure constructed along the square lines of an apartment building, identical to hundreds of others in their neighborhood. Which neighborhood he made fun of constantly to Marinda, although whenever she made even the smallest joke he became utterly defensive and told her that this particular neighborhood, in addition to producing the best Jewish athletes in the city, sent the highest percentage of students on to the selective public high schools in New York and from there to the best colleges in the Northeast. Which colleges, he explained to Marinda, were even tougher to get into if you were Jewish and from that particular part of New York City, because there were these unspoken quotas, everyone knew it, just look at all the kids who had gotten into Harvard (Jason had not been accepted by Harvard as an undergraduate, those were always the words he used, *They didn't accept me*) from Iowa and Texas and Hawaii whose grades and board scores and achievements didn't touch the ones of these fast-talking smart kids from Queens and Long Island, these kids who went to N.Y.U. and Columbia and University of Pennsylvania and Cornell and who would, Jason further explained, have to work twice as hard once they got out of school simply because they didn't have a Harvard degree.

None of which Marinda really cared about. College seemed like a million years ago. *It's just a place, it's no big deal*, she had once told Jason, and he had argued with her, saying *Don't you see, it's all part of the system, it's all part of the way the system maintains itself, the way the powerful retain their power.* She had been so naïve when she first met Jason, she thought, it was incredible how much she had learned in the almost-a-year they'd been going out.

"Because it was Friday night?" Marinda asked. She had learned from Jason, for example, that even if a Jewish family wasn't—what was the word he used?—*observant*, they still made certain public gestures in deference to their community, such as not holding weddings on Saturday afternoons and not going to work on certain important Jewish holidays.

"Because it was a German car. That was one of the differences between Queens and Long Island. In Long Island they drove German cars, served bacon at breakfast, and ordered lobsters in expensive restaurants—stuff like that."

"Oh," Marinda said, not knowing whether it was the lobsters or the expensive restaurants that defined the differences between Queens and Nassau County, neither of which she had ever been to until she had met Jason. They both looked exactly like New Jersey to her, but Jason had disagreed violently and launched into a complicated analysis of the differences between the two places, which had to do with the difference between blue collar and white collar, working class and service class, uncontrolled industrial development and planned bedroom community. It was all political, he had explained, and Marinda had agreed, although until she met Jason she had always thought politics had to do with government and running for office and the sort of things her father did.

But politics was everywhere, Jason had taught her. Politics was where you lived (New Jersey or Long Island, for example) and what you wore (T-shirts or *chemises Lacoste*) and what you played (tennis versus baseball versus bowling). Politics could be heard in the kind of music you listened to (rock and roll could be either extremely political or the exact opposite). Politics was there in bed with men and women, with Jason and Marinda, and he had given her a couple of books to read on this particular subject, books his last girlfriend had left behind when she moved up to Vermont to work at a shelter for battered women.

"I can just picture you in high school driving this car to the country club," he said, pronouncing "country club" the same way he'd pronounced "German," raising his voice and speaking a little louder for the first syllable.

"Actually my father just bought this last year," Marinda said. "We always had big American cars, like Pontiacs." It was one of the things that had changed about the Vincents while she was in school. They'd sold their Cadillacs and Oldsmobiles and bought expensive foreign cars. The men had begun wearing looser conservative suits with narrow lapels, and the women had bought sling-back shoes and pearl jewelry. Some of the ornately carved furniture had been replaced by simpler and darker woods, and chintz had appeared around windows, needlepoint pillows on chairs. It was as though in some way they'd all gone to Harvard with Bobby and Marinda and were continuing to go now with Bobby's and Marinda's younger brothers and sisters. When she'd gotten her diploma, she'd handed it to her father, who'd accepted it without comment, as though it were rightfully his (he'd paid for it, so it was, Marinda felt), had had it framed, and hung it on his office wall.

When they got to the 7-11, Marinda picked up the items she'd been sent for (three bags of ice, a carton of True blues for a visiting cousin, diet soda, Kraft mayonnaise), and Jason piled the counter with things he said everyone might want later (ice cream sandwiches, taco chips, smoked almonds, Pepperidge Farm cookies), and Marinda paid for everything with the new fifty-dollar bill her uncle had given her before she left.

Back in the car Marinda turned up the heat. She hated this tradition they had of opening up the summer house off-season for Thanksgiving and Christmas and Easter dinners; the big old house was poorly insulated, and its radiators clanked and hissed all through the night. At home she had her own bathroom, but here she had to share one with her brothers, carrying her diaphragm (Jason had made her switch from the pill, it was unhealthy and made her gain weight, he said) back and forth in a little flowered cloth bag she stuck up under a bulky sweatshirt so no one would notice. At least, she thought, or rather: at last, they had let Jason stay in the same wing of the house as she, in a narrow bedroom originally designed for a servant, though maybe that was just because they'd needed the sunnier, larger guest room at the last minute when Bobby had announced he was bringing Katie Lee.

When they got back nearly everyone had gone to sleep. Marinda unpacked the groceries while Jason made drinks for them to take upstairs.

"Just Tab for me," she said, and then, patting her hips, "I'll probably gain five pounds tomorrow." She liked getting high with Jason, but she hated the way it made her so hungry, especially when he was always making sandwiches thick with mayonnaise and buying things filled with butter and sugar.

"You look great in those jeans," he said as he followed her up the stairs, his head nearly level with her waistline.

"Thanks. I couldn't barely fit into them when I bought them. Now they're almost loose." Ten more pounds and she'd reach her ideal weight, a weight she hadn't been since she was seventeen years old. Jason was a self-described "fat fascist," and she had started dieting in earnest as soon as she'd met him, last January, at a party uptown near school. Her gradual but nonetheless dramatic loss of weight over the past year had run parallel to their getting more serious about each other, and Marinda had begun to believe that when she reached this miraculous milestone of her Ideal Weight they would also reach a turning point in their relationship. Jason would never propose, of course, because he didn't believe in the institution of marriage, but still Marinda ached for some kind of declaration, something along the lines of I-don't-believe-in-marriage-but-if-I-did-I'd-marry-you.

They had passed from the initial phase of making love more than once a night, through the phase of making love once every night and occasionally in the morning, through the phase of making love once at night *or* once in the morning, to where they were now: once at night unless they had stayed out very late or both of them were drunk or one of them was sick or it was really hot out or one of them had fallen asleep while the other was watching television. He was so different from Peter, who had always been looking for new ways (let's just kiss each other for an hour and see who gives in first) and new places (what do you mean, you've never done it on a boat) and new times (if we're late to the reception no one will notice) to begin, but no matter how differently they began, it always ended the same way, with Peter exhausted and distant, and Marinda wide awake and wondering what he thought of her.

With Jason it always began the same way, but it always ended diffently: in mischief (he was tickling her on the kitchen floor, he had hidden her bra somewhere in his apartment but pretended not to remember where) or in tenderness (he had spilled sweet liquored cream all over her and licked it up like a cat, he was giving her a massage afterwards and asking her about her childhood). As competitive and ambitious and obsessed as Jason could be in the classroom or on the tennis court, so he was in bed.

They undressed down to their underwear (jockey shorts for him, white lace briefs and a front-hooked bra—Jason insisted—for her), and Marinda curled into his arm, waiting for his hand to come up over her breast. They were listening to a medley of old Drifters on the clock radio, and every so often he kissed the top of her head. He slowly moved his hand upward over her nipple and rubbed it through the smooth, almost glittery fabric, hesitantly, like an uncertain teenager waiting to be slapped down.

"Did I ever tell you you've got great tits?" he said.

"I do?" she said, though he'd told her countless times. "What's so great about them?"

"This part here," he said, running a finger along the side of her, "we used to call it armpit cleavage. It's the best thing about bikinis and tank tops." He unfastened her bra and laid it across the sheet. "It makes strong men weak."

"I'll keep that in mind," she said as he kept on stroking her.

"This part right here," he said, cupping one breast from below, giving her a little squeeze, "cannot be duplicated by science or silicone. Excuse me while I swoon." He ran the flat of his palm across her and then he extended his hand, like a pianist reaching across a wide and difficult chord, and with his pinky and thumb fluttered both nipples at once.

"And their taste," he said, leaning over and taking one stiff nipple into his mouth until she reached down and held him, he was already hard, and she held him tighter until he caught up with her, until he crossed the line from wanting to urgency.

Only then did he raise his head and breathe in deep like a swimmer surfacing for air and kiss her, for the first time, his free hand moving down her belly, down to see if she was wet, to guess, from the heat and movement of her, what she wanted, his hand or his mouth, to feel his weight on top of her or to be lifted up by her shoulders, to be pulled over across him, so he could watch her swivel in the moonlight coming through the uncurtained window of her parents' house, her breasts bobbing above him, their hands still going at each other wherever and whenever there was room, was time, her eyes closed but his open and watching her until tonight, in the bed she had first slept in as a small child, he came first, and then he was moving his hand faster, trying to make her come while she could still feel him strong inside of her, before he had softened back into himself, and she was moving a little differently now because she was moving only for herself. She was working for it, he had had to teach her that, to work for her own pleasure, and he watched her come, he saw her lips purse together and her neck arch back and her jaw clench, and then he pulled her back down to him.

They rested for a while, and listened to the news, and Marinda filled him in on the past adventures and embarrassments of the various relatives (forty in all) who would be coming for dinner tomorrow. Their talk grew softer, the pauses between sentences longer, until finally one of them, Jason, said good night and the other, Marinda, began to fall asleep.

• • •

In the morning Marinda awoke to see Jason pissing out the window onto her mother's flower garden and hear Katie Lee, in the driveway, asking Bobby if they hadn't arrived too early.

"Get away from the window! What if Katie Lee looks up!" Marinda hissed.

"I think she's seen one of these before," he said, holding himself in his hand, grinning as Marinda took aim and flung his shorts squarely at the middle of his chest. He knelt on the edge of the bed and bounced up and down on his knees. "You were pretty cute last night," he said.

"So were you," she said, thinking he still was. His thick, straight, nearly black hair had been angled by sleep and stuck up from his head, revealing the high forehead that would eventually became higher. His eyebrows, dense and archless above round brown eyes, gave him the expression of judgment even now, when he was barely awake, and his tan skin shone before his morning shower. He looked more like the rebellious hoodlum in a grade-B British movie than a nice Jewish boy from Queens, and he cultivated this impression by slouching slightly and by shaving before he went to bed, so that he carried a rakish stubble throughout the day. It was a private joke they had, that everyone had always told Jason he looked Italian and Marinda that she looked Jewish, but what they never said was that they both enjoyed being mistaken for something other than what they were.

Jason flexed his arms and let out a litte jungle yell. "Tarzan hungry. Tarzan want breakfast," he said.

Marinda tilted her head and pulled the sheet up over her breasts. It was the thing she had not yet learned from him, to be unashamed and naked in the daylight. It was something boys learned in locker rooms, she thought, and Jason had obviously spent a lot of time in locker rooms. Before him she had gone out only with thin, fleshless boys made soft by money, but Jason, from years of softball and track and lifting weights and summer jobs in construction and gardening, was hard and muscular. He looked great in T-shirts and blue jeans but uncomfortable and constrained in suits, which he swore he was never going to have to wear anyway, except to funerals, since he was going to be a public-interest lawyer and would be able to get away with the old tweed and corduroy jackets he favored.

There was a knock on the door and then Katie Lee's stage whisper. "Are you decent, sweetie?" she asked. "Do you have that big gorilla in there with you?"

Marinda got up, pulled on her robe, and tossed Jason his jeans.

"We're semi-decent, if you can handle it," she said, opening the door for Katie Lee.

Katie Lee peered around the door and gave Jason a smile. "Honey, why don't you put your shirt on, thank you, and then Marinda can give me the scoop on everyone before they wake up." She crossed the room as if to sit down on the bed and then changed her mind, swept a damp towel from a chair, and sat there. "I'm exhausted, you know, your cousin drives like an absolute maniac." She picked up the Scotch Jason had brought up the night before, now watery and warm, sniffed it, and then swallowed it in three gulps.

"Do I need to change before breakfast?" she said. She was wearing a plaid kilt, a yellow Shetland sweater, and high-heeled brown leather boots.

"We're pretty casual here," Marinda said. "You can borrow some jeans if you want."

"Oh, I brought some," Katie Lee said. "How casual is casual?"

"Just wear something comfortable," Jason said. "Though Marinda won't be taking out her tiara until after sunset."

"Very funny, Mr. Feld," Katie Lee said. "I'd just like to fit in if I can. You wouldn't understand."

"I guess not," he said, picking the towel off the floor and hanging it over his head. "Well, I'm going off to my morning prayers, and then to the showers," he said as Marinda giggled.

"You know that isn't what I meant," Katie Lee said after he was gone.

"Relax, Katie Lee. We're on your side, remember."

"As opposed to who?"

"Nobody. Listen, I just woke up and I haven't had any coffee. Let's go down and start breakfast."

"In a minute," Katie Lee said. "I just want to know whether I'm walking into a den of lions here. Bobby said his mother wasn't thrilled when he said he was bringing me. You can imagine what she'll say when we tell her we're getting married."

"She won't say anything. First thing you have to learn: the Vincent women are not allowed to have opinions. It's his father, and probably mine, you have to suck up to."

"You're picking up some of Jason's less pleasant expressions."

"Look, just flirt with them and try to say as little as possible and the men will like you. Compliment my mother on the house and help out in the kitchen and everything will be fine," Marinda told her, though she knew that nothing would ever be fine between Katie Lee and the Vincents. "Don't talk about politics, and whatever you do, don't talk about money."

Katie Lee lifted her eyebrows. She wasn't sure what subjects were left.

"And don't freak out if they start speaking Italian."

"They won't be talking about me, will they?"

"No, of course not," Marinda said, knowing that Katie Lee would never recognize the Italian words for witch, temptress, and whore. "Look, do you want a Valium or something?"

"No. I just want everyone to like me. I've had an absolutely awful week, you know, with Schuyler and all."

"Have you."

"He's taking it very hard. He actually got down on his knees and begged me not to leave him. He called Rosaline up in the middle of the night and told her if she didn't come over he was going to do something drastic. She had to hold his hand, and she said he just cried like a baby, and she said she took all my things out of his apartment because she was afraid he was going to do something crazy, something violent. Trevor won't even speak to him, he behaved so badly. Poor boy. He really loved me."

"Yes, well, he'll get over it," Marinda said. "He's a big boy."

"Oh, I don't know," Katie Lee said, running a hand through her hair. "I think I just broke his heart to pieces. It was worse than after Rosaline."

"Was it," Marinda said.

"He was terrific, but he was still second best, you know what I mean? He said something rather vicious about you, actually, in the middle of this big fight we had. When I told him about Bobby."

"And what was that," Marinda said, turning away and making the bed.

"Oh, he said you'd set me up with Bobby because you were trying to break me and Schuyler up, because you wanted Schuyler for yourself. Imagine! You see what I mean, he was being totally ridiculous. He thinks you're to blame for all of this," she said, waving her hand around the room, which Marinda noticed she and Jason had made a complete mess of. She picked a pair of socks off the floor. "He actually tried to call you, he was going to yell at you, I guess, but I made him promise not to call you until he'd simmered down."

Marinda sat down on the bed and drew her knees up to her chest. "Where's your ring?" she asked.

"Oh, it won't be ready until next week. It's a real rock—Bobby insisted."

Jason returned, dripping, a fresh towel wrapped around his hips. "I'd ask you to stay and watch me change," he said, "but I don't want you to get too excited on your big day."

Katie Lee stood up and sniffed. "He is so unfunny," she said to Marinda. "I really don't know how you can stand to go out with him."

"Because I've got this great big steaming hunk of kosher salami that goes throbbing up her love roll every night," he said, dropping his towel and putting his hands on his hips.

Katie Lee blushed and stood up. "I've seen bigger," she said in a shaky voice, and she left the room.

"Jason, that was mean, she's really nervous about being here."

"You think me cruel," he said in a fake British accent.

"Me think you funny," she said. "Now get dressed and come downstairs. You don't want to miss the fireworks when Bobby tells them the news."

"They like me," Katie Lee said as she and Bobby walked back from the pond. "I can tell." She held her hands up to her nose. "Ugh, they stink. I can't believe I washed all those dishes."

"I thought you were wearing gloves," Bobby said, putting his arm around her waist.

"The gloves are what smell the worst. And I can't believe I ate all that food. You should have warned me that everyone brought a different dish. I had to eat *everything* so no one would be insulted. Did you and Jason get high before dessert? He couldn't stop smiling at me. I don't think he's right for Marinda, do you? I think she has this self-destructive tendency to go out with men who push her around, don't you?"

"Jason's okay," Bobby said. "He's been great for Marinda. She's lost all that weight, for one thing."

"I hope they don't get married, I mean, do you think they will?"

"No. Jason's too smart for that."

Katie Lee stopped and pointed a finger at him with a school-teacher's wag. "Well Bobby, just what do you mean by that? You're marrying me, and you know it will be the smartest darn thing you ever do."

"It probably will be," he said, giving her a smile that showed a lot of teeth. The evening had been a complete disaster, though he couldn't tell if Katie Lee hadn't caught on (she didn't speak Italian) or if she was just trying to pretend otherwise. Jason and Marinda had made it worse, exchanging giggles and glances with each other every time Katie Lee made a wrong move. "Come on," he said, pulling her back to him and kicking up the dead leaves, "let's head back. It's getting cold."

She leaned her head into his shoulder. "I want them to like me so much, Bobby, sweetheart," she said. "I'm going to make you so happy, they'll see, they'll see, I'll be the best thing that ever happened to you."

He felt her shiver and took off his heavy wool scarf and wrapped it around her neck. His family had behaved like the narrow-minded clannish peasants they really were, he thought, closing ranks against an outsider, judging Katie Lee before they even got to know her. It should have been enough that he'd told them he'd chosen her, that he said he was going to marry her, that should have been all they needed to hear. But no, they thought they knew what was best for him, they always thought they knew what was best for everyone in the family. His father had taken him for a long walk down by the pond and explained that Katie Lee wasn't a suitable wife for the kind of man he expected Bobby to grow up to be.

Expected: that's what his father did best, telling Bobby what he was expected to do without giving him the least sense that he was actually capable of doing it. His father expected everything and made Bobby feel like nothing at all.

Katie Lee was the only one who really understood. When she'd given him a speech on the drive down about how someone as smart and talented as he, with so many opportunities, had an almost moral obligation to serve the public, to do big things with his life, to live up to the responsibility of his ability and heritage, at first he thought her ridiculous. Just imagine, she'd said, just imagine if Franklin Delano Roosevelt had decided it would be more fun to stay home and count his money and give parties, where would the country be then, she said, people like you have to go out in the world and do your best.

Her plans (he could run for office, he had the connections, he had the money) were both silly and inspiring to him. She really believed he could do it, and when he was with her, he believed it too. He was in love with this woman: the woman who was in love with the man she knew he could someday be.

He stopped walking, turned away from the house and, holding her by the shoulders, gave her a squeeze.

"Do you know how much I love you?" he asked.

"Well," she said, "sometimes I guess I wonder. Sometimes a girl likes to hear it."

"I love you," he said. "I love you, Katie Lee. I'll always love you."

"Oh, do you promise?" she said, a tear spilling over and down her cheek. *Senator and Mrs. Robert Vincent,* she thought, *I know I can do it,* and then she caught herself: *I know we can do it.*

"I promise."

"Oh, Bobby, I love you too. I love you so much. I always have." She fell into his arms, and he held her for a while, looking over her head up to the starless sky, lit to a dull gray from the full moon hidden behind the clouds.

20

"*D*o you want the good news or the good news?" Alex asked, pushing the button on his electronic telephone console that told his secretary he was accepting none but the most urgent calls.

December propped her feet up on his desk. "I think Felicia disapproves of me. She never offers me a drink. She never even offers me coffee."

"Felicia is under orders not to offer stimulants and alcohol to pretty young clients. And she happens to be the fastest typist on the West Coast."

"Not that you ever write letters, as far as I can tell, it's all done over the telephone. I thought you'd be my manager and my pen pal."

"Darling, don't be flirtatious so early in the morning. It gives me a headache," Alex said. "You can tell me that you love what I've done with my office."

"I love what you've done with your office," she said, glancing around. It looked just like a library at Harvard, right down to the red leather chairs and standing brass ashtrays. "Hey, you know what? I really love what you've done with your office."

"Thank you."

"No, really. I think I'd like to do my bedroom this way. Find myself a wacky professor. We'll read Milton to each other by candlelight."

"*Paradise Lost* or *Paradise Regained*?"

"Oh, I hate sequels, they're never as good as the original. I'll take the good news—no, wait, give me the good news, I'm a strong girl, I can handle it."

"All right. The Mustang is yours. It will need an oil change in another eight hundred miles."

"Terrific! I love you—have I told you that recently?—I really do."

December sat up and put her hands on top of her head.

"And *I* love *you*, my darling."

"We're such a happy couple."

"That we are."

"Okay, now give me the good news and give it to me straight."

"I've found him," Alex said, pulling a folder out of his second left-hand drawer.

"Found who?"

"The answer to all your problems, or have you forgotten. He's perfect. Handsome, successful, not quite thirty, and needs publicity as much as you do, or so his agent says."

"Oh. My boyfriend."

"His name is Tory Robinson, and he is a semi-rock star."

"Tory Robinson, Tory Robinson," she said. "I have one of his records at home, the Red Album, I've even listened to it a few times. It's pretty good. So how cute is this guy," she asked. On the album cover he was photographed in sunglasses through the streaked store-front window of a run-down surf shop.

"I wouldn't know. What I do know is that he sells lots of records, although the last one didn't do as well as they hoped, and if the next one doesn't hit the top ten he's in serious career trouble. He likes pretty girls, a little too much for his own good—there was a paternity suit last year, totally unfounded I'm sure, but his agent would like to install a steady girlfriend on the scene, at least for the public record. You can go to parties with him once a week or so, and we'll arrange for some candid photo opportunities before Christmas."

"Great. I feel like I've been given into white slavery. I suppose you told him I'm a great fuck."

"Please do give me a little credit. He doesn't know a thing about you. All we're going to do is have you taken backstage after a concert tomorrow night, and you'll be introduced, and you can take it from there. You're a very charming girl. I'm sure you'll know what to do. Go buy something glittery."

"So, do I have to fuck him?"

"Not if you don't want to."

"I'll have to fuck him, won't I. Oh, God, what a drag."

"December, darling, I believe that half the adolescent girls in this country would sell their mothers for just such an opportunity." The telephone buzzed and Alex picked it up. "Hello, yes, just a minute," he said, and then he put the call on hold. "I don't want to keep you," he said to December. "Be ready tonight at seven. Robinson's agent's name is Bill Forbes, and he'll be picking you up."

Felicia appeared in the doorway. "It's going to be one of those days," she said to December as Alex waved goodbye and returned to his call. "Mr. Child said you should keep this in the car at all times."

December opened the envelope Felicia had handed to her. It was the insurance card for the Mustang. The policy had been effective and the car had been in her name for the last four weeks, from the day after she'd first asked Alex to buy it for her.

December drove the Mustang up along the coastline, playing the radio at top volume. It was hers, hers at last, Alex had bought it for her, or rather, he had bought her with it, but either way, pressing the pedal down to the floor, she drove with the singular joy of a woman who, for the first time and at a comparatively advanced age, owns her own automobile.

She stopped for lunch at a roadside fried chicken stand and then turned back. She was going to have to buy something fuzzy to hang from the dashboard. She was going to need large dark sunglasses in brightly colored frames. A new tape deck, for sure. On the way home she stopped by the gas station, but the manager told her that Tom had taken the week off.

Although each time they met—three or four times a week over the past month—they never made plans to see each other again and they never talked about the future, she felt annoyed that he had left for a week without warning her, and then she felt annoyed with herself for being so annoyed, for it meant that she was getting dependent on him.

He's turning into my drug, she thought, my love drug. But it was true: in the last few weeks she had pulled into the gas station as if looking for a fix. He always reacted the same way, tossing his dirty rag onto a pile in the garage, coming over and leaning into the window of the Mustang, telling the manager to keep an eye on her while he washed up so she didn't get into trouble. Sometimes, if the owners were away, they drove up behind the house overlooking the canyon. Sometimes, at night, they went to the beach. Once they had done it on a high school baseball field, and another time they'd done it right in the gas station in the backseat of a '72 Cadillac that had been dropped off for a tune-up and new hubcaps.

Once home, she did her daily laps and then, dropping her wet suit in the doorway, spread a towel on the living room floor, put on one of Robinson's albums, and began her regimen of one hundred sit-ups, three sets of ten push-ups, and a routine of stretches and calisthenics that Alex's trainer had designed especially for her.

Though she knew the melodies by heart, she had never really listened to any of the words to the songs, which were mostly about girls, with an occasional car, dead best friend, hometown, or topical current event thrown in: the standard stuff of top-forty rock and roll. But now as she listened, crunching her stomach two beats to the bar, she thought she heard something else, the thing she had been trained in her literature classes to look for—symbol and structure, poetry and art. She stretched out and bent her leg, pulling her foot up across her hip. Yes, it was really there, hidden by the drone of the bass line, the whining arc of an electric guitar, the crack and growl of a voice reaching beyond its range, there it was. Damn. This guy was smart. He certainly understood women.

She stood up and twisted around from the waist. So what else was he, she thought, believing like a good schoolgirl that the writer could be revealed by his text and that if she only listened long enough she would be able to figure this one out, would know what to expect and how to behave later tonight. She flipped the record, put the turntable on repeat, and struck the lotus position. The first time through she could barely make out all the lyrics. By the third time through she had picked out all the words and was beginning to see connections between the songs, was beginning to feel that she knew what made Tory Robinson tick. By the sixth time around she was questioning whether love between men and women was possible in the modern world, whether there was such a thing as a love worth searching for, worth waiting for and traveling around the world for, the way Tory Robinson seemed to think there was. In the middle of the seventh time through the doorbell rang. She got up, tying the towel around her in a sarong, and opened the door.

It was Schuyler Smith.

"Hello," he said. "I just happened to be in the neighborhood. Looking for good Mexican food."

She looked down at her bare feet. She held the towel tightly to her, crossing her arms and clenching her fists, the way an unsure driver clutches the steering wheel on a dark, wet night, as though if she let her concentration drop, the towel would fall with it and she would be standing there, naked, her body damp from exercise, scented with chlorine.

"Schuyler, come in," she said, wondering if without makeup she looked older or younger than what he had expected. What had he expected? "How did you find me?" she asked.

Schuyler followed her into the living room, inhaling the chemical blue scent of pool water, and folded his arms, so that they faced each other like two soldiers, like two warriors about to do battle, or two palace guards protecting the same royal treasure.

"Rosaline gave me your address," he said, thinking that she looked completely different from her photographs. He had forgotten how it was, the play of sunlight on pale skin and hair that the camera could not catch, he had willed himself to forget it. He had seen the pictures, all mascara and contouring and backlight and artful posing, and he had come to believe the pictures were the girl. "Is this a bad time?" he asked, watching the rhythm of her breath in the rise and fall of the towel.

"No, sit down, I was just doing laps," she said. "What time is it?"

"Six."

"Oh, Jesus, someone is coming by at seven, and I'm supposed to be dressed and ready and gorgeous and everything."

Schuyler stood in front of a wide picture window, the sun throwing a long shadow across her carpet. "This is a bad time. I should have called. I'll call tomorrow."

"No, wait," December said, turning down the music so it played soft as a sound track. "So. Anyway. What brings you to L.A.?"

"You." He was wearing a pure white dress shirt. His pale-yellow tie was loosened and a lightweight gray jacket was slung over his left shoulder. His trousers were cut loosely and fell to a narrow cuff over unpolished brown boots. His hair seemed longer and his sideburns shorter, almost shaved away to the tops of his ears. He smiled.

December giggled.

"I'm serious," he said, and she stopped laughing and looked into his hooded gray eyes for the first time. And in that moment everything came rushing back to her, everything she had felt in that one night long ago. It was a bond that could never be broken, not by all the distance, not by all the years, they would always be connected, she would always get this feeling, standing so close to him, that they shared something, not something emotional or intellectual or sexual but something as deep and unchanging as their spirit. When I breathe in he breathes in, she thought, watching him, sure it was just as true when they were divided by a continent. When I breathe out he breathes out.

"Look," she said, "I have to go to this *thing* tonight, but it should be over by midnight. I'd get out of it if I could, but I can't, it's too stupid to explain. Why don't you wait here for me?"

"Why don't I go back to my hotel and you can give me a call tomorrow?"

"No. Please. I'll be back by midnight, just like Cinderella. Please," she said, and he nodded, and she walked up five steps to the level that held her bedroom and bathroom and closet full of clothes. She chose a floral perfume and covered herself with matching bath powder. She made up carefully, her hand shaking so hard she could barely draw the cobalt blue eye pencil across her lower lid. She shimmied into a tight silver dress with buttons up the back that, in the absence of a dresser's helping hand, required a yoga contortion to fasten. And to unfasten, December thought, and she imagined herself later that night bending her head to her chest, holding her hair up off her neck, as someone slowly released each tiny button from its silver loop, as someone breathed in the perfume she'd dabbed in the hollow of her shoulders. Someone. The powder had something sparkly to it that picked up the silver of the dress. Among all the glitter and splash of the backstage scene she was going to make sure she was noticed. She slipped into silver ballet flats, turned around in the full-length mirror, kicked them off and put on high-heeled silver sandals with thin straps that crossed and fastened around her ankles. She guessed Tory Robinson was just about her height. Schuyler Smith was not.

She descended the stairs to find Bill Forbes helping himself to a drink and explaining to Schuyler about what he called simply "the business."

"The future's all in merchandise, that's what the kids want, charge them ten dollars for a concert and they'll spend twenty on T-shirts and buttons and posters," he said. "Hey, December, you look terrific," he said. Either he was forward or he did not want Schuyler to know that they'd never met, but either way December curtsied and gave Schuyler a wave.

"Midnight," she said, and he stood up and bowed back to her.

"I'll be here," he said, and he watched through the window as December was led into a long baby blue limousine and driven off into the city.

December had looked forward to her first backstage pass, but now, as she sat with Bill Forbes and a few record company executives and the drummer's second wife and her daughter by her first marriage and the girlfriend of the lead guitarist and the record producer and the record producer's boyfriend, in an over-air-conditioned room somewhere behind the stage where the audio was piped in off the soundboard and the visual, out of focus and full ōf static, was limited to one long camera angle that did or did not follow Robinson as he leaped around the stage, she was mildly disappointed, but too polite to say so.

"Is this your first time?" asked the daughter, whose name was Cecily. "I've been to twenty-two concerts, and each one gets better. Wait, you have to watch this part, he's going to do a somersault. Oh. Well, take my word for it, he does this somersault off the piano."

"I guess you don't have to go to school tomorrow," December said.

Cecily shrugged. "My teacher's a total Robinson freak. Even though she's really pretty old. He's not my real father, you know."

"Where is your real father?"

"Salt Lake City. He's a numbers cruncher."

"Would you like a drink?" Bill Forbes asked December. "Would you like to go out and take a look?"

"Sure," she said, and he led her to a small platform behind the drummer, from which she could view Tory Robinson in his tight black jeans and sweat-soaked red-and-white-striped T-shirt from the back only, which was not disappointing, and from which she could only guess, because the lights shone so brightly toward the stage, at the size and behavior of the crowd. They cheered wildly not just at the end of the songs but after the instrumental solos, or for the opening bars of familiar songs, or for lyrics that seemd to alternate between passionate anthem and soulful torment. December tried to imagine what it would be like to have all those people shouting and clapping and dancing at you. It was easier, she suspected, if you couldn't see them one by one.

"That's singing," Bill Forbes said. "Come on back, we've got a great spread laid out, and I'm starved." He took her back across the hall, where people were forking up salmon onto thin crackers and dipping elaborately carved raw vegetables into something light-green and creamy. The crowd roared louder, and there was some movement in the hallway.

"They'll do two more encores and that'll be it," he told her, looking at his watch. "It'll be over by eleven at the latest. I've got to meet with these people from the radio station. Then we want to get a picture of you and Tory. Come on, you can wait in his dressing room," he said before she'd had a chance to swallow the one thin strip of gutted cucumber she'd picked up.

"See you in two seconds," Bill Forbes said, and then, waving at the bar, "help yourself."

She looked around the dressing room, which held a few deck chairs, a narrow single bed, a portable tape player on which were piled cassettes of Ray Charles, Dusty Springfield, and Tommy James and the Shondells, a rocking chair, a stack of thick, fresh white towels, and a duffel bag filled with what she assumed were Robinson's clothes. There was a familiar smell in the room, something she couldn't identify but that seemed to her utterly male. In the bathroom, a shaving kit and a half-smoked pack of foreign cigarettes. On the floor by the bed, a biography of Mark Twain. She picked it up; the corners were turned down every twenty pages or so—he'd been reading it in spurts.

"Don't go losing my place now," he said, and she turned around.

There he was. His hair lay wet and flat against his neck. A small gold earring caught the light. He was breathing hard. His black leather belt buckle was bordered with metal studs. Through the white bars of his striped T-shirt, made transparent by sweat, she could see his chest rise and fall.

He took her in with a single sweep down to her sandaled feet, back up to her widened eyes. He smiled, looking at the dozen thin bangle bracelets hanging loosely over her wrists, the lapis beads that circled her neck and brightened her eyes, the large silver Saturns she'd clipped to her ears, her hair held back with a blue satin ribbon. She was still pale pink, the palest person in California, and with her white skin, sheathed in the thin silver fabric, with her light hair spread out behind her shoulders, and just a touch of pink blush across her cheekbones, she looked like the gift wrapping for a baby present from a very expensive and exclusive department store.

"Tory Robinson," he said, extending his hand.

"December Dunne," she said, taking it. It was warm, and sweaty, and he didn't let go. She recognized the odor now. It was the smell of a gas station.

"You can call me Tom," he said, grinning, pulling her toward him and kissing her in that place, on the back of her neck, where he'd found on their second time together she so liked to be kissed. She slipped her hands in his back jeans pockets.

"And you can call me Deirdre," she said.

When he woke up it was nearly dawn and he was alone. He stretched his legs out and pushed his hair off his forehead. The corduroy of her couch had left jail stripes across one side of his face and on the palms of his hands, which had clutched the pillow tightly in sleep.

Schuyler stood up, folded his jacket and tie into his backpack, and left the house without checking to see if the door locked behind him. He walked for a mile or so until he felt awake and the sun was fully up, until he found a telephone booth from which he could call a taxi to pick him up and take him to the airport.

At the counter the reservation agent frowned when she pulled up his name on the computer.

"Round trip seven-day advance is so much cheaper," she said, taking his credit card between ink-stained fingers. "Your flight should begin boarding in an hour and a half. I'm just telling you, you know, for next time."

"There won't be a next time," Schuyler said.

"This way costs the most," she said as she handed him his ticket back to New York.

He bought something called a Miniature Executive Travelkit at the newsstand and washed up in the bathroom. He smoked half a dozen cigarettes before his breakfast of a single scrambled egg and French fried potatoes arrived, and a half a dozen more as he drank his coffee, watching the planes take off from the window of the airport restaurant. The glass was grimed with exhaust fumes. Someone had written something on the outside with a finger, the way kids scrawl CLEAN ME on the hoods of dirty cars, though Schuyler couldn't figure out how anyone had gotten three flights up to do it.

JIMI LIVES, it said, and then below, KISS THE SKY. Schuyler placed his palm across the word SKY and left it there, watching everything waver in the heat and push of departing planes, until he heard his final call for boarding. He paid the bill twice over and left.

• • •

When they'd driven off together after the show, up and around the familiar roads to the house overlooking the canyon, December and Tory had sat silently together, neither one wanting to be the first to ask the kind of questions that, their anonymity gone, it was time to ask. He knew her name now, and what she did, and where she was from, and whatever else his manager had told him in the briefing session she imagined he'd gotten before the show. And she knew his name and suddenly so much more about him, and she felt all this information like a weight that might crush whatever it was they had made together in the last few weeks.

It was as though they were riding over a long, low suspension bridge, a bridge that bore the heavy wheels of trailer trucks and rush hour traffic, a bridge held together by countless delicate cables intertwined. And with every little thing she had learned about him she felt the thin wire of a cable fray and break. His name was Tory Robinson—snap. He had written those songs she nearly knew by heart now—snap. His friends, his band, his vintage Thunderbird, his fans, his money, her money—snap, snap, snap. When he parked in the clearing she had to stop herself from saying Wait, we don't have to do this anymore, I've got a nice, clean, comfortable house with a wide bed and smooth cotton sheets and we won't have to pick bits of dried leaves and broken grass out of our hair and clothes when we're done.

But she said nothing as he killed the lights and turned off the engine. Maybe he had a girlfriend stashed away someplace. Maybe this was what he wanted, that they would continue as they had before. She got out of the car and unbuckled her sandals; the ground felt damp and scratchy through the thin mesh of her stockings. Maybe this was what she wanted too, because maybe what they had wouldn't hold up under public dinners together in fashionable restaurants, the carefully planned candid photographs that Alex had already scheduled for the weeks ahead, the parties where it seemed that the more established you were as a couple, the more you were flirted with, the harder someone tried to seduce you upstairs in an unused guest bedroom or downstairs, over a game of billiards, or in the host's climate-controlled wine cellar.

December folded her arms across her chest when he walked up behind her and placed his hands on her shoulders. Tonight for the first time there were no parties, and in the quiet dark houses around them December imagined a couple sitting together reading on a couch with their feet in each others' laps, parents putting their children to bed, a husband carrying aspirin and a mugful of hot chocolate to a wife suffering from the flu, a woman with a hangover falling asleep with a cold plastic compress over her eyes. Something was shutting down all around them, something was shutting down inside her. It was like one of those madcap forties movies where the butler is really a railroad baron in disguise and the maid turns out to be the long-lost daughter of European royalty. The movies always had to end after the scene where everyone learned who everyone else actually was, December thought, because no one could ever figure out what could possibly happen after that. She wished it were yesterday.

"Are you nervous," he said.

"No," she said, like a small child walking nervously past a fierce dog, afraid she might reveal herself with one small gesture, or scent, or sound in a register that only the animals heard.

"You should be," he said, picking her up and carrying her to the edge of the clearing, where for one terrifying moment December thought he might just toss her onto the rocks below. "You definitely should be," he said, and then he turned and carried her past the car, along a dirt path, to the back of the house.

"There's a key on that ledge over the light," he said, and she reached up and, feeling a nail chip over the rough slate, found the key and opened the back door. He carried her through the dark kitchen, up a flight of stairs, and dropped her on a soft unmade bed. Besides the bed the room held very little: a small dresser with the bottom drawer open to reveal a jumble of underwear, sweatshirts, and socks; a vinyl-topped card table stacked with a schoolboy's composition notebooks, a portable tape recorder, and a lamp made from a Chianti bottle filled with colored sand; a framed photograph of a roadside diner hanging over peeling flowered wallpaper; a heap of used towels; a wicker wastebasket overflowing with empty beer bottles and old newspapers.

"Who lives here," she asked as he got into bed beside her.

He ran a finger across her collarbone. "Needs new wallpaper, don't you think?" he said. "And some lamps or something."

"Who lives here," she repeated, as he unclipped her earrings and dropped them onto the floor.

He leaned back against a pillow and folded his arms behind his head. "And curtains. Curtains always make a big difference."

She rolled over and sat across his stomach and put her hands on her hips. He reached around her and began to unfasten her buttons, from the bottom up.

"Who lives here," she said.

He pulled her down by her shoulders and kissed the top of her head.

"We do," he said. "You and me."

To get a fresh bottle of champagne out of the refrigerator. To take a bath, brush her teeth, run a comb quickly through her hair. To put a new tape in the cassette deck. To call Alex from the single black rotary phone in the kitchen, just to say not to worry, everything was okay. To hand a twenty-dollar bill to the delivery boy (pizza, Chinese, more pizza). Other than that, in the first few days, there had been very few reasons to get out of bed.

Like a romantic novel left poolside in the rain, face down and unfinished, Schuyler was remembered too late to be retrieved. December telephoned her house and heard her own voice, lowered a sultry octave against a background of Buddy Holly, telling her to leave herself a message of whatever length she desired.

"It is three o'clock on Sunday afternoon, and I have achieved a state of perfect happiness," she said, looking out at the cloudless sky, and then she hung up. Schuyler had appeared suddenly out of nowhere and had disappeared just as quickly back into it. I've found something that I never believed existed, she wanted to tell him, and if they made one for me they made one for you. She's out there somewhere, baby I promise you she's out there somewhere, just keep looking, you'll find her. Someone who's been waiting for someone like you.

December got a fresh beer out of the refrigerator and returned to the bedroom, where Tory was sleeping curled around a king size pillow. She sat cross-legged on the tabletop and watched him sleep. You don't realize how hungry you've been until you sit down at the table and smell the food that's been put in front of you; you don't know how thirsty you are until you tip the glass of water up to your lips; you can't admit how cold and tired you really are until that first moment when you walk into the warm house and pull off your stiff damp boots and shake the snow out of your hair. She hadn't known what she was looking for until she found it. Her waiting was over.

21

They were the last link with what he had come to think of as his previous life, these packages that Rosaline sent every month or so. Schuyler drove into town only once or twice a week to pick up his mail at the two-room red brick post office, but when the padded manila envelopes arrived, postmarked 10028 and addressed in Rosaline's curling bright-blue script, the clerk always telephoned him by lunchtime to let him know something had come in from New York City.

His first Christmas there, right after he'd moved back to Montana, she sent him a picture of Scotty on a rocking horse, photographs from Katie Lee's wedding, and a bottle of cognac from a case that Trevor and Philip had been saving for five years.

Just after Valentine's Day she had mailed him snapshots of Agamemnon's first four foals, with a letter telling him that they'd booked him to some really fantastic mares this season and next year's babies, if they looked at all decent, should fetch nice prices in the auction ring. She was pregnant again, but he please shouldn't tell anyone yet, whoever was out there to tell or not. Marinda had transferred to a law school in Florida and would be setting up house in Miami with Jason, who had gotten a job in some sort of do-good law clinic down there, and Rosaline was going to try to visit them before she got too big. Trevor enclosed a bottle of champagne and a list of some halfway decent California wines that he thought Schuyler might be able to find in the nearest large city. The nearest large city was a three-hour drive on a good day.

In June she thanked him for the photographs of his ranch, which looked splendid to her, although didn't it ever get lonely, with just a few horses and all those cows and a couple of dogs, but of course it must be lovely to be able to keep big dogs around after all those years

279

in New York. She sent him a magazine article about how the New York Hopewell House was exceeding everyone's expectations, including Katie Lee's. Marinda sent her best, she and Jason were living together in an apartment that Rosaline thought was perfectly awful (and imagine leaving Columbia Law for a school that was most famous for the sordid death of two of its most promising football players during a fraternity hazing, something to do with bourbon punch and a plastic coffin), but they seemed very happy, even if there was no talk of marriage. *Different strokes*, Rosaline wrote, and Schuyler smiled to read it, remembering how silly she always sounded using slang. Trevor, in a postscript, apologized if the champagne had turned out flat, as a few of the bottles had, but then what did Schuyler expect from a country that had made such a mess of itself in the last war.

In September Rosaline wrote that the baby, now a week late, obviously knew a good deal when he saw it (she was sure it was another boy) and had no intention of leaving the womb for the big bad world. Had Schuyler heard from Marinda, who'd asked three times for his address. Rosaline thought there might be some problems with Jason. It wasn't really her business of course, but a corporate law firm (Trevor said it was the absolutely aces place to be if you had to be in Florida) had offered Marinda a fantastic job at an absolutely insane salary after she graduated next spring, whoever would have guessed, and Jason worked those awful hours defending welfare mothers who knifed their boyfriends and drug dealers who couldn't speak English, political convictions were important of course, but as Trevor had pointed out, this wasn't what the Founding Fathers had in mind when they wrote the Constitution and besides, he was making no money at all, just living off Marinda, was she being too terribly old-fashioned, did Schuyler think, well it wasn't really her business. Marinda said she was happy, and she was still thin, so Rosaline supposed they should all believe her. Trevor would be sending something special after the baby came.

In October Trevor sent a case of Scotch that he said was just the thing for winter in Montana. He promised that Rosaline would write as soon as she was up to it, the birth had been difficult, Charlie weighed in at nearly nine pounds, a true Goodwood, and unlike Scotty, this one knew how to make noise. Had Schuyler bought that stock Trevor had recommended last winter, because now was a good time to sell. He supposed Schuyler didn't see much television or magazines, which was just as well, Rosaline had asked him to send Schuyler the enclosed clipping about that old roommate of hers who was launching some sort of acting career. Thank God she hadn't been invited to the wedding, though Trevor had never met December, he could tell she was the sort of girl who liked to make scenes, of course Schuyler didn't see the New York tabloids, but now that this Robinson fellow was on tour, well, it was amazing to him that Rosaline could be friends with such a person. *Women,* Trevor wrote, *they'll fly off into outer space if they haven't got a good man to tie them down. Speaking of which, you ought to give some consideration to this marriage and fatherhood business. Not getting any younger, as they say, and there must be some fine old-fashioned girl in your neighborhood who can be hoodwinked into taking a chance on a crusty old cowboy like you.*

I hope this reaches you before 1979, Rosaline wrote at Christmas, sending him another family picture, this one including Charlotte dressed in bright red and a frail Joseph smiling just to the left of the camera. *And here's a copy of Tory's new album, Trevor refuses to let me play it, which is just as well because it's all noise to me, I can't make out the words at all.* December had been cast as the chief girl in the new James Bond movie and would be posing for a poster in a bikini that Rosaline said was smaller than one of Charlie's diapers. Trevor sent two bottles of Russian vodka without labels, this was the rare stuff, it had to be smuggled in these days, and shouldn't be defiled by anything other than a single ice cube of pure distilled water.

On a late Friday afternoon toward the end of March, Schuyler drove into town to pick up mineral spirits, a new set of hinges for his back door, shaving cream, and the latest arrival from New York.

He tossed his purchases into the backseat and read Rosaline's letter in the fading light.

This is the one, she had written, sending him a blurry Polaroid of the Agamemnon–Chronic Joy colt, *the one we're going to keep and race.* Even Parker, who never displayed any enthusiasm about horses before they reached his barn, had come by the farm to check him out. They were going to call him Orestes, if the Jockey Club approved. It was lovely of Schuyler to invite Trevor out, he'd hardly had time to touch a gun since Charlie was born, but the market was going crazy so they'd just have to wait and see. Katie Lee and Bobby had been over last night for dinner, Katie Lee had looked absolutely disgusted when she watched Rosaline change a diaper, it was clear she didn't want kids, but then Bobby was such a big baby, maybe that was enough. Had it made the Montana papers about that client of Jason's who'd given the FBI all sorts of information about the cocaine trade in return for a new identity and federal protection? He'd been found dead somewhere in Arizona, his face still swollen from plastic surgery, his blond wig turned backwards, a pack of expensive Cuban cigars in his pocket. Jason was taking it very badly. Rosaline thought she might go down to visit Marinda at the end of the month and take in some of the good three-year-old stakes. *Trevor is being very sweet about all the time I'm putting into Blue Smoke—he's started calling me his "career girl" and had his secretary call to ask if she could help me with arrangements for my "business trip"! I wish my father were well enough to come with me, but the trip to New York at Christmas took a lot out of him, it will be a long time before he has the energy to travel again. I promise to send you a postcard with pink flamingos on it. Love, Rosaline. P.S. Something disgusting and bourbonish coming from Trevor under separate cover.*

Schuyler looked at the photograph of the colt: a long-legged thing with a nicely shaped head, his chestnut coat a perfect match to Rosaline's own mane. If they were lucky, in a few months he might fetch somewhere in the low six figures in the auction ring; if they were even luckier, and they kept him, he might win more than that on the racetrack and prove himself to be a valuable stallion. Or they might run out of luck altogether and end up as most breeders did, with an animal as useless as it was beautiful.

He tucked the picture up into the visor and tried to guess what kind of bourbon Trevor might be sending. Considering all the letters and photographs and liquor he'd gotten from the Van Schotts, he'd sent back relatively little: a baby present for Charlie, two Christmas presents for Scotty, and a handful of postcards, all showing the same tourist office vista of a winter sunset.

It's colder here than any man deserves was just about all the first card said. *They've got five Roy Orbison tunes on the jukebox here, what more could anyone want,* he wrote a few months later, and then *On a bad day nothing at all happens here and on a good day even less* a few months after that. He telephoned them once to offer an invitation he knew they'd never be able to accept, and they called him once, slightly drunk on New Year's, on the chance that he was expecting their call and alone. He was neither. The women came and went, as warm and easy as the land was cold and the winter hard, drinking Trevor's liquor out of blue ceramic coffee mugs, asking nothing more from Schuyler than what he was prepared to give: a comfortable bed piled with Hudson's Bay blankets, gentle hands, and a smile that stayed friendly the morning after.

Across the street from the post office was the town's only bar, owned and run by a mail-order minister who believed that income taxes were a violation of God's will. Schuyler took a seat on a worn and cracking leatherette stool and signaled for a double Dewar's just as the flip side of "Pretty Woman" began to spin.

"Smith, my man, hard day at the office?" said a dark, bearded man in a red-and-black checked jacket two stools down.

Schuyler smiled, though he'd heard the joke from Nelson before, nearly every Friday afternoon in fact. Nelson was the closest thing to a local celebrity, a tough-guy writer whose slender novels about guns, drugs, and heartbreak won prizes in New York and were made into movies in Los Angeles. He had moved here just before the real estate boom of the early seventies—he alternately bragged and cursed himself as being the one-man reason for the boom—and he served as a sort of ambassador between the locals and the more recent arrivals. In the East he had a reputation as a professional bad boy, though Schuyler could hardly think of a naughty thing that Nelson had ever done, except sometimes getting a little too drunk and telling off-color jokes involving feminists, Indian chiefs, and various farm animals.

Nelson was a sort of cultural artifact in these parts. People were arriving unannounced on Nelson's property all the time. A college student with ten dollars to his name and an unpublished manuscript in his canvas backpack. A narcotics agent hoping to find the five kilos of cocaine that were rumored to be hidden somewhere back of the barn, pending the release from federal prison of Nelson's ex-wife's second cousin Ramon. A teammate from Nelson's high school football team back in Mississippi, a draft dodger on his way home from Canada at last—people passed through and Nelson put them up. Nelson had adopted Schuyler as a sort of pet dog/lost cause when he first arrived in Montana. Schuyler would rant drunkenly about how he'd found and lost the story of the century, how he'd been just about to nail down all the hard evidence for his organized-crime story when the whole thing collapsed for no apparent reson, and Nelson would listen, for hours and hours, until he'd finally suggested Schuyler turn the thing into a screenplay, if only to exorcise the ghosts. Which Schuyler did, handing the finished work to Nelson, who passed it on to his agent, who sold it for a small amount of money to an independent producer in Hollywood. The project had pretty much disappeared, as far as Schuyler could tell, but he would always be grateful to Nelson for helping him get through a bad winter. There had been some social shrewdness in it, Schuyler guessed later: Schuyler had grown up there, after all, and was the genuine article that Nelson aspired to be.

"I think I got spring fever," Nelson said, frowning at his open left palm as though he were trying to tell his own fortune.

"Doesn't feel like spring to me," Schuyler said, though spring had officially come to Montana, and everywhere else in the country, exactly three days ago. The ground was still covered with snow.

"These spots are definitely spring fever," Nelson said, "and there are just two known cures for spring fever. One of them involves the venom of a poisonous snake that only makes its home on the banks of the Amazon."

"And the other?" Schuyler asked. It was just about the only thing Nelson asked of his friends, besides that they didn't throw up on his furniture and they didn't make passes at his ex-wife, whom he swore he still loved: that they play the straight man.

Nelson smiled slowly. "It's arriving sometime tomorrow afternoon. Why don't you stop by after dinner?" he said, very casually, to let Schuyler know that he had probably extended the same invitation several times over in the last few days. Nelson never came out and announced that he was giving a party. He just suggested that people stop by, if they didn't have anything better to do. "One of the cures is a department-store heiress from Atlanta. The other is a graduate student at Berkeley, which apparently still exists, in some unknown form."

"Graduate student in what?" Schuyler asked.

"Archaeology," Nelson said, pronouncing it archie-ology, "the study of North American hamburger stands."

"Or red-headed comic-book characters."

"Whatever. We could always use a few good men."

"Well, thanks," Schuyler said. "Though the very thought of it fatigues me."

"I'm not going to have to sit through another maybe-I-should-find-a-good-woman-and-settle-down monologue, am I?" Nelson half barked. "You get another CARE package from the perfect couple today?"

An old Eagles song came on the jukebox. Schuyler stamped an Olympic symbol on his cocktail napkin with the damp bottom of his nearly empty glass. "Maybe. If they still make them."

"They do. Their fathers are either preachers or war heroes."

"And they still cook you meat and potatoes. Prime rib. Loin of pork. Broiled lamb chops."

"They don't diet, they don't eat yoghurt, and they don't wear nail polish. Are they virgins?"

"Nope," Schuyler said. "There was that captain of the college football team. And that medical student, the one who died tragically in a boating accident." He was getting a little drunk on his second double. It felt great.

"They're all named Mary or Margaret or Maureen," Nelson said, turning his open hand in the dim light.

"Try Martha," said a low female voice.

"Martha!" Nelson exclaimed, patting the empty barstool between them. "How the hell have you been?"

"Fair to middling," she said. She had last seen Nelson three hours ago. She rented a cottage and a little bit of land from him, where she bred and trained hunting dogs for a living. The real thing: the ones that were born to scent and point, the ones that made no sense indoors, the ones that could be sold for several thousand dollars when Martha was through with them. Martha had been a social worker at some point and was hanging out at Nelson's waiting for her divorce to come through.

She gave Schuyler a wink and he bought her a drink. Finnish on her father's side, pure Cheyenne on her mother's, Martha had bones you could hang a hammer on and was everywhere neither light nor dark but something creamy in between: thick, smooth skin naturally the tan that others spent hours on the beach trying to acquire, a heavy braid of hair that began brown at her scalp and ended two feet later in a blond sun-streaked curl in the middle of her back, and eyes the color of adobe, opaque, a poker player's eyes—you never knew what she was thinking. And you would never know, save for the long legs and square shoulders, what her body was like under the baggy men's jeans and bulky Fair Isle sweaters she wore, unless you undressed her, as Schuyler did from time to time, when they were both feeling friendly.

Tonight Schuyler was feeling suddenly friendly. He rested his chin on a fist. "Nelson here has Rocky Mountain spotted spring fever," he said. "It may be contagious."

Martha peered over at Nelson's hand. "That's not spring fever," she sniffed. "It's stigmata. Hysterical in origin, probably. Happens in South America all the time."

"But I'm not Catholic," Nelson protested.

"Doesn't matter," Martha said. "Check your ankles when you get home."

"*You* check my ankles," Nelson leered. It was a game they had played in this bar before: Nelson flirted with Martha, Martha rolled her eyes in a prom queen's grimace of rejection, Schuyler took Martha home.

"What am I drinking?" she asked Schuyler.

"Love Potion number nine," Nelson sang.

"Dewar's," Schuyler said.

Martha stuck out her tongue. "It's disgusting. What happened to that great single malt you got from New York?"

"I've still got a bottle or two left," Schuyler said, putting his arm around her waist just an inch or two up under her sweater. He ran a finger over the beehive corrugation of her thermal undershirt.

"Don't make me beg for it," Martha whispered just soft enough so Nelson couldn't hear, "I come from a noble breed."

Schuyler knocked back the last of his Scotch and stood up. Martha handed Nelson her car keys. Martha and Schuyler would drive home together in his truck and Nelson would take Martha's car back to the ranch—it was one of the niceties she insisted on, that her car didn't sit out overnight in front of the bar where everyone in town would see it and know she'd left with a man. It made no difference if Nelson's car sat out in front of Mason's all night, all week, all month: he was always lending his cars to people and besides, guessing where Nelson slept and with whom was one of the few games in town, a game Nelson encouraged everyone to play.

Nelson hung his head at an angle and stretched out his arms, as if on a cross. "Be careful, my children," he said.

" 'Night, Dad," Martha said. Schuyler gave a silent salute.

It was always the same with Martha. She didn't like to kiss much. She would weld her cheek to his, murmuring into his ear, keeping things slow, until the murmur rose in pitch into a constant hum of pleasure and she would roll him over onto his back, his thumbs in

the deep hollow made by her hip bones, her hands over his. She kept
her eyes open and her socks on. Sometimes she made it over the edge
but usually she just watched him, smiling, and then placed a single
finger across his lips, giving him a look that said she wasn't asking
for any favors, this was part of the deal they had made, the deal they
always made, to spend all night in a slow exchange of pleasure, not to
count the days or weeks or months between their times together, to
be friends. They would fall asleep with only the tips of their fingers
touching. In the morning she'd bring him burned coffee, and he'd
drive her home before dawn, the dogs lined up against the tornado
fencing, barking for their breakfast.

When he got back from dropping Martha off the next morning
Schuyler set up a fresh pot of coffee and, running a hand along his
jaw, decided to put off his daily shave until the evening, before he
went to Nelson's. He'd briefly considered a beard last autumn, but
when it came in half gray he'd changed his mind: it made him look
too much like something that was about to get sent down into a coal
mine or decked in a barroom or shotgun-married to a first cousin and
a trailer park.

On a low table next to the fireplace his large calfskin-covered
family album lay face down. It held more than the usual posed
family portraits and vacation snapshots; it went back for generations
and contained a yellowed newspaper article about a great-great-
grandfather who had developed a disease-resistant hybrid strain of
sweet potatoes, the woven silk decorations his paternal grandfather
had earned for acts of heroism in Europe during World War I, a lock of
hair from his great aunt Althea, who had claimed to be the very first
flapper in Baltimore, birth certificates, deeds, a pressed flower from a
bridal bouquet, an obituary, a child's first scrawl. Generations had
observed the tradition of adding a page to the book with every major
family event. When a Smith married, his wife was supposed to
present him, on his wedding night, with a page that represented the
best of her family. The book had been opened to the page Schuyler's
mother had made, a collage that included the final paragraph of her
valedictory high school graduation speech, a clipping about an aboli-
tionist great-great-grandmother of hers who had run a safe house on
the Underground Railroad, and her father's recipe for crab cakes.
Martha must have been looking at it before he woke up. She had once
said that this book was the best thing in the whole house, that it

reminded her so much of her own Native American and Scandinavian traditions, where family histories were recounted over and over to each generation so that no brave deed would ever be forgotten, no precious lesson ever unlearned. The last page in the book had been created when Schuyler was born and the next, he supposed, would come when he got married.

Outside it really was nearly spring, though it would be some time in late May before these straggly trees—he still hadn't found out what kind they were—showed any signs of life. Schuyler crossed his arms against the cold and sent smoke rings up into the cloudless blue. The land here stretched nearly flat in all directions, and on a day like today how far you saw depended only on the strength of your own vision. Sometimes Schuyler thought he detected the curve of the planet in the haze of the horizon.

As he stood there in his yard Schuyler had a sense of his exact location on a map of the world. The state stretched from time zone to time zone (the only state to do that, schoolchildren noted with pride), from the Rockies in the west to the east, where Schuyler lived. *Scale*, he said to himself, that was what he'd lost track of in New York, how a single man was just a pinprick on this surface that glaciers had shoved and shifted into mountains, canyons, and flatlands, had veined with rivers and washed with oceans. Considered against this particular landscape, everything human shrank to nothingness: a man, his house and his animals, his ambitions and longings, his love and his anger, it all just disappeared. A woman walking in the distance, even a woman as tall and strong and beautiful as December, would vanish in a blink.

Schuyler blinked again. Something moving against the snow had caught his eye, what was it. Just birds, dark birds fluttering up across the sun, fooled by this year's early southern spring into thinking Montana was ready to receive them.

22

Mondo Condo, Marinda thought, turning off the vacuum cleaner and picking a penny out of the soft wool twist of the green wall-to-wall carpeting. It was one of the few things that distinguished these otherwise identical—what were they called? the broker had said "town homes" but the legal papers said "residential units"—condominiums from each other: the color of the carpet and of the smooth Sheetrock walls and of the narrow venetian blinds that hung from every window, blocking out the fierce Florida sun that would fade anything unprotected to a pale pastel within months. If you don't keep the blinds drawn, the broker had told them, the carpet will fade around the furniture and you'll never be able to rearrange anything, because you'll always have to worry about hiding the bright patches. *As long as you live,* the broker had said, and then quickly apologized; *I meant as long as you live here,* she'd said. Marinda had known exactly what she meant: so many people came to Miami to die. These oceanfront condominiums were their last stop on their way to the great unknown. Jason thought the whole thing was ridiculous, paying all this money for a great ocean view that you couldn't enjoy because you were worried about your rugs and upholstery fading. He was right, as usual.

Marinda punched up the pillows that lined the couch she and Jason had ordered from the Contemporary Design Center in the Crescent Creek Mall. The green of the carpet was everywhere: in the narrow stripes of the pillows, in the flecked tweed of the couch, around the rims of their plates and coffee cups, in the framed silk-screened charts of herbs and wildflowers that hung over the butcherblock kitchen table, in the abstract swirl of the plastic shower curtain, in their bath towels, on the ceramic bases of the ginger-jar lamps that sat on either side of their platform bed (another Contemporary Design Center acquisition), and even on their bed sheets. Marinda hadn't noticed when she'd bought them, but now she was sure of it. Little houndsteeth of this green, barely discernible, in the plaid pattern she'd picked out because Jason had said he refused to sleep on anything too femmy. In the sale catalogues that arrived with their Sunday papers, tucked between the comic section and the television supplement, this color was usually called seafoam. But to Marinda it was poverty green, because it was this exact candy-mint shade that covered the rickety wood frame houses in the poorer districts around where she'd grown up. She arranged the pillows in planned randomness along the back of the couch. There was a poverty-green house in New Jersey they had always passed right before the ramp up onto the Parkway, and in front of the house there had always been a late-model Pontiac of matching hue. Once Marinda had pointed this out to her parents, and her father had just said, *Yeah, that's nigger green all right,* and her mother had protested, saying it was nearly the same color they'd used in their very own living room, but her father said no, their green was definitely classier, closer to the color of money.

The condominium had been a present from her parents when she'd transferred to law school down here so she could be close to Jason, who'd gotten a job in a storefront law clinic representing people who couldn't afford the more expensive criminal and immigration law firms downtown. Her father had bought the apartment as an investment, he said, but his real motivation was to make sure that Marinda didn't move into Jason's apartment in a run-down, dangerous part of the city. Instead Jason moved in with Marinda, though he continued to pay the extremely low rent on his city apartment. When Rosaline said she was coming to visit and asked whether Marinda and Jason were living together Marinda said they weren't, Jason had this apartment in the city. She didn't tell Rosaline that Jason stopped by his apartment only once or twice a month, to pick up mail and clothing.

Not that Rosaline ever would have stayed with them: she took a suite overlooking a golf course at a hotel nearer the racetrack, with a small sitting room and two bedrooms in case Trevor came down with the children, which he never did. During her two-week visits Marinda would invite Rosaline over for an elaborate dinner at home with her and Jason, and then Rosaline and Marinda would share a couple of more casual dinners or lunches where they took turns with the check, and then, usually on the last weekend of her visit, Rosaline would take Jason and Marinda to the most expensive seafood restaurant on the waterfront, as if thanking them for the hospitality she never asked them to extend.

Rosaline had arrived yesterday and was due for dinner in an hour. Marinda poured herself a small brandy and drew a bath. Jason would be picking up flowers on his way home; to Marinda's great surprise it had turned out to be Rosaline, of all her friends, whom Jason liked the best. Straight, rich, Republican Mrs. Trevor Van Schott, whose family had built its fortune on the backs of the very people Jason fought so hard to defend. But Jason—who raged against Marinda's family, who tortured Katie Lee at every opportunity, who had rolled his eyes at December's television commercials for a line of cosmetics that were perfected through laboratory testing that involved cruelty to small, helpless animals—just doted on Rosaline, opening doors for her, rising from his chair every time she entered the room, refilling her wineglass with a gentle turn of the wrist. Well, thank God he doesn't hate *all* my friends, Marinda had thought the first time she watched them together, with an emotion somewhere between jealousy and relief.

"I'll get the dishes," Jason said, taking the remains of the chicken sautéed with sherry, shallots, and mushrooms into the kitchen.

"He's so sweet," Rosaline said when they were alone.

"It's all for your benefit," Marinda said, trying to calculate how many tablespoons of butter she'd used to cook the meal. Twenty-four, which, when divided by three, meant she'd managed to put away an entire stick by herself. "Usually everything sits out overnight. In the morning it looks like a bomb struck."

Rosaline fluffed up her hair, which she had had cut into soft gamine curls that fell just to the bottoms of her ears. The style made most young mothers look suburban and sexless, but on Rosaline it just looked French.

"Great haircut," Marinda said. "You can really wear some fantastic earrings with that kind of haircut."

"You think?" Rosaline said, fingering one of the large emeralds ringed with tiny diamonds. "Not too boyish? I feel rather like Mia Farrow, *après* Sinatra."

"Oh no," Marinda said, feeling her own heavy twist of dark hair coming undone. "I'd do it myself if I had the guts." She had this fear that cutting her hair would cause her to grow old. The women Jason represented all had their hair cut before they went to prison, and he had described to Marinda how amazing it was to watch these young women transformed into older, harder versions of themselves.

"But you have such lovely hair," Rosaline said, raising her voice over the whir of the dishwasher. Marinda winced: she would have waited until after Rosaline had left. "You really look terrific."

Marinda laughed away the compliment. "This sounds like some kind of mutual admiration society," she said.

"But it's true!" Rosaline protested, smoothing out the tablecloth in front of her. "Look at how—how improved we are. Just last week I was going through old photographs with Trevor, and we found all these pictures from freshman and sophomore year, and if anything, we looked older then."

"Come on, Rosaline," Marinda said.

Rosaline shook a finger at Marinda. "I'll make copies for you. Everyone had practically the same haircut, center parts, their hair glued to the sides of their heads. And so much makeup! Jason, you wouldn't believe how much makeup Marinda used to wear."

Jason placed her coffee before her, light with one sugar, as he remembered she liked it. "Most women look better without makeup," he said, "and sometime I'll tell you about the companies that manufacture and market makeup. You've all been brainwashed."

Rosaline giggled. "Yes, they took me into a small room and knocked me out with drugs and planted electrodes in my head and sent me messages telling me Buy makeup! Buy makeup! Marinda, he's just as extreme as ever. Marinda, tell him why women wear makeup."

"Why do women wear makeup," Marinda asked, taking a sip of the strong blend, feeling the shock of sugar after months of Sweet 'n Low.

"To make themselves feel better of course," Rosaline said. "To make themselves more attractive to men, I suppose. To make themselves more desirable."

"Right," Marinda said.

"Marinda," Jason said, sitting down between them, "tell Rosaline how fucked up it is the way women spend so much time and money on their appearances."

"Right," Marinda said. "Uh, Rosaline, it's extremely fucked up the way women spend so much time and money on their appearances."

"It is? Why? I mean, I can guess what you're going to say, but why don't you say it first."

"Oh, I don't know," Marinda said, scraping the table with her teaspoon. "Because Jason can say it so much better."

"Jason?" Rosaline said, and Marinda watched Rosaline's face as Jason explained our society's false and oppressive notions of female sexuality, and how women used their appearances as scapegoats, failing to focus on whatever their true obstacles were, and how the time spent on how they looked could be spent more productively in improving their lives in other ways.

"Oh," Rosaline said. "Well."

"Think about it," Jason said.

"Oh, I will," Rosaline said. "It's a very nice theory, but, you know, it's *your* theory. Someone else might have another theory."

"Such as?" Jason said.

"Oh, well, everybody has to decide for themselves—excuse my error, for herself," Rosaline said. "I wouldn't tell Trevor to shave his beard, for example."

"Trevor would never grow a beard," Jason said.

"But what I mean is, I think each woman should be able to make up her own mind. Is that a pun? Not just do things to please her husband."

Or boyfriend, Marinda thought.

"Don't you want to please your husband?" Jason asked, and Rosaline began to blush bright red.

"How did we get onto this topic?" she said in a high voice. "Weren't we just talking about old photographs?"

"We were," Marinda said. "And about how much better we all look now."

"I found one of Schuyler with such long hair. And one of you, you looked so different, I can't exactly put my finger on why."

Marinda was filled with a sudden panic, that Rosaline was going to say in front of Jason: your eyebrows, remember how you used to tweeze your eyebrows into those thin black lines? It was the danger of introducing old friends to new loves, the danger that they would reveal you, impart some seemingly harmless bit of information that would put an irreparable crack in this new perfect self you'd created and presented. *You used to tweeze your eyebrows?* she could imagine Jason saying later when they were alone. Rosaline might reveal any awful old thing, it terrified her to think of it. *You had a complete set of Judy Collins records? You drank Black Russians? You said "okey dokey"? You signed your letters with quotations from Kurt Vonnegut novels?* How much longer would Rosaline stay? An hour? Two? They were nearly through with dessert.

"Was she thin then?" Jason asked.

"What kind of question is that," Rosaline said. "Of course she was."

"You know what it was," Marinda said, believing that she would be absolved of a sin if she confessed it before it was discovered, "my eyebrows. I used to tweeze them. Can you believe it?"

"Aaargh," Jason said, like a character in a horror movie who has just begun to watch his beloved become transformed into the One-Eyed Antwoman from Outer Space.

"We all used to do it," Marinda said.

"Did it hurt?" Jason asked.

"Sort of," she said. "Well, no, not really, I guess. I can't really remember. It wasn't any big deal."

"It must have hurt," Jason insisted. "It couldn't have felt good, right? It must have been painful. Rosaline, this proves my point. Women are brainwashed to the point of enduring extreme pain just so they can go around with these eyebrows that make them look like transvestites."

"I didn't say *extreme* pain," Marinda whined.

"Marinda never looked like a transvestite," Rosaline said.

"Okay, it doesn't matter," Jason said. "Okay, minor pain. But pain is pain, right? Am I right?" He pounded the table.

Lawyers, Rosaline thought, sighing to herself.

"Pain is relative," Marinda said.

"Fine, I'll concede that," Jason said. "Tweezing, excuse me, plucking your eyebrows is less painful than being hacked to death with a buzzsaw. But I'm sure if I plucked a hair from my eyebrow, I'd say 'ouch.' Who wouldn't say 'ouch' when they're in pain?"

The women said nothing. Jason wouldn't have settled for anything less.

On Thursday, Marinda skipped a class and accompanied Rosaline to the races. They were sharing a box with Trevor's cousin Taylor, who had come down to settle a client's estate in Palm Beach; with the client's daughter Jacqueline, who was still undecided as to whether Taylor's firm should continue to handle her family's business; and with two breeders (one from Texas, one from Atlanta) who were considering buying shares in Agamemnon.

Marinda had drunk her two vodka tonics a little too quickly and now, just before the fourth race, she was trying to decide whether she was drunk. Possibly she was: teetering to and from the paddock in the midday sun in beige sling-back heels had left her drained and sweating, and she found herself laughing a little too loudly at Taylor's jokes, which were mostly directed to Jacqueline. And possibly she wasn't: the others in the box spoke very little between races, and having ascertained Marinda's role there (college roommate, can't tell the horses apart, not one of us, won't see her again), felt free to ignore her, but it was easier for Marinda to blame her self-consciousness on a few ounces of alcohol than on the way these people, her dear friend Rosaline's dear friends, were failing to behave.

What hadn't yet occurred to Marinda was this: that the loveliest people from the nicest families were capable of a kind of bad manners that, over the years, had been completely perfected. The rude and obvious had been centrifuged out, leaving only a pale mixture of a graceful refusal to respond to others, and a subtle display of the position that allowed them to do so.

Taylor and Rosaline had gone out to the paddock to look at some promising three-year-olds, leaving Marinda with Jackie and the two southern gentlemen.

"I do admire your *chapeau*," said Richard, the thin one from Texas, who at age fiftyish was nearly bald, his few strands of hair brushed confidently back from his brow in a manner that suggested he had lost his hair long ago and was patiently waiting for his peers to catch up to him.

"Yes," seconded Robert, the younger and heavier one from Atlanta, who had also lost a great deal of hair but did not quite yet believe it. The smooth, healthy tan of his face ascended into an angry red sunburn where he had left the top of his head unprotected by sun block during the recent fishing trip he had earlier described. "Such a lovely shade of pink."

Jackie smiled and touched the wide brim of her hat. "Thank you. It belonged to my mother, actually."

Marinda looked away. She suspected it was rather extreme, even during the season in Miami, to wear such a hat: bright pink, the crown circled with white silk flowers, with white and pink satin ribbons running down the back. There seemed to be some leeway, though, for heiresses from Palm Beach. Perhaps they were expected to drink more, to wear more jewelry and have more husbands, to curse occasionally (though always in a second language).

"I love that kind of romantic old-fashioned hat," Marinda said, which was not true. "I wish I could carry them off," she continued, which was.

"Yes?" Jackie said, and then, "Richard, who do you like in this race."

"Oh, well," Richard said, frowning at his program, "I guess I'll put some money on Leaping Lief." He'd been hoping Taylor and Rosaline would return from the paddock in time to give him some guidance he could turn to profit. Richard and Robert had been taking turns making trips to the windows, placing each other's bets and occasional wagers for Jackie and Marinda. Taylor and Rosaline could never be spotted at the window but had both clutched winning tickets after the second race was made official. Richard could not tell if there was someone here at the track running their bets for them or whether arrangements had been made in advance or whether perhaps there was some secret place, not available to him or Robert, where Rosaline and Taylor bought and cashed tickets.

"Yes, Rosaline was saying in the car that Leaping Lief was a horse to watch," Marinda said. "She said that last year the owners were hoping this was their Derby horse, but then he got injured, and they couldn't get him back into training in time."

"Is that right," Robert said, lifting his binoculars and examining the horses as they paraded onto the track. "Well, no one will beat Spectacular Bid."

"Here's hoping," Richard said, raising his glass. "I placed two thousand dollars with the winter book."

"What's the winter book?" asked Marinda, of no one in particular, so that none of them felt obliged to answer, and her question hung there in the warm air like a badly blown smoke ring. *I hate these people,* she thought, *Jason is right about every last one of them.* When she got home and Jason asked about her day she would put on a fine performance, and this prospect buoyed her spirits, and she began to turn the others into cartoon characters who now existed only for her and Jason's later amusement. Richard, who wore cowboy boots under his seersucker suit and had spent half an hour discussing how his Mercedes-Benz, shipped directly from Germany, had been rebuilt to American specifications. Robert, whom Marinda had caught stirring his drink with an index finger and then running his hand through the hair he no longer possessed. Taylor, who according to Rosaline had discovered on his wedding night, when they checked into a hotel in Bermuda and the desk clerk confiscated her American Express card, that his bride was two hundred thousand dollars in debt. And Jackie, who had invited Richard and Robert out for dinner as though Marinda were as invisible as a servant, who had told vicious gossip about Charlotte and Joseph as soon as Rosaline had left the box, who two weeks after her mother's funeral had dressed herself up in cheerful fuchsia, piled on her recently inherited jewelry, and come to the races wearing the dead woman's favorite straw hat.

They were completely awful, Rosaline knew, but business was business. When her father had first bought Agamemnon and Rosaline was hoping to reduce Blue Smoke's exposure by selling off shares, Richard and Robert hadn't even returned her telephone calls. Now that Agamemnon appeared to be something short of a disaster at stud—he'd gotten several nice mares in foal after just one cover, and the babies even at this early stage all looked so nice and strong, and a couple of the old-line Kentucky breeders, the ones who knew Joseph's father and grandfather, were advising Rosaline to put together a syndication so she wouldn't be so much at risk—the newer investors, such men as Richard and Robert, had begun to call, hoping that Rosaline might still be a bit panicked and sell too low. Their money came from businesses Rosaline knew little about—the manipulation of land values in states whose capitals she couldn't even name, the sales of machine parts to Third World countries still under colonial regime—but it was nonetheless money, money that Blue Smoke needed to purchase new mares, to renovate its training facilities, and to pay the enormous insurance premiums that had doubled and then tripled in the last couple of years.

The paddock was filled with friends of Joseph and Charlotte who came down during the season. The men talked of sport fishing and the women of a Latin American singing star who, during his first winter in Palm Beach, had played very minor roles in three very major scandals. The Divorce Scandal (accusations of homosexuality, the seduction of the federal judge in whose jurisdiction the trial might be held, a rifle that may or may not have been loaded). The Stock Fraud Scandal (who had bought when, on whose advice, at whose investment firms). And the Jackie thing (the kiss at the funeral, the golf course, some of the jewelry she was wearing was rumored to have been left to the New York Public Library, though the singer couldn't have known that or possibly wouldn't have cared). Rosaline hadn't known Taylor was bringing Jackie, and she was a little annoyed at him—it would appear that Rosaline was somehow vouching for Jackie, whom she had met only once before, at her wedding to Trevor, and who would now probably send Rosaline all kinds of invitations to dinners and outings she had no interest in attending.

Parker came over (he trained for a few other owners besides Blue Smoke, the same owners, not coincidentally, who had been the first to agree to send some of their better mares to Agamemnon) and gave Rosaline a little kiss on the cheek.

"How is your father doing? Will he be coming down?" Parker asked. It was the charade Parker maintained, that Joseph had some temporary ailment and Rosaline was just carrying the ball until he could return to take command of Blue Smoke. It was what allowed him to take direction from a woman less than half his age.

"Oh, I don't think so," Rosaline said. "Travel tires him so. He's following everything, though."

"Still off the sauce? Can he get the *Form* up there?"

"We have it flown in for him."

"Well," Parker said, smiling over her head at another trainer, "place can't be too bad then. Hope we see him soon." Like most who had a serious and daily relationship with the bottle, Parker refused to accept the consequences of alcoholism in his former drinking partners. "Next time you see him, tell him Coronet Blue will be ready to run in a couple of months. Tell him we're deciding between this little stake at Keeneland or something they might write for him in New York. See what he thinks."

"Oh, I will," Rosaline said. It was how she and Parker did business: Parker giving her information in the guise of questions for her father, Rosaline making suggestions or asking advice as though she'd just gotten off the telephone with Joseph.

"You might come by the barns tomorrow," Parker continued. "We might work that Northern Dancer filly. Francisco said he wasn't even letting her run the day she did forty-seven and change."

"Really?" Rosaline said, knowing that Parker asked Francisco Gomez, now Blue Smoke's regular rider, to work only those two-year-olds he had serious hopes for. The rest were ridden by exercise riders who, for reasons of weight or age or lack of skill, could not make their living as jockeys, or by jockeys less successful than Francisco who hoped that by riding for Parker in the morning they might pick up the mounts that Francisco didn't take. Rosaline was pleased that the filly was doing so well but annoyed that Parker hadn't told her ahead of time that Francisco would be getting on the horse. She might have wanted to come watch. She was sure he would have told Joseph, if Joseph had come down.

"Yes, I would definitely like to come by," Rosaline said.

"Well, come around seven. She'll be going out onto the track around seven-fifteen. Excuse me," Parker said, nodding toward a jockey wearing bright red silks, "I've got to go give the boy his instructions."

The boy was nearly forty, but Parker and his generation still insisted on describing their riders this way. Rosaline stood still for another little kiss and studied her program.

"Mrs. Van Schott," said Gomez, coming up and shaking her hand. "How nice to see you."

"Hello Mr. Gomez," she said, knowing how silly she sounded— everyone called the jockeys by their first names—but she still couldn't help it with Francisco, whom she hadn't talked to since Saratoga, what with the baby and all, there was something so correct about him, she had to respond in kind. "It's nice to see you. How have you been?" she asked, and they replayed the same conversation they always had. He said how much he always enjoyed being at (whatever track he was at). She said how happy they were with (whichever Blue Smoke horse had most recently won). He said how disappointed he was that she didn't have a horse in (whatever the major upcoming stakes race was, in which he would ride, nine times out of ten, one of the favorites, a mount he wouldn't have traded for a Blue Smoke horse even if Parker had asked, which he never did). She said, Well, we won that race in (a distant year, long ago, when stables such as Blue Smoke dominated American racing). He asked after her father and her husband and (either her mother or her children, but never both). She gave a brief report, telling him Trevor was in (whichever place, never here, that his business demanded he be, though of course he would always rather be here, and of course she would always rather be there), and she asked after Francisco's brother, who ran a restaurant in the Keys and who was the only relative Francisco had in this country. Francisco had been engaged, just briefly, to the sister of his brother's business partner, but the engagement had been broken when his brother discovered that his partner had been skimming cash out of the register to take to the blackjack tables in Atlantic City.

"My brother is very well, thank you, and he says I should remind you to come to his restaurant if you are ever down that way."

"I'd like to, in fact, I'm taking some friends out for dinner on Saturday and I was going to take them to the same old boring place I always go to, but they haven't been in Florida very long, so maybe they'd like—where is it exactly?" Rosaline asked. Of course Jason would prefer someplace—what was the expression?—*off the beaten track*, that was how she thought of it, rather than where she had planned to take them, a restaurant filled with men like Marinda's father and women who overdressed.

"Islamorada," Francisco said. "It's called the Tortoise and the Hare. For the tourists, who do not like to eat there if the name is Spanish. But they don't serve tortoise or hare. Here comes my horse. Definitely a tortoise," he said, giving her a wink.

"Oh, well," Rosaline said, flustered by his tone. He spoke as though he were confiding a secret to her, something much more important and dangerous than the probability that his mount wouldn't win, which anyone could have told from a brief look at the *Form*. She folded her arms across her chest. Though Francisco was always formal, even distant, she thought he was standing perhaps just a little too close to her. She had heard all sorts of stories about his womanizing but had dismissed most of them as rumors, there were always so many rumors about the top jockeys, and Francisco in the last couple of years had become one of the very top jockeys in the country. His face, now creased slightly with age and sun, appeared from time to time on magazine covers, in part because of his riding achievements and in part because he was, quite simply, gorgeous. Even Trevor had noticed (calling him not "gorgeous" but "photogenic") how Francisco carried himself with a grace and strength that belied his 112-pound, 5'4" frame, how his green eyes, the color of some powerful and perhaps illegal liqueur, were set like a magnificent surprise in his browned, weather-lined face.

"Are you coming to the works tomorrow?" he asked. "I'm getting on that very nice two-year-old."

"Yes, Parker told me, the Northern Dancer. I'll be by around seven."

"No." Francisco frowned. "Not that one," he said, pursing his lips, realizing that he had made a mistake, that, for whatever reason,

Parker had not told Rosaline that the best two-year-old in the barn would be worked a little after six A.M. "The other. The Damascus."

"Oh, well, yes, I'd like to see him too," Rosaline said.

Francisco gave her a look that she interpreted to mean: if you come by early, pretend to Parker it was just by chance.

Rosaline gave him a look that she hoped said this: of course, it's understood.

And Francisco nodded just before he walked off, for he understood much more than she had intended, more possibly than she understood herself. But then, he had been watching her for such a very long time. The girl, now the lady, with the eyes just as green as his own and the skin with that touch of sallow gold that said maybe there was some small part of her that came from a place he knew. Though he knew very little about Rosaline's background and had thought of her only briefly, unanalytically, between their rare encounters, he believed he understood her in some wordless instinctual way, the same way he could sometimes just predict, without any real clue, how a horse was going to behave on the track. He understood that she was attracted to him (but then, he thought, weren't most women?) but that she had no idea of it, had no idea that it was even possible for a lady like her to think such thoughts about a man like him. He understood the implications of such an innocence: there was a part of her that had never been tapped, that might never be tapped, like an underground river that runs swiftly and silently for hundreds of years until someone thinks to sink a well. And he understood this too: that the well had to be built in just the right place, at the exactly correct time of year, and that then, and only then, would the cool, clear water come bubbling up happily to the surface.

He drank her in with a final look and then forgot her and went off to exchange courtesies with the owner and trainer of his mount in the next race. After the horses were led out Rosaline returned to the box, where Taylor was explaining to Jackie what the procedures were, here at Hialeah, for making a claim. Rosaline sat quietly through the next few races until there was a commotion in the infield as a man in a small rowboat waved his oar at the colony of flamingos that lived there.

The bright birds flew up in a burst of pink and coral and black, and Rosaline stood up with them, clasping her hands to the middle of her chest.

"Do they do that often?" Marinda asked.

"Yes, I've seen it a hundred times before. It just seemed different today, I don't know why," Rosaline said, taking her seat again. The birds settled back exactly as they were before, exactly as she knew they would. Just once, she thought, she'd like to see them take off and fly away, over the track and the tops of the carefully groomed palm trees and the city beyond, out over to the sea, or down south toward the Keys, to the Everglades, where flamingos lived in the wild. But such a thing of course would never happen, and it was probably for the best. Rosaline had read somewhere that a bird or animal, once taken in captivity, was no longer capable of surviving in the place where it really belonged.

23

They'd been arguing this way for over two hours, Katie Lee and her father and the art director from the advertising agency, as if the fate of the free Western world depended on which accent color would be chosen for the new Hopewell House campaign. They had all agreed to spend the money for a metallic ink (this had taken a little more than an hour) and were now discussing just which precious metal best represented the growing chain of Hopewell Resorts.

"Nothing compares with gold. Absolutely nothing," Katie Lee said, pointing a schoolteacher's finger up toward a higher authority. "Since the beginning of history gold has represented the ultimate. The same way we're offering the ultimate in luxury and service. People will respond to that." She gestured toward the sample layouts, which used an illustration of the same beautiful woman in a variety of scenes: fastening an earring in front of a full-length mirror in an opulent hotel room, loosening her hair and dipping a toe over the mosaic edge of a long swimming pool, picking out an elaborate pastry from a cart wheeled by a smiling waiter in a perfectly cut dinner jacket. "And we could use gold not just in the lettering and the border but also to pick up elements in the pictures, like jewelry, for example, or the gilt frame of the mirror."

Henry Hopewell poured himself another inch of the bourbon he hadn't offered to the others, though his secretary had appeared at precise twenty-minute intervals with fresh ice and soft drinks.

"Well, gold would have been perfect, honey, except—" he said, and then he took a long pause, sipping his drink, confident that no one would interrupt him until he signaled, with a familiar look or gesture, that he was ready to entertain comment from those less experienced or knowledgeable than he. The art director kept his eyes trained on Henry, who was looking out the window, while Katie Lee stared at sample ads.

"—except that everyone uses gold. It's so overused it hardly gets noticed anymore. We need to differentiate our product by going in another direction. Now, what makes a Hopewell Resort different?" he asked, though they knew better than to try and answer. He put down his drink and folded his hands.

"I'll tell you what," he said. "The current trend in marketing is a sort of remember-ance of things past," he began.

I'll bet he doesn't know that's from Proust, thought Katie Lee, correctly.

I'll bet I'm the only person here who's read the damn thing, thought the art director, also correctly, though he was the only person there who'd never been to Paris.

"People are buying up old hotels and renovating them with period furniture. Even the new buildings have this sentimental architecture that's supposed to remind guests of the past, of more luxurious and less complicated times. We're the only folks who are keeping things modern. Using lots of glass. Maybe we'll put in some fancy kind of marble, but we won't cover it up with Oriental rugs. The fact is, most of our business comes from people who have made a lot of money all by themselves, and pretty damn recently, and we're not going to put these folks in a situation where someone comes into their room and asks them about the reproduction Chippendale and which museum has the original of whatever art we've put on the walls," he continued, leaning back in his high leather chair. Henry had completely redone his office last year after a banker had asked a difficult question about a Chinese lacquered screen.

"To me," he said, "silver is contemporary. Clean. It says who we are: the first people to put strength-training machines in every hotel and whirlpool tubs in every luxury suite bathroom. Chrome fixtures. What do you think, Kevin," he said, turning toward the art director.

"Well, both gold and silver have definite advantages and disadvantages," Kevin said, not sure how the argument would be resolved and knowing that while Henry had been paying his bills for the last three years, Katie Lee would be the one giving him work in the future. "But it's not really just a question of gold versus silver," he said, nodding toward Katie Lee, who he suspected was going to lose this particular battle. "You have to consider the context, the entire visual package. For example, will we be using mostly interior or exterior shots? Day or night? And the most important thing: what will the model look like? Blond or brunette?"

"Blond," Henry and Katie Lee replied in unison, and then they looked at each other and smiled.

"Have you approached anyone in particular?" Kevin asked.

"Not yet," Katie Lee said. "Right now we're getting tons of publicity just from that one announcement. We'll wait for that to die down before we take the next step. Though a few people have called us to say they're not available, if you can believe it." Meaning that for the right price they were willing to be bought out of whatever contract they were currently obligated under.

Kevin nodded. Though the Hopewells hadn't yet said so, he guessed that they were thinking about television advertising in addition to print, and that meant huge commissions for his agency. It also meant they had to find not just a top model but one who could talk, which narrowed the field considerably.

"Well, we'll let you know next week what we decide," said Henry, who never allowed decisions to be made in front of the help.

Kevin stood up, followed by Henry and then Katie Lee. Henry stayed behind his desk while they all shook hands and Katie Lee walked Kevin to the door of Henry's office, where he was met by Henry's personal secretary, who took him out to the reception area, where the junior secretary would retrieve his coat and ask the receptionist to call the underground garage to have his car brought up.

"He's right about the girl," Henry said when they were alone. "She'll define the entire look of the campaign. What kind of progress are we making?"

Katie Lee gave him a report on where they stood. An actress who had at first sounded enthusiastic had then used their offer to negotiate a higher price from a national cosmetics company, whose current model had just turned thirty and would be shunted off to a line of anti-aging skin preparations. They'd sent another model to New York for four weeks of intensive speech training, but preliminary reports from her coach indicated that you could take the girl out of Detroit but not vice versa. And then there was December, who perfectly embodied the look Henry was after but whom Katie Lee had argued against, saying her image was too wild.

"Now, I know men may respond to her," Katie Lee said, pointing a finger at her father, "but the feelings women have about her are, well, less than warm. She's just not *us*."

"Maybe, maybe," Henry said. While he had been picking the sites, in newly developing urban centers and along suddenly fashionable coastlines, where the most successful hotels had been built, it was Katie Lee, he openly admitted, who had come up with the marketing and staffing techniques that had made their ventures so successful. Though their New York hotel advertised itself as the epitome of urban sophistication, Katie Lee had insisted that the front-line staff —the desk clerks, the restaurant captains, the lounge hostess—all be very obviously *not* from New York in appearance and accent. Most of their guests were out-of-town businessmen easily reassured by a fresh, clean appearance and open midwestern vowels or a lilting southern cadence. In Florida and Los Angeles it was the same. The chambermaids and porters could be dark and Hispanic, but the visible staff all looked and sounded like something straight out of a cornfield.

Katie Lee had enticed her All-American staff into seemingly dead-end jobs by creating a training program that recruited heavily at the large state colleges and that promised a lucrative career in the expanding and exciting hotel business for those who weathered five years of service in the Hopewell ranks. She'd hired three of her best service managers by handing her business card to the flight attendants in the first-class section of her weekly flights from New York to Lexington and back. The discotheques and nightclubs all boasted sexy names and dark, sensual entrances; inside they were fairly well lit, with smiling and friendly staff and familiar, unthreatening music. The visitors walked in with the feeling that they were doing something unusual, glamorous, even dangerous, and then were made to feel instantly comfortable and accepted. This was the contradiction upon which the Hopewell's success was now being built: the image was sophistication, even decadence, but the reality was the rosy-cheeked girl next door.

Which was why Henry thought December would be perfect. But the idea would work only if Katie Lee wanted it to work, and that was the one problem he had left: getting Katie Lee to make the approach.

"The thing is, sweet pea," Henry said, "eighty percent of our reservations are made by men, or by their secretaries. Maybe some day women will represent an equal portion of the business trade, but right now our primary customers are men, some of them bringing their wives along, for socializing or shopping or theater or whatever. So what you're saying is really an argument in December's favor."

"I just don't think she's right," Katie Lee said.

"Well, sugar, you do know her best," Henry said. "What I really worry about is her tendency to—to act up. We need someone who will respect the Hopewell image. Who won't embarrass us. If I could be sure we could control December, I'd have those contracts out in a minute."

"Control isn't the problem," Katie Lee said.

"I think it would be. She has to be handled in just the right way."

"Oh, that would be easy," Katie Lee said.

"You think so."

"Honestly, now, you know I've done it before. I was her roommate, remember?"

"She's a very strong personality."

"And I'm stronger."

"Of course you are, sugar," Henry said, "I know that. I just don't want to put you into a position where you feel uncomfortable. Now that you're married and, if you'll allow me to hope, there may be a few little ones on the way, I just don't want you biting off more than you can chew. You've got other priorities now. You don't need the headache of keeping our spokesperson in line. You should be picking your spots. This is going to be a huge campaign for us. I want you to give some thought to hiring additional staff."

"What did you have in mind?" Katie Lee asked.

"I've been thinking about creating a new position. Some kind of marketing position. Possibly a vice-president if we find the right person."

Katie Lee said nothing. As vice-president in charge of development and sales she also ran the marketing department. One of her brothers was vice-president in charge of finance, and they'd also hired from within the ranks their vice-presidents in charge of construction, management, and real estate. Development would always be the "favorite son" position, the one that Katie Lee hoped would lead to eventual presidency of the company when her father retired, but she didn't want to take her chances with still another player in the game, someone who would be taking away some of her territory, even in a relatively minor way.

"Anyone in mind?" she asked. Henry shrugged. She had a sensation of panic; perhaps, without telling her, he had been asking around quietly within the industry, conducting his own private headhunt for a new executive.

"Nothing's been decided yet. If we do hire someone," Henry said, though Katie Lee knew in this case "we" meant "I," "we should get him on line from the very beginning of the campaign. Don't want to switch horses midstream."

"The campaign starts in November. It's already June," she said. They would need to have their print ads ready by the end of July. If they could accelerate their schedule, choose the model and final designs in the next week or so, shoot by the end of the month, Katie Lee figured she could take control of the campaign before her father had a chance to find his new vice-president. She'd be happy to let him find additional staff over the summer. Staff that reported directly to her.

But it was impossible: to find the right model, to negotiate and sign the complicated exclusive contract, to make all the arrangements with photographers and stylists in so little time. Unless she agreed to use December. She could simply phone December tomorrow—it was that simple. December would certainly agree to rearrange her summer schedule for an old friend and college roommate.

Katie Lee smiled and shook her head. "So I suppose we don't have very much time, do we."

"I guess not," Henry said.

"Well, if you'd like, I could ask December sort of casually if she'd be interested. With no commitment from us of course, because I do think we can find someone better. I just don't know if we can find someone in the little time we have. We could have December as a sort of last resort. Just in case."

"Sounds good," Henry said, pushing back his chair from his desk.

Katie Lee stood up and walked over to one of the illustrations. "You're right, Daddy, you always are," she said, "it's a man's reaction that we're worried about here."

"Well, you know what this man's opinions are," Henry said. He would have the legal department send a draft contract to Katie Lee by the end of the week. A contract with December's name on it.

Katie Lee laid her briefcase on the small round table of the airport cocktail lounge and began, in the dim light, to take notes on December's contract. In the week she'd spent in New York since her meeting with Henry she'd managed to negotiate all the major points of the deal with Alex; tonight, if this damn rain ever let up, she would fly out to California to tie up the few remaining loose ends, get all the papers signed, and make the announcement to the industry press at the luncheon she'd scheduled at the Hopewell House in Los Angeles.

It had taken an enormous amount of work to put the event together on such short notice. The invitations had been printed up and pasted, in the form of labels, onto bottles of French champagne. Kevin's staff had worked around the clock, hand-lettering the invitations in silver ink, tucking each relabeled bottle into a box filled with silver ribbons of Christmas tree foil, wrapping each box in silver paper patterned with the familiar Hopewell bluebirds, flying the twenty cases out to California, and arranging for each invitation to be hand-delivered by would-be actors and actresses dressed as Hopewell doormen and singing "Bluebird of Happiness."

The one advantage of working so fast was that there hadn't been time for anyone to leak the identity of the new Hopewell spokesperson. Katie Lee had wanted to wheel out an oversize version of the gift box each guest had received and then pull off the ribbons and open the box to reveal December inside, dressed in an evening gown made from fabric of the same pattern as the gift paper. Alex had refused even to discuss the idea with his client, saying it had all the dignity of a syndicated game show. He insisted that he and December be seated at the head table with Katie Lee. He reminded Katie Lee that December had not yet signed the contracts and that he would advise her not to do so until Katie Lee promised to treat his client in the appropriate manner: as a respected and valued member of the Hopewell promotional staff.

Katie Lee had sighed and given in. She'd assured her father that she knew how to handle December. But she'd underestimated Alex, who had simply worn Katie Lee down during their negotiations by dragging out their discussions endlessly, arguing over every damn thing, tossing out outlandish hypothetical situations for the mere sake of argument, even insisting on correcting the grammar of the contract, substituting semicolons for commas where appropriate, as if he had nothing better to do than spend all day on the telephone torturing Katie Lee. Well, he probably didn't, Katie Lee thought the last time he'd said "So it's all agreed, love?" and then hung up before she had a chance to protest. Surely December would be better off with one of the larger agencies, the ones that understood how to do business with people as important and powerful as the Hopewells; in fact Katie Lee might suggest this to December when she saw her for breakfast tomorrow. As one old friend speaking to another. She had only December's best interests at heart.

Katie Lee looked up at the video monitor. Her flight had been delayed an additional hour: time for another drink. She was sure she hated waiting more than anything else in the world. She blinked, and her flight was delayed another twenty-three minutes.

She seemed to have done a lot of waiting in the last seven days. One of the elevators in her apartment building was out of service, so that one had to stand in the lobby sometimes as much as five minutes until a car became available, and then one had to pile into it with ten other anxious residents and stand there smiling, listening to talk about the weather, while the elevator stopped at nearly every floor.

Her first day back in New York she'd waited nearly twenty minutes in the Tiffany repair department. Though it was her favorite place in the entire store—tucked up on the mezzanine, away from browsing tourists, a tiny room with comfortable chairs where you signed into a guest register and then, when your name was announced, watched a woman in a high-necked dress and a worn cashmere cardigan gently arrange your jewelry on a spotless black velvet board—Katie Lee had caught herself tapping her toe against the wooden chair like a schoolgirl at 2:58 P.M.

She was there to pick up the pearls Bobby had given her for their first anniversary. The pearls themselves had been beautiful—huge, glowing, slightly pink baroques that fell just below her collarbone—but the clasp had been rather ordinary, and Katie Lee had picked out an antique emerald fastening and had dropped them off to be restrung. The emerald clasp had probably cost more than the pearls themselves, but it could always be worn in the front or, if she got that short haircut that looked so good on Rosaline, it would certainly be noticed.

The next day Bobby had been half an hour late for their weekly lunch together at the Harvard Club. It was a dreary place, she thought, so noisy and such boring food, but she liked to make an appearance with her husband in front of all their friends from school. She always put on a first-rate performance there, resting her foot against his under the table, giggling endlessly at his every joke, taking his arm or his hand as they left, picking their way through the clutter of tables in the lobby, where people drank and played backgammon and read newspapers as if this were a true gentleman's club instead of what it was: an alumni organization for men who hadn't been asked to join one of the select, traditional private men's clubs and for women who didn't feel comfortable drinking in hotel lobbies.

Bobby had finally arrived, breathless and with his hair out of place, pleading a meeting with a deputy mayor on the other side of town that had gone into overtime. His family had installed him, just two months before their wedding, in the newly created New York office of the family law firm. Very little actual legal work got done there—it was more of a political base of operations where the Vincents could extend their influence, call in favors from old friends and entertain new ones, and most important, give Bobby a highly visible job but very little real power, keep him in the family fold without having to deal with him on a day-to-day basis, and let him play attorney without any real responsibility for the legal decisions that, both his father and uncle agreed, he was not yet ready and probably never would be ready to make.

Katie Lee, picking at her cold poached salmon with a dull and heavy dinner fork, listened to her husband's evaluations of next year's political candidates as if she were hearing everything for the first time, as if he weren't just reciting, nearly word for word, the article Carter, now a free-lance political writer, had published in last Sunday's paper. It was obvious to her that Carter and Bobby got their ideas from the same place: from the elder Vincents, who paid the bills both at Bobby's office and for the elegantly restored Greenwich village brownstone apartment where Carter "house sat" for Marinda's parents, who had spent fewer than five nights there since the place had been rented, a week after Carter's graduation from law school.

And later that day she'd had to wait nearly an hour at the hairdressers. The receptionist apologized every ten minutes, she knew how busy Mrs. Vincent was, but two of the head staff had been summoned to Saratoga at the last minute to take care of Charlotte and her various guests, who were attending a party in celebration of a ballet premiere. Charlotte had wasted very little time, after that first difficult year, in resuming her old ways of entertaining and spending. Two hours later Katie Lee had emerged with a subdued, conservative version of Rosaline's tousled gamine cut. The dramatic change in style would make it less noticeable that she'd had her hair lightened three full shades, to something just short of platinum.

On Thursday she spent a little over an hour reading back copies of *People*, waiting to see her gynecologist, Dr. Trout. An Italian former race-car driver who now sold shoes to the wives of senators and congressman posed in front of a pile of patent leather sandals and made cautious comments about the feet of the married-to-the-rich-and-famous and described to the reporter the five pairs of low-heeled navy pumps a senator's wife had bought to wear to her husband's bribery trial. (Yes, she'd previously paid in cash; no, the credit card she'd offered him hadn't been in her husband's name; and yes, he'd called in for an authorization code, though he'd done so from the back of the store so as not to embarrass a valued customer in her time of public distress.) There was a picture of December pouring champagne over Tory's head backstage after a concert the day his album was certified platinum. A story on a French movie actress's eighth marriage was accompanied by a sidebar on the advantages and disadvantages of various plastic surgery techniques.

When the nurse came out to fetch Katie Lee she did not apologize for the wait, and after complimenting her on her new haircut (this worried Katie Lee; the nurse had a dreadful haircut and wore clogs of perforated white leather) held out a stiff hand for the urine sample Katie Lee had been instructed to take first thing that morning. Katie Lee took out of her large suede shoulder bag a tiny shopping bag embossed with the logotype of an imported-chocolate shop; inside was the distasteful jar, originally intended for marinated artichoke hearts, its label scrubbed off with hot water but its bright-blue top still listing ingredients as required by federal law.

She'd been coming to Dr. Trout once a month ever since he'd taken her off the pill a few weeks after she was married. She'd been retaining water weight and getting rashes across her forehead; after trying several different doses of contraceptive hormones, the doctor had explained that sometimes, in rare cases, people developed sudden allergies as they grew older. He fit her with a diaphragm and told her that she might not get her period on a regular basis for several months and probably would not be able to become pregnant for as long as a year. In the months since then she had developed all sorts of strange ailments—an infection with a long Latin name that resisted antibiotics, sharp aches that seemed to move from one side of her body to the other, and what the doctor delicately called "spotting." The prescription was usually the same: low-dosage painkillers and no sex for at least two weeks. Lately Katie Lee had felt bloated and tender, and the doctor had moved up the appointment for her thorough annual examination.

At the end of this Trout retreated to his office, giving Katie Lee time to dress and reapply lipstick before he gave her the results of the exam and his usual lecture about her resting pulse rate being twenty beats too high for a woman her age.

"Don't tell me to exercise again," Katie Lee said when he came back and frowned at her chart. "I tried running, and it was a total bore."

The doctor smiled. "Heart disease is also a total bore. Have you been having problems with your diaphragm?"

"Yes. It's disgusting."

The doctor nodded, waiting for the speech he heard five times a day, the one that began "If they can put a man on the moon."

Katie Lee sniffed. "If they can come up with an artificial sweetener that tastes nearly as good as sugar, they should certainly be able to figure out a better way than this."

"You'll be the first to know," Trout said. "Have you been using the diaphragm?"

"As needed. Pretty much. Though it's an awful pain, since I can't get pregnant anyway."

"Well," the doctor said. "You are pregnant. About seven weeks. It's only ninety-nine percent definite before we get lab results, but I'm as positive as I can be."

Katie Lee said nothing, and then, "You'll understand, of course, if I don't pretend this is good news, because it isn't." It had taken her less than a minute to make the decision, or rather, for her there was absolutely no decision to be made. It was simply a matter of bad timing: she couldn't afford to take even a couple of months off from work this year, not with the ad campaign just getting off the ground, not with her father dropping hints about hiring additional staff at the executive level, not with so many new hotels in the works. Bobby wanted lots of kids, and it was a constant battle with him; if he found out she was pregnant he would never allow an abortion.

Well, she just wouldn't tell him, that's all. Trout's face was a perfect blank as she asked him to schedule an outpatient procedure for the next Tuesday, when Bobby would be in Washington on business. She waved goodbye to the nurse, who gave her a bright smile of newly capped teeth. It would be the simplest thing in the world, she told herself. As simple as a surgeon's tools pulling smooth the wrinkles on the face of an ancient actress. As simple as a hairdresser's chemicals turning her from blond to blonder. The word "unnatural" did not occur to Katie Lee, for her natural state was this: to have things happen exactly as she planned them, to control her business and her husband, to solve problems, remove obstacles, ignore doubts, forget mistakes. What she felt, as she pushed open the heavy brass door before the doorman had a chance to rise from his chair on the sidewalk, as she strode out from underneath the dark-green canopy with its blinking taxi light and gave a wide wave to a cab halfway down the block, what she felt was simply this: she was proud of herself, of how she stood strongly on her own two feet. She was the only one of all of them, she thought, who knew how to take care of herself.

Katie Lee was halfway through her second drink when the monitor flashed an additional delay of seventeen minutes; her flight to California, originally scheduled for 8:45 P.M., was now due to depart just a few minutes short of midnight. The bar was filling up with customers whose late arrival in New York had caused them to miss connecting flights. Some of them would be staying in the motels near the airport. A few of them, those more adventurous or enabled by less restrictive expense accounts, would venture into the city, transforming their bad luck into a serendipitous night on the town. A young man, a college student, Katie Lee guessed from his dirty running shoes and nylon backpack, took out a notebook and began to write. A mother dressed in a yellow-and-white seersucker sundress cooed her cranky two-year-old daughter into a precarious sleep and then, the child at last calm and quiet in her lap, stared off into space, unable to fetch a magazine or a drink for fear of waking up her precious bundle. A man and a woman, dressed in nearly identical navy blazers and pink oxford shirts and gray trousers (a blue and maroon rep tie for him, a pink paisley bow tie for her), ordered Gibsons and leaned their heads together over a sheaf of computer print-outs. Katie Lee watched as the gentleman emphasized his points with gentle nudges to the lady's gabardine elbow. The lady played with her bow tie, dropped her pencil onto the floor, and as she bent to retrieve it brushed her fingers against the loose cuff of his trouser. Drawing a circle around a set of figures, the gentleman dared the briefest connection, his left hand, the one with the broad gold band, against the bare inside of her wrist, just below her striped cotton watchband. She wore no rings or bracelets, just a pair of plain gold squares clipped to her unpierced ears, and now she pulled at one, lifting her eyes from the table, stabbing at the onion in her drink with a green plastic toothpick and holding it up to the gentleman with a girlish smile, as though they were children sharing a single slice of birthday cake and she were offering him the precious sugary blue rose. He drew it off the toothpick with his teeth. The lady suppressed a giggle just a second too late to conceal her self-consciousness and sudden lack of nerve.

The man smiled, sat back, and reached for his wallet. Katie Lee suspected that they would be clever enough to show receipts for separate hotel rooms on their expense reports, though not clever enough to go through the motion of checking into separate hotels. The desk clerks at Hopewell hotels seemed to develop a sixth sense about which visiting businessmen would leave their rooms virtually untouched, the bed unused, the bath towels dry, the drawers unopened, no sign at all that they'd been there except a single smear of toothpaste on the countertop, and assigned them the rooms with lesser views or faulty heating units or stains in the carpeting. The chambermaids changed their linens anyway, sometimes finding a generous five- or ten-dollar bill tucked into the pillowcase, the only visible residue of guilt, along with a ring of whisker shavings around the sink basin, the adulterer's trademark proof of purchase.

Katie Lee replaced the cap on her hot-pink highlighter. She'd been drawing thick lines across a working copy of December's contract: pink for changes that Alex had demanded, yellow for additional language required by Katie Lee's own lawyers, and green for revisions that might cost the Hopewells money. The ten-page contract was striped everywhere with pink, occasionally interrupted by a short burst of yellow, but Katie Lee could count only three green paragraphs. On those points she would not yield. She would give in to Alex on everything else, kicking and screaming the whole way, hoping that if she let him win ninety percent of the battles he might not detect that, in those three little paragraphs, she had managed to win the war.

A departure for Atlanta and Miami was announced, and the mother rose, cradling her sleeping child, kicking over a canvas book bag and spilling its contents—a soiled terry-cloth bib, an unopened package of peanut butter and cheddar cheese cookies, a tube of mascara, a rubber doll in the shape of an elephant—onto the smooth plaid carpet of the bar. The woman in the pink paisley bow tie extended a perfectly polished navy kidskin toe to block the progress of a half-consumed package of butter rum Lifesavers as it rolled under her chair. While the mother stood apologizing, looking as if she might burst into tears at any moment, the lady and the gentleman repacked her bag, the gentleman chucking the baby under the chin and the lady slinging the bag over the mother's shoulder. As the mother trundled off toward her departure gate, pausing briefly under the frame of a metal detector, the lady and gentleman exchanged self-congratulatory smiles over their display of concerned citizenry, this shared good deed that proved them to be generous, considerate people. Their bill paid, they hoisted up garment bags and briefcases and proceeded into the night.

As Katie Lee watched this exchange she felt a flurry of nerves in her stomach. Something was going wrong. Maybe her flight would be delayed, and delayed again, and then canceled, leaving her stranded in her least favorite airport at two in the morning. Maybe the flight would take off into this unrelenting rain only to be forced down in some bleak midwestern city, or even worse— Katie Lee contemplated the very worst and decided to wait until tomorrow and clearer skies to fly to California. Something bad was about to happen, she thought, and although she knew her premonition was completely irrational, the result most probably of maternal hormones whizzing through her bloodstream, she was at the same time totally sure of it. Maybe she should chase after the mother and her child, find them at the check-in counter or even follow them up into the plane, where they might already have buckled in, and warn them: don't fly to Atlanta tonight. Or maybe it was the couple who needed warning; perhaps the gentleman, once tired of his conquest, would ship his subordinate out to the fulfillment department in Akron, Ohio, perhaps the lady would begin telephoning him at home, leaving suspicious and cryptic messages with his wife. Katie Lee packed up and telephoned her car service. Within half an hour she was back on the bridge, the lights of Manhattan a blur of yellow through the smoky, rain-streaked glass.

Her panic only increased the closer she got to home. Perhaps this driver—she didn't recognize him, was he new, there was something she hadn't liked about the way he'd smiled at her, showing a mouth-

ful of uneven yellow teeth—would make a wrong turn after the
bridge and land them in Harlem on some deserted, unlit street where
they would be surrounded by hoodlums who would press their faces
against the windows and demand things at gunpoint. No, he had
made the correct turn, but he was driving too fast, she had never
noticed before how narrow the lanes were on this highway, how dan-
gerously close the cars came, and here they were nearly at her exit
and he was still driving in the far left lane. Off the highway, he accel-
erated left through a yellow light and Katie Lee clutched at an
armrest and pressed her foot against an imaginary brake. By the time
they reached her building (one doorman held open the door as she
signed the driver's chit, the other carried her bags to the lobby) she
was sweaty and nauseated and praying that she would reach her
apartment without running into jewelry thieves, Albanian terrorists,
and other agents of violence.

But when she opened her door and saw an unfamiliar trenchcoat
flung across the arm of her chintz loveseat and heard giggling from
the red guest room at the far end of the gallery she realized that it
was here, in her own house, that the awful thing was happening.
They hadn't heard her, and she swiftly weighed the alternatives.

She could make a scene. Bobby, who she assumed was drunk,
might humbly plead forgiveness but might just as easily become abu-
sive, insulting her in front of whoever owned the trenchcoat. Katie
Lee lifted the coat: new, Aquascutum, with a silk Hermès head scarf
tucked into one pocket. Its owner might emerge unembarrassed and
half-dressed from the room just last month redecorated in red velvet
and polished mahogany, taking in the bedraggled Katie Lee with a
long smirk, gossiping about it afterwards, giggly and sarcastic, with
her friends or her hairdresser or her shrink.

Katie Lee pocketed the scarf, quietly left the apartment, and from
a telephone booth across the street telephoned Bobby to say that her
flight had been canceled and she'd be home in about an hour. She
opened the door of the telephone booth just enough to turn out the
light and then waited, for twenty minutes, until the woman, wearing
her raincoat and holding a newspaper over her head, left the building
and headed south on foot. What will I do, what will I do, she said
to herself, leaning against the glass wall of the phone booth, taking
her pulse every five minutes until it was nearly back to normal and
the hour was up. And then it came to her: the solution was so simple, the oldest trick in the book really, a woman's trick, tested effec-

tive for centuries in the cold, dark laboratories of failed marriages. The doormen greeted her with the barely discernible nods of an auction room. In the elevator Katie Lee applied another coat of coral lipstick and sprayed herself with *eau de toilette.*

Bobby was waiting, lying with his legs flung over one end of the loveseat, cupping a tumbler of cognac, reading a magazine with a picture of a Porsche on the cover.

"Hello darling," he said, getting up and giving her a quick kiss. He smelled of toothpaste, rum, and tobacco.

"Hello sweetie," Katie Lee replied, dripping onto the carpet.

"You look beat. Want a drink?"

"No, thanks. I just want to sit."

Bobby lifted his eyebrows. "Not even a little cognac?"

"Not even a little cognac," she said, stepping out of her wet shoes and dropping her coat and luggage into a pile by the doorway. "It's a mess out there. It took them four hours to decide to cancel the flight, and there were hundreds of people all over the place getting hysterical about missing meetings, losing a day of their vacation—one girl just burst into tears and said she was going to be late to her own wedding."

"Alex called a few minutes ago. He wanted me to tell you there'd be someone waiting at the airport no matter how late your flight got in."

"Oh, how nice," Katie Lee said, sinking into the loveseat, patting the cushion beside her.

"I told him I thought you'd be taking the first flight out tomorrow morning," Bobby said, sitting next to her and combing her hair with his fingers. "He said he'd confirm your hotel reservation and meet you for lunch instead of breakfast."

"Oh, good," she said. "Darling, did I ever tell you you'd make a marvelous secretary?"

"Is that a job offer?" Bobby asked.

Katie Lee smiled and tipped her head to one side. "How's your shorthand?"

"Pretty terrible," he said. "Would you settle for fast longhand?"

Katie Lee lifted her feet up onto his lap. "What I need is a really great foot massage," she said, leaning her head back and closing her eyes. As Bobby rubbed her arches she calculated his mood: he was both solicitous (he didn't want to rock the boat) and relaxed (he'd been fooling around for a while, his calmness told her, and he planned to be fooling around for a while more). Some part of her had known this all along. Still, the expensive coat and scarf disturbed her—she would rather have found a vinyl department store raincoat or one of those umbrellas given free by the local public television station to anyone who sent in a check for twenty dollars or more: proof that she was competing with someone of lesser resources. Tomorrow she would give the scarf to MacKenzie in personnel; if it had been bought in the city with a credit card he would be able to track down its owner. There were any number of ways Katie Lee would be able to take care of her once she knew the situation, once she knew whether the woman was married or in need of money or working for someone who owed Katie Lee a favor, someone who needed just the right person for the fulfillment department in Akron, Ohio.

Holding onto Bobby would be easy, she thought, turning her feet outward so that he could knead the tense spots on both sides of her heels. He might notice that her feet had swollen slightly from the summer heat or he might ask if there was some special reason why she wasn't drinking, why tomorrow morning the smell of bacon frying would make her queasy, why she was making an appointment with her decorator to redo the red room in something pale and floral from Laura Ashley.

Isn't it wonderful, she would say, isn't it just the most wonderful thing in the world? She would wrap her arms around him and weep a little into his shoulder. Isn't it going to be the best thing that ever happened to us, she'd say, and of course he would have to agree.

24

"*D*o they make business suits in maternity sizes?" December asked. The only person she had more difficulty imagining pregnant than Katie Lee was herself.

"I'll have to have a lot of things made special," Katie Lee said. "How's the ice cream?"

"Ice-cream-like," December said, offering Katie Lee a spoonful.

"No thanks."

"Well, I have to say, you're being really good about everything. It must be hard not to drink."

"Not really," Katie Lee said. "What is that, vanilla?"

"Coconut."

"I hate coconut."

"So, when will you start showing?" December asked.

"In a couple of months. How does the dress fit?"

December smoothed the long sleeve of the cobalt-blue wool knit dress Katie Lee had ordered for her to wear at the announcement luncheon. With padded shoulders, a cinched waist, and rhinestone buttons, it made December feel like a forties starlet.

"I had to take it in a little, but I really love it, thanks."

"Well, you look terrific in bright blue," Katie Lee said as December spooned up the last of her ice cream. "I hope they lay you out in that color."

"Who's that fat guy in the gray suit?" December whispered into Katie Lee's ear as the waiter brought another plateful of delicate cookies. "The one who keeps staring at my chest."

Katie Lee rolled her eyes. "A freeloader from one of the trades," she said, smiling briefly for the flash of a camera and then returning her attention to December. "They're always trying to get a picture of you when you've got a fork in your mouth or you're chewing some really

320

disgusting piece of meat. The announcement went pretty well, don't you think? They actually seemed surprised."

"Alex and I know how to keep a secret," December said, though she knew the real reason the press was so amazed at her being named the inaugural Hopewell girl was that Katie Lee had leaked, through a syndicated gossip columnist, the exclusive news that a certain former Miss America was going to get the job. Right now the secret they were keeping was this: while Katie Lee and December had stood on a tiny wooden platform in the corner of one of Los Angeles' favorite French restaurants, making their announcement to the press, Alex had placed an icy pat of butter on Katie Lee's chair. When she got up from dessert it would be stuck to the seat of her skirt. The thought of it had kept December smiling all through the announcement and subsequent questions from the audience.

From across the table Alex threw December a wink as he asked the woman on his right, the newly hired in-house director of promotion, another question about her son in medical school. Where did Katie Lee find these people, he wondered, these people who, no matter how sophisticated and important their work, all seemed to come from a simpler place and a simpler time. This woman, a former fashion editor on a midwestern daily, wore her hair in a style Alex hadn't seen in years: a soft pageboy, sloping down in the back, with short sideswept bangs that curled across her pink forehead. Alex was doing his best to be extremely charming, because it was Louise's responsibility to supervise December's work on a day-to-day basis and to make sure December was living up to her end of the contract, including that dreadful morals clause he'd been unable to get deleted. Look, Katie Lee had argued, though we know it would never happen, if December becomes a crazed drug addict and attempts to assassinate the president of the United States and otherwise embarrasses the company because of immoral conduct, we want to be able to cancel her contract, no questions asked. But of course that will never happen, Katie Lee had said, so what are you worried about? Alex had sighed. When Katie Lee had left his office briefly to make a phone call he'd gone through her folder and seen that this paragraph, along with the only other two items she'd refused to give in on, was highlighted in green. All right, you win, he'd said, but you know about the boyfriend going in. He assumed that Louise knew about Tory as well, though she had the look of someone whose age lines had come not from hard living or too much sun but from a stern and continuous disapproval that over the years had molded her face into a permanent frown.

December winked back, thinking what a wonderful flirt Alex was and wondering what Louise's reaction would be if she knew that the wine steward, the one who had graciously held his face expressionless as Louise inquired after their selection of rosé, had spent the better part of his last Thanksgiving holiday with Alex in a hotel on an island off the coast of Mexico. Alex had explained to her that Louise was going to become sort of a housemother, taking care of December's travel reservations and accompanying her to the more important public events. "Housemother" was the right word, December thought; Louise seemed a relic from the age of monograms and sorority rushes, white turtleneck dickeys and pink elastic napkin belts, wrist corsages and Pat Boone.

When Katie Lee stood up at the end of lunch and turned to give the art director a celebratory goodbye kiss on the cheek, it was Louise who leaped up from her chair and whispered in Katie Lee's ear. Katie Lee immediately returned to her seat and waited while Louise went off to fetch Katie Lee's jacket from coat-check.

"Now, you won't tell anyone, will you?" Katie Lee whispered to December.

"Tell anyone what?" December asked.

"You know. What I told you before. About the baby."

"Oh. I didn't know it was a secret."

"Well, it isn't really a secret, sweetie, but we're not going to announce until I'm three months on the way. Just in case, you know."

"Well, sure. You told Marinda, though, didn't you?"

"Of course, darling, she's family."

"What about Rosaline and Trevor?"

"Well, of course I told them—Rosaline's only absolutely my best friend in the whole wide world."

"And your family, right?"

"Well, sure. You can tell Tory and Alex but no one else—promise?"

Tory will hardly be interested, December thought, and Alex will wonder, as I do, why Katie Lee wants to make sure the entire world knows she's going to have a baby.

"I've got to run," Katie Lee said, "I've oodles to do before I leave town." Such as figure out how to make it up with an extremely annoyed gossip columnist before her next column went into print and see if there weren't some way to smooth things over with the former Miss America, who had represented a state where the Hopewells did a fair amount of business. Honestly, the things I do for December, Katie Lee thought, I just hope she appreciates what a lucky girl she is.

"What a lucky girl you are," Tory said as he pulled on a black leather jacket (one of five he owned) and picked up a handful of twenty-dollar bills, a set of car keys, and a half-smoked pack of cigarettes from the top of his dresser, "getting to go out with a handsome dude like myself."

"Fuck off," December said, smudging her eyeliner with her right ring finger. The blue dress Katie Lee had sent her was lying in a heap on the bathroom floor. She had changed into the last clean pair of blue jeans she could find and a plain white man's undershirt with the sleeves rolled up.

Tory lay down on the bed and faked a snore. "Wake me up when you're ready to roll, princess."

"I'm ready, I'm ready," December said. "Remind me again, where are we going?"

"We're going over to Billy's to hear some of the stuff for his new album, half of which is a ripoff of the Red Album, the other half of which totally sucks. But it will probably sell a zillion copies, mostly to girls who think Billy is the handsomest man in the universe."

"Which we know not to be true," December said, grabbing him by the cuff and pulling him up off the bed.

"There can only be one handsomest man in the universe."

"You're so modest," December said.

"Modest, modest, I don't think I know that word," Tory said, holding the door open and waving her through. "What is it, one of those female hygiene products? They sell it in the aisle I never go down in the supermarket, between the air freshener and the dish detergent?"

"You never go to the supermarket, period," December said. "You have slaves to go to the supermarket for you. The car sounds funny."

"December Dunne, girl mechanic," Tory said, shifting up into fourth gear. "What you hear is the sound of old-fashioned V-8 power."

"It sounds like it's working too hard. What's Billy's wife's name again?"

"Billie. Billie Sue, actually, I think, is her real name."

"Pretty funny."

"Billie Sue, a legend in her own mind," Tory said. "Did I ever tell you how they met?"

"Maybe."

"Billy was on tour, and things weren't going so well. First few dates were sold out, then word got around, and they were having trouble filling the places up. Anyway, they were due in New York in a couple of weeks, and the record company was totally panicked, because the press was just lying in wait, you know, it was like supposed to be his comeback tour, he had already used up all the aces in the deck, it was lay-it-on-the-line-or-kiss-it-all-goodbye time."

"When was this?" December asked.

"Seventy-five. Billy was around twenty-four, I think. Anyway, the record company, they have this secret weapon, this woman named Billie Sue who lives somewhere outside of Oklahoma City. She's, I don't know what, whatever people like that are—she works at a clothing store or a beauty salon or something—but what she really is is a hired gun. Gets called in from out of town five or six times a year when some tour's in serious trouble. Very professional. Worked with the best in the business. Will do the whole band if that's necessary. So they call her in to take care of Billy."

"This is so romantic," December said.

"So anyway, the joke is, Billy falls in love with this girl. He knows all about her, he doesn't care, he keeps her around for a couple of weeks, and one night they drive down to Tennessee and get married. Of course the record company makes them promise to keep it a secret until the tour's over because Billy's fans will have a fit if they find out he's married. They gave a huge party when they got back to California."

"You introduce me to the most charming people."

"They called it Billie Sue's Retirement Bash. It lasted five days. Here we are," Tory said, pulling up behind an old Volkswagen mini-bus.

December got out and pulled her jeans down over her boots. Billy's house looked like an oversized log cabin. How many nights had she spent listening to his music; how many parties had ended with the sun coming up behind the window shades and someone scraping out the last lines as Billy played in the background; how many times had she sat at a bar losing at liar's poker while someone bumped up Billy on the jukebox; how many long-distance drives had been punctuated by the sounds of Billy coming suddenly over the radio, with someone she'd thought had been sleeping in the backseat saying turn it up, we've finally found our station. Billy and his friends had been the ultimate California good-time boys, injecting a little bit of country heartbreak into old-fashioned rock and roll. No one except adolescent girls and aging rock critics wanted to hear them anymore. British punks had come along and with a rusty safety pin burst their pretty harmony balloon.

Still it was a thrill to be here. December took the large snifter of brandy offered her and sat quietly next to Tory as Billy's soundman rolled the tape.

"Is that Curly again on keyboards?" asked Billy's saxophone player, one of the two men in the room (along with Tory) who did not wear a mustache. Like nearly everyone else, Billy had begun recording songs on separate tracks, at different times, sometimes in entirely different studios, so that what sounded like a band on the final recording might in fact be musicians who had never even met each other.

Billy looked upward, as if to check that Curly weren't perched on top of a bookshelf before he said something uncomplimentary. "Yeah, last thing he did before detox."

"How's he doing, anyone heard from him lately?" Billie Sue asked.

"This isn't the reggae thing, you promised me at least one reggae thing," said a man in bright-purple cowboy boots.

"I lied," Billy said.

"Reggae sucks," said a man with very short red hair.

"Oh, I love it," Billie Sue said, and again no one responded. "Don't you just love it?" she said a little louder, looking at December.

December smiled at Billie Sue and shrugged, not wanting to join the men in their rudeness but not feeling like speaking up either.

Billie Sue gave her a huge smile back, the warm smile of an eager hostess, perhaps, or maybe just the hungry expression of the least powerful person in the room in search of an ally. December looked quickly away, first at her boots, then at Tory, whose eyes were closed, and then back at her boots.

"Sounds good, old man," Billy said after a brief guitar solo Tory had laid down one night when they'd happened to be renting rooms at opposite ends of the same sound studio.

Tory opened his eyes. "Thanks," he said, and then he whispered into December's ear, "I can see right through your shirt."

"Is there more ice?" someone said. Billie Sue got up and fetched a salad bowl full of crushed ice and gestured to December from the doorway to follow her into the kitchen.

"What do you think?" Billie Sue asked.

"Sounds great, but what do I know," December said.

"Yeah, we don't know shit, do we," Billie Sue said. Her frosted platinum hair was held up at the sides with plastic yellow barrettes in the shape of dachsunds. She was wearing a yellow suede camisole and tight black jeans with bright-yellow socks and high-heeled black patent leather pumps. Her deep tan was set off by heavy frosted eye makeup and pale-yellow nail polish. She was absolutely gorgeous and kind of disgusting and seriously sexy and sort of self-mocking all at the same time. December admired her and wondered whether Mae West had been born too early for her true calling.

"I gotta show you something," Billie Sue said, taking December into what looked like a guest bedroom. Billie Sue opened a closet and pulled out a cardboard box. "If I hear that tape one more time I'll go nuts. Wait a minute. Here it is. What do you think?"

Billie Sue was holding up a white plaster cast of a male sexual organ.

"Um, it's lovely," December said. "I didn't know you did sculpture."

Billie Sue laughed. "It's Billy, silly. From life. He's something, isn't he?"

"He sure is," December said, sitting down on a soft velvet ottoman and taking a large swallow of brandy.

"He's the greatest. Oh, look, here's Travis Jones," Billie said, taking out a slightly smaller plaster cast. "Cute, hunh? He was sweet. Wait, I've got more. Pass me my brandy? This one'll kill you," she said, tilting her head back as if contemplating Yorick's skull.

"Alas, poor Duane, I knew him well," she said. "I did my minor in English."

"What was your major?"

"Agricultural administration." Billie Sue laughed. "Man oh man. I'm thinking about writing a kind of rock opera, you know, I'm good at poetry. You ever think about what you'll do when you're done with this?"

"Done with what?"

"Actressing."

"Not really," December said. Sit around counting my money, she thought. "One step at a time, you know?"

Billie Sue pulled out four autographed plaster cocks. "Franklin, Kingman, Smith, and Burns."

"No shit," December said, wondering which was which. "Can I

see?" she said, and she held each cast in her hand, turning them round one by one. The blue ink of the signatures had faded with age to a paler purple. "Wow. How many of these do you have?"

"Oh, I used to have more," Billie Sue said, "but when I married Billy I gave some of them away."

"This is the weirdest thing I have ever seen," December said. "Billie Sue, you are a remarkable woman."

"Nah, we all used to do it. These women in Chicago started it. Really, everyone did it. It was a big deal, you know, to get certain guys."

"Like which guys?"

"Jimi Hendrix," Billie Sue said, rolling her eyes. "He was like, well, you know."

"Like what?"

Billie Sue giggled. "The one you needed the most plaster for."

"How did you get them to do this?"

"It wasn't any big deal. Getting them to agree, I mean, that wasn't any big deal, and getting them started, that wasn't such a big deal, but you had to, you know, keep them in the mood long enough for the plaster to set. That was the challenge."

"I'll bet."

Billie Sue smiled and stuck out her tongue. "It's where I got my training, honey. I was the Vaseline queen. Here's Jimi."

"Oh. I see what you mean." December finished off her brandy and stood up. "This is American history. They should have a museum for this stuff."

"Tell me about it," Billie Sue said, putting her collection away. "Things were fun before everyone got so old and boring and into real estate. Well. Anyway." She led December silently down a different hallway, its walls covered with framed photographs of Billy in performance, and back into the living room.

Tory pulled December onto his lap and lit up a joint. When he passed it to December she made a big show of inhaling but held the smoke in her mouth. It was a game they played when they wanted to leave a party: Tory brought killer dope, which they only pretended to smoke and which rendered everyone else just short of catatonic. Tory and December would wait until people were too wrecked to care and then they would slip out, often without even saying good night. Of the twenty people here most worked for Billy's record company, and December suspected that Billy had wanted Tory here not for his advice or suggestions but simply to show him off to what December had nicknamed the-men-in-the-black-leather-pants.

Billy ran the tape again, and one of the A&R people from his record company got up and began to dance. "This has got to be the first single," the man said. He was wearing a vintage bowling shirt that said "Springfield V.F.W." with his black leather pants.

"You think?" Billy said, turning up the bass. "It doesn't really sound top-forty to me."

"Oh sure, sure, add some synthesizer, some gospel girl backup, it'll be great. Speed it up a little, maybe."

"I guess," Billy said.

"Or do it as a duet," Billy's producer said. He was wearing an embroidered Mexican shirt and a wide copper cuff bracelet with his black leather pants. "Maybe we can get Ronstadt?" he said.

"You think?" Billy said, looking at Tory.

"Why not," Tory said, taking December by the elbow and walking backwards toward the door. "Fuck Ronstadt, go all the way, add a disco beat, get Diana Ross, get Diana Ross and the Supremes, get that dead Supreme, that's it, you've got a major hit on your hands. A major hit. Billy, we gotta go."

"Yeah, I'll see you out," Billy said, putting his arm around Tory as December brought up the rear with Billie Sue.

"It sucks, don't tell me, I already know," Billy said, running a hand over the waxed fender.

"No, it's great, but don't let them fuck it up for you," Tory said, pulling Billy over to one side and talking to him so softly that December couldn't hear.

"Billy can fuck it up all by himself," Billie Sue whispered to December, "he doesn't need anyone's help for that."

"It'll be a great album," December said.

"You're sweet. So much sweeter than his last girlfriend," Billie Sue said.

"Well, thanks, I guess."

"Are you going to marry him?"

"I haven't really thought about it."

"Don't bullshit a bullshitter," Billie Sue said, leaning over so that December could smell the brandy on her breath.

"Well, I mean, we haven't really talked about it."

"Tory's a sweet, sweet man. Billy adores him. I adore him, and I haven't even slept with him. He's crazy in love with you." Billie Sue had grabbed the sleeve of December's shirt and was twisting it between yellow-tipped fingers.

"I guess," December said.

"But whatever you do, honey, don't marry him. Promise Billie Sue?"

"Gee, Billie Sue, this is weird to be talking about."

"Yeah, I know you," Billie Sue said, lifting up a hank of December's hair in the moonlight. Out here in the darkness Billie Sue's bottled blondness looked no different from December's natural own, and the fine grain of her skin was smoothed out so that if one were seeing her for the first time, one might think her pretty and somewhere close to December's age. "Yeah, I know you, college girl, got your own money, think you're the one who's going to be different, think you don't have to play by everyone else's rules. Think you're gonna live forever, right? Won't have to grow old like the rest of us? Think you're that special?"

"Let go of my hair."

"Think he won't fool around when he's on the road? Think you can compete with every hot little girl between here and Madison Square Garden? Think love lasts forever, right?" Billie Sue said, dropping December's hair and covering her mouth with her hands. "Oh honey, I'm sorry, I'm stoned, I didn't mean it."

"Yes you did," December said. Billy and Tory returned from the darkness laughing at a joke the women hadn't been able to hear.

"December, thanks for coming by," Billy said, opening the car door for her.

"Any time," December said, pulling the door shut, turning toward Tory.

"Get me the fuck out of here fast," she said.

"No such thing as fast enough," Tory replied, backing onto the street without checking for traffic.

It was times like this, when they were just a man and a woman driving fast on a dark empty road, that December felt she was exactly herself: nothing more, nothing less.

Nothing more than this: the daughter of a bad-news guy who was lucky enough to be born pretty and smart enough to use it for what she could get, which right now seemed to be nearly everything. Sonny had been beautiful, and beauty was the gift he gave to her. December had other things going for her, she knew, but she was no fool: her face was what was taking her through life, and it was her father's face.

Though December never talked about Sonny, she thought of him almost every day. By now she thought she had a pretty good idea of what he had been like. She believed that there was a line that people cross, and once they've crossed it, they can't go back. Her father had crossed that line and when he got to the other side he realized it just didn't make a difference anymore what he did.

Getting as close to that line as you can without going over: that was the ultimate kick. It was like walking to the edge of a cliff, just inches between you and the long whistling fall, that's when December knew she was alive. Most people she'd met spent their whole lives being scared and backing away, and she didn't blame them for anything: why take a test if you know you're going to fail? But December had to prove to herself that she could walk that line. She thought of Sonny, and wondered if it was just something in her blood.

And no one else had understood it, no one until Tory. All her friends from school were always worrying about doing the right thing, thinking the right way, afraid of getting hurt, afraid of having to deal with hurting someone else. Like Rosaline, with her centuries of Christian conscience, or Schuyler, who at eighteen had carried the guilt of generations of rich white men on his poor narrow back. What a burden. December had never felt that way. Her people had been treated like shit as far back as anyone cared to go, and she didn't owe anything to anyone. It was the private joke that she and Tory shared: only the poor can ever truly be free.

And nothing less than this: a girl who'd started out with nothing and had therefore learned early that she had nothing to lose. Nothing except Tory, who she knew would never leave her, who she knew she'd never be able to leave. From the first time they'd made love they'd been living inside each other's skin. Even before she'd finally pieced together the sad history of his life from the stories he occasionally told about his friends and family, she felt she'd known everything important about him. Some of it was common knowledge, how he'd gotten knocked around a whole lot before he'd made it big. December had seen how people who'd been through bad experiences often got extremely self-protective, so worried about being hurt again that they never took any risks. But Tory had been knocked around so much that it seemed to December he'd reached a higher place where it just didn't matter anymore, he too had nothing to lose. He was always one hundred percent there for her because he felt he had lived the worst that there was to live and survived it. He felt kind of invincible and when December was with him she felt invincible too.

They were speeding along a freeway that may or may not have been named after a saint when Tory said he was going to take the speedometer as far as it could go. When he got up to eighty December unbuckled her seat belt and unzipped his fly and went to work. He kept his foot hard against the gas pedal, and she was doing him every way she knew how, trying to make him come at the exact moment the needle of the speedometer hit its right-hand limit.

After he came she just held him in her mouth, waiting until he was ready to start again. There was a grit to him like fine sand, or like a powder of ground-down bones. Sometimes men had asked her, What do I taste like, women were supposed to come up with something flattering like pear nectar or vanilla yoghurt, she knew, but she could never think of anything to say. Come tasted like come. If they wanted to know they should check it out themselves, but she guessed they never did no matter how many women demonstrated the edibility of the stuff. December could feel them turning off the freeway and cruising along the rough, dark streets of the city. Tory pulled over and put something quiet on the tape deck and she began again, more softly this time, there was no need to hurry, and Tory slowly braided and unbraided her hair.

When December sat up she saw they were parked on a burned out street in Watts. The kind of neighborhood where white people never go and even the blacks who live there keep their doors locked and windows rolled up after dark. There they were, half undressed, the top of the Thunderbird down, Van Morrison piping softly from the speakers above the backseat, looking up at the full moon.

But she was safe. She was with Tory.

25

*S*he stayed on her side of the bed long after he had left. Some days he remembered to reset the clock radio for seven, and she would wake up to the morning traffic report as called in from a helicopter high over Interstate 95 or to the insistently cheerful voice of Elton John or to an advertisement for a brand of undistinguished beer that tried to pass itself off, with its Germanic name and untwistable bottle cap, as a premium import.

This morning, like most mornings, Jason had forgotten to reset the alarm, and when Marinda woke up, narrow slats of sunlight already stretched halfway across the bed, and she was due at the office in less than an hour.

In the next thirty minutes she took a shower (lather, rinse, no time for repeat, pale-yellow discount-store balsam conditioner doing its work as she soaped only where she might offend, she'd shaved her legs the day before yesterday, and that would have to do); dried herself off and dressed in her second-to-last set of clean clothes (the cotton shirt sticking to underarms still damp from deodorant, the tight mesh of her nylons unwilling over legs unsmoothed by her usual lotion and powder); applied what she considered to be the minimum acceptable makeup (one neutral shade of eyeshadow across lids, mascara on top lashes only, blush, a squeeze of medicated lip balm); checked her bag for the necessaries (keys, license, ten dollars, spray cologne, credit cards); and with the bed unmade and last night's dishes still sitting in the sink, locked the door and tried to remember where she had parked her car. Each town house in their complex came with only one adjacent parking space, and since Jason was always the first to get home from work, by the time Marinda arrived, his dusty blue Volkswagen bug was already backed into their designated slot, number twenty-two.

Marinda stood in the empty parking space and, lifting a hand to shield her eyes from the sun, searched the row of cars parked on the far side of a concrete divider until she found her own silver Toyota wedged between a department store delivery truck and a navy Delta 88 with Connecticut plates, just in front of the sign that said OVERNIGHT GUEST PARKING, 20 MINUTE LIMIT ON ALL SERVICE VEHICLES. She pulled out into the height of rush-hour traffic and tuned in to news of hostages in Iran, prisoners from Cuba, and scandal at the zoo. She combed her fingers through her damp hair at each stoplight and, at the last red light before she drove up the ramp marked RESERVED AND VALET ONLY, pinned it up with mismatched bobby pins she'd fished out of the toll-change compartment. She found her space, to the left of the dark-green BMW that belonged to the partner whose name appeared third of six on the firm letterhead. The Toyota complained as she turned off the engine. She'd come the whole way without hitting high gear.

When she got to work there was not much to do besides wait, look busy, and find some way to kill the boredom. Marinda had made few friends here and sat alone in her square office; she opened a file folder and held a ruler across a randomly chosen line of print, so that if anyone looked in he would think she was in the middle of reading a document with slow and special care. She wondered whether the color of the fake suede wall covering was called mushroom, taupe, or beige; if the lawyer who sat next door really did, as rumored, have six toes on each foot; what her colleagues were like in bed and which one (if the entire world were destroyed by nuclear war except for this one concrete and glass skyscraper) she would be most willing to sleep with.

For the last four months Marinda had been working with two partners and one paralegal on a complicated estate case. A shipping heir who had in less than ten years built his inheritance into a vast and complicated fortune involving precious metals, South American real estate, and computerized communications systems had died shortly before his fortieth birthday, leaving a will he had written over a decade earlier when all he had owned was some stock in his family's corporation, a vintage Stutz Bearcat, and twenty percent of an apartment building in Brooklyn Heights. His ex-wife, three children, business partners, and live-in fiancée had all retained separate lawyers to protect their various interests. He had named his college roommate, a lawyer who worked for a politically connected real estate firm, as executor of his estate. His children had retained Marinda's firm to make sure that none of what they perceived as family holdings would fall into the hands of outsiders. Marinda had spent most of the summer reading loan documents, partnership agreements, tax returns, drawing up charts showing what stock or property had been pledged as collateral to finance which endeavors of which overseas corporation; his family would be able to keep their holdings intact only by releasing any claim they had to his cash, bonds, and collection of American primitive art. This morning the attorneys representing all the parties concerned were meeting for the fourth and final time, before lawsuits were filed, to see if they could work out a settlement to everyone's satisfaction. Since the girlfriend had been advised not to move in with her new boyfriend until the disposition of the estate was resolved, and the ex-wife needed capital for her interior design firm, and the business partners were unable to move assets from company to company or sell off unprofitable ventures until their legal right to do so had been established, it was likely that Marinda's clients would receive the greatest satisfaction of all. They could afford to drag things on for years, pay the exorbitant rates that Marinda's firm charged, sit through a long court case if necessary, their position only strengthening as their opponents resources dwindled.

Marinda hoped the case would be settled today. She knew people from college and law school who had devoted years of their lives to the AT&T anti-trust suit or to defending a single corporation from hostile takeover. It wasn't as though any of the heirs were in danger of not having enough money to eat, was how Jason had put it to her, and he was right: she was spending sixty hours a week defending the greedy from the even greedier.

She was drinking her third cup of coffee and pretending to read an in-house memo soliciting players for the firm's bowling team when Thompson came in and sat down without being asked, his prerogative as rising young star and her immediate supervisor on the estate case.

"We should hear in about half an hour," he said, picking up a jumbo paper clip and tapping it against the edge of her desk. Last week, during an interminable staff meeting, Marinda had imagined him tying her secretary, Wendy, to a four-poster canopy bed in a dark hotel room.

Marinda set her coffee mug on top of a steno notebook she'd been using as a telephone log. It would be impolite to continue drinking without offering Thompson some coffee. But Wendy (whom Marinda shared with one other attorney) wasn't at her desk, and if Marinda offered to fetch the coffee herself, he would make a huge production of it, telling her he liked exactly an inch of half-and-half and one third of a packet of artificial sweetener. Wendy had a way of disappearing down the hallway into the mailroom or the copy center or the word-processing room or one of the other places where Marinda never went, though the people who worked there—old hippies who traded stories about Key West, Cubans who told jokes with punch lines in Spanish, women her own age who still talked about how they'd gotten tickets to some hot rock concert at the last minute and discussed the ingredients of various rum or tequila concoctions and dressed in the bright fashions advertised in *Glamour* magazine— seemed a lot more interesting than any of the other young attorneys Marinda hung out with.

Marinda was sure these people led fascinating secret lives that they kept out of sight like hair tucked up under a hat. She always went out of her way to be especially nice to them. She joked with them about the Miami Dolphins. She complained with them about the weather or the traffic. She agreed with them that the president was a jerk—all the people down here, no matter what their politics, seemed to believe that the president was a jerk, although Marinda saw him more as an intelligent, capable man who had simply signed up for a task that was turning out to be too much for him, a man who had backed himself into a corner and was recognizing, just like herself, that every job, no matter how important and highly paid, is still a job.

Marinda noticed Thompson staring at her coffee cup and realized how incredibly uncool and femmy it was to have bought this set of mugs decorated with field flowers.

"What a pretty mug," Thompson said, as if he could read her mind, as if he knew that she'd spent several minutes deciding just what he'd used to bind Wendy's wrists and ankles. Scarves were too cliché. Neckties were impractical—he wouldn't have been carrying spare neckties around, and Marinda demanded from herself a copy editor's attention to detail. What was called for was pantyhose, the kind that sold for under two dollars a pair at drugstore cash registers; such a sensible woman as Wendy might easily pack a half dozen extra pairs in case of emergency. Marinda herself was never quite organized enough to do so (extra pantyhose was in the same category as dental floss and sewing kits), but then Marinda rarely figured as a character in her own fantasies.

"Thanks," Marinda said, "a gift from my friend December." He couldn't blame her for the taste of her friends, and she couldn't resist reminding him just who her friends were.

"If we settle today," he continued, "it should take about another two weeks to get all the papers signed. And then you can finally take some vacation time if you like." Thompson was husky and muscular, looking more like an ex-high school wrestler than what he was, an excellent squash player who routinely beat more talented players with his superior stamina and power to concentrate. He had a farmer's round face and blunt features and a head of thick gray hair that at forty showed no signs of thinning.

"That would be great," Marinda said, but when Thompson smiled she had the feeling her employers would frown on her taking any time off at all, even though she'd worked without a break, sometimes on legal holidays and weekends, ever since her first day there. Jason wanted to go to France and Italy ("check out the continent" was how he'd put it), and last month he'd gotten his first passport and told Marinda he was tired of waiting for this case to be resolved, he was going to go by himself if she couldn't get the time off. An empty threat, Marinda had thought; he'd be able to scrape up the money for air fare and rooming houses, but he needed Marinda and her credit cards if he wanted to eat at any decent restaurants and stay at the better hotels. "Jason and I have been talking about a little trip to Europe," she said, and Thompson described in detail the trips he had taken with his wife, a museum curator, to London and Tuscany and the more picturesque provinces in France. He told her that of course it would be impossible for her to do much of anything in two weeks, and she had to agree, afraid to say *But I have three weeks coming to me*, the way Wendy or any other member of the support staff would have felt free to insist. Wendy had been drunk when Thompson tied her up. She had giggled; it had taken her a few minutes to realize what was happening. He had promised her he wouldn't do anything that didn't feel good. He made sure she was comfortable. He closed the window so she wouldn't get cold.

Marinda supposed she should have been flattered that Thompson took the call in her office. That made her the second to know: the case had been settled, and they'd even gotten a little more than they expected in exchange for agreeing not to share certain details of the settlement with the press.

Thompson stood up and extended his hand; Marinda took it firmly, maybe too firmly, she thought, maybe he'd think she was trying, once again, to prove something. He invited her to a celebratory dinner at a newly fashionable Italian restaurant with everyone else (except the paralegal) who'd worked on the case, and she declined, saying she and Jason were having guests, suspecting that he didn't really want her there anyway.

He raised his eyebrows. "Well, if you change your mind, Botticelli's Garden, we're meeting there at eight," he said, and he asked her to have drafts of certain waivers and releases on his desk by tomorrow morning. It was total monkey work, Marinda knew, just a matter of pulling forms from other files and inserting new dates, names, land descriptions, and dollar amounts, something Wendy could do if anyone would trust her enough to teach her how.

And suddenly she wished that, just for one day or even a few hours, she and Wendy could trade places. Marinda could come into work in a pretty flowered dress and high heels and dramatic eye makeup and take phone calls and gossip with the other secretaries and eat a fifty-eight-minute lunch (soup du jour, cheeseburger deluxe, Tab) in the coffee shop downstairs. The guys in the mailroom would give her advice about buying a new car. She could plan birthday parties and baby showers on company time with the other secretaries, and when one of them got sick they'd ask her to sign the oversized get-well card they'd bought at lunch hour in the gift shop in the lobby. On Monday mornings they'd trade stories about how drunk they'd gotten over the weekend, and on Friday afternoons they'd discuss what they were going to wear on their dates. Someone would recommend a specific brand of waterproof mascara, and she'd return the favor by giving the name of the oil-free sunscreen that didn't clog your pores and make your face break out. Thompson would flirt with her, and if she made a mistake, he wouldn't notice, because he expected so little of her. Just that she show up on time every day, and not chew gum in front of the senior partners, and wear nice clothes, and laugh at all his jokes, and fetch his coffee, and not get mad when he called her his girl.

• • •

By the time Marinda got home it was after seven, and she had to park all the way at the other end of the lot, in front of the trash bins. She carried the shopping bag full of imported beer and softening pints of ice cream slightly away from her body and, too tired to search for her keys, rang her own doorbell with the middle finger of her left hand.

Jason, his bare feet tapping to an old James Brown record, peeked inside the bag, nodded approval, and gave her a kiss that tasted of garlicky cheese.

"Mmm, Boursin," Marinda said, slipping out of her shoes, dropping her purse next to the door and dumping the groceries in the kitchen.

"Gretchen and Felipe brought it," Jason said, pointing with his elbow toward the living room. "I invited them at the last minute."

Marinda calculated as she shoved the ice cream between a stack of ice trays and a box of frozen macaroni and cheese. Mary, who worked at the legal aid clinic with Jason, and her husband, Jack, who was still in medical school. Luis, a friend of Jason's from college, and his girl-friend, Yolanda, who had worked as a manicurist until Jason got her a reception job at his office. And now Gretchen, who did absolutely nothing as far as Marinda could tell, and Felipe, who worked with Mary and Jason and lived with Gretchen off Gretchen's father's money, which was mailed to them once a month by Gretchen's father's secretary. That made eight for dinner when she'd counted on only six. Which meant that instead of six people getting six shrimp each, four people would get four shrimp and four would get five, unless all eight people got four and Marinda saved the extra four for later, to eat while they were cleaning up, after everyone went home.

"Well, that's the thing about linguini, it stretches," Marinda said. "Guess what."

"What."

"We won the case."

"Well, great. Congratulations. I guess that means now you can live like a normal person for a change," Jason said.

"It means I can take a vacation is what it means. God. I don't think I remember how to have fun."

"Hey Marinda," someone called from the living room, "how old is James Brown?"

"Older than you think," she called back. "I didn't know Tommy was coming," she whispered to Jason.

"Oh, yeah, I thought I told you. He brought some guy who's visiting him from Texas, a real asshole, keeps telling us how lucky we are not to have to deal with Mexicans. Says Mexicans are the worst. Why don't you change into something more comfortable?"

"Good idea," Marinda said, and she waved a hello as she tiptoed over wineglasses, beer bottles, and ashtrays on her way through the living room to the bedroom.

"Five dollars says James Brown is at least fifty," Yolanda said, dropping a cigarette butt into an empty Michelob bottle. "Marinda, you look so cute all dressed up. Do they make you dress like that every day?"

"Yup," Marinda said. "I'll be back in a minute, just let me pull on some jeans." In the bedroom she counted: four people get three shrimp, six people get four shrimp. She listened to them argue about how old James Brown was and whether any of the Three Stooges was still alive and why the speed limit should be raised back up to pre-Ford levels. Mary was saying how expensive it must be to have to wear a different suit to work every day, and Jason said he thought Marinda appeared ten years older in her work outfits. Marinda looked at herself in the full-length mirror. She looked tired. Her jeans felt snug and her thin cotton sweater pulled across her breasts—she must have gained five pounds working on this case. She didn't feel like going out and sitting around drinking with Jason's friends, and she certainly wasn't up to cooking them dinner. She considered ordering in pizza but knew that Jason would say she was offending people if she offered to pay for it, and that if everyone chipped in six bucks, more than one person wouldn't have carfare in the morning.

"Bet you ten dollars," Felipe was saying when she went back to the living room.

She sat down cross-legged next to Jason and took a sip of his beer.

"Make it twenty. I can have one of the librarians look it up," Jason said. "Chevy, Buick, Oldsmobile, Pontiac, Cadillac."

"No way," Felipe said. "It's Chevy, Pontiac, Oldsmobile, Buick, Cadillac."

"You telling me a Skylark has more class than a Cutlass?" Jason argued, ruffling Marinda's hair..

"You see those new Pontiac compacts?" Felipe said. "Those cars are for shit. Marinda, what do you drive?"

"A Toyota."

"Another for-shit car. With all the money they pay you, you should go out get yourself some nice wheels."

"Marinda won a big case today," Jason said, lifting his bottle of beer. "To my favorite capitalist tool," he toasted.

"Hear, hear," Mary said, and they all lifted their glasses and bottles. "May the rich get richer."

"'Cause the poor is sure getting poorer," Yolanda said, and then Luis said something in Spanish, and everyone laughed except Marinda, whose only languages were German, Italian, Latin, and a little bit of conversational French.

She went into the kitchen and started the heat under the water. She wished she'd taken off her stockings; they itched under her tight jeans, and her little toe was poking through a run in the left foot. She wanted to be celebrating her victory and was sorry now that she hadn't gone to the restaurant with the others. Maybe she should call Rosaline and tell her they'd won—surely Rosaline would understand what this meant to her, Rosaline had even sent her flowers at the office to congratulate her when they'd won the first round of negotiations. Marinda picked up the phone and had gotten as far as 212 when she felt Jason's hands on her shoulders.

"Hey," he said, "who are you calling?"

"Rosaline. I should have called her from the office. She'll kill me if I wait until tomorrow."

"Come on, we're all starving out there. If you call Rosaline you'll be on the phone at least an hour." He took the handset and replaced it on the hook. "Did you put salt in the water?"

"I thought you wanted to cut down on salt."

"Man, it's going to take forever to boil. You could have at least covered it." He banged the lid on the pot and left. Marinda followed him as far as the archway that separated the kitchen from the living room and stood there, watching her guests try headstands against the far wall. There were two wet spots on the carpet from spilled wine (white, she hoped) and a streak of ashes across the back of the couch. It seemed amazing to her that these were her friends: six months ago she hadn't known any of them, and if they all disappeared tomorrow she didn't think she'd mind a bit.

"Hey baby, get me a beer," Jason said, as he steadied Gretchen's ankles, in a voice that implied that she should have known enough to bring him one without his asking.

Marinda got a Beck's from the refrigerator. Each couple, it seemed, had brought one six-pack, though they easily drank more than three beers apiece. She carried it to the archway and held it out to Jason, who was tickling Gretchen's feet through her hot-pink anklets. She was giggling, and as she squirmed, her loose plaid shirt fell down from her hips, exposing a sliver of leopard-print briefs below her black jeans and a pale-pink rounded, untanned stomach and an inch of matching leopard-print bra. Marinda held the beer out stiffly in front of her as if she were posing for a statue, a statue of a soldier carrying his flag into battle. When Jason finally looked up he frowned at Marinda and let go of Gretchen's feet.

"If you would be so kind," he said in a bad imitation of a British accent, "if you would be so kind, madame, as to bring me a bottle opener."

Marinda felt her arm swing down and back, and with an overhand perfected in countless family softball games flung the bottle of beer across the room. It hit without breaking just inches from Jason's head bounced at his feet, rolled across the carpet, and came to a wobbly stop in front of Gretchen, who had covered her mouth with one hand and appeared to be stifling a laugh.

"Get your own fucking beer," Marinda said.

"Oh, hey," Yolanda said, rising to her knees, "hard day at the office, it happens to everyone, let's just—" She stopped mid-breath as Jason held out his hands like an orchestra conductor signaling for silence. Everyone was looking at Jason, who said nothing, and then everyone was looking at Marinda.

Who said, "And make your own fucking dinner."

She grabbed her bag and shoes from the front hallway, slammed the door behind her, and ran out to her car in stockinged feet. The evening breeze held the first hint of autumn, a chill that was both a surprise and a relief to Marinda and made her homesick for the North. She sat in her car and flipped through a news report and the live call of the World Series before she found a station playing exactly what she wanted to hear: something loud and angry by the Rolling Stones. By the dashboard light she picked bits of gravel out of her pantyhose and wondered where to go. There was no one she knew well enough to drop in on unannounced. By the time she got to the nearest mall the stores would be starting to close. She had a key to Jason's apartment downtown, he would never think to look for her there. If he came looking for her.

But of course he wouldn't, she realized; she could sit right there in her car all night, just yards from her door, and Jason wouldn't come out to get her. The dinner party was going to proceed just fine without her, just fine in spite of her—in fact, they would probably have a better time with her gone. Everyone would be able to have four shrimp. They could speak Spanish without having to translate for her. They could stay up all night listening to James Brown without her complaining that she had to get up early and go to the office the next morning. They would make a huge mess, and then they would all stay and help Jason clean up because they felt a little sorry for him, going out with a stiff like her.

Marinda pulled out onto the highway. There was no traffic, and she cruised along in the left lane, passing trucks with confidence and shifting into high gear as she approached the city. At Botticelli's Garden they were probably just starting on their second round of drinks. If she made the lights she'd be there before the first course arrived.

"Oh, but I am too," Marinda said, and she closed her eyes and spread her arms and then slowly touched her fingers to her nose. "See? If I were drunk I couldn't do that."

"Some people can *only* do that when they're drunk," Thompson said, "like some people can only fuck when they're drunk."

"What?" Marinda said. "What did you say?" She was the only one who'd heard him. Someone was in the bathroom, and someone else had gone to another table to say hello to a client, and someone else had gone home long ago to his wife, and someone else had just left after settling the bill. They hadn't seemed to mind when she'd shown up late and in blue jeans; the large round table accommodated six as easily as five, and they said they were happy to have someone there who could translate the menu for them. They had all proceeded to order strange combinations of things, dishes that Marinda's family would be disgusted to hear about—spinach linguini covered in marinara sauce and topped with crumpled bacon, veal in heavy cream sauce that had frozen peas and oregano in it—and they seemed disappointed when Marinda ordered, in English, a simple boneless cut of chicken sauteed in lemon butter. But Marinda had matched them drink for drink. She was someplace past tipsy, short of drunk, pleasantly anesthetized, totally capable of driving home despite Thompson's insistence that he would give her a lift. Well, she wasn't going to fight about it with him in front of a senior partner. Maybe he had something important to tell her, some good news, and she'd bet he'd be impressed when he saw where she lived, and she couldn't wait to see Jason's face when she stepped out of Thompson's large German car. She could take a cab in tomorrow morning.

They all said their good nights in the parking lot, Marinda pulling at the side seams of her jeans in an attempt at a curtsy. Thompson's car smelled of mint. Though it had gotten even chillier in the last few hours, he opened the sunroof.

"You look great in jeans," Thompson said, fiddling with the sound system. "Do you like Barbra?"

"Oh sure, who doesn't," Marinda said, hoping he didn't play any of Streisand's recent attempts at pop—she wouldn't be able to keep a straight face if he did. The sky looked so small through the sunroof. She sat back against the smooth leather and found his hand there, just below the headrest.

"Ooops," she said, leaning forward, and his hand went with her, circling softly around her neck, pulling her gently back against the seat.

"You are a little drunk," he said, rubbing her neck with his thumb. "Also very nervous."

"Oh no, not me, I'm nerver nevous," she said, and she giggled and closed her eyes. "Jesus, Thompson, are you making a pass at me?"

"No."

"Then why are you giving me a neck massage?"

"Do you want me to stop?"

She didn't. It felt great. "I don't think this is such a good idea," she said.

"Just relax. Nothing will happen that you don't want to happen."

"How do you know what I want to happen?" she said. Thompson was smarter than she was. Most of the time she hated him for it.

"You're so beautiful," Thompson said. "Does your boyfriend ever tell you how beautiful you are?"

"Yes, all the time," she lied. What a line he had. He leaned over and kissed her, a kiss just the far side of innocent, his lips slightly open but no tongue, no teeth, a dreamy teen kiss.

"That was nice," he said, and he moved away from her, and for a few minutes they sat there quietly, listening to old standards. "When you go to Europe I have the names of some great little restaurants outside of Paris. You'll love Paris."

"Everyone loves Paris," Marinda said, and he kissed her again, more insistently, his hand sliding down around her rib cage. He was a terrific kisser, Marinda thought, and then she began wondering what it was exactly that they were doing. I am making out in a car with a man I don't want to fuck and it's the most delicious feeling in the world, she said to herself. *Delicious*, there's a word, how long has it been since I kissed a man just for the sake of kissing him, just for the delight of it, not as the requisite preliminary to the main event.

"You're full of fear, little girl," Thompson said, pulling back again and stroking her hair.

"I am not, and I'm not a little girl, and I don't want to fuck you."

"No one asked," he said, and he began kissing her again, and she twirled her tongue around his to show him she wasn't afraid, and knew that was exactly why he had accused her of being afraid, and knew that he wouldn't ask of her any more than she was prepared to give, because one thing Thompson wasn't going to be: rejected.

"What's it like, with your boyfriend," he said.

"Stop calling him my boyfriend, it sounds so dumb. He has a name."

"Yes, I know, the only guy named Jason who's over six years old and doesn't have a sister named Jennifer or Jessica. What's it like."

"It's just fine. It's just absolutely incredible, if you really want to know."

Thompson smiled in the dark and started the car. They drove home in silence. He found a space right in front of her unit and turned off the engine.

"I just want you to remember one thing," he said. "You're a warm, beautiful, intelligent, very special woman, and if he doesn't appreciate you he's a worse fool than I thought."

I bet he says this to everyone, she thought.

"Tell me more," she said, and he began to kiss her again. He had one hand up under her sweater and another between her legs, pressing against her, trying to find her through the layers of jeans, pantyhose, underwear.

"You're wet, I can feel it," he said, and he took his hand off her breast and reached across her and pulled the lever that released her seat back.

"I can't, you know I can't," she said, finding the lever and straightening the seat back up. There was something exciting about playing the protesting female, God knows she'd never done it at the age when it was appropriate, never with Peter, she'd been so eager to lose her virginity she'd gone all the way with the first boy who managed to find his way to second base, did anyone talk about bases anymore, she wondered, how much older than she was Thompson, he probably had had years of experience at this sort of thing, getting girls drunk and feeling them up in fancy cars.

"You know you want to," he said, and he took her hand and placed it over his fly.

Not very romantic, she thought.

"I want you so much," he said.

That was better.

"You can't send me home like this," he said.

"Please, I can't," Marinda whispered, realizing that there was some possibility that she might begin to cry and that it might not be such a dumb thing to do, given the circumstances.

He took her hand and began to kiss it, sucking slowly on each finger, and with his other hand he unzipped his fly, and when her hand was wet all over he placed it over his cock. Boxer shorts: she never would have guessed.

"I'm pretending it's you," he said, as she circled him and tried, with a firm thumb and trilling fingers, to make things happen as fast as she could. *I'm pretending it's not you*, she thought, though who else could it be? Was there any man at all she really wanted? Was that why in her fantasies, as she killed time at the office or tried to push herself over the edge with Jason or pleased herself in the mornings sometimes after he'd left for work, was that why she never appeared in her own fantasies?

I did once, she thought, and then, when he came, God, what do married men say when they show up at two in the morning with come all over their expensive pinstriped suits? I did once. A long time ago. Thinking about old fantasies was like remembering old boyfriends: they were sweet and heartwarming and so unbelievably naïve.

"You're so sweet," Thompson said, zipping himself up. "I owe you one."

"Sure thing," Marinda said, opening her door.

"Wait," he said, pulling her back in. "Where's my good-night kiss?"

She gave him a peck on the cheek.

"You can do better than that," he said, and he gave her a full open kiss, and damn it, she felt herself getting excited again, how could that possibly be, but there it was. Delicious. She could kiss him all night. There ought to be a law. Well, there was, she thought, and a commandment too.

She felt herself giving in to it. That was Marinda, on the bed, the bed was covered with a thickly quilted coverlet, they were in the newest hotel in the oldest part of a city (Houston, Atlanta, San Francisco), he had drawn the curtains so that she couldn't see the water, their drinks sat unfinished on the dresser, he had turned up the heat so she wouldn't get cold.

Part of her was thinking: she had been so nice as to jerk Thompson off right here in front of her house, where anyone could see if anyone was awake, and now it was her turn, she was just going to keep kissing him and concentrate on this scene in her head and let him do whatever he wanted with his hands, it all felt great, she lifted up her hips so he could pull her clothing down to her knees, she spread her knees a little, a little more, it was totally her turn and she was going to take her time if she felt like it.

And part of her was thinking this: he had spread her out against the covers, he was whispering in her ear all the things he was going to do to her, some of them she had never done before, and then there was light coming from somewhere, someone had opened the door, who was it, he had gotten rid of Thompson, he was loosening the knots and curling her into his arms and then he was making wonderful wonderful love to her.

Marinda opened her eyes. Thompson was covering her mouth with his hand.

"Jesus, are you hot," he said. He pulled his hand back tentatively. "Don't want to wake the neighbors," he said.

She blinked and tried to reassemble herself.

"Thanks for the lift," she said, opening her door again.

"I don't think you want to go up just yet," he said, and he twisted the rear-view mirror around so that she could see herself in the moonlight.

"Oh God," she said, laughing, "I see what you mean." It showed, even in the dark.

"Can I ask you just one little question?" he said.

"Shoot," she said. He was going to ask something awful, she knew, like did she do this often, did she and Jason have an "arrangement," could she be trusted to keep her mouth shut, when could he see her again. He was going to ruin it.

"Who's Schuyler?" he said.

26

*H*e hadn't been surprised when Marinda called. Rosaline had telephoned a few days before to set him up for it. They'd spent a few minutes talking about her horses and his cows, his friends and her children, and then she told him about what she politely referred to as Marinda's situation. Marinda had broken up with Jason, telling him she was taking two weeks' vacation and when she got back she wanted every sign of him gone from her apartment: his corduroy jackets and khaki trousers, his Ray Charles albums, the bottle of dark-green antidandruff shampoo, the embossed books of matches from restaurants they'd been to together, everything. Then Marinda had called Rosaline to ask the name of the hotel Rosaline and Trevor had liked so much the last time they went to Bermuda (she'd hoped to go to Europe but didn't have the energy).

"I gave it to her, but I don't know," Rosaline said, "I didn't quite know how to tell her the place will be full of newlyweds at this time of year. I think it's the most depressing place she could possibly go to. I offered her the house in Saratoga, and of course she's always welcome at the farm, but she said she wanted to go someplace she'd never been, she wanted to go somewhere that didn't have any memories. I never knew Marinda could be so dramatic. Don't tell me you're still smoking?" She'd heard the rip and pull of a match being lighted.

Schuyler laughed. "It's my only vice. Honest." He was wondering if he should make the offer or wait until Rosaline came right out and asked him to put Marinda up for a couple of weeks. There was plenty of room, too much room if he really thought about it, and how many times had people from the East promised they'd visit him? But they hardly ever did, except for Teddy.

"So, anyway, I was thinking—and you just say no right away if you

want to, because it may be the absolutely worst idea I've ever had—"
Rosaline began.

"—but can Marinda stay here?" he finished for her.

"Oh, forget I even thought of it. It's a silly idea. I just thought, you
know, wide open spaces, fresh air, clean living, and all that."

Schuyler looked at the dozens of beer bottles stacked in an oversize
wastebasket, the residue of last night's entertaining. "We specialize
in clean living, ma'am," he said. "It's sort of bleak here, actually. The
leaves have already fallen."

"Wait, here's Trevor, he wants to say hello."

"Schuyler?" Trevor boomed into the telephone. "What time is it
there? Is it dark yet?"

"It will be in a few minutes."

"I'm sending you some really terrific port. Stuff that will put hair
on your knuckles. Rosaline told you about Marinda?"

"Wants to reserve her a room at Heartbreak Hotel."

"Did you ever meet Jason? Most arrogant son of a bitch I've ever
encountered. Smartest thing she's ever done. Don't make faces, Rosaline, you know I'm right. Could you take care of the baby, darling?"
Trevor said, and then he began to whisper into the telephone, "Listen, old man, if you don't take Marinda she's going to end up staying
here driving us all crazy, and I just won't have it, but you know how
Rosaline is with lost causes."

"But it's all right if she drives me crazy?" Schuyler asked.

"Ah, but she won't, you know she's a charming girl, it's just that
Rosaline's been working so hard, and even with the staff the kids can
really wear you out and I won't have Marinda here keeping my wife
up all night talking about this fool she should never have given the
time of day to."

"I hardly know Marinda," Schuyler said, and it was true: they had
never really been friends. She had always been Rosaline's roommate,
Katie Lee's sidekick, he had always seen her in terms of someone
else.

"That's what makes it so perfect. You'll be able to ignore her. All
she needs is a place to stay."

Rosaline took back the phone. "Baby sends his love. It sort of
sounded like this," she said, beginning a series of gurgles and sighs.
"Don't let Trevor boss you around. He's only allowed to boss me
around—don't make a face, sweetheart—but listen, Schuyler, forget

I even brought it up. When are you coming to visit us?"

"Maybe in February," Schuyler said. "That screenplay I sent off into outer space seems to have come back into orbit. They want to shoot as much as they can on location."

"But that's marvelous news!" Rosaline said. "Can we all be extras?"

"Can you look like a gangster's moll?"

Rosaline giggled. "What do they look like?"

"I haven't the faintest idea," Schuyler said. "I don't even remember having any female characters." He'd been completely shocked when Nelson's agent called him with the offer: surely there'd been enough movies made about the mob, Schuyler had said, and the agent had said exactly, exactly, it's exactly *because* there have been so many that the movie company wants to do more. It made no sense to Schuyler. The money, though, that made a terrific amount of sense.

Schuyler half listened as Rosaline told him about her babies, meaning her yearlings, and how they'd sold nearly everything off at auction and were for the first time in years in the black. After taxes, she means, Trevor called from the background. Schuyler didn't know why he was being so ungenerous about Marinda. She would probably be a perfect houseguest. Nelson took in strays all the time, he told Schuyler it was the only thing that was going to get him into heaven; though, Nelson said further, he had no idea why anyone would want to go to heaven since everyone knew that's where all the ugly women were.

"Listen," Schuyler said, interrupting her, "it's fine with me if Marinda wants to hang out here for a little while. Tell her there's plenty of room."

"Oh, you don't have to. Really."

"No, I'd like to see her. I think she'd like it out here. Fewer lawyers per square mile than any state in the union. Does she ride?"

"No."

"There's not much else to do. Please tell her if she won't be bored I'd be happy to see her."

"I'll tell her to call you. Oh Schuyler, this is so wonderful of you, it really is. I'm jealous that Marinda will get to visit you before we do. I'm going to make her promise to take lots of pictures."

"Hope you like pictures of cows."

"There must be something else there besides cows."

"Just me and the cows, ma'am. Honest injun." They said their good nights. Schuyler walked through the house trying to decide which of the three extra bedrooms would most suit Marinda. He chose the one with the pale-blue flowered wallpaper that looked out onto what had once been his mother's vegetable garden. The one that was farthest from his own.

The first night nearly nothing happened. After three connecting flights and a long drive in a rented Dodge, Marinda arrived late and tired in the middle of a rainstorm and went straight to bed. Schuyler had planned to stay up late reconciling third-quarter statements. As they said good night Schuyler wondered to himself what she was sleeping in, a flannel nightgown perhaps, or men's pajamas, or an old sweatshirt. He'd warned her about the cold.

The second night they watched a bootleg video of *Guys and Dolls* and ate a supper of grilled cheese sandwiches and Campbell's tomato soup. Marinda had spent the day reading Charles Dickens and taking naps with her clothes on. Schuyler had driven two towns over to the nearest hospital, where one of the stable boys was recovering from a burst appendix. When Marlon Brando sang, Marinda put on a silly face and held her hair out from her head in thick fistfuls. She had more hair than anyone Schuyler had ever seen. He imagined it lying against a pillow—long dark curls spreading wildly in every direction.

The third day it rained again, and they stayed inside drinking Trevor's brandy, listening to Merle Haggard tapes, and playing Monopoly with an old game Schuyler had found in the attic. Most of the Chance cards were missing. Marinda acquired expensive properties and spent a lot of time in jail. Schuyler rolled big numbers and favored railroads, utilities, and the properties around Free Parking. Whenever Marinda landed on Reading she clutched her hands to her chest as though she had been stabbed and dropped her head onto the table. The second time she did it Schuyler flashed that she was dropping her head into his lap, that she had pulled down his jeans and her hair was lying across his bare thighs. This sort of thing happened all the time, though less frequently as he got older; he dismissed it more easily than he had as a teenager, when he had seemed to mentally undress nearly every beautiful woman he got within spitting distance of, sometimes having to switch check-out lines at the hardware store or change seats on a train because he was afraid the object of his brief and unplanned fantasy might somehow pick up on what he was thinking. By the sixth time Marinda landed on Reading she was broke, and Schuyler had never been so happy to win a game of Monopoly.

It wasn't until the fourth day that Marinda mentioned Jason, and then it was only in passing. Schuyler was explaining that out here the sport people cared about most was football and that it was one of the things he'd liked about coming back after all those years in Boston and New York.

"That was something Jason was always complaining about when we moved to Miami," Marinda said, lacing up her hiking boots. She had announced that morning that it was her turn to cook, and after an inspection of Schuyler's kitchen cabinets it was clear she had a lot of shopping to do. "Miami's a real football town, it's incredibly southern that way, you know, they follow all the college games. I grew up watching football, it was this big family thing on the weekends, but Jason could never get into it."

"Katie Lee used to fly down to Kentucky for basketball games," Schuyler said. "I went down with her once. Unbelievable, how much money gets bet."

"Yeah, Jason was always saying how pure baseball was because there wasn't all that betting. Bobby told me, he warned me once, he said an entire generation of New Yorkers had been ruined in 1969, that they would never recover until the Mets won another series."

"Jason was a Mets fan?" Schuyler asked, following her lead of speaking about him in the past tense. He was feeling pumped up from the extra cup of coffee he hadn't meant to drink. Marinda had done something different with the coffee, he was going to have to ask her what it was before she left.

Marinda smiled. "Uh hunh. Queens, remember?"

"He has a serious wait ahead of him," Schuyler said.

"Like forever," Marinda said. "They'll never get past the Pirates." She zipped up her down jacket and put on a black baseball cap with horizontal yellow stripes. "I wore this the night of our last big fight just to torture him. Dinner at seven?"

"I'll be there," Schuyler said. "Can I pick up wine or anything?"

"Nope, this one's all on me," Marinda said.

"Isn't there anything you want me to do?"

"Just get lost until seven," she said. For the first time in a long time she was actually looking forward to spending time in the kitchen. She was going to make everything the way her mother did, from scratch. It would take her hours to wash and peel the potatoes, to simmer down the stock for gravy, to trim the beef, to blanche the vegetables and grate the orange peel for the chocolate mousse.

She hit the highway in pursuit of food perfection. She drove miles between stores, listening to the only station that came in without interference. Marinda usually didn't like country music, but out here, driving in her rented American car, wearing a baseball cap, shopping for a big old-fashioned supper of meat and potatoes, it seemed like the right sound track. A man she couldn't identify and a woman who sounded like Dolly Parton sang about having nothing left to hold onto. Another man sang about being so lonesome he could die. By the time Marinda pulled back into Schuyler's driveway she was humming along as a man and woman alternated verses of past heartbreak and then agreed, in a final chorus, to give love one last shot.

I'm just an old-fashioned girl cooking an old-fashioned meal for an old-fashioned man, she thought as she lifted the heavy brown bags out of the trunk. She'd had to go to three towns to find everything she needed. She unpacked her purchases and found a note from Schuyler saying he'd be back around seven.

Marinda arranged the food across the kitchen counter. Coming here had been the right thing to do, she thought, she was already dreading the day, a week from now, when she'd have to head home. Schuyler seemed to expect nothing from her, not even conversation, and in the last few days she'd begun to realize how much pressure she'd been under, from Jason, from Thompson, from her family. What an ordeal it was in Miami just to drive to work in the morning, just to get through the day in one piece.

Out here it seemed life was as simple as a recipe. If you had the right ingredients and followed the instructions, nothing could go wrong. Marinda got her camera out of her knapsack, loaded it with color film, and shot a roll of this food that seemed suddenly wonderful, its colors as bright and reassuring as a box of children's crayons: lemon yellow, apple red, rich chocolate brown, orange, and the most remarkable find of all, fresh Italian parsley. She wanted to be able to remember this exact moment and just how she felt, before the washing and cutting and heating and serving, just how it felt to be looking forward to doing something as simple as this. She folded up the bags she'd use later to hold the refuse. At the bottom of one something rattled, something she'd forgotten. She'd tossed them into the cart on impulse while wheeling down an aisle in search of an eggbeater—a pair of long navy-blue candles, the same color her mother used to buy.

The candles had burned three quarters of the way down. Marinda had cooked too much meat and not enough gravy. The mousse looked cool and sweet but tasted slightly bitter. Schuyler held each spoonful on his tongue until it warmed and melted. Buddy Holly was singing about something that seemed so easy. As Marinda cleared his table, Schuyler debated whether or not to open another bottle of wine. One more glass and he'd be wondering how much of a mistake it would be if the evening ended up in her bedroom. Two more and he wouldn't care. Another after that and he'd be too lazy and happy to do much of anything besides pull off his boots and collapse into sleep.

Marinda brought in coffee and turned up the tape.

"Don't let me drink too much of this," she said, "I'll be up all night."

Schuyler took two sips of coffee and four large gulps of wine. It wouldn't be gentlemanly, he told himself, it would be downright dishonorable to take advantage of her when she was at her most vulnerable. He'd known a few men who specialized in this sort of thing, seducing women who'd just broken up with boyfriends of long standing. He'd known Marinda too long for that. In the morning she'd be expecting something besides another week in Montana.

"Nelson's having some people over tomorrow night, it might be fun," Schuyler said. Nelson would be surprised to see Marinda after what Schuyler had told him about her. She took a tan well. Under the weight she had lost there turned out to be a real old-fashioned waist, narrow hips, and long athlete's legs. He'd forgotten about her breasts —like smooth skin and a friendly smile, he'd begun to see them as just another sad, useless bonus that God gave fat women, but now that she was thin, there they were still, moving easily inside what he imagined was a rather flimsy bra made out of some shiny thin knit fabric. Like most men with light eyes, Schuyler projected all sorts of sad knowingness and sensual sophistication onto a woman with eyes as brown and thickly lashed as Marinda's. Italian, Spanish, Jewish, Greek—it was all the same to him: she was dark, exotic, a mystery he might never figure out.

"Is it a party?" Marinda asked.

"You never know until you get there whether there'll be eight or a hundred and eight," he said.

"It sounds like it'll be fun," Marinda said. It sounded sort of terrifying, actually; she couldn't remember the last time she'd been to a big party without a boyfriend to protect her. She supposed Schuyler would be the sort of perfect gentleman who would be sure to introduce her (which Jason hardly ever did) to everyone who joined them in a conversation and who wouldn't abandon her (which Jason always had) when there was someone important he had to talk to. Like most women with dark eyes, she saw in Schuyler's steel-gray eyes an honesty, a simplicity of motive, a lack of guile. She inferred from his rugged looks and cowboy mannerisms that he lived by some old-fashioned masculine moral code that the rest of the country had sadly forgotten. She heard in his long and many silences a thousand things he'd never say. He's the real thing, Marinda thought, I never quite believed it until I saw him here.

"I didn't really bring any party clothes," she said.

Schuyler poured himself another glass of wine. "We don't really get too dressed up around here," he said. He told himself that this elaborate dinner had simply been Marinda's way of thanking him for his hospitality. And even if it were something more, right now she needed a friend more than a lover.

Except they weren't really friends, he reminded himself. He'd always thought it was bad form to take up with people on the rebound, but when you thought about it, nearly everyone over the age of sixteen was on the rebound from someone or something. It was just a question of how long it had been, days or weeks or months or even sometimes years. Nelson had a friend, a divorce attorney, who slept with more than half his clients. He'd told Nelson that he thought these women were incredible—especially the ones who felt rejected—trying to prove in one night that they were still attractive and desirable. Maybe it was just what Marinda needed. She was a big grown-up girl. She knew what she wanted by now. He emptied his glass and told Marinda about some of the people who would be at Nelson's.

"She sounds pretty neat," Marinda said after Schuyler had described Martha. She was sure from the softness in his voice that he'd slept with her. She was jealous and too drunk to hide it. She felt incredibly foolish, having traveled so far, having fussed over her hair and her clothes and her tan in the days before she left, having cooked this elaborate Cosmo girl feast, only to have this man, this man who she now knew was the only man she would ever be able to really love, the only man who would ever be able to love her back the way she really wanted, to hear him talk about his new girlfriend. While she'd been two thousand miles away, wasting time on a dumb boyfriend and a dumb job, Schuyler had been falling in love with this Martha person. Who was probably prettier and thinner than Marinda, and possibly older, she guessed, and definitely not as smart.

There was no way to let Schuyler know that she would be as perfect for him as she knew he was for her. She didn't exactly know how she'd blown it, but she'd blown it, her life from now on would be the kind of compromise she read about in magazines: trading love for companionship, romantic devotion for mature commitment, soulful gazes for generosity and reliability, wild abandoned sex for my-turn-your-turn and a sense of humor. She was going to have to be just like everyone else. She was going to have to grow up. She was going to have to take what she could get.

"Are you all right?" Schuyler asked. Her eyes were getting glossy and her bottom lip was trembling. He wanted to kiss her, to hold the quiver of that lip between his, to feel her melt and soften beneath his warm hands. He placed one hand over hers and with the other emptied the last of the wine into their glasses.

"I guess so," she said. He was caressing her palm with his thumb. Buddy Holly was saying how it went faster than a roller coaster. She looked up into his eyes and saw there that with one sign from her he would take her to bed. If she gave up the last thing she had left, this little bit of pride that even Jason hadn't been able to wrest from her, this pride that was the one thing that was holding her together, keeping her this side of teary collapse, if she gave that up she would get from Schuyler all she'd ever wanted and less: a sympathy fuck.

She pulled herself up on tottery legs and brushed her hair back from her face. "I've made a huge mess," she said.

Schuyler stood up and walked around to her side of the table. She took a step back and pointed toward the kitchen.

"It looks like the end of the world in there, and I don't have the energy to deal with it," she said.

Schuyler stepped back too and smiled. "Me neither," he said. "It can wait until tomorrow. Dinner was fantastic."

"Well. See you tomorrow," Marinda said. She bent over and blew out a candle.

"Make a wish," Schuyler said.

It was the same wish she'd made on countless birthday candles, on dandelion seeds scattered into the sun, on fallen eyelashes blown off fingertips, and on the star that was really a planet, the one you could pick out even in the city-brightened skies of New York and Miami. She wished for him.

"Your turn," she said, pointing at the other candle.

"I have to think about it," he said. She shrugged and went off to bed.

He sat there wishing that he hadn't drunk so much wine. Wishing that he'd kissed her when he first thought of it or that he'd never thought of it at all. Wishing that she'd leave tomorrow or that she'd stay long enough so that he could be sure he had failed to do whatever it was he wanted to do not from lack of nerve but rather from lack of desire. Buddy Holly was asking what she'd done to him, guessing that it didn't matter anymore, he was sick of trying, she didn't matter anymore.

Fall: he hated it. Everyone bustling around, planning Thanksgiving dinners, talking about Christmas, and here he was, again, alone, in this big old house. He blew out the last candle and wished for winter.

"She's madly in love with him," Martha said to Nelson across a bowl of punch. People had begun dancing just after midnight and were working themselves into a collective frenzy as the Raylettes told Mr. Charles just what to hit. "What's in there, anyway. It looks disgusting."

"Damned if I know," Nelson replied. "When I put it out five hours ago it was empty. People've been putting in whatever they want. Could be anything in there."

Martha dipped in a finger and licked off a taste of punch. "Not bad. Can't figure out what makes it so purple. Nice bowl."

"Wedding present," Nelson said. "That bitch left everything behind."

"Don't they all," Martha said. "I envy the people who get cleaned out. They don't know how lucky they are. If there's weird drugs in here I'll kill you."

"Get in line," Nelson said. "How do you know she's in love with him? Maybe she always looks that way."

"What way?" Martha asked. She felt a little frumpy in her Irish fisherman's sweater and worn brown corduroy jeans. Marinda was wearing a light pink sweater that had sparkly silver threads woven through it and black velvet jeans that stopped a few inches short of her immaculate black suede ballerina slippers. Outside, the ground was cold and mucky; Martha guessed that Schuyler must have had to carry his date from the car.

"That way women look, like they know more about you than you do yourself. I've seen you look that way on occasion."

"Have not," Martha said. Schuyler looked his usual self, only better, in a bright-red chamois cloth shirt that had softened down with age.

"Have too. Jealous?"

"Maybe," Martha said. Nelson hadn't dressed up much either, she noticed, except for the orange satin bow tie he'd clipped to his plaid flannel shirt.

"Well, that's the deal, isn't it," Nelson said.

"Yeah, that's the deal."

"You're prettier than she is. If that helps."

"Thanks," Martha said, but she wasn't sure it was true. She watched Schuyler and Marinda dance together and guessed they hadn't slept together. Yet. Schuyler was falling for Marinda, Martha could see that, in the way Martha felt herself to be just a little too old to be fallen for. There were too many things Martha knew, things about men, things that she couldn't even pretend to forget.

"You're not going to get all weepy on me," Nelson said. He was trying to think of something he could say that would make Martha feel better. That only trash wore glittery clothes. That there were a dozen men here who'd been asking after her. That Schuyler wasn't worth it. The first two statements he'd be able to say with some semblance of conviction.

"Wouldn't dream of it," Martha said. "You know, I always have this feeling about Schuyler, like he's a jigsaw puzzle with one of the pieces missing."

"Think Marinda is the missing piece?" Nelson asked.

"No," Martha said. "But I'll bet you she knows where it is."

"Come on," Nelson said, grabbing her by the hand, "we're cutting in."

"I don't know if I'm up to this," Martha said as they closed in on Marinda and Schuyler.

"May I?" Nelson said to Schuyler as he put an arm around Marinda's shoulders.

"This is a wonderful party," Marinda said to Nelson, who had turned her around so that she was facing the stereo system. She was trying to follow his lead.

"It's all in the feet," Nelson said. "There. Like that. This is how white people are supposed to dance. Great perfume. Are you fucking my best friend?"

"What?"

"Didn't think so. Right-left-right, lean back, right-left-right, lean back—there you go. Are you the girl who broke his heart?"

"What?"

"You heard me."

"No."

"Didn't think so either but had to check."

"That was Katie Lee. She's married now. You're drunk."

"I hope so," Nelson said, giving her a twirl.

"Hope you're drunk?" Marinda asked, watching for Schuyler and Martha in the spin.

"Hope she's married. Means she'll be punished."

"I guess that means you're married," Marinda said.

"Was once. Ever seen a single man with a three-gallon lead crystal punch bowl?" He spun her round again, and she saw Schuyler laughing as Martha whispered into his ear.

"One thing I like about you, Mr. Smith," Martha was saying, "I can always count on you to laugh at my dumb jokes."

"Guess I'm easily pleased," Schuyler said.

"Are you?" Martha said, holding him slightly away from her and giving him a solid stare.

He lost the beat of the music for a second, and when he found it again the song had begun to merge into another.

"That girl has a serious crush on you," Martha said. "In case you hadn't noticed."

Schuyler pulled her closer though the music hadn't slowed. "Jesus, I'm sorry, Martha. We shouldn't have come. I didn't really think."

"You never think," Martha said. "It's one of the things I like best about you."

"You're not going to let me off the hook, are you."

"Sure I am, cowboy. I just want to watch you squirm a little first."

"I'm squirming, I'm squirming."

"So that's the girl who broke your heart," Martha said. "I thought she'd be prettier," she continued, not really meaning it. It would be easier for him to leave her there, she knew, if she gave him a little something to hate her for.

"No, that was the fair Rosaline. She's married now. Martha, look—"

"Don't say it, cowboy. We both knew the deal." She was leading him slowly back to where Marinda and Nelson were attempting a jitterbug. It was something she had learned in the all-girl dance classes given at her high school, where the bigger girls had always been made to lead.

"Trade?" Nelson said to Schuyler.

"He's all yours," Martha said to Marinda.

"Thanks," Marinda said to Martha.

"Thanks," Schuyler said to Nelson, who took Martha to one of the back bedrooms, where a better quality of drugs and liquor was being shared by two songwriters and a wall-eyed bartender who'd driven from Key West without stopping.

Dancing in her sweater was making Marinda uncomfortably warm. It was always this way, for she had been putting together different versions of this party outfit for years, fuzzy sweaters and velvet jeans, what nice girls wore when they tried to be casual or what casual girls wore when they tried to be nice. Each year the neckline got lower or the shoulders broadened or the waistline gathered up into pleats or the cuff tightened around the ankle. Marinda thought it might be time to get rid of all her old clothes and start completely new. Her favorite part of fashion magazines was the make-over section (she wished there were a magazine full of nothing but make-overs), and she wondered if there were some way she could apply to be made over. She needed an expert opinion. It was possible she was doing everything wrong. Perhaps she should be wearing warm peaches and corals instead of cool pinks and mauves. There might be some little trick with a charcoal-blue eye pencil that would turn everything around. Her hair was either too full or not full enough. She had applied her blusher to the wrong parts of her cheekbones. Men said they never noticed these things, but they were lying. Her perfume (too floral or too spicy, too sweet or too musky) might be driving Schuyler into an erotic frenzy but just as likely might be reminding him of his least favorite elementary school teacher, the one whose Rachel face powder ended in an abrupt line just below her jaw.

Schuyler was wondering, did she smell that way all over or was she one of those women who just wore perfume behind her ears and on her wrists. The room was warm and full of too many smells—the women's perfumes, the beer, smoke from the fireplace, cut flowers arranged in empty wine bottles, sandalwood incense—and when Schuyler told Marinda he needed some fresh air she said she was ready to go any time he was.

When they got home Marinda put up a fresh pot of coffee.

"I think we need to talk," Schuyler said, watching the filter soak up the hot water.

"I guess." Marinda said, turning off the flame. "I'm not very good at talking. You first."

Schuyler pushed his hair back from his face. "I'm not quite sure how to put this," he said. "Well."

She poured him a cup and offered it to him. "Whatever you want. Really. Whatever you want, it's okay. Nothing. Or everything."

Schuyler took a sip. "And what's in between?"

Marinda tore open a packet of sweetener. "Trouble, probably. Nothing we can't handle, I guess. Who knows."

"What do you want?" he asked.

She looked at her shoes. They were covered with mud. "I don't know most of the time."

"I know what I want," he said, "I want everything."

She looked up at him. "Do you," she said.

"Everything," he said, pulling her to him. The top of her head came just up to his heart. He held her for a while, weighing the mix of passion and comfort. With Marinda in his arms Schuyler felt himself growing younger, more confident, for that was the way she saw him still: as he had once been, years ago, before he realized that the more you learned, the more you knew you didn't know anything at all. Marinda could make him happy, that was clear to him now, happy not just in bed but in this house, on this ranch, in this place in the middle of nowhere. It was time to connect, time to settle down, time to start building something besides a stack of tear sheets and a herd of healthy cattle.

It's happening, Marinda thought, at last at last at last. *At last*, she thought as he carried her to bed, *at last* as they made love slowly, quietly, *at last* there was no pressure, no worry, no rush, because they had all the time in the world: not just this night but every night to come.

After the second time Schuyler pulled back the covers and Marinda nestled into the crook of his arm. They talked first about nothing at all (she would show him how she made coffee, he would teach her how to ride Western) and later about everything they could think of (her family, his family, she'd need to go back to Florida to finish up loose ends at the office and rent out her apartment, he knew of a lawyer who represented a couple of Indian reservations and was looking for someone to help him with research), and when they were all talked out it was dawn and they were too tired to start again.

27

*T*he week before her fourth wedding anniversary, with two perfect children and an adoring husband, against all her finer instincts, contrary to everything she had been brought up to believe in, perhaps without even realizing what was happening, unexplainably, uncontrollably, undeniably, irrevocably, Mrs. Trevor Goodwood née Rosaline Van Schott began falling in love.

At first she dismissed her feelings for Francisco Gomez as a schoolgirl's crush. In those years when Rosaline actually could be described as a schoolgirl she had never carried on any sort of flirtation, and so it seemed possible to her that this was nothing more than a passing phenomenon, a sort of emotional flu that could be waited out with plenty of bed rest and soothing warm beverages. A more experienced woman migt have recognized the early symptoms and laughed them off, but Rosaline, never having waited anxiously by a high school coat locker or on the sidelines of a varsity baseball field, carried no antibodies within her system and was therefore totally susceptible to the charms of the Panamanian jockey who rode her horses daily.

It began, of course, in Florida, where it was warm all winter. She had trouble meeting his gaze. She blushed when he said her name, lowering his voice half an octave, rolling the *R* on his tongue. She said nothing intelligent in his presence. She drove to the barns every morning knowing he would be there and then, having arrived, tried her best to avoid him. She remembered every word he had ever said to her. She spent her evenings playing with her children (who were installed, along with a nanny, in adjacent rooms in her large hotel suite), wondering where Francisco was and whom he was with, and sending her husband silly postcards full of love.

What Francisco noticed she could not say. Mostly she hoped he knew nothing: she did not flirt, after all, she had not shared so much as a cup of coffee with him, and she knew her manners were impeccable. She was just the rich American lady who gave him a lot of business, and it was his job to be nice to her, especially now, with all those lovely yearlings she was keeping to race next year.

But other times she thought she might have given herself away with a single gesture or glance. It was often thought of people who spent most of their time around animals that they put little stock in language and instead could "read" someone intuitively, in the toss of a head or the wave of an arm or a foot tapping nervously in the gravel. How could she possibly hide feelings as strong as this, Rosaline thought, how could he not somehow guess that the few moments she spent with him each day were the most wonderful and terrible times of her life? Not that he would ever acknowledge what he knew: she was the rich and married American lady of a class that never stooped to his, and it was especially important that he not do anything to create a problem, now that she was giving him so much business.

Sometimes Rosaline thought that if things continued in this impossible way for one more minute she would die or go insane or become a Papist and enter a convent.

Things went on this way for one year.

In those months Rosaline began for the first time to take closer notice of those around her, of those couples who she believed were madly in love, to see if she had anything at all in common with them.

When she and Trevor went to parties in New York she saw that one minute a couple were waltzing around the floor and the next minute they were capable of calm and rational conversations, he about stocks or hunting, she about children or decorating. When Rosaline imagined what it might be like to have Francisco take her in his arms and whirl her around a dimly lit room, she began to shake and sweat.

When she went to visit Schuyler and Marinda in Montana, she saw that if Schuyler called Marinda by name from a distant room, Marinda could still complete sentences without missing a beat, and that if Marinda tapped Schuyler on the elbow, he did not drop his lit cigarette in the middle of the living room carpet. They both said it was at long last true love and it was merely the formality of introductions to both sets of parents that was holding off an engagement announcement. When Rosaline imagined living in the same house as Francisco, opening the door in welcome when he came home from work in the evening, she had to close her eyes and be very still. It was a treat she saved for herself, this imagining, it was the story by which she fell asleep each night.

When Rosaline flew to Lexington for a weekend with Bobby and Katie Lee, she saw that for some people children were simply children, that they did not necessarily bind a man and woman closer together. It seemed that, if anything, Bobby and Katie Lee had drifted further apart since Bobby junior had been born. Rosaline could tell that Bobby was drinking heavily—she knew the signs from her father—and she had suspected that Bobby was fooling around, but she wouldn't have guessed about the cocaine if Katie Lee hadn't complained about it. Rosaline couldn't tell what upset Katie Lee more— that Bobby was developing a dependency on drugs or that he was spending so much of Katie Lee's money on it. Katie Lee didn't trust Bobby to supervise the child, and she traveled too much to do it herself, so most of the job was left to a live-in nanny and someone Katie Lee called a day governess. Katie Lee couldn't believe that Rosaline telephoned her children twice a day and usually arranged for them to travel with her. They won't remember any of it anyway, Katie Lee said, how much do you remember of anything that happened to you before you were twelve. When Rosaline imagined having a child with Francisco she nearly fainted.

Only once did she ever believe that there was another person who would have the slightest idea of what she was going through. December had called her with an invitation to see Tory perform in New York, "two tickets fifth row right of center, bring earplugs and wear comfortable shoes." Trevor refused to go, but Grace said that if Rosaline didn't take her, she'd never speak to her again. So Rosaline put on the only blue jeans she owned and an old pair of deck shoes and sat between December and Grace drinking lukewarm beer, thinking: here I am, twenty-six years old, going to my first rock concert.

During a break between sets Grace ventured out for a concession stand in search of T-shirts for her children, her nieces, her nephews, and her cleaning woman, who listened to Tory as she scrubbed Grace's floors with a short-bristle handbrush.

"He's wonderful," Rosaline said to December, "I can't believe how much energy he has."

"He's pretty great," December said. "It's kind of fun to sit out here, I haven't done it in ages. Usually I just stay in the back and watch on monitors. I forget what it's like for the fans."

"Isn't it strange to think about all these people obsessed with Tory?"

"Kinda," December said. "You ought to see some of the letters. They're crazy in love with this guy they've never met."

"Sometimes that can happen," Rosaline said, turning down the cuff of her pale-blue Shetland sweater.

"Has it ever happened to you?" December asked.

Rosaline blushed. "No, of course not," she said. "But it would be possible to fall in love with someone, don't you think, without knowing them very well?"

"Sure. In fact it's probably easier the less you know."

"Oh, that's so cynical! Tell me how you fell in love with Tory."

December smiled. "It's a long story. At some point I was just thinking about him all the time, even when he wasn't there, you know, I'd be tossing my socks into the hamper and I'd be thinking, I wonder what kind of socks he has on right now, or I'd open a beer and I'd think, last night I had exactly this same brand of beer with Tory and it's kind of like 'our' beer—dumb stuff like that. So then I guess I kind of knew I was in for it."

"That sounds so romantic," Rosaline said.

"Socks and beer instead of moonlight and roses? Maybe."

"Did you feel like you were, I don't know, doing things you didn't mean to do but you couldn't help it?"

"Out of control, you mean?" December asked.

"That makes it sound so extreme."

"Rosaline, are you in love?"

"I'm married."

December put her arm around Rosaline's shoulders. "You didn't answer me, sweetie. Are you having an affair?"

"I could never have an affair. Let's change the subject."

"It's done all the time, you know," December said.

"Not by me it isn't. It doesn't matter. I have these thoughts, that's all, but that doesn't mean I'll do anything about it."

Having thoughts is the first step, honey, December said to herself, and I wonder if you have the guts to take the second.

December patted Rosaline on the head. "Well, you don't have to do anything about it if you don't want to," she said, "but if you do want to—"

"I don't."

"Well, if you ever did. It wouldn't be the worst thing in the world. I don't mean to be getting all philosophical on you, but, you know, there's a certain kind of love that's pretty incredibly great and that most people never get a chance at. So if you have a chance at it, even if it's not with your husband, you know, it may be your only chance. So if it ever comes up, you ought to think about taking that chance."

"I love Trevor, December."

"Of course you do. He's a great guy," December said, thinking, he's a boring stiff, you're going to spend the rest of your life with a boring stiff, and maybe five minutes before you die you'll realize that's it, you blew it, it's all over, you fucked it up, you missed the moment. Still, it was hard for December to imagine Rosaline succumbing to passion. Probably some banker friend of Trevor's had sent her a dozen roses and invited her to a very proper lunch in some boring French restaurant and now Rosaline was having a moral crisis about it.

Rosaline looked behind them up into the balconies. "If Trevor were here, he'd be estimating the gross."

"It's not that much for tickets, really, when you think about it. Lots of the money is in the merchandising. You know, people pay fifteen bucks for their seat and then spend fifty on T-shirts."

"Like Grace," Rosaline said, for Grace had just returned carrying a laundry load's worth of brightly colored shirts.

The lights went down, and Tory launched into a series of love songs. The audience sang along, and Rosaline realized that everyone knew the words, even Grace, everyone it seemed but her. Then Tory began singing about searching for someone to love, and he pointed to different women in the audience, shaking his finger in time to the beat.

"What if he asks you to dance?" Grace shouted in Rosaline's ear.

"What?"

"He always picks someone to dance with—there she goes," Grace said as December leaped onstage. Rosaline watched Tory and December dancing together as the band traded instrumental solos. It was dancing as she had imagined it. It was hard for her to believe that the same word was used for both things, for what Trevor had learned in classes and for what Tory and December were doing together now in front of thousands of people. There was something that existed between Tory and December, something that Rosaline had been trying to pretend didn't exist at all, was only a schoolgirl fantasy, and now that she saw it there was no going back.

Rosaline remembered a night Trevor had taken her to the opera. A dozen singers had been dressed in drab peasant colors, browns and dark greens and muddy reds, moving slowly against a background scrim painting in the same murky tones, an outline of their dreary village. And suddenly the lights had come up behind the scrim and Rosaline realized she had been seeing only the first half of the stage, and the violins got louder and the screen lifted, and there were a chorus dressed in bright silks and velvets, and rows of ballet dancers spinning under arbors of glittering flowers, and the audience cheered at what was revealed to them, and forgot what had gone before, and the opera began in earnest.

As Rosaline rode up in her elevator she remembered that moment and felt that some screen had lifted, that a possibility of beauty had been revealed to her. Before she had a chance to get out her key Trevor opened the door and gave her a hug.

"Hello, darling," he said, "was it wonderful."

"You would have hated it," Rosaline murmured in his ear. "Grace thinks you're the best for giving her your ticket, and she bought you this hideous thank-you present—she said she looked but they all had polyester."

Trevor took a step back. "Parker called," he said. "There was an accident at the track this afternoon."

Rosaline looked at Trevor and tried to gauge from his face how awful this news could be. He was wearing his bad-luck-but-that's-life-let's-move-on expression. A horse, she guessed, a nice one but not one that was winning a lot of races.

"Orestes?" she asked. "I knew we'd been working him too hard."

"Gomez," Trevor said. "Don't worry, he's all right. Had a spill. Parker says they've been complaining about the condition of the track at Hialeah for years, but no one will do anything about it. He was on a horse that had just been shipped from California, and the horse got spooked and took a bad step, and Gomez had to bail out. There were a few horses right behind him, and he got knocked around some, but Parker thinks he'll be all right."

Rosaline believed herself to be doing the hardest thing she had ever done in her entire life: she smiled at her husband, slowly removed her coat, leafed through the mail as if looking for an awaited invitation, and said in a calm, cheery voice, "Well, thank goodness—I suppose we should send flowers. Perhaps I'll call Francisco in the morning."

"I don't think they have telephones in intensive care, darling," Trevor said, scratching himself just below the collarbone.

"Intensive care? I thought you said he was all right?" Rosaline said, marshaling all her energy and yet sounding no louder than a kitten crying for milk.

"Well, he could have been killed—the man's alive, he suffered a concussion, but Parker said they don't think there's any permanent damage to the head. He's a very lucky little boy."

"His head. What about the rest of him?"

"Parker said too early to tell."

"Did he break any bones?"

"Yes, I think so."

"Well, which bones?"

"Darling, I didn't ask for all the gruesome medical details. Parker said he'd call you in the morning. I didn't realize you'd get so upset."

"Well darling, of course I'm upset."

"Darling, you're nearly hysterical, I'm going to pour you a nice big brandy to help you calm down."

"I am not hysterical."

"You always tell me this kind of thing happens all the time, and everyone knows it going in, and it's just part of the game. You must have seen a hundred spills worse than this one."

"Well, maybe," Rosaline said. Trevor was staring at her hard. She wished she had married either someone much smarter or someone as stupid as a stone. Someone she didn't have to explain things to, or someone too dumb to require an explanation. "It's just that there are all these big races coming up, and we were going to start Orestes in three weeks, and if Francisco isn't in shape by then we'll have to get another rider, who may not know the horse as well. Spring is when we make all our money, darling, and Francisco has been riding so well."

"From what Parker said I don't think he'll be back in three weeks. I don't think he'll be back ever. He'll be lucky if he doesn't have to spend the rest of his life in a wheelchair."

"Jesus," Rosaline said, sinking into a chair. It may have been the first time her husband heard her curse.

Trevor brought her a brandy and sat on the arm of her chair. "Well, no use your getting upset. There's nothing you can do about it." He began massaging her shoulders. "I didn't realize this was going to be so tough on you. Poor little Rosaline."

Rosaline closed her eyes as his thumbs pressed into her neck. It was what Trevor did best, being sweet and taking care of her. Except that she didn't need him to take care of her anymore, and she'd lost her taste for sweet. Francisco was lying in a hospital—who knew where, in who knew what condition. Perhaps he had broken his spine, perhaps he'd be paralyzed for life—it had happened a few years ago to that nice Canadian who'd ridden Secretariat.

She wanted to be with him. She wanted to sit by the side of his bed and hold his hand and feed him soup and read his get-well cards to him and tell him silly jokes about the doctors and the nurses.

He would probably be surprised to see her. He would think how polite she was, the nice American lady, visiting him in the hospital, promising him he could have all his mounts back when he returned to the track. She imagined him saying, after ten minutes, that he was getting very tired, that he thanked her so much for stopping by. It was silly of her to think there'd be any more than that: a few courteous hospital visits and then she would never see him again.

And then she remembered a race he had won for her last fall on a filly that had gone off at thirty-to-one. In the winner's circle she had given him a congratulatory handshake, and he had held her hand for an extra few seconds and had stopped smiling and had just looked at her with this look that said, I know what you're thinking, I know everything, I have known everything for a long, long time, before you even knew it yourself, and I am waiting for you. I am here. When you are ready.

Rosaline shook off Trevor's hands and stood up.

"I have to go down there," she said.

"Darling, there's nothing you can do."

"I have to. There's too much going on."

"You've got a million things to do right here. You're supposed to take Scotty to the circus, and we've got that dinner at Eleanor's, and I told your mother we'd drive her up to Connecticut."

Rosaline dug a toe into the Persian carpet. There was Trevor, in his proper gabardine trousers and tan cashmere cardigan, leaning against a mahogany sideboard, pouring expensive brandy from a crystal decanter. There she was, in her tight blue jeans, the soles of her deck shoes sticky with beer, the words of rock and roll still running round her head, get off of my cloud, it's my life and I'll do what I want. She felt like a rebellious teenager, and Trevor was her father, pretending he knew best.

"I don't care. I have to go pack," she said.

Trevor did not believe in arguing with his wife. It was one of the ways he knew they had a happy marriage. He would help her get her luggage down from a high shelf in a hall closet, and he would call weather information in Florida and tell her if she needed to take rainboots and an umbrella, and he would arrange for the car that would take her to the airport, and tomorrow morning he would see her off, buttoning her up at the collar, wishing her a good trip, kissing her goodbye.

From underneath a mummy's wrap of white gauze bandages and hardened plaster, with hanging tubes, Francisco smiled and said, "I knew you would come to see me."

"The last time I was in a hospital I was having a baby," Rosaline said. Francisco had been moved to a private room overlooking the hospital parking lot. Flowers were everywhere. "You look sort of awful, but you sound fine. What does your doctor say?"

"The doctor is a fool. He knows nothing. I pay no attention to him."

"Do you want me to get someone from New York?" Rosaline asked. "Do you want another opinion?"

"I need only my own opinion," Francisco said. "Watch my feet," he said, and Rosaline saw him wiggle his toes. "You will see, I will be out of here in four weeks. I will ride for you at Saratoga."

"Oh, I hope so," Rosaline said, but she had seen the X-rays, had been shown where his left leg was broken in twenty places, and knew that he would never race-ride again.

"Did you see Parker?" Francisco asked.

"We had lunch," she said.

"What an old woman," Francisco said. "You know he almost fainted when he saw me. He thought he was looking at a dead man. He came to see me and said he was going to say a prayer for me. I said, 'pray for yourself, old man, because when I walk out of this hospital the first thing I am going to do is belt you one for putting me on that crazy horse.'"

Rosaline didn't tell Francisco that Parker had said he wanted to retire at the end of the year and that he had recommended that Rosaline hand her string over to a friend of his who had been training successfully in England, a man whose list of favored riders did not include Francisco. Francisco needed to believe that everything would be kept waiting for his return.

"He's very worried about you," Rosaline said.

"Well, I don't need worried old women fussing around. I need beautiful young women to hold my hand and look into my eyes and tell me they are counting the minutes till I get out of here to take them dancing."

Rosaline giggled.

"So?" Francisco said.

"So?" Rosaline repeated.

"So. Hold my hand and look into my eyes. There. Thank you. What are you doing the first Saturday in May?"

It was two months away. "I don't know," Rosaline said, "that's Derby day. I'll be in Louisville, I guess."

"Next year you will be in Louisville, I will ride Orestes for you. We will look good in roses, don't you think?"

"Orestes hasn't even started yet. So much can happen between now and then."

"So I am hoping. But this year you must come back to Florida and watch the Derby with me, and then I am going to take you down to the Keys for dinner. In eight weeks."

Rosaline dropped her head. "You know I can't."

"Please, I don't want to hear about your being a happily married woman and your wonderful husband and silly talk like that. I am a man who has returned from the brink of death. Don't talk nonsense to me. You did not come all this way to talk nonsense to me."

"It's complicated," Rosaline said.

"No. It is the simplest thing in the world."

"I'm sorry. I can't."

"Then please leave," Francisco said, turning his head slightly away. "I don't need you to come here to be polite."

"Francisco, my life isn't like that, you know it isn't."

"You can leave now. Come back when you are ready. Or don't come back. I will need all my energy to put myself back together in one piece and walk out of here. I don't have time for little dramas. Either you will be with me, all of you, or I don't want you here at all."

She put on her coat. "I'm sorry," she said, "if you need anything."

He said nothing. She couldn't see his face. As she left, a nurse brought in a basket of fruit and an arrangement of freesia and tulips. In the parking lot she started her rented car and then sat for a few minutes, listening to the engine hum.

Perhaps it was true what December had said, that some people got only one chance, and perhaps Francisco was that one chance. If she pulled out of the parking lot and onto the highway she would be driving away from the one man who could give her what she wanted. She would forever be in the audience, watching other people dance, knowing she had given up her opportunity to be one of the dancers. She would be one of the drab villagers forgotten in the darkness while just a few feet away Francisco sang and danced with a pretty girl in a pink chiffon ballerina gown.

It was sad, but she knew what she was. A good person, who could tell right from wrong. She was loyal and generous and kind, and her family could always count on her. She would fly back to New York this afternoon, and she and Trevor would start going to church again. She had lost her way, she had almost strayed, but she knew she could find the path back.

She shifted the car into drive, keeping her foot on the brake.

And then shifted back into neutral. Before she and Trevor were married she had spent several afternoons taking instruction from the minister. They'd sat in his parlor drinking tea while he explained that the ability to love was a gift from God, a gift to be cherished, a gift with a lesson to it: that in our love for each other we could see the reflection of God's love for us, a love that was forgiving and ennobling, that made us strong. Rosaline hadn't really been listening. At the time she'd thought he was trotting out an ancient speech that was supposed to gear virgins up for their wedding night, convince them that they should approach the physical burdens of their marital obligations with a sense of higher purpose. She'd giggled about it afterwards with Katie Lee.

But now Rosaline thought she was understanding the minister's words for the first time in her life. Her love for Francisco was a gift. What was the greater sin: returning to Trevor and the lie of their marriage or wasting this precious gift that had been revealed to her?

By the time she reached his bedside her face was streaked with tears.

He opened his eyes. "I prayed for you to return," he said. "You see, the angels are with us. Look in the drawer. Parker brought some things from my apartment."

"Your lucky cookies?" Rosaline asked, holding up a package of vanilla wafers.

"Not that. In the leather bag."

Rosaline zipped open what looked like a shaving kit. Inside were a Bible, a photograph of a man she guessed to be Francisco's father, a seashell, and a small square of silk with flowers hand-painted around the border.

She drew out the scarf. "So you knew," she said, tying it around her neck.

"Always," he said.

When she kissed him, gently, carefully, she could feel the strength that was there underneath the bandages and the plaster, the strength that was knitting bones and mending muscle, that was pulling him through this incredible pain. She felt blessed as a newborn baby, as blessed and innocent and frightened and wondering as someone who has just, in the last few seconds, begun to live.

28

"**I**t's going to be the most excruciating social event of our entire lives," said Katie Lee, long distance from Lexington, "I wouldn't miss it for the world."

"Has Rosaline decided?" Marinda asked. Katie Lee must have some sixth sense, Marinda thought, because she telephoned only when Schuyler was out of town.

"Trevor said she was in Florida, but I keep missing her. I left a message with the nanny."

"Tomorrow's the Derby, she probably has a million parties to go to."

"Don't we all," said Katie Lee, who had done the Louisville circuit for a few years running with Charlotte and Rosaline and was distressed to find that, without Charlotte and Rosaline in attendance, she hadn't merited any interesting invitations on her own. Most of her friends in Lexington had left for Louisville yesterday but Katie Lee had pleaded too much work to make it this year.

"Anyway," Katie Lee said, "of course Rosaline is going to come. Fifth college reunions were made for people like Rosaline. I'm making reservations at the Ritz, and I have to know by next week whether or not you're coming if we want to be guaranteed rooms on the same floor."

"I thought they put us up in Currier House or someplace equally wonderful."

"Sweetie, if you think I'm going to stay in some yucky dormitory and share a bathroom that's been used by some awful computer nerd who probably has a disgusting disease, think again."

"What disgusting disease would that be, Katie Lee," Marinda said.

"You know. We should bless our lucky stars we all got out of there and got married before the Era of Running Sores."

"I'm not married, in case you forgot."

"I haven't. It's been almost a year, hasn't it, sweetie?"

"More than a year, actually," Marinda said. When she talked to old friends she noticed that she had picked up some Montana in her voice.

"Well, I'm sure you'll have something to tell me any day now. Maybe when Schuyler gets back from California. December said they've finished the casting for his movie."

December said: Schuyler had called Marinda every night in the ten days he'd been in L.A. and he hadn't mentioned seeing December. Marinda wished she'd accompanied him to California, but there'd been so much to do at the office, there was no way she could have taken the time off. I hate having a job, she thought. As soon as we're married I'm going to get pregnant and quit.

December said: Katie Lee could tell from Marinda's silence that she had scored one where it hurt. When Katie Lee had called December about booking hotel rooms, all December had said was that Alex had told her an amusing story about how Schuyler's producer had canceled lunch with Alex so he could meet Schuyler at the airport and that Alex was devising various forms of social torture to punish this man for daring to think that anything could possibly be more important than lunch with Alex Child. Still, it was what Marinda deserved. Marinda had lent her Florida condo to Bobby over the winter, and Katie Lee knew for a fact (the detective had photographs) that Bobby had entertained at least three women in what she now thought of as the Vincent whorehouse-by-the-sea.

"I'll let you know in a few days," Marinda said. "Is December coming?"

"If she can tear herself away from Mr. Dreamboat. What a cretin."

"He's actually pretty smart from what I can tell," Marinda said.

"A regular nuclear physicist," Katie Lee said. As far as she was concerned, December's affair with Tory (her highly publicized affair was how Katie Lee referred to it in conversation) was a complete joke. Here was December, her elegant spokeswoman, her Radcliffe roommate, tooling around with a man who had barely made it out of high school. Okay, so he'd read some novels—he always worked that into his interviews, Katie Lee noticed—but so what, that didn't make him smart. That was why he needed December, Katie Lee figured, to prove to the world he was smart. And December was attracted to Tory out of her same tired old rebellion thing. He was a loser, he was a greaser, he came from a no-account family, he was as close as you could get to a black man without actually crossing over.

Katie Lee had figured out the secret of Tory's music: he appealed to people who liked black music but didn't have any black friends. Bobby agreed with her: you could take all the blacks December knew and put them in a room together and you still wouldn't have enough to sing four-part harmony. Katie Lee told her friends she was proud to have several blacks on board at Hopewell, and she didn't just mean people working for her, she said, she meant executives who had stock options that validated their ownership point of view. They were assets to her company, every one of them. December had never given a black man the time of day. Culturally, Katie thought, Tory was a total ripoff artist. She had to admire him for that.

"Well, I'll call you in a couple of days," Marinda said.

"It's not like we're negotiating world peace here," Katie Lee said. Honestly, if you put a peanut in that girl's path it would take her three weeks to figure out how to jump over it. She'd better get that Smith boy to marry her right quick if she has a brain in her head. If they spend one more minute Discussing Their Relationship they'll talk themselves out of whatever it is they think they're doing. Nothing made Katie Lee crazier than whiners and wonderers, people who couldn't make up their minds about what they wanted. People like Marinda waste their best years figuring out what they want, and by the time they decide, they're drooling in their wheelchairs wondering where it all went.

When she got off the telephone Katie Lee took out a compact and checked that her makeup hadn't turned too orange under the fluorescent office lights. And I'll have gotten more done before my thirtieth birthday than most men accomplish in their whole lives. Not because I'm so special. I just work harder, that's all. Katie Lee doesn't fool around. Life is serious business. You get up early every morning and give it your best effort. You keep on going till you're too beat to move. Trying to stop Katie Lee is like standing in front of a fast freight train and holding up a little red flag. I'll run right over anything and anyone so foolish as to get in my way. That's the way my daddy raised me.

She took a deep breath. She was psyched. She was pumped. She was ready to meet with her father and go over the final numbers for the casino hotel she was planning in Atlantic City.

"Looks good," was all Henry said at first, though the compliment may have been directed only at the report's typesetting and bar graphs. Katie Lee had kept the staff in word processing on overtime past midnight to get things exactly right. Henry had cleared the top of his desk of everything except Katie Lee's folder. "We'll have another zoning fight on our hands."

"We can pull it off," Katie Lee said. "Bobby's father can help us on this one."

"He said he'd step in?" Henry asked, swiveling in his chair and looking out the window. In profile Katie Lee could see how much he had aged. The skin of his neck had loosened away from his jaw. His hair had thinned into a reddish gray fringe that could not be described as distinguished.

"Not in so many words. But I know I can count on him."

"Good. Good. I like it. I never thought we'd put our name to a gambling establishment, but times have changed."

"They certainly have, Daddy," Katie Lee said. "It's the eighties." May 1981, to be exact, just a few weeks short of Henry's sixty-fifth birthday, the day he'd always said he'd retire. But he showed no signs of slowing down. He hadn't mentioned retirement in months, not even when Katie Lee had given him an extravagant set of new golf clubs at Christmas with a card that said "All work and no play makes your handicap go up up up." In the last few years Katie Lee had secured her position as the next head of the family business, and pretty soon she knew she would get tired of waiting around, of having to ask Henry's permission to do every little thing, of not being able to sign checks in amounts greater than half a million dollars, of not getting her formal portrait in the glossy annual report, of having to drag Henry along to meetings with bankers and partners who believed themselves too important to sit down with anyone other than the "top guy."

"Things sure have changed in these modern eighties," Henry said. "How much of your own time will you be able to give to this project? How much on-site?"

"Whatever it takes, you know that," Katie Lee said, leaning an elbow on his desk. "I'll give it one hundred percent. This is going to be a very exciting move for us."

"You sure are an eighties kind of gal," Henry said. "You know, twenty years ago you'd be home with three kids making yourself pretty for the man of the house. You wouldn't even have your own credit cards."

A good definition of slavery, Katie Lee thought, not being able to have your own credit cards. "I'm a lucky girl, I know that," she said. "Born in the right place at the right time. I've tried to make you proud."

"I'm proud, sugar, I'm proud, any father would be proud to have a son like you."

"Or a daughter?"

"Well, now, maybe I'm just too much of an old-timer, you have to forgive your father if he has a little trouble adjusting. I do worry some about Bobby junior. A boy needs to have his mother around. My mother was there for me, a great woman, I'm sorry you never had a chance to get to know her. And your mother was there for you."

Because she practically had to get a signed note from you every time she drove to the shopping mall, Katie Lee said to herself. She had been forced to sit through this same lecture the last time she visited Bobby's family in New Jersey. Bobby's parents complained that they didn't see their grandchild enough, that he was being raised by strangers, that he should be spending more time with his cousins, learn what it was to be a Vincent. "Junior's doing just fine," Katie Lee said. "When Rosaline was here she said he was doing things months ahead of her kids."

"Sweet little girl, Rosaline. She said she takes her kids with her nearly everywhere she goes. She told me we ought to put baby food in room service. Get someone to look into that." Henry lifted a hand to run it through his hair and then, realizing that he might disturb the lacquered arrangement of his few remaining strands, settled for rubbing the back of his left ear.

"Well, I certainly couldn't do that with my kind of travel schedule. I don't want to bring up my kid in airports."

"True, true. The thing is, sweet pea, I think you should be spending more time at home. That's the only thing that worries me about this Atlantic City business. There must be someone else we can get to handle it."

It's my baby, Katie Lee thought, you can't give it to someone else after I've done all the work of putting it together and figuring everything out. "There just isn't anyone else now. You know that," she said.

"Then I'm afraid I'm going to have to put this on hold, sugar. You know, as I get older I realize there's more to life than dollars. When you're my age you'll understand better what I'm talking about. You'll look back and you'll want to remember the time you spent with your family. I sure wish I'd spent more time with you when you were little."

"What do you mean, on hold?"

"Three, four years."

"But that's crazy. Casinos get a lot of return business. We're already jumping in at half time here—in three years there'll be even more competition."

"That's my call," Henry said, taking the folder and placing it into his "out" basket. "You better start paying attention to what's happening on the home front. I've been hearing things about that husband of yours. He'll make fools of us all. You get things under control, I'll reconsider."

Katie Lee tried for another hour to convince her father otherwise, but it was hopeless. When she got back to her desk she was incapable of concentrating on the work she'd scheduled for that afternoon. She told her secretary she had something to take care of outside the office and would return in a couple of hours.

The gateman at the horse farm recognized her car and waved her through. Katie Lee parked neat the stallion paddocks, where Agamemnon had been turned out for a little exercise. She leaned on the wooden fence and watched him run from one side of the paddock to the other.

It was hard to believe that this big dumb animal had completely changed Rosaline's life. Sweet, quiet, passive Rosaline, who had been raised to do nothing other than be a perfect wife and mother and who was now running a multimillion-dollar business. Katie Lee gave herself more than a little credit in this department. If it had been up to Trevor, Rosaline would still be at home doing crosswords and needlepoint.

You find out what the rules are and you do your best to follow them, and then they change the rules on you in the middle of the game. It isn't fair, Katie Lee thought, you're raised to be one thing and then suddenly you're supposed to become something else entirely—in her case, one of those career moms she read about in magazines, the ones who take their children to the pediatrician on their lunch hour and schedule their business trips around their husband's calendar, the ones who, Katie Lee had a strong suspicion, didn't really exist. Or if such women did exist, they all worked on these magazines and wrote about themselves. You couldn't pull it off in the real world, you couldn't compete against men and be on a first-name basis with the salesclerks at Toys "Я" Us.

All her life she had believed the way to win her father's love and approval was to be as much like him as possible. Here she was, following in his footsteps, and suddenly he had turned around and said go back, go back, this path is not for you.

She watched Agamemnon dip his head to the grass. Pretty simple deal, she thought, the animal's bred to run fast and all he has to do is run fast. She'd been born to take over Hopewell, and she was going to do it with or without her father's approval. She could do it on her own. She would do it for herself. Eventually he'd see that she was right, and if he didn't, she couldn't spend her life trying to make him happy.

It was all Bobby's fault. That was what was upsetting her father most, that she'd made a bad marriage. She could add up on her fingers all the nights they'd spent in the same city since Christmas. He was her husband in name only, but after all, that was the best part, being Mrs. Bobby Vincent, that had been the main thing all along.

She would make a deal with her father. She'd find a way to keep Bobby in line if he let her do the Atlantic City project.

She would make a deal with Bobby. She would get off his case if he agreed to stay out of Lexington. He could do whatever he wanted, and she would pay for it, as long as her father didn't catch wind of his misbehavior.

She would make a deal with Bobby's father. They could have Junior all summer if they helped her with the zoning in Atlantic City. She would tell Henry she was staying with Junior at the Vincents and commuting (it was a reasonable drive) to Atlantic City.

"Let's Make a Deal"—probably the greatest game show that ever existed, Katie Lee thought as she drove back to her office. At the end of the program someone traded away a valuable prize or dollars for a trip to Hawaii or a set of dining room furniture or maybe just a big shaggy mutt and a carton of old-fashioned peanut brittle. You took a risk and you made your choice. Door number one: success and a career. Door number two: husband and family. Door number three: you lose—if you're lucky the shaggy dog can eat the peanut brittle.

Door number one, Katie Lee wants door number one. I've got a large silver safety pin in my handbag, I wore this crazy costume of bird feathers just for you, Monte, I've got a white handkerchief in the bottom of my coat pocket, and I'm ready to trade everything for what's behind door number one.

29

After she had dusted herself with a second coat of Chanel talc and changed into the pale-beige lace nightgown and rubbed a bit of pink rouge across her cheeks and given her hair twenty strong strokes and brushed her teeth and applied some flavorless lip balm and hung up her street clothes on the back of the bathroom door, Rosaline noticed her first gray hair.

There it was, springing up from her side part. She had no idea whether she was ahead or behind her genetic schedule: her father had been gray as long as she could remember, and her mother's carefully streaked ash blond was always teased up just enough to conceal the first few weeks of undyed growth. Rosaline twisted the hair around a finger and pulled.

Francisco would be up in a few minutes. She'd done the driving down to the Keys—his left arm was still a little stiff and he had trouble turning his neck—and in the bar of his brother's restaurant they'd watched Pleasant Colony win the Derby. Dinner was champagne and crabmeat. Francisco explained that in order to protect the supply of local seafood, the fishermen were allowed to remove only a limited amount from each crab they caught and then were supposed to toss the crabs back into the waters, where they would regenerate themselves. Then Rosaline asked how long it took until the crab was whole again, Francisco said he didn't know, probably not much time, for a crab's life was very short. Rosaline said, So it's possible that you could order crabmeat days or weeks or months apart and it could turn out that you're eating the same crab. It's a reasonable question, she said, why are you laughing so hard? Because you are always wondering about everything, he said, because I enjoy watching you wonder. He slipped her the key to one of the rooms upstairs and said he was going to take a short walk by himself along the beach.

Like an old-fashioned bride, that's what I am, Rosaline thought as she wrapped her first gray hair (along with her wedding band, which she'd removed in the bar to the opening strains of "My Old Kentucky Home") in a blue linen handkerchief and stowed it in the bottom of her suitcase. She turned down the covers and got into bed.

Francisco let himself in with a duplicate key and sat down on the edge of the bed.

"You look like the girl in the fairy tale," he said, pushing her hair back from her face.

"Which one is that?" Rosaline asked.

"The one where she needs the kiss of the prince. Sleeping Beauty. Snow White. I don't remember which."

"All the fairy tales sort of end the same way, don't they?" Rosaline asked.

"It seems that way," he said. "The ones they told us when we were children."

"Everyone learns the same ones," she said. It didn't matter where you were from, which country on what part of the map, whether you were rich or poor, whatever language you had been taught as a child, everyone had been fed the same dreams. She watched him undress. He was going about it awkwardly; perhaps he was nervous or perhaps it was the injuries, but he did not ask for help. In the darkness she could see no signs of the accident, the skin had not been broken, the scars were all on the inside.

He got into bed and they lay on their sides, facing each other.

"You are so beautiful," he said, "so delicate."

He kissed her. She felt his chest rise and fall against hers, they were lined up with a precision that spoke to her of fate rather than coincidence, it was as though they had been formed exactly and only for each other, their knees touching, his toes curling against hers.

"Open your eyes," he said. "There. Keep them open. There."

She was looking at him looking at her looking at him pull off her nightgown and fold it in quarters at the foot of the bed. It might have been the most marvelous thing she had ever seen a man do; there was time to be careful and tender of everything fragile, her spirit and his body, care would be taken, not a single thing would be left undone, unnoticed, unconsidered, unremembered.

He laid his lips against the curve of her jaw and moved a hand over her breasts, stopping only when she closed her eyes, starting again when she reopened them. She had the feeling of being trained, of learning to do what he wanted so that the pleasure would continue, until the lesson and its reward merged into one, and the doing became the pleasure. She traced the muscles of his shoulders, his arms, his chest, his waist, first with just her fingers, then with the full force and surface of her palm. It was something she had always known enough to do, it was something that pleased them and that showed them you were being pleased, but it was turning into something different, her hand was moving with a curiosity that was new to her. She wanted to know what he was like everywhere. She wanted to find the pulse point in his neck, to locate the cut of a bicep, to feel the hard press of his gut, count his ribs, measure the temperature of his skin.

He was telling her things, words in Spanish she did not understand, words in English, the same ones over and over, in the softest whisper, she was so beautiful, what everything felt like to him, her skin, her bones, her hair, her breath. He did not stop talking until she kissed him, her tongue seeking out every surface, she wanted to find a way to get beyond the surface, the skin, to feel the heft and tug, what was rough and what smooth, cool bone and pumping muscle, to find his warmest place. He ran his lips down her body, lifting his head to meet her gaze, to tell her everything he noticed. The scent of flowers. A taste of salt. There had always been some part of her brain that a man could not engage, that was thinking about the color of the wallpaper or a draft from the window or a child in a distant room, but now that part was forced to listen to him, to respond to his words, to concentrate completely on what he was doing, so that the talking became not a distraction but the way that he focused her every sense and thought exactly where he wanted it to be.

"Love," was the first word she uttered when he ran his tongue down either side of her. "Love, love, love," she said, as if it were his name. He circled her and laid his lips against her, murmuring, forming words she could not hear, she could feel only the hum and hiss and pull of the letters, the curl of his tongue, the breath in a consonant and the suck of a vowel. She saw how his hair fell as he moved his head from side to side, she saw the flutter of an eyelid, the knitting of his brow. She was changing, she was heating up, she was melting, she had softened from solid to liquid, soon she would evaporate into the warm air, she grasped his shoulder with shaking fingers to pull him up to her. She was ready.

"Tell me what you want," he said.

"I want you," she said. She was ready for him. She was waiting for him.

"Here I am," he said, setting his mouth to her again.

"Come here, come to me," she said, pulling on his shoulder.

"I want you this way," he said.

For a few moments she felt a clutch, fear's little tickle under the ribs, she was not sure what he wanted or even what she wanted—she was ready to move forward and he was insisting on pulling her back, pulling her back to him. He was waiting for something, she knew that, she thought she had given him the signal, but it had been the wrong signal. He took her hand from his shoulder and held it, lacing his fingers through hers.

"Don't move," he said. "Don't try. Don't rush. Don't think. Don't move." He continued, on and on and on, it was going to go on forever, there was nothing she could do, he didn't care, it was going to go on forever, she was going to receive this forever, and just when she had gotten used to this idea she felt herself seize up in pleasure, he continued on and she came again. Now she knew. After eight years, three lovers, two children, now she knew.

They made love once. When he came, she wrapped her arms around him and held him as hard as she could. Now she knew, now she knew some version of what it felt like for him, of what it felt like for anyone, for everyone, for all the people who were making love, who were rearranging their lives for it, flying across the oceans for it, counting the days to it. People married for it and divorced for it and drove all night for it and lied for it and begged for it and paid money for it, and Rosaline at last understood why.

Francisco had his head on her stomach and was staring at her neck.

"You have such a beautiful long neck," he said. "Like a swan."

"I read somewhere swans are extremely stupid. As birds go."

"A swan is only as smart as a swan needs to be," he said, "any more is useless. Listen. I want to have children with you."

"What?" she said.

"Don't you want more children? Two is not so many."

"Yes, I do, but, I don't know. There's so much to think about," she said. All our children will have bright-green eyes, she thought. "Children are hardly appropriate pillow talk."

"Appropriate. Pillow talk. Silly expression. Everything is pillow talk."

"What I meant was, I don't know if I can have a serious, sensible conversation now. Not the way I'm feeling."

"What way is that?"

"You know," she said, giggling.

"Now is the best time to talk about children. Bed is the best place to talk about everything serious. We will never be closer than we are here. You want to talk about children while we are driving in a car, worrying about the traffic, about whether the windshield wipers work if it rains, about how many miles till we get there? Or what— when we are having dinner? Is there a piece of bone in my fish, will the waiter hear us?"

"Maybe I just mean because it's so soon," Rosaline said. Twelve hours ago she'd been sitting in a bar, sipping champagne, slipping her wedding ring into her pocket.

"What will be different tomorrow or next week? What do you think is going to change from right now?"

She tilted her head sideways on the pillow. Nothing was going to change. She knew everything she needed to know. She loved this man. Just thinking about the last few hours made her gut wrench up inside, as though it were trying to wrap itself around her heart. She would never give him up.

"Nothing will change," she said.

"Promise me."

"Nothing will change. Nothing will ever ever change."

"Your husband will be very angry. We will have to find a smart lawyer, an expensive lawyer, to take care of your papers."

"My children," Rosaline said.

"They will like me," he said. "They are too young to know better."

"Sweet," she said.

"It will be an enormous scandal."

"Well," she said.

"Our children will be very short. They will have yellow skin and speak behind your back in Spanish."

"Sounds wonderful," she said.

"Your friends will say you are making the biggest mistake in your life. The newspapers will be snickering. Your mother will cry and your father will disown you. I am a terrible, terrible man. They will tell you all the stories of how terrible I am. That terrible, terrible Gomez. He is ruining your life."

"I don't care," Rosaline said. Her fairy tale was coming true. He gave her a kiss to send her to sleep.

30

When was the last time she had seen a lightning bug? If everyone hated drum solos, why did bands still do them? Had there been some year, somewhere in the early seventies, when people stopped using the word "horny"? Or was it just a word that people outgrew, did kids still say they were horny, and had December and her contemporaries simply outgrown it? Who bought all the dark-brown blush and lipstick she saw dangling from pressboards in the drugstore? If none of her friends admitted to voting for Reagan, how had he gotten elected? Was it still illegal in New Jersey to pass on the right?

December was wondering about these things, she had time to wonder about these things, because they were setting up between shots and there was nothing for her to do. It was another spy movie, and once again she was the beautiful villainess. But it's going to be totally different, the director was telling her, totally terrific, because of the music and the quick cuts and this location, in Alaska.

December adjusted the elastic thigh band of her dyed-mink bikini. Exactly what country am I supposed to be working for, she had asked the director. Is it a communist country? A fascist country? Is it technologically advanced, or are its people living in wooden huts, practicing ancient folk rituals involving dried berries and fragrant essences?

"Was I born evil, or have I been coerced into it?" she said.

"Why do you need to know," the director asked.

"It would help my motivation," she said, knowing he would roll his eyes (why did directors, in conveying their own emotions, use the hackneyed facial expressions of farce?) as soon as she said "motivation."

"It doesn't matter," he said. "You are acting in the best interest of your country. You believe you are a good person. Pretend your country is America. Pretend you are saving the world from nuclear war."

There was only one good thing to be said about shooting in Alaska the first week of June. It meant she didn't have to go to her fifth college reunion. Katie Lee would probably ask December to reimburse her for the nonrefundable down payment on the hotel room.

December calculated that if interest rates didn't fluctuate too much after this movie she would have enough income to live on comfortably for the next twenty-two years. In 2003 she would be forty-eight years old. She didn't know which possibility was more absurd: the year or the age. There was little point in providing for either. When this job was done she was going to take a long vacation. Tory's current tour would be over. It would be just the two of them — no band, no managers, no photographers, just she and Tory driving who knew where in the Mustang, which had just gotten a brand-new transmission. (Maybe they would drive to Vegas and get themselves married. Well, maybe not. Maybe definitely not.) A long, long vacation. Like how about for the rest of her life.

Marinda didn't know why they had to call them vacation days when it wasn't going to be any kind of vacation. It was just a trip to Cambridge for a few days. It was going to be like a family wedding: something you looked forward to for a long time and then when you got there you drank as much as you could to get yourself through it.

"How did you manage to wriggle out of yours?" she asked Schuyler as he watched her pack.

"It never occurred to me to go in the first place," he said.

"Smart move," she said. People were going to ask her what she was doing, and she'd watch their eyes glaze over as she tried to explain how surprisingly fulfilling her work in water distribution and tax certiorari had turned out to be. People were going to ask her whether she was married, and she'd watch them smile condescendingly as she said no, everything was fine just the way it was, did they remember Schuyler Smith, yes, he *did* used to go out with Rosaline, yes, Katie Lee too, well, it's a long and complicated story.

Maybe she would just lie once she got there. I work for the government, she would say, consulting, a lot of travel, I can't say exactly where. Then she'd wink. There's a man, he's in government too, and then she'd wink again.

"Which sweater?" she asked, holding up one in lilac cotton and one in navy silk.

"They're both great," Schuyler said. "Take both."

"I can't, not enough room."

"That pink one," Schuyler said, though it made no difference to him.

"It's not pink, it's lilac."

"Is that the same as lavender?"

"Lilac has more blue in it."

"What's heliotrope, then?"

"A euphemism for lilac."

"How about mauve?"

"Mauve is more like rose."

"I say it's pink and I say to hell with it," Schuyler said. "You don't have to go if you don't want to."

"Katie Lee's already paid for the rooms," she said. Marinda wondered if the real reason she wanted to go was to check out December, whom she hadn't seen in over a year and whom Schuyler never mentioned. Still. During his last trip to California she'd called his hotel room a few times late at night and gotten no answer. She didn't have any proof of anything. She scanned the long-distance pages of their telephone bills for any unfamiliar cities where December might have stopped for a shoot or as part of her work for Katie Lee. When Schuyler answered the telephone she listened carefully to see if he might be talking to someone other than who he said it was, to see if "No rain this week" really meant "I can't talk, Marinda is in the room" and "We sold five head at auction" meant "I love you madly and always will." There was nothing in the mail. Still. It was just a feeling. He could be calling her from the post office or a bar or from a phone booth along the highway. She knew he wasn't calling December from Nelson's because the last time Marinda was there she'd also checked Nelson's telephone bills on an extended trip to the upstairs bathroom.

She just couldn't stand December being out there, anywhere, anywhere at all on the face of the earth.

"Well, we wouldn't want to waste Katie Lee's hard-earned money," Schuyler said. He guessed December might be there. He knew better than to bring up her name. He hadn't talked to her in years, not since the sorry night he'd spent on her living room couch, but with Marinda there was no such thing as a casual conversation about December Dunne. He'd seen her face when Nelson or some other unsuspecting friend had brought up December's name: you went to school with *her*, she was your *roommate*, are you still in touch.

When he saw her tense up like that he wanted to fold her in his arms and say, don't worry, silly girl, I would never do anything to hurt you, all the hurting is over. He had changed so much in the year they had been together; he had relaxed into the simplicity of setting up house with a beautiful woman who loved him, who took care of him, who, if he came home one night and said, honey, I just took my shotgun up to a rooftop and showered bullets on helpless schoolchildren, she would say, honey, how awful for you, how terrible you must feel, come here and let me give you a hug, come here and let me make you feel better.

He wanted to move on to the next phase of his life, away from the ache and the hungriness, on to what was supposed to come next: building a life, a family, and knowing how to sit back and enjoy what you'd built. Marinda understood that, without rushing him, without expecting anything he was not yet ready to give. She made everything easy. Sometimes he sat up in bed at night and asked himself: when was the last time we had a conversation—yesterday, the day before that—and what was it about? Then he realized it didn't matter. He was understood. He would lie down and fall asleep. When he woke up again she'd be sitting on the edge of the bed with a friendly smile and a hot cup of coffee.

"It should be fun," Schuyler said. "I wish I'd gone to mine."

"No it won't and no you don't," she said. She thought this might be the first trip in ten years that she wasn't going to pack her diaphragm for.

Schuyler opened the top drawer of "his" dresser and pulled something out from underneath a pile of thick gray wool socks.

"Here. I got you something to wear," he said.

Marinda took the dark-blue velvet box. Inside, a small emerald cut diamond in an antique platinum setting. She knew that whatever she said next he would remember till the day he died, but she couldn't think of a single thing to say. She certainly wasn't leaving now, she wasn't going anywhere, she was going to stay right here and give him the most wonderful weekend of his life.

"This is the part where I get down on my knees and tell you I love you and can't live without you and want to spend the rest of my life with you," Schuyler said, lowering one leg into a kneel.

She got down on the floor with him and laid her head against his chest.

"Is that a yes?" he asked.

"Yes," she said. "I'm going to make you the happiest man who ever walked the face of the earth."

"I already am," he whispered into her ear, "I already am."

Katie Lee was about to leave for Newark Airport when she got the call that Bobby had been in a car accident, no, don't worry, nothing serious, a broken arm and a few cuts is all, he just got out of ER at Riverside.

She cursed her husband all the way to the hospital. Twenty more minutes and they wouldn't have been able to reach her until tomorrow morning. Her suitcase was lying across the backseat. She'd ordered up a large arrangement from the hotel florist. It was just like him, as usual, to interfere with one of her rare opportunities to have a good time.

She parked her car in a space reserved for visiting surgeons, removed her tape deck and laid it under the front seat, slid the sign that said *No radio* into the window on the driver's side, picked up her suitcase, activated the burglar alarm, and locked the car door behind her within the ten-second security window. *BMW stands for Break My Window*—that's what the repairman told her the fourth time she'd brought in the cream-colored sedan for new cylinders.

She identified herself at the front desk, trying to adjust the tone of her voice so that it would be appropriate to both a receptionist and a nurse, for the woman in pale blue wore no name tag.

"Room 802," the woman said, and then she pointed at Katie Lee's suitcase. "Oh, I'm sorry, but you can't. Hospital policy."

"It's just clothing, not a bomb," Katie Lee said.

"Well, I know that. Please don't get upset."

"I'm not upset."

"Anyone would be upset if their husband got in a car crash."

"*Her* husband, *her* husband," Katie Lee corrected.

"He's not your husband?" the woman asked.

"Of course he is."

"Well, it doesn't matter. You can't stay overnight in his room."

"Did I ask to stay overnight in his room?" Katie Lee said.

"Well, it isn't a bomb in your suitcase. Lots of wives want to sleep over while their husbands are here, they think it will help the men get better soon, but really, what the patient needs most is rest."

"Why would I want to stay more than fifteen minutes in this

dump?" Katie Lee said, grabbing the visitor's pass out of the woman's hand. She had never heard a more ridiculous idea. She was relieved to find she had the elevator to herself—you could catch something awful just breathing the air in places like this—and when she found Bobby he was sitting up in bed watching Rocky and Bullwinkle cartoons.

"Hello, sweetheart," she said, leaning over and giving him a kiss on the forehead.

"Two point oh," he said.

"What?"

"I registered two point oh. That's nearly twice the legal limit. I thought I should tell you before they did." He turned up the volume with the remote. He had the kind of good looks that were improved by the suggestion of bad times. Two days' growth lent a hardness, an implication of danger, to the childish curve of his mouth. His jet black hair, uncombed, curled in all directions, as though someone had just run her fingers through it.

"My goodness," Katie Lee said, "what were you drinking?"

"Alcohol. Ha ha. Bourbon. Thought that would amuse you. The car was totaled."

"I'll call the insurance company. And a lawyer, do you need a lawyer?"

"I am a lawyer, in case you forgot. Not necessary, they were absolute gentlemen as soon as I pulled out my license. Aren't you going to ask me how I am?"

"They said you were fine," Katie Lee said. Sometimes it was a shock, to be reminded of just how handsome Bobby could be. He was surely the handsomest man in the hospital. She didn't want to think about what the nurses did here, besides tuck the patients in at night. "Just some cuts and a broken arm," she said. "Does it hurt?"

"Off the record or on the record?"

"What's the difference?"

"Off the record, don't worry, I'm a little sore is all and would probably be in the middle of a monster hangover if they hadn't given me such mega-painkillers."

"On the record?"

"Very bad. Very bad. Renewable prescription, please."

"Bobby, you're terrible. You should be spanked."

"You volunteering for the job?"

"Naughty boy. I was supposed to go to my college reunion. I was all packed and everything."

He turned away. "I don't really need you here. You can still go if you want," he said in a soft voice.

"No, I can't," she said. It wouldn't look right. She sighed. "When do they let you out of here?"

"Soon. It's not such a bad deal here, really. Quiet. Good place to think."

"You've only been here a few hours, Mr. Serious-head, you'll get the jimmy-jammies by tomorrow morning. You'll be begging me to take you home."

"Yeah, well, we have to talk about that," Bobby said. "I don't want to go home."

"Where do you want to go?"

"Someplace. Anywhere. I want to be by myself for a while. I think —I think I've got some thinking to do."

"That was three 'think's in one sentence."

"Well, I've got some catching up to do."

"Bobby, you have a broken arm. You need someone to take care of you," Katie Lee said, hoping that one of the maids would agree to cancel her vacation at the last minute so that the other help wouldn't complain about putting in extra hours.

"It's not such a big deal."

"Oh, honestly. Sometimes you are so dumb, it makes me scream."

"Look, I just can't face everybody right now. You know, I realized I could have been killed in that car. Or killed somebody else. Or both. Because I was drunk on my ass in the middle of the afternoon."

"We can get you help. You know I've wanted you to get help for a long time," Katie Lee said. Wasn't that the way, she thought, people never give you credit for your ideas, they just take them and pretend they made them up themselves. She'd tried to make Bobby go to a therapist back in Lexington. He'd said he didn't need one.

"That was then. This is now," Bobby said. "It's not the same when other people want you to do it. You have to do it yourself. Katie Lee, I'm fucking up my life here, it's the only one I've got, I want to get myself together before it's too late."

"I'll help you, sweetheart. That's what wives do best."

"It's not like that."

"What isn't like that."

"You don't get it, do you."

"Get what? I'm trying to understand what you're saying."

"Katie Lee, I've got a lot of problems. And one of them is our marriage."

"Why don't you just come out and say it."

"Say what?"

"Say it. Say I'm driving you to drink. Say it's all my fault. I make you do all these awful things. If you hadn't married me your life would be just one big bowl of Georgia peaches right now."

Cherries, cherries, Bobby thought.

"Say it," Katie Lee continued. "Say it, say it, say it."

"Katie Lee. Listen to me. I want out. I'm leaving."

"You're Catholic. You can't."

"Wake up. You can't make me stay married to you."

"Oh yes I can. You ever want to see your kid again? You want me to keep my mouth shut about all your sleazy slimy whoring around, every slut with two teeth in her head between here and Pensacola, you want me to keep quiet about all those drugs you've been taking, you think I'm going to let some crazy drug fiend get near my kid? You want to get home and find more than ten cents in your bank account? Damn straight I can make you stay married to me. Anyone around here does any divorcing, it's going to be me."

"So you divorce me. Say anything you want. Take anything you want."

"I don't want to divorce you," Katie Lee said. "You can just forget about *me* divorcing *you*."

"Why do you want to stay married to someone who doesn't love you?"

"Oh please, spare me the drama. You don't know who you love or what you want. You've ruined your own life, but I'll be damned if I let you ruin mine and Junior's," she said. I have two children, she thought, Junior and this one right here, this one watching pictures of a moose and a squirrel and something called a dinkleberry.

"There's no point in talking to you," Bobby said, closing his eyes. Arguing with Katie Lee was bad enough, but arguing with Katie Lee sober was excruciating.

"And there's no point in talking to *you*," Katie Lee said, picking up her suitcase, thinking how much she hated carrying her own luggage. In the elevator were a Pakistani dressed in white tie and a blond girl dragging a teddy bear back and forth along the handrail. It was making her crazy, this elevator was so slow, and the girl was just pulling her toy that way to annoy her.

"You better be careful with that bear," Katie Lee said. The Pakistani took a step closer to the fire alarm button. "You play with him that way, someone might just have to take him away from you."

The girl began to cry. The Pakistani put on a pair of gold-rimmed sunglasses. Katie Lee was the first one out of the elevator. When she got to her parking space, someone who actually may have been a visiting surgeon was leaning on the hood of her car, writing something on a piece of shirt cardboard.

"You're in my way," Katie Lee said, unlocking her door and starting her engine before the man had a chance to register her presence. She pulled back in reverse. As she left the lot, her security alarm went off, and it wailed like an ambulance until she punched in her four-digit protection code. The piece of gray cardboard was still sitting on the hood of her car. *Some people think they can* was as far as the man had gotten before being interrupted by Katie Lee.

"How long has this, this, I can't even say it. How long has this been going on," Trevor asked. They were sitting catty-corner at the dining room table. The cook had gone home and the nanny, like the children, had gone to bed.

"Just a few weeks," Rosaline said. It was true, but it felt like a lie.

"How sure can you be after just a few weeks," Trevor said.

"I'm sure," Rosaline said. She was shocked by his calm. She didn't know what she had expected—that he would scream, that he would curse, that he would cry, that he would hit her. But he was the same old Trevor: considered, logical, trying to do the right thing.

"This has happened before," he said.

"No, it hasn't," she said. How dare he accuse me of having affairs, she thought, and then she caught herself. Having an affair—that's all he thought it was. That's what he meant: it had happened before, a wife cheating on her husband, he was telling her that she wasn't special, that Francisco wasn't special, that the thrill of it would wear off, that he expected it to wear off, and that he expected to be waiting for her when it did.

"It has. I never dreamed it would happen to us, though," he said.

Us. There is no more us. He was wearing a brown cashmere cardigan over the shirt and tie he'd worn to the office that morning. He seemed suddenly ridiculous to her, a man not quite thirty wearing an old man's clothes, and his being ridiculous filled her with love for a moment, just long enough for her to remember all the silly things about him that she would miss. How he always sent her carnations, even though she didn't really like carnations very much, because he knew when he got home she would say, Trev, you're the best, and tell him he was so romantic, and pluck a flower from the bouquet for him to wear in his buttonhole, and he couldn't stand wearing anything other than a carnation. How he kept crushed cloves in the glove compartment of his car so that when they stopped at a gas station they could hold the little satchels of spice (he sent away through the mail to a place that sold equipment for making tea) under the children's noses so they wouldn't get sick on the fumes. How he always wore pajamas to bed and sometimes, after making love, would dress himself again but in a different, more brightly colored pair. How he followed the exercises suggested in a worn volume published by the Canadian Air Force, how he had made her promise that they would have the exact same marvelous dinner with the exact same marvelous people every New Year's Eve for the rest of their lives, how he still called all his friends by their boarding school nicknames, how he managed to waltz to a four count, how he refused to tell anyone, even her, how he voted in national elections. The confidential ballot is the cornerstone of democracy, he said. She knew all his phrases, all his tastes, all his dislikes, all his jokes.

He was telling her not to rush into anything.

She was telling him that there was no point in waiting, she wouldn't change her mind.

What he wasn't telling her: she was breaking his heart. She was the only girl he had ever loved. Still, it wouldn't do to get all weepy. A woman didn't like a man who showed weakness. She'd feel sorry for him, that was all. Nothing that would help his case.

What she wasn't telling him: that it was he who had become the other man. In the last month, in the time she had spent with him (it had been easy to avoid sex, he never pushed her) she had felt that she was cheating on Francisco, that the only deception lay in her pretending to be Trevor's wife. She hoped that by setting Trevor free she would make it possible for him to find someone who could love him better, he would be able to have for himself what she had with Francisco. If he found it, she would cheer him. If he never did, would it prove that he was some kind of hopeless case? Or that she had dealt him an irreparable blow?

It was Trevor who raised the practical questions first. The dissolution of their marriage involved intricate trusts, land and houses and horses and paintings and carpets and all sorts of what Trevor referred to as "tangible assets"; it wouldn't just be a divorce, it was something complex and corporate.

"I haven't really thought about a lawyer," Rosaline said.

"Well, Davis will handle it for you of course," Trevor said.

"Oh, let's leave him out of it," she said. Davis had taken care of her family's business for so long he was nearly a relation. And retaining Davis seemed like an unfair advantage: his taking her on would imply a moral right she didn't believe she deserved.

"No, no, I insist. It wouldn't look proper otherwise. We're not going to have one of those awful messy divorces, are we?"

"All divorces are awful," Rosaline said.

"Well. As civilized as a divorce can be. Don't worry about me. It's not as though we're never going to speak to each other again, is it?"

"Of course not. I'll bring the children here as much as you want."

"Bring them here? Won't you be staying here?"

"Where will you go?" she asked.

"Where would you go?" he said.

"I don't know. Where am I supposed to go?" she said, and she nearly giggled. It was impossible, she would always be asking him what she was supposed to do.

And he always knew. "The woman is supposed to stay in the house. Don't want to uproot the children."

"Where are you supposed to go?"

"I'm supposed to take an apartment at the Carlyle, I say it's just temporary, although I believe it's acceptable for me to do this for as long as five years, however long it takes, until I find another place."

Until you find another wife is what you mean, Rosaline thought. Of course Trevor would remarry. Why wouldn't he remarry? He'll remarry in a snap.

"The Carlyle is close, so it will be easy about the children. I'm supposed to take some of the paintings with me and a favorite old chair but none of the wedding presents."

Rules for everything, Rosaline thought. People like us even have rules about how to break rules. Trevor laid out his plans for her: he would be sleeping in a guest room for a week, which would give them time to share the news with their friends and families, and then he would move to the hotel. She and the children should arrange to be out of town when he left.

"What are you going to say? In the papers?" Rosaline asked.

"The last thing either of us will do is talk to the papers," Trevor said.

"I meant you have to say something in the papers, like mental cruelty, or incompatability, something for the legal record."

"I won't say anything, darling. You must sue me."

"How can I possibly sue you? On what grounds?"

"The woman always asks the man for a divorce. Always. A gentleman grants it without protest or complaint. If I were to divorce you, people would think, well—I just couldn't."

"But you haven't done a thing," Rosaline said.

"No need to make that public, darling," he said. "It's the one thing I ask of you. Davis will know how to word it. *You* must sue *me*."

"This is ridiculous," Rosaline said. "It's all meaningless convention."

Trevor stood up at last. "It may well be ridiculous, but it certainly isn't meaningless. Do you think I'm enjoying this? Do you think this is easy for me? If we didn't have conventions we'd be screaming and yelling and going at each other like animals, like the rest of the world does."

"You're shouting at me."

"I'm sorry."

"Don't be sorry. I deserve it. I've been waiting for it. It's rather a relief, actually."

He dropped his voice again. "I'd like to be alone for a while."

She stood up. He had his back to her. Leaving the room without giving him a good-night kiss was like going to Mass without Communion.

When she had left he sat down, holding his head in his hands. He would never be able to change her mind—he had seen that from the first moment—but he'd had to try, he was the kind of man who could always say he'd given it his best efforts.

She was the most wonderful thing that had ever happened to him. She was special in a thousand ways he would never find again. In a thousand ways he probably didn't deserve, she probably thought he didn't notice or appreciate, because he wasn't like her, he didn't have that gift, he could love it in her, but he would never possess it himself. So she'd gone off and found someone who did. A scandal. He would be in the middle of a scandal. It would be an opportunity, he knew, to show the world what he was made of. He wished he were dead.

All his life he had felt as though he were swimming in choppy ocean waters. It was tough work staying afloat, but he was confident, he knew he was a strong swimmer, he knew to find a point on the shore and keep swimming toward it, to kick, to breathe, to keep the rhythm. When Rosaline came along she was like a tiny figure in a wooden dinghy, a little girl in an oversized yellow rain slicker tossing him a rope with a bright-orange life preserver at the end of it. He still had the life preserver, but when the storm came she'd let go of her end of the rope. He was floating, without her, in the middle of nowhere. He'd lost his sense of direction. He almost wished she'd left him with nothing, that he could relax and go under; it was widely believed that a drowning man experienced a tremendous euphoria in the moments preceding death.

But he would keep kicking, he would go on. There was so much to do. Arrangements. Reservations. Telephone calls. Meetings. Divorce would keep him a very busy man. Too busy to feel sorry for himself. Too busy to think too hard. Thinking was the worst thing he could possibly do right now. He laid his head against the cool oiled grain of the mahogany table and wept.

31

*S*chuyler had returned to Montana just after Christmas. Marinda had been amazed at her own family: now that she was getting married to someone they approved of, had officially announced a date of Valentine's Day, the fourteenth of February 1982, now that she had the ring—the rock—her family was treating her rather well. It was nice of course, but she suspected that it also made Schuyler wonder if she hadn't been exaggerating some of her earlier complaints.

She'd quit her job, and her father teased her about it, "such a modern girl, you were always giving us such a hard time, and now look at you. Your mother will be proud." "But I'll have plenty to do," Marinda had said, "it takes a huge amount of work to put together a wedding in less than two months." The invitations were ordered and would arrive in a few days. One of Marinda's aunts had taken courses in calligraphy and would help her address them so that they could all go out just after New Year's. Marinda had picked out stamps with drawings of state birds on them. It would be fun to decide which stamp to use on whose invitation: Kentucky for Katie Lee, Montana for Nelson, but each sheet came with only one New York and one New Jersey. Someone less favored would get stuck with Idaho or West Virginia or Rhode Island.

She'd driven to New York with her mother to order fabric for the wedding dress, ivory velvet with pearl beading around the sweetheart neckline; she was going to sew it herself, a family tradition. Where did I learn these things, Marinda asked herself, why was I ever paying attention to this? She didn't remember learning how to bead velvet or which fabrics should be ironed through handkerchiefs on the wrong side or that you could fix an oversalted soup by throwing a potato into it or that you could remove blood from cloth with cool water only—anything else would leave a permanent stain. Some part of her had been memorizing all these things. The part of her that stayed awake at night trying to decide what music she should walk down the aisle to and how it should be played.

On the last day of the year Marinda took out the blank vellum page Schuyler had given her at Christmas and began to plan her contribution to his family's album. After a breakfast of half a grapefruit and one slice of salt-free Melba toast she took a flashlight up to the large unfinished attic, a huge, disorganized open storage space of corrugated cardboard cartons, old wooden filing cabinets, standing metal closets, shoe boxes, bookcases, and a few pieces of discarded furniture. Everything was here: chiffon evening gowns from the sixties and cotton bathing suits from the forties reeking of mothballs, a set of imported china both too ugly and too valuable for everyday use, old legal files that hadn't made the move when the family firm expanded its offices into a modern glass building just off the Parkway, a round hatbox from Margaret's of Boston in which all her cousins' baby teeth had been saved in brown plastic prescription bottles, Bobby's swimming trophies, photographs, child-sized baseball mitts, a broken ironing board.

Marinda wiped the dust from her hands and pulled the masking tape off a packing carton that had her name on it. Lying on top, her head turned at a gruesome angle, was Marinda's Barbie Doll, dressed up in a pink satin gown with a white fake-fur stole. A book no bigger than a passport, a calorie counter she'd picked up at Woolworth's when she was thirteen. Letters from Peter. A pair of white go-go boots with red, blue, and yellow patent leather rectangles appliquéd to the front. A troll doll with bright-green hair and amber eyes. Articles she'd written for her high school newspaper. A photograph of Marinda marching against the Vietnam War—wearing turquoise and silver jewelry, her right hand raised in a fist, her left hand clutching a white kitchen candle. This will be great for the album, she thought, though the picture was really a lie: Marinda had marched only once, mostly because all her friends were doing it and it was an excuse to get out of a family excursion to the seashore.

Next she opened a box of her grandfather's papers. She could hardly remember him, but she recalled the crowd that had attended his funeral, and she knew there would be something here—a letter from the governor, an article about a case he'd won—that would let Schuyler know she came from a family he could be proud of.

Sagamore, Ava, 1962–64 was the first file she found. A woman had murdered her sister, a three hundred-pound soft-drink distributor improbably named Bootsie, by bludgeoning her repeatedly about the head with a not-so-blunt heavy object: a hubcap from her Chrysler Imperial. She had then replaced the hubcap and had driven the car for months while the police tore up her house in search of the murder weapon. Marinda's grandfather had gotten her acquitted on a technicality involving the manner in which the police had transcribed her confession.

Crichton v. *Martin, June 1934–October 1942* was next, a suit against a pension fund represented by her grandfather, involving a woman who had told her employer her true age but presented herself as much younger to the man she had married. By the time the courts resolved in precisely what year she was entitled to retirement benefits the woman was dead and her husband had remarried.

Marinda took a sip of cold coffee and set the Styrofoam cup on top of a bookcase full of an outdated set of the *Book of Knowledge.* Somewhere among all these cartons and files there had to be something presentable about the Vincents, just enough to fill one page of an album, just enough to make sure Schuyler knew that whatever it was he'd heard, whatever he'd learned when he was doing that piece on organized crime, the Vincents were basically fine people, the good outweighed the bad, Schuyler would not be marrying into a family that would embarrass him, that he would someday be ashamed of.

Triplister Industries, 1946–48. A builder had managed, with her grandfather's help, to violate nearly every provision of the construction code. In the lower left-hand corner of a few carbons of transmittal letters attached to applications for variances were three- or four-digit numbers penciled in by hand. They could have meant anything: part of a forgotten filing system, a code for how much was owed the bookie, or the amount the variance was going to cost.

She felt a little light-headed (who wouldn't, she thought, on eight hundred calories a day) and took another sip. The coffee got sweeter as it reached the bottom of the cup—it was the one thing she hadn't given up this time, the sugar in her coffee. The attic was overheated and smelled of insecticide. Marinda stood up, did some stretching exercises, and opened the one window that hadn't been painted over. She watched Bobby brush the snow off his car. Katie Lee had gone back to Kentucky. All during Christmas they had taken turns pulling her aside, trying to enlist her support: Bobby wanted a divorce, and Katie Lee refused absolutely. Bobby's parents were on Katie Lee's side—they'd become awfully fond of Katie Lee over the summer. It was all too boring for words.

Schuyler hadn't called her in four days. It made her depressed and cranky: all she wanted to do was sit around eating double chocolate-chip ice cream and Heath bars and peanut M&Ms. That was the problem with choosing velvet for a wedding dress: the old seams showed if you let them out. This diet was going to kill her, but it was part of the program to be absolutely stunningly gorgeously beautiful on her wedding day. She drank eight glasses of water daily and jogged around the pond for half an hour four times a week. At night she coated her hair with mineral oil and her body with Vaseline, a regimen Doris Day had said was responsible for her glowing good looks during the height of her popularity.

Getting married made her want to immerse herself in women's magazines full of advice. She tested herself in a quiz that told her whether she was a romantic, a classic, a modern, or a natural. She learned about the secret lives of hairdressers. She found out you could prepare your own facial soufflé from packets of frozen garden vegetables. Broccoli, spinach, and green peas for dry skin. Orange and yellow vegetables for oily. Pearl onions and lima beans for combination.

A woman had written to a magazine saying that now that she was engaged, her fiancé seemed to be paying less attention to her than usual. She had tried talking to him about it (every letter made this clear—*I tried talking to him about it*—because they knew from these magazines that this was the first line of defense or perhaps because they didn't want the advice columnist to respond *Try talking about it*), but he denied everything. The magazine told her this was not unusual. Many men asserted their independence in the final months before marriage. They didn't call when they had said they would. They stayed out late. They looked up old girlfriends in their high school yearbooks and called to see if they were still around. It was just their way.

That was all Schuyler was doing, Marinda thought—just his last dash at bachelorhood. Staying out late, drinking with Nelson and the boys. What kind of trouble could he get into in one week?

Oh, just about every kind of trouble there was. A particular kind of trouble that began with the letter *D*. Marinda thought she understood how you could hate someone enough to murder them, hate them so much you just reached for the first available weapon, even a hubcap. She didn't actually want to kill December, she just wanted to render her powerless, to kill what she thought existed between December and the man she loved, to discredit December somehow in his eyes, make him see December for what she was: unworthy, unloving, selfish, beneath him, a girl whose page in his family album would hold nothing but a long list of lovers and star billing in some of the worst movies ever made.

Marinda moved on to the file cabinets. She ran through *B. Leonard v. C. Leonard, Springwood Toy Company, Mercy Hospital Association, The Lucy Rush Trust.*

In a bottom drawer was a folder marked *Background* containing newspaper clippings with little notes from her grandfather attached to them. Something about an inventor whom he might be able to use as a witness in a patent case. An article about a police department that used a Gypsy fortune-teller to locate corpses. A front-page spread with a big picture of a man who looked just like December.

Who looked just like December. It was uncanny. Marinda read, the yellowed newsprint falling apart in her hands, about the murders, the investigation, the trial, the victims, she turned over the page and found photographs of the victims, their houses, the murderer smiling at the camera—he looked so innocent they nicknamed him the Choirboy Killer—his wife, his little girl. Gloria. December. Of course.

December said she'd moved around a lot as a child. Willie Dunne at some point had adopted her. Marinda wanted to know for sure, and she wanted to know fast. There would have to be records somewhere, some kind of proof, people just couldn't disappear and reappear with new identities, though some of it might be confidential, sealed up by the courts.

Her father would know how to get it for her. People owed him favors—people who had access to sealed records, who could make copies for her, who would do it tonight if necessary, if her father asked for her.

Marinda stood up and drank the sugary last of her coffee. Her hands were streaked with dirt. Two things occurred to her. That when she got married she would still retain her maiden name. And that the newspapers in California wouldn't close until three hours after those in New York.

"Whatever you do, don't answer the telephone," Alex told December.

"All right."

"If I call you, I'll let the phone ring once, hang up, and then call you back in exactly two minutes. Otherwise don't even touch the telephone."

"All right."

"And whatever you do, don't answer the door. Don't even look out the window. Don't be upset if you see people camping out on your front lawn. They'll say they're sick, there's an emergency, they need to use the telephone, they need to use the bathroom. You mustn't let them in. You mustn't even speak to them."

"All right."

"Katie Lee is canceling your contract, you know. She says the publicity about your father has ruined her whole campaign. She says she has a file folder three inches thick with memoranda from Louise about what she termed 'inappropriate episodes.' I don't think we're going to be able to fight her on this."

"All right," December said. The newspapers would say she was unavailable for comment. Alex was holed up in his office fielding telephone calls, offering carefully worded statements, convincing Gloria that inviting the tabloid photographers in for a tour of her house was not the cleverest thing to do.

"When does Tory get back?" Alex asked.

"In a couple of hours. They left Philadelphia at two."

"It shouldn't take nine hours to fly in from Philadelphia," Alex said.

"They have to change planes twice. It's New Year's Eve. Everything's all booked up."

"Have him call me when he gets in."

"All right."

"You can hold up till then, can't you? Promise me you can."

"All right.

"You know I'll forever love you madly. Whoever you are."

"I'm the same person I always was," December said, hanging up the telephone.

She got a beer out of the refrigerator. Here it was, the moment she'd been preparing for all her life, and now that it was here she had no idea what she was going to do. In two hours Tory would be here. One step at a time. She only had to worry about how to get through the next two hours.

She took a scalding hot shower, balancing a fresh beer on the plastic mesh shampoo rack. She rubbed herself down with baby oil and then baby powder and put on some light-pink cotton underwear, a pink T-shirt, and a pair of bleached-out blue jeans.

She found an old black-and-white movie on television, something reassuring with Jimmy Stewart in it, and commercials for discount carpet warehouses and friendly neighborhood car dealerships. She

turned down the sound during the news break. There was footage of
the president's wife waving to reporters. A bearded actor wearing a
button that said FRIENDS DON'T LET FRIENDS DRIVE DRUNK. A weather
chart. A plane in flames on a hill overlooking a desert. A map of Las
Vegas with a flashing red flag on it. A man with a microphone standing in front of the burning plane. An old picture of Tory. The man
with a microphone talking to a firefighter who was shaking his head.
Another picture of Tory, this one more recent.

She turned up the sound in time to catch the last thirty seconds of
the broadcast, in which the announcer listed by name who, along
with Tory, had been killed in the crash, and said that the cause of the
accident was being investigated, that the station management
wished its viewers a Happy New Year, and now, the heartwarming
conclusion of *It's a Wonderful Life.*

The Crossroads Café was neither a café nor located at a crossroads. It
was a run-down wood frame rock-and-roll joint halfway down a street
that dead-ended into a narrow creek and, beyond that, railroad tracks.
In between sets you could sometimes hear the trains go by. Tory had
played in the house band before he got his first record contract and still
showed up a couple of times a year on the odd empty weekday night,
sometimes joining a local cover band for its last set of the night.

His picture was hung prominently over the bar in the special spot
that, where December was from, was usually reserved for Frank Sinatra.
The stalls in the women's bathroom were covered with graffiti, a call
and response of felt-tip pens, mostly about Tory. When he was here,
people lined up at the public telephone to alert their fellow followers, to
describe what he was wearing, what he was drinking: *yes, he pays for his
drinks himself, no, she's not with him, I think he's gonna play, I think
he's gonna play.* When he wasn't, people pretended it didn't matter and
danced to his songs, featured heavily in the nightly mix, and bought
Crossroads Café souvenirs at the coat-check window and stuck quarters
in a foosball game that had two of its grips missing.

By the time December got there, the parking lot had turned into a
vast spontaneous wake, a tailgate party of fans who'd dressed up and
taken off for New Year's Eve parties and then, hearing the news on
the radio, had headed here instead. A dozen blaster boxes sat on car
roofs, all tuned to the same FM station that was playing commercial-
free sets from Tory's albums. Some people were crying. Some people
were dancing. Some people were crying and dancing. Others sat si-

lently in their cars, drinking out of translucent plastic cups and bottles wrapped in paper bags. A girl in a Red Album tour jacket wandered from car to car, sobbing, asking people to sign a condolence poster made of oaktag that she was planning to send to Tory's mother. Players from the local high school football team had shown up fully suited and were ramming into each other, over and over, at the edge of the creek. Two uniformed officers leaned against a police van, arms folded, their headlights shining into the crowd, smoking cigarettes and watching for signs of a possible disturbance.

A bartender came out and set a tin of ice at the edge of the lot. When he recognized December he gave her a hug, and though she couldn't remember his name, wasn't sure if she had ever met him, she hugged him back and let him lead her inside, where those who had arrived first on the scene were taking advantage of the open bar. She joined him behind the counter. The disk jockey was playing the bootleg tapes of live performances that he had been pretending for years he didn't possess.

If it hadn't been so noisy, if she hadn't been so busy pouring drinks, she might have noticed how drunk she'd become. She sloshed cheap Scotch over the countertop, she started cigarettes and then abandoned them half smoked in half a dozen ashtrays, she kissed a boy whose face was streaked with tears, she lost her shoes among the empty beer cans and cut her feet on the broken glass. But December didn't care, all she wanted was not to have to be alone. Tomorrow she would be alone, and the day after, and the day after that. For the first time in her life she knew she was going to be alone for a long, long time. And for the first time in her life she was scared.

When she could no longer stand up, the bartender carried her to a back room and placed her on a pile of paint-stained dropcloths, where she covered her face with a dish towel and passed out to the sound of firecrackers and people singing "Auld Lang Syne." When she woke up it was light out, and she was twenty-seven years old.

"Do I hear a party?" Rosaline asked, unclipping an earring so it wouldn't clack against the handset.

"Sort of," Schuyler said. "Nelson found some cross-country skis in the attic, and we're all going to have a try on them at midnight. I'll probably spend New Year's wrapping turned ankles in Ace bandages. My cousin Teddy came out with the little woman."

"What's she like?" Rosaline asked, giving Francisco a smile as he brought her a glass of champagne. The children had been tucked into sleeping bags at the foot of the Christmas tree, which Rosaline had promised to keep lit all night long. Something Trevor would never have allowed, she thought. He would hear about it when he came visiting tomorrow after Francisco had left for the track and would make some comment about safety hazards and electrical wires.

"Her name is Joan, and she's just like Teddy's mother, but we're all too polite to mention the resemblance."

"Men will be like that," Rosaline said.

"Some men."

"Well, I don't suppose you've been watching television?"

"No."

"Well, Katie Lee just called. December's in some sort of jam."

"Is she," Schuyler said, taking the telephone into the quietest corner of the room.

"I don't know why, I thought she might have called you."

"I haven't talked to Katie Lee since Christmas," Schuyler said. "We're going to be related, if there's such a thing as cousins-in-law."

"It's twice removed, I think," Rosaline said. "Anyway, I didn't mean Katie Lee, I meant December."

"I haven't talked to December in a long time," he said. A little over four years, though it felt like longer; 1977 seemed a century away.

"Just this silly feeling I had," Rosaline said. "It will be all over the papers tomorrow. Do you remember—I mean, I had completely forgotten, but apparently she was adopted?"

"I remember," he said. *I remember everything,* he thought.

And Rosaline repeated to him the story as she'd heard it first from Katie Lee and then from television reports and the early editions of the next day's papers that Francisco had picked up while Rosaline gave the children their baths.

"Killed on impact, they said," Rosaline told him.

Schuyler said nothing.

"It's so strange—you think you know someone, and then it turns out you don't know her at all. It must be awful for her. I feel like one of us should be out there."

"One of us?" Schuyler said.

"Oh, Sky, you know what I mean. Someone who cares about her. Someone from before California."

"Are you going out?" he asked.

"I meant you."

Schuyler looked out the window. In the headlights of an idling pickup truck Nelson was demonstrating a downhill turn for Joan; they looked like teenagers from an early sixties dance show, twisting silently in the snow.

"It's impossible," Schuyler said.

"Oh, forget I asked, it was silly of me, I know you must have your hands full with work and houseguests," Rosaline said, like a hostess who, having extended a last-minute invitation to a previously over-looked guest, quickly and graciously accepts the regret.

"That's not what I meant," he said. It was so like Rosaline, politely letting people off the hook, asking for something and in the same breath retracting her request. Schuyler couldn't believe that she'd been able to summon the nerve to ask Trevor for a divorce, didn't believe it until he met Francisco and Rosaline for dinner in New York just before Christmas and saw what they were like together. The next day Schuyler had had lunch with Trevor, who had been promised by his attorneys that the divorce would be final before the end of the tax year, and sat for two hours in the small dining room of a midtown club as Trevor discussed an upcoming auction of treasury bills and never brought up Rosaline's name.

"No, I know, you don't have to tell me," Rosaline said.

And like a poker player who exposes his flush in hearts after he has already conceded the hand to a full house, Schuyler told her anyway.

"I went to her once. In California."

"I didn't know."

"Once was enough, Rosie. It's over. In six weeks I'll be married."

"Marinda showed me a sketch of her dress, I'm not allowed to say anything, but it's going to be absolutely gorgeous," Rosaline said, thinking that she had nearly forgotten her role as loyal matron of honor, how close she'd come to turning Marinda's life on end. "I'm coming back to New York from Florida a week early, I thought maybe I'd have a little lunch for her—do you think she'd like that?"

"I'm sure she would," he said. Teddy had pressed his face against the windowpane and was waving his hand, signaling Schuyler out into the cold.

"Well. Have a happy new year and all that," Rosaline said.

"And all that."

"So. Happy whatever, and sweet dreams," she said, hanging up.

"You too. Rosie?" he said, but she was already gone. He'd been about to tell her what a lucky girl she was, or what a lucky guy Francisco was, something sentimental and New Year's Eve-ish. It was just after ten, and he sat there, the phone in his hands, trying to remember Marinda's code, punching out the 201 and then stopping. He pulled his boots on and put on a pair of leather gloves that were still slightly damp from the afternoon's shoveling.

"Do I see America's answer to Jean-Claude Killy?" Nelson said, tossing Schuyler a pole.

"Different sport," Schuyler said. Joan kept falling down and blaming it on the champagne. Teddy pulled her up, singing an improvised medley of old show tunes in a drunken baritone.

"Skis is skis," Nelson said.

"The girl that I marry will have to be," Teddy crooned.

"A person who knows her psychiatry," Joan sang back.

"As soft and sweet as a nursery," Teddy continued. Joan fell again, and Nelson shook his head.

"There goes America's hope for the silver," Nelson said.

"Hold my hand," Teddy sang, offering her a blue plastic insulated mitten, "and we're halfway there."

"Somewhere," Joan and Nelson joined in.

"Somehow," the three of them sang together as they pushed off toward the woods. Teddy turned and cued Schuyler with an outstretched arm.

"Someday," Schuyler said in a voice just short of singing, like an old British actor who, being best known for his serious classical roles, is not quite ready for the music, for the comedy, for the fun.

In her family's large warm house on the distant coastline a woman waited for a telephone call that never came. She fell asleep cradling the pink princess trimline her father had installed on her sixteenth birthday. When she woke up it was noon, and Schuyler was watching her from a rocking chair, drinking a glass of water.

He was giving her a look full of bad news and pity and a decision reached on a sleepless night on the first plane out of Montana. He had come to break her heart. He didn't need to say a word, she could see it in his eyes, in the way he held his shoulders, in the way he had rocked forward and was resting his arms across his knees, as though he were trying to explain something very complicated and adult to a small and trusting child.

Marinda picked up the princess and threw it at him. When he registered no surprise, she knew it for sure. On her dresser was a box of envelopes sitting in gift tissue, stamped with the colorful birds of every state in the union, their faces covered with graceful curves of India ink, ready for sending; she'd stayed up late last night sealing them, dragging them across a moistened kitchen sponge as she watched the news from the other side of the Rockies.

The hangover wore off after two days. Alex had visited, bringing telegrams of support, baskets of fruit with sympathetic cards tucked into them, offers of help and reassurances of continued working possibilities. Tell them to call back in twenty-two years, December had said. Longer, if the interest rates keep going up.

It wasn't lonely in her house overlooking the canyon, just peaceful. Everything reminded her of Tory. His music was on the radio all the time. She felt that some of the wildness had gone out of her the day he died. Was it possible, she wondered, that one person was put on this planet just for you, that she had been lucky enough to meet hers, that it would never happen again. She cut her hair to just above her shoulders and sold the Mustang at a slight loss.

For the first time in her life she could see her days stretching out before her. On a sunny morning in March she would start a garden of tomatoes and herbs and different varieties of hot peppers. In the heat of an August afternoon she'd begin an organized program of reading, Tolstoy and Dickens and Proust. On a cool October night, when the hills are dry and the fires that no man has figured out how to stop can come through and burn it all down, she'd open the windows wide and smoke a Lucky. Tory's music would be blasting on the stereo, and when the songs he wrote for her came on, she'd turn the volume all the way up. His music would fill the canyon and the house would begin to shake and only then would she lie down and, feeling the vibration of the bass come up from the floor, up through the bed, fall into a deep, dreamless sleep.

32

*N*ed Vincent had to admire Marinda's work. It had been his brother's idea, taking her on board at the family law firm, and at first he'd resisted, reciting a list of disadvantages: Depressed by a broken engagement, his niece might not be able to give them her best. She hadn't passed the New York or the New Jersey bar exam. She had had no experience in the kind of cases they handled. Women made lousy lawyers, they didn't know how to go for the jugular.

Ned had agreed to take her on a trial basis and had watched Marinda put in fourteen hours a day, six days a week. He'd read every document she drafted, sat in on her meetings with clients, even surreptitiously listened in on a few of her telephone conversations. He saw that she knew how to keep her mouth shut; Ned had learned that the people who were best at keeping secrets were the ones who had the most horrible secrets of their own. What Marinda did to the Dunne girl wasn't very pretty—Ned had watched his niece suffer some after it—but it was a good lesson for Marinda to learn early: every victory has its price, and there's no space in the winning locker room for the least bit of guilt. Yesterday Ned had made it official: she had made her father proud, she had a great future ahead of her, welcome to the club. It was the same speech he had given his own son when Bobby got out of law school. Only this time he'd meant it.

Ned took off his bifocals and massaged the bridge of his nose. His eyes could no longer take eight hours of fluorescent office lighting; he would have to ask his wife to see about picking out some desk lamps for his office. He heard Bobby junior crying in an office across the hall; the child had been staying in New Jersey since Christmas, and he had asked his sister-in-law to bring him into the office so his mother could see him when she came by for her appointment at one o'clock. The secretaries abandoned their work whenever a child came in for a visit, and now, even though there was a two-hundred-page loan agreement they were trying to get out by tomorrow morning, there were five women playing with his grandson on the floor of the smaller conference room. Ned took a bite out of one of the heart-shaped butter cookies with pink icing that his secretary had left on a plate at the edge of his blotter just before leaving for her lunch hour. The secretaries always seemed to be celebrating something: Groundhog Day, the mailman's birthday, the anniversary of the end of World War II—they were always baking these awful dry cookies, and he was always eating them so they wouldn't be offended. He wrapped all the cookies except one in yesterday's sports pages and tucked them inside his briefcase.

"Mrs. Vincent is here," said the temporary receptionist over the intercom.

Ned picked up the handset. "Which Mrs. Vincent?" he asked.

"The blond one."

"Show her in," he said, quickly piling stacks of files on the more comfortable guest chairs so that Katie Lee would be forced to sit on a hard pine ladderback. He did not want this visit to last one second more than it had to.

"Papa Vincent, how are you," Katie Lee said, coming around his desk and giving him an air kiss.

"Nice to see you, Katie Lee," he said, noticing as she sat down that she had had her hair cut in the same style his wife had attempted last week, something short and boyish made popular by the girl who had married Prince Charles. It looked terrible on his wife but fantastic on Katie Lee, and it was one of the few things he hoped his grandchild would inherit from his mother: that thick, straight, golden hair.

"Did you see Junior?" Ned asked.

"On the way in," she said. "He's coming with me to Kentucky next week for my father's birthday. Don't those women have any real work to do?"

"Cookie?" he said, pushing the plate toward her.

"Oh, no thank you, diet."

"I insist."

"Really, no, thank you."

"It's bad luck to say no to something in the shape of a heart. Old Italian proverb," he improvised.

"Well, in that case," Katie Lee said, taking a small bite. Tiny crumbs flaked off onto her frosted coral lipstick and stuck there as she spoke. "You called just in time last night, I was about to leave for the airport."

"I'll have someone drive you to Newark when we're finished."

"Bobby sends his love," Katie Lee said, though she hadn't talked to her husband in weeks.

"I spoke to him yesterday," Ned said. "He called from Lexington."

"Did he?" Katie Lee said, dabbing at the crumbs with a pale-pink tissue.

"We talked for a very long time. It was a very interesting talk," Ned said. Ned had told Bobby of Marinda's progress and that if Bobby kept up his lackadaisical attitude he would be working for a woman someday. When Bobby had broken down on the telephone Ned could barely believe it: he hadn't heard his son cry since he had been eight years old and had fallen from the roof of the garage.

"I know I'm a failure," Bobby had said, "you don't have to tell me."

"I didn't say you were a failure," Ned had replied.

"But you think it. I can tell. You let me know. Every fucking time I talk to you, you have some incredibly subtle way of letting me know."

Ned said nothing. His wife was in the bathroom, twisting the long bangs of her new haircut into an electric curling iron.

"It's all that bitch's fault," Bobby said.

"I doubt that. You're almost thirty years old. You can't go around blaming your mistakes on other people for the rest of your life. I thought I taught you that."

"You don't know what she's really like, you only see her when she's putting on an act. She's ruined me."

Ned scratched his ear and examined a fingernail. "I know exactly what that wife of yours is. If you remember, I tried to tell you before you got married. You make your bed, you lie in it." *Be a man*, he thought, *why can't you grow up and be a man.*

"She won't divorce me."

"I don't want to hear that word."

"It's 1982, for Jesus' sake."

"She's your wife and the mother of your child."

Bobby had laughed through his tears. "Yes, and let me tell you, a great mother she is. By the time she gets through with that little kid he'll be as much of a monster as she is. You know what he said to me yesterday? He said he liked it at Papa Wop's house—that's what she's taught him to call you. Last time Katie Lee came home from a business trip he bit her on the ankle."

Ned flicked his fingernail clean over his wife's side of the bed. He had no sympathy for Bobby, but he knew Bobby was right about the child. He'd seen enough of it since Christmas. The child was spoiled and weak and didn't know how to play with kids his age. He was going to grow up into the thing Ned hated most: a sissy, a wimp, a boy who always wanted his own way but had no idea how to get it. Maybe Bobby was right about some other things too, maybe if Bobby got free of Katie Lee he might have a chance to straighten up and make Ned proud. Marinda was his niece, but Bobby was his oldest son. Marinda was capable of running things, there was no question of it, but the thought of his son working for Marinda made something inside him, something much deeper than concern over the future of his business, twist into an angry knot. And it was Marinda, after all, who'd introduced Katie Lee to the family. Who was this girl from Kentucky who thought she could manipulate them all like little marionettes? Who did she think she was, the queen of Spain?

After Ned had hung up he had gone down to his study and called his brother. Katie Lee had become what the Vincents called a Problem, and his brother always knew exactly how to make a Problem go away.

His brother had made a few calls before he telephoned Ned back with an idea, the idea that Ned was proposing to Katie Lee now.

"I thought you didn't believe in divorce," Katie Lee said.

"There are ways," Ned told her, "when there is no other choice."

Katie Lee tried to push back her chair, the legs resisting against the woven carpet. "Let me get this straight," she said. "If I agree to a divorce, with no financial settlement whatsoever, then you'll make sure I get all the green lights I need for the project in Atlantic City?"

"Easy as pie," he said.

"The extra hundred rooms?" she asked.

"No sweat."

"No trouble with the unions?"

"They wouldn't dream of it."

"How about the license?"

"Not a worry in the world."

Katie Lee breathed in. "And if I don't?"

Ned breathed out. "Then you have just bought the most expensive piece of undevelopable swampland this side of the Delaware River."

"I see," she said, and she saw it perfectly: she was going to have to trade it all away, her husband, her marriage; she had no choice but to do as Ned asked. She could hear her father telling her, *When they have your ass against the pavement, sometimes it turns out to be the yellow brick road; every bad thing has a good side to it if you're smart enough to see it.* Maybe she was better off without Bobby; he hadn't turned out the way she'd expected at all. She could remarry, maybe not in Lexington, where she'd be considered too old for anyone this side of fifty, but she could find someone in New York or Chicago, there were plenty of men, and she had plenty of money. *Never give in without a fight; when in doubt, negotiate.*

"My lawyer will call you tomorrow," Katie Lee said, standing up, though she had already made up her mind.

Ned stood up with her and held out her ankle-length mink by the shoulders. "Tomorrow," he said. "I look forward to it."

At the door she turned and ran a coral fingernail along the olive-green wallpaper. "I've always thought this color was very unflattering to people with your type of complexion," she said. "Let me get this straight, no settlement at all?"

"I don't think alimony is called for," Ned said.

"Well, goodness, no need to be spiteful. Business is business. I'd like some child support at the very least."

"I don't think that will be necessary."

"A symbolic gesture," Katie Lee said.

"It won't be necessary, because my grandson is staying here."

"What?"

"Did I forget to mention it?" Ned asked. "Of course Bobby will be retaining custody. We all think the child will be happier here, he's used to it, and you can rest assured you'll be welcome to see him whenever you like."

Not hardly, Katie Lee thought. "I won't have it."

"It's best for the child. Everyone agrees."

"Everyone?"

"We spoke to your father last night. He said he was very grateful that the Vincents were able to provide his grandson with a stable family environment. Your father is a remarkable man. He's very proud of what you're doing in Atlantic City. I hope he'll be able to spend some time with us this summer."

"I don't believe this."

"Your lawyer, tomorrow. A pleasure seeing you, as always."

"Oh, stuff it up your sausage grinder," Katie Lee said, storming down the hall and finding Marinda, in a suit and paisley bow tie, leaving her office.

"Marinda, honey, you look positively manly, and I mean that as a compliment."

"Then thanks," Marinda said, leaning against the conference room door.

"You do look a little pale," Katie Lee said. "It must be the air," she continued, wrinkling her nose. "Did you know there's more pollution and toxic waste here than in the next three states combined?"

"Cancer alley, they call it," Marinda said.

"Charming. Think about a sunlamp, sweetie, it does wonders. Is today Valentine's Day?"

"I believe so."

Katie Lee gave her an exaggerated wink. "You wouldn't be one of those single girls I read about who gets so many valentines she can't keep track of them?"

Marinda said nothing.

"You were supposed to get married today, honey, weren't you? Of course you were, how could I forget. I have it circled on my calendar. Marinda and Schuyler, it says, and I drew some little hearts around it."

"Well, you know what they say, you can always wear the bridesmaid's dress to a party."

Katie Lee sniffed. "Not to any party I'd want to go to. But, Marinda, enough girl talk—I've just had the most awful conversation with your uncle," Katie Lee said, blinking fast so that the smallest tear spilled over onto her cheek. "He's a monster, everything you ever said about your family is true, all they care about is themselves."

"They're not so bad," Marinda said, shifting her weight from left foot to right, "I mean, *we're* not so bad."

"Do you know about this terrible thing they're trying to do?"

"Pretty much," Marinda said. She'd gotten her father's call late last night, just after she'd returned from dinner with an extremely boring state senator who told her, between courses, that her eyes reminded him of Ida Lupino's. She'd begun dating again in early January, business and political friends of her family at first, then people she met through cousins and old classmates, and last night the state senator, who was thinking of making a move to a national office. As soon as he gets a brain transplant, Marinda thought. It was amazing how many men wanted to date Marinda Vincent now that she was thin and available and the apple of her uncle's eye.

The conference room door opened and Junior came crawling out, dragging a wooden roll toy behind him.

Katie Lee bent down and mussed his hair.

"You've got to help me, Marinda," she said when she straightened up. "I know they'll listen to you. A divorce is one thing, but taking my baby away from me, that's downright immoral."

Marinda smiled. "Actually," she said, picking up the boy and balancing him on her hip, "the custody thing was my idea. A lot of fathers get custody these days."

Katie Lee slapped Marinda hard, knocking her jaw against the child's head, so that he began to wail, and three secretaries emerged from the conference room clucking maternal comfort.

"You're a bitter little bitch," Katie Lee whispered before she turned and marched away.

"What has she been eating?" said the secretary who'd baked the cookies.

Marinda shrugged and gave the boy a little bounce.

"Aunt Marinda knows best, doesn't she?" Marinda said in baby talk. "Doesn't she, sweetie? Are we wet?" she said, feeling the seat of his terry-cloth playsuit. "We are wet, aren't we, cookie?" She handed Bobby junior to her father's secretary and went back to work.

33

*R*osaline laid a wooden board across the arms of her father's wheelchair and spread out the pictures of Agamemnon. It was April, and the first time Joseph had been wheeled outdoors since last September.

"Doesn't he look fat and happy?" she said.

"Don't we all," her father said. He'd grown bald and heavy as a Santa Claus up in New England; it was one of his few remaining pleasures, Rosaline guessed, the hearty country meals the clinic staff prepared for those who were not too depressed to consume them.

Rosaline was fat too: she was five months pregnant, and this time around she was going to gain as much weight as she wanted. When she got up at five in the morning she stood in front of the mirror, queasy and tired, and said to herself: cleavage. Her husband came up behind her and placed his small strong hands over her breasts. He told her he had dreamed they were going to have a daughter and they were going to name her Josephine. Then he left for the stables; he said it made him laugh every morning to sit in Parker's old office, in Parker's old chair. Parker had told Rosaline, at the retirement dinner she had helped throw for him last summer, that she was making a terrible mistake: Gomez would make a lousy trainer of horses—retired jockeys always did. In the fall Blue Smoke horses won eight graded stakes, and at the end of the year Agamemnon was ranked as the fourth leading sire of two-year-olds.

"How is your mother?" Joseph asked. "She never calls me."

"The same," Rosaline said. "She never calls me either. She sends messages through Trevor, who's her new favorite cause. I actually think she's trying to marry him off."

421

Joseph sighed. The people up here had organized for him a program of counseling and pep talks and soothing drugs to help him fight the depression. They were training him to accept what he had made of his life, or rather, what he hadn't made of it. He listened as his daughter showed him pictures of horses and told him how each one was coming along, what their personalities were like, whether they would be pointed for the races or the breeding shed, the dirt or the turf, routes or sprints. He hated all of it. He wished he had never heard of Agamemnon, never been to the racetrack, never even seen Paris, because then he might have had a shot at happiness.

"And now everybody's saying what a genius you were," Rosaline continued. "And last week I got the most outrageous offer for a share of Agamemnon. A million dollars. For less than three percent of the horse! You're not listening."

"A million dollars," Joseph said. He wanted to tell her that she already had a million dollars, a lot more than that, in fact.

"But I'm going to hold out for more."

"More than a million dollars," he said.

"Because after the Derby that's what it will be worth."

"The Derby?" Joseph said.

"Oh, I know everyone thinks they're going to win the Derby, but I just have this feeling about Orestes. Like he's just fated to win. Francisco had a dream about it. He said it was like watching television, the image was that sharp."

"The Derby," Joseph said. "We've never won the Derby."

"I know. I wish you could come down," she said. She wanted to say, it's all for you, it's all been for you, we showed them you were right, everyone who laughed, everyone who pitied, all for you.

Joseph picked up a snapshot and held it out at arm's length. Little Rosaline, what had she done. Created a scandal worse than his own, ruined her marriage, made a wreck of a fine gentleman he'd been proud to call his son-in-law. All because of a horse.

But the Derby.

It didn't matter what anyone said—he knew there were richer races won by better horses, but the Derby was the only one that counted. If you went to your grave and the only thing you could say you'd done was win the Kentucky Derby, you'd die a happy man.

"Can I keep this one," he asked, showing her the picture of Agamemnon shot through the familiar blue picket fence.

"You can have all of them, I brought them for you," she said.
"Just this one," he said, "I only need one."

Rosaline's morning sickness lifted on the first Saturday in May. From her box at Churchill Downs she surveyed the infield: hundreds of drunken college students creating a scene that made Fort Lauderdale at spring break look like a convention of Future Librarians of America. A girl in a white dress came up and said her name was Beth and she was from the network and would Rosaline mind if she placed a yellow sign on the front of her box so that the cameraman could locate her quickly. Francisco's brother offered her the mint from his julep. Davis asked what instructions had been given to the jockey, a veteran California rider who'd flown in two nights earlier. Let him go as fast as he wants, Rosaline said, and then make him go a little faster. When the horses passed the stands for the first time, she clutched the railing in shock, she could not believe that Orestes was so far back. He wasn't a closer, he was the kind of horse who had to get out in front early and then be whipped hard into staying there. At the top of the stretch, just a fraction of a mile to the finish line, he was still eighth in a field of fourteen. *Do it, do it, do it*, Rosaline whispered, *do it, do it for Francisco, do it for my daddy, do it for your daddy, do it for Joseph, do it for Agamemnon. Do it*, she said. *Do it for me.*

They'd wheeled the television set into Joseph's room and propped his head up on a pillow. He could barely see, he had barely been able to do anything for the last three days, but he'd made them promise not to tell Rosaline about his condition until after the Derby. A nurse stood by and took his pulse. Another nurse adjusted the thermostat and offered him juice. He could feel the life going out of him. It was easier than he had thought it would be. You just relaxed into it. You just learned to let go.

There was something wrong with the television set. He thought he saw Charlotte on a commercial, holding up a squeeze tube of artificial margarine. He heard the music to "My Old Kentucky Home," but the words were different. It was the president talking. The president was hoping he'd feel welcome here in the White House. Then he couldn't hear anything at all, just his own breath, the thin pathetic wheeze of it, and he couldn't really see anything either, just a sort of glow, like when you're lying on the beach and you close your eyes and turn your face up to the sun.

Welcome to the White House. Welcome to the White House. And for a final second the television picture came nearly into focus. He saw a swatch of chestnut coat. A boy in white pants and a shirt the color of blue smoke. And roses, a blanket of deep-red roses, he tried to breathe in their smell, but no breath would come. Roses, roses, Rosaline.

34

There was nothing but static on the radio. The oil-gauge light was still blinking, though December had stopped off in Utah to put in a fresh quart. The ashtray had gotten stuck three quarters of the way open. She'd thought it would be fun driving cross country in a rented car, it would lend a carefree top note to a trip concocted of musky and heavier scents. She'd left California on Independence Day, all heavy symbolism intended. The house felt hot and confining, and Alex was on her case to get back to work.

"You don't seem to understand," he told her, "if you sit around Los Angeles not working, people think it's because you can't get any work."

"I don't want to work," she said.

"Well then what do you want," he asked.

"I don't know," she said. "I haven't figured that out."

"Well get off your lovely little ass and figure it out. Take a trip. See some splendid sunsets. Visit a famous gravesite. I love you, you know that, I only want what's best," he said.

"I love you too," she said. "You sex-crazed faggot."

"Don't try to offend me, it won't work."

"I could go to New York, visit Rosaline," she said.

"Sounds decent," he replied.

"I could go to New Jersey," she said. "Stick around for hurricane season."

"Sounds less than decent," he said. "But whatever. Kiss kiss."

"Kiss kiss," she said.

She packed a knapsack full of clothing and called the banks to get the limits raised on her credit cards. She rented a pale-blue Cutlass sedan with twenty thousand miles on it and bought five pairs of expensive imported sunglasses.

425

When she got to Las Vegas she registered in one of the older down-town hotels with a gleaming neon marquee and proceeded to lose thirty-five hundred dollars at the blackjack tables. She drove to the site of Tory's plane crash and placed her bouquet of purple freesia next to what others had left behind: a plastic arrangement of daisies set in a green aluminum flowerpot, an American flag, a Matchbox dump truck. She stopped at the local shopping mall and racked up forty dollars' worth of merchandise at the discount drugstore.

When she got back to her hotel room she gave herself a facial rub with an apricot-scented gel, and took megadoses of vitamins C, B-6, and B-12, and dyed her hair pitch black with Loving Care Color Foam. She was now unrecognizable, even to herself.

On to Utah, where the radio gave out. In the silence of another state it occurred to her that, her limits raised, she could drive on like this for months, undetected by friends and family, drive anywhere she wanted or nowhere at all. She didn't really want to go to New York, she'd always hated New York. It had been months since she'd stayed up till dawn, so there was no longer any point to the Atlantic Ocean.

The next time she stopped to refill the tank she telephoned Rosaline, collect, from a telephone booth near the diesel pump.

"Hi, it's me," she said.

"December!" Rosaline cried. "I was just thinking about you. This very minute."

"You were?"

"You sound so surprised. When will you get here? Oh, forget I said that, you told me I'm not supposed to ask."

"I'm not sure," December said, waving away a truck driver through the dirty glass. "I don't even know what state I'm in."

"Well that's silly. Where are you, a motel?"

"A gas station."

"Well, look at the license plates. What do they say?"

"Pennsylvania. Idaho. New Hampshire, live free or die. Indiana has the best one."

"Wander," Rosaline said. "I've never been to Indiana."

"I should get there tomorrow or the day after," December said.

"What do they do in Indiana?" Rosaline said. "Is it a corn state?"

"Stone, I think," December said. "How's everybody?"

"Just great. Just great. And I'm as fat as can be," Rosaline said.

"I doubt it."

"I am, I am," Rosaline said. "I'm wearing size seven shoes."

December had this feeling, watching the traffic go by, that there was something she needed to tell Rosaline. Something she wanted Rosaline to know in case December didn't make it to New York.

"You did good, Rosie," December said. "With Francisco, I mean."

"Yes, I know. I mean, not only do I know that I did good, I know that you know."

"I don't think I ever called you, you know, when things got tough. I got the messages and everything, but, I don't know, there was so much going on out here, I mean, out there," December said. The truck driver was pointing to his watch. "I should have cast an absentee ballot, or something," she said.

"You didn't have to," Rosaline said. "Are you all right?"

"Sure. Just checking in."

"Well, I was thinking of you, even if you didn't call. Do you remember that time we went to see Tory?" Rosaline asked. When December said nothing, Rosaline thought it had perhaps been a mistake to bring up his name over the telephone, when she couldn't see December's face.

"Yeah," December said. She remembered everything.

"Do you remember what you told me?"

"Nope."

"You said people didn't get that many chances, and they should seize the chances when they could. Or something like that. You were talking about a special kind of love, I didn't really know what you meant, but when things got awful, with Trevor and all, I kept thinking back to what you said. About taking the chance."

"I said that. Well. I used to be a pretty smart girl, I guess," December said. The truck driver had made a face and left.

"Oh, I know what you mean!" Rosaline said. "Do you ever feel you know less now than you did then? I mean, that you used to think you knew everything, but now you don't know anything at all? Am I making sense? Is there some reason I always get absolutely incoherent when I'm pregnant?"

"Hormones," December said.

Rosaline giggled. December heard everything in that giggle: girlishness and innocence and a touch of sex.

Fifty miles down the highway she turned on the radio and found it tuned perfectly to a country station. Had she really said that to Rosaline, given her that kind of advice, how long ago had that been? The oil gauge appeared to have cured itself. Tory had taught her, follow the road, let the road tell you where to go, forget the careful directions and the street maps and the dashboard compass and just drive on simple instinct. She gave a knock to the ashtray and it sprang wide open.

Somewhere in Colorado she took a left turn. North, up, toward Montana.

Without making a telephone call to prepare him or taking a drink to prepare herself, she arrived, a few minutes short of sundown.

At first he didn't recognize the woman with black hair in oversized sunglasses. When he did at last, he stood there in the doorway, his face expressionless.

"Aren't you going to invite me in?" she asked.

"That depends."

"On?"

"On why you came."

"I don't really know," she said. "I was driving—well, it's a long story, it just felt like the right thing to do. I'll leave if you want."

"No. I don't want."

She felt a surprising and marvelous relief that there were no indications of a receding hairline. He was one of those men who would look better as time went on, as though his gaunt, lined face were catching up with something much older within him, a knowledge that seemed beyond years. Today he was all of a color: his light-brown hair, his cowboy's tan, his worn suede jacket, an old pair of narrow corduroy jeans over boots the color of butterscotch. Everything about him seemed warm and touched by sunlight except his eyes, still the same cool, metal gray, the color of steel, it was as though this steel ran everywhere through him, as though his bones were formed from it, and the only place it showed was where it glinted in his eyes.

She wanted the strength of that steel, wanted to feel it in her hands, wanted to lean against it and have it hold her up. And once he had wanted her—twice, in fact—but she hadn't seen what he was offering. She had been so hungry, she had reached out for something that would fill the place that was hungry. But maybe the point was to find the thing that stopped the hunger. It was something Schuyler had discovered somewhere along the line, something that he couldn't share or explain. That they could weld themselves together, forever, and build something out of this foreverness.

She pulled at a strand of her dark hair and twisted a sneakered toe into the woven doormat.

"I don't know why I came here," she said.

He smiled at last.

"Well. I do," he said.

She followed him up the stairs.

They peeled away the layers slowly as it grew dark. His suede jacket. Her cotton sweatshirt. His boots. Her hightop basketball sneakers. His workshirt. His T-shirt. Socks. Watches. When she started to pull her T-shirt over her head he stopped her, and did it himself. When she moved to kiss him, he placed his palm across her lips.

"I want to look at you," he said. "First."

He stared at her, and motioned for her to take off the rest of her clothes. He stood there another few minutes.

"The hair," he said. "So dark."

"The darkest they make," she said. "On the box it says it will wash out in four to six shampoos."

He lifted her up and carried her into the bathroom, where he sat her down in the tub and ran the water just short of hot. He unhooked the showerhead hose, turned its action up strong, and began to lather her hair. The suds, at first golden, took on the color of the dye, which when wet showed itself to be not black but simply a very dark brown. He rinsed her out and lathered her up again. She was sitting in an inch of discolored water. Her hair was growing lighter. He massaged her scalp and twisted the ends of her hair between his fingers. The shampoo smelled of lemon. Again he rinsed, and lathered, and rinsed, and soaped, until her hair was clean of the black and the water ran clear as a spring. He soaped her all over, rinsing her down, until she was completely clean and her fingertips began to pucker. When he toweled her off and carried her to bed, she felt a chill even though it was a warm summer night, the feeling of a draft against wetness, as if the house had a weather all its own.

In bed she closed her eyes, and finally he kissed her. She felt herself growing younger under his kiss, as young as the girl she had been the first time he kissed her. She had forgotten, she had forgotten, she had forgotten not just what he would be like but what she herself was like, because forgetting him had been the same thing as forgetting herself. She felt some of the steel in that kiss, she was growing strong and happy, she was remembering what it was like, not just the pleasure of it but the spirit: it had nothing to do with bodies and passion and power and control, it had everything to do with spirit, with leaping outside yourself.

When he took the tip of her breast in his mouth, when he ran his fingers along her, she thought, he knows exactly what that feels like for me, and when she took him in her hands she knew, precisely, what her touch had done. She thought she would float off the bed, and then he put her where he wanted her, and pinned her down.

It had been so long. She moved against him, not just for his pleasure or her own but just to know, after all these years, what he was like. If a deaf woman learned to listen with her eyes, if a blind woman learned to see with her hands, was it possible that all the senses could be reduced into this, could she discover it all right there: feel the pulse in a narrow vein, the measure of a curve or angle, the smooth part, the softer part, the pull of warm skin.

Could he discover it too, for he was moving, not a simple in and out, not the fancy hip tricks that could be practiced into a pillow, but as deftly as a finger, rubbing into places that she had never thought of as just that: this place here, a slow and gentle pushing. This place, something quicker. This place, and this place, and this. And then one place where she wordlessly begged him to stay, and he did, because it was the place that knew as sure as a tongue how to receive him, to know the temperature and taste and stick of him.

He tipped up her chin with his thumb and gave her a kiss and raised his eyebrows in question.

She said nothing. She never did.

He smiled, and formed a shape of sound with his mouth, his top teeth slightly exposed, his lips moving forward, as though he were teaching speech to someone who didn't know how to hear him.

She mirrored his mouth and breathed out.

"I," she said.

"I," he repeated. Then he stuck his tongue behind his top teeth.

"L," she said.

"L," he repeated, holding the sound, and then they said together: "Love you."

*A*t one point or another he had been in love with all of us—Rosaline, Katie Lee, Marinda, and me. We couldn't help but love him back.

It's been almost ten years since we were all together in the same place, but it doesn't matter: everyone always thought of us as a quartet, they'll probably think of us that way until the day we die. It's sort of nice, it's the way a woman in her fifties, a hundred pounds overweight, a life of hard luck showing on her face, her cheap dress matching her skin-tone support hose, can show up at her high school reunion and there'll always be some guy named Barry saying, *Cheryl? Remember me? Well, it's been a long time, but I remember you. Everyone remembers the captain of the cheerleaders. I remember you did splits down onto the cold winter ground with a smile on your face. Care to dance?*

There's Marinda in a version of purple. I believe in Victorian times this particular shade was suggested for the final stages of mourning.

And there's Katie Lee in taffeta polka dots and ruffles. There's going to be a lot of noise when that girl moves. I hear she's been getting awful chummy with Trevor. She does like to reheat Rosaline's leftovers.

And there's Rosaline and the proud new papa. Josephine. Imagine.

So here we all are. Four daughters of four of the most famous men in America. (Maybe that's what my father taught me: that you can get famous for being naughty. He was a murderer. I took off my clothes in front of a camera.)

Four beautiful girls who thought the world owed them everything.

Four women who found out it didn't quite work that way.

Four smart cookies.

Though I had to do some pretty dumb things before I got this smart. It's as though I thought life was as large and round as the globe itself, and that by turning and walking away from the thing I wanted most in the world I would eventually come upon it again, from a different and surprising angle.

Why do I love him? I have no idea. I really know very little about him, when you get right down to it. I couldn't tell you the make of his first car, or what his number was in the draft lottery, or the topic of his senior thesis, or why his movie never got made, or how come he likes being around cows and horses so much. He just is the way he is.

Look at him now. Admit it. He's the most wonderful man you've ever seen. The rosebud was my idea, it matches my dress, which is just about the most virginal thing I've ever worn. Except for the color. Yellow's the color they used for welcoming back the hostages, and that's just how I felt when I got to Montana. Like there were yellow ribbons hanging from the trees and the windows and the antenna of Schuyler's dirty red pickup truck, like I was someone who'd been held captive for so long I'd stopped counting the days, stopped believing I was a prisoner at all.

What it does to me, seeing him there at the far end of the aisle, taking a long step toward me to the sound of something classical.

Here I am.

Closer. Closer.

Here I am. The one who loves you best. The one whose love is going to outlast them all.